COTTONWOOD FALL

COTTONWOOD FALL

A Novel

by

GARY SLAUGHTER

Library of Congress Control Number: 2005929245

ISBN -13   978-0-9744206-2-2
ISBN -10   0-9744206-2-X

Manufactured in the United States of America
Cover design by Michael Lang
Interior layout and design by Danita Meeks
Editing and proofreading by Sharon Yake
Printing and binding by Falcon Press

Published by Fletcher House
P.O. Box 50979
Nashville, TN 37205-0979

For additional copies of *Cottonwood Fall*, contact www.fletcherhouse.com.

For Joanne —

Whose boundless enthusiasm,
timely encouragement,
and just plain hard work
ensured that
Fall followed Summer this year.

CONTENTS

COTTONWOOD FALL

1 THE ADVENTURES RESUME

SUMMER OF 1944 WAS A CHALLENGING TIME FOR MY best friend Danny and me. For our bravery, we'd been proclaimed town heroes on at least three occasions. We saved the citizens of Riverton, Michigan, from sinister Nazi spies, enemy air raids, nasty escaped German POWs, and the ravages of fire. I'd elaborate further but modesty forbids.

But, as we would learn before Thanksgiving, our heroic summer was a walk in the park compared to the dangerous obstacles that would confront us in the fall. On Don McNeil's *Breakfast Club* radio show, President Franklin Delano Roosevelt and FBI Director, J. Edgar Hoover, told everyone in America that Danny and I were lucky to be alive to share our story. That's why they awarded us the Medals of Courage.

And Governor Thomas E. Dewey, a native of nearby Owosso, said he was very proud to be our friend. We'd gotten to know each other when we helped him during his campaign for President of the United States. Of course, we also helped President Roosevelt with his campaign. Since Danny and I liked them both, we were glad we didn't have to choose between our two friends at the ballot box. Sometimes being too young to vote has its advantages.

But I'm getting a little ahead of myself.

BY THE END OF August, Danny and I were ready for fall. But Michigan summers are fickle. Sometimes they give way to autumn in late August but not this summer. The Farmer's Almanac predicted that warm weather would linger until mid-September. So we had to be patient, but patience was not one of Danny's virtues.

We were sprawled haphazardly on my front steps keeping tabs on the Forrest Street neighborhood. A bee buzzed at us from a white clover blossom in the grass next to the porch. Danny absently *buzzed* back. The startled bee flew off in a huff. Danny waved goodbye with the thin blade of grass he was using as dental floss.

The familiar sound of the lunch whistle floated our way from the Burke Factory, far out New Albany Avenue, where Dad worked as a tool and die maker. I imagined him closing his tool box and carrying his lunch pail down to the cafeteria where he played his daily game of gin rummy with Don Paulus.

Following the practice of many Riverton men during the war, Don worked a second job as a security guard at our neighborhood canning factory. Danny and I held Don in high esteem because of his role in our capture of the two tough POWs who had escaped from the confines of Camp Riverton with the help of the Libby sisters. Those two young women, who lived just down the block from us, were charged with treason, punishable by hanging in times of war. But mercifully the judge allowed them to plead guilty to a lesser charge. Nonetheless, the women were sentenced to long prison terms, a high price to pay for what started as an overnight lark. Everyone in the neighborhood agreed that it was their mother, Louise Libby, who ultimately paid the price for their folly.

As we waited for the day to unfold, we were lazy and more than a bit bored. "Whatcha wanta do?" Danny asked.

I had come to learn that Danny wasn't really expecting an answer to that question. It was just his way of breaking the silence. So I answered with a question of my own, "Are you all packed?"

"Yep!"

"Are you taking everything that's on the list?"

"Nope! Not taking a Bible."

"But, Danny! We're going to a church camp. You gotta have a Bible."

"Don't need one. Awredy read it."

"Aw, for gosh sakes, Danny," I sputtered with exasperation. "Sometimes you're just plain stubborn."

"Judge not, 'less you be the judge," he quoted with authority. At that, I guffawed.

Danny peered at me through his wire frame glasses. His eyes, as black as his closely cropped hair, sparkled with amusement. Then he gave me one of his patented grins that stretched from one enormous ear to the other. Suddenly he stood up, snatched the Detroit Tigers cap from his head, and bowed deeply from the waist. I smiled and tipped my own Tigers cap right back at him. Not surprisingly, I forgave my best friend's idiosyncrasies one more time. Who wouldn't?

Just then we heard the familiar sound of squeaking gears emanating from beyond the giant cottonwood tree that stood in the middle of the sidewalk at the crest of the Forrest Street hill. Each summer, that magnificent old tree covered our neighborhood with a profusion of white fluff, making us sneeze and wreaking havoc on laundry hung out to dry. The base of the cottonwood was the meeting place of the Forrest Street Guards, a secret anti-Nazi spy organization founded by Danny and me. It was so secret that membership was limited to the two of us plus a snotty, neighborhood kid named Sherman Tolna.

"Wonder if we could get one of those bikes?" Danny asked wistfully.

"Why don't we ask Mr. Long when he gets here?"

Langford Long had been our mailman ever since I could remember. Each afternoon, during fair weather, he covered his long delivery route, including our part of town, on a very special bicycle.

This unique vehicle, appropriately painted wartime khaki, had a special frame designed for a normal size bicycle wheel (26 inches) in the back and a much smaller wheel (about 14 inches) in the front.

This configuration allowed for the installation of an oversize basket that was attached to the handle bars and positioned above the front wheel. The basket comfortably accommodated Mr. Long's huge, leather mail pouch that was always fully stuffed with letters, magazines, and parcels destined for the mailboxes of homes and businesses in our part of town. His special vehicle allowed him to cover his route more quickly by reducing the need for return trips to the post office to refill his pouch.

By the time Mr. Long arrived at my house, Danny and I were standing at the end of the sidewalk under the box elder tree in whose highest branches our secret, air-raid observation post was hidden. "Gotta special package for Master Jase Addison today. Whatcha thinka that? Hafta sign here." He handed me a clipboard and pencil. "Looks like this one came from overseas. Wanta guess who it's from?"

Of course, we both knew it could only be from one person. "Uncle Van!"

"Yep! You're as right as rain."

"Thanks, Mr. Long," I said as I signed for the precious parcel.

"Jase, tell your Aunt Maude that was a fine article about your Uncle Van in the *Riverton Daily Press*. Would ya?"

"You bet, Mr. Long. I'll tell her!"

A few months earlier, to save money and to help Mom around the house, Aunt Maude, my mother's older sister, had come to live with us in our small two-bedroom bungalow. She and I shared my miniscule bedroom. I loved having my very favorite aunt as a roommate, and she seemed to enjoy it as well.

Her husband Van had enlisted in 1942. Because of his work experience at Riverton Central Telephone, he was assigned to the Army Signal Corps. After landing at Normandy, he headed a team of communication technicians whose job was to wire-unwire-and-rewire the Allied front line as it progressed eastward toward Germany.

After slugging it out in the hedgerows of Normandy, Uncle Van was assigned to General De Gaulle's Free French Army that had recently succeeded in liberating Paris. Despite the danger involved in carrying out his special assignment, there were a number of sniggers around the supper table about his taking time off from fighting the war to "vacation with the Great General in Gay Paree."

"Oh, Jase! Don't forget the rest of your family's mail." Mr. Long handed me a fat bundle. Then he turned to his bicycle.

Danny watched the entire exchange with exaggerated indifference, his eyes pegged at half-mast. I knew him well enough to know that he was about to launch into his impersonation of Edward G. Robinson. "Listen here, Mr. Long. We gotta special request. *See?*" Danny slurred, sounding as if he had a fat cigar in his mouth.

I gave my gangster friend a dirty look. As usual, he ignored me and plunged ahead. "I wantcha to tell me, *see?* How would two enterprising young gents get their mitts on a couple a them fancy bikes, *see?*"

Mr. Long spun around and stared at Danny. He looked confused. His mouth fell open. "Whatta you askin', young fella?"

Danny evidently concluded that postal service employees were not conversant in gangster dialect. So, in plain English, he asked, "Your postage bike. Do they sell those to boys like us?"

"Oh, I see. This is a Victory Bicycle. People use these instead of burnin' gas in their cars. But this particular one is Government Issue. G.I., you know? Jus' like the soldiers," Mr. Long explained, trying to be helpful.

"Okay. Just wonderin'." I had never seen Danny give up so easily. Usually, when he wanted something, he pursued his prey until the poor victim dropped of exhaustion.

Mr. Long looked relieved. "Well, I'll be off then. Be good, boys!" he admonished, pedaling away as fast as he could.

"Hey, Mr. Long," Danny hollered after him. "Do you like sauerkraut?"

Mr. Long looked back and gave Danny a bewildered look. He didn't respond. But I did. "Sauerkraut?"

"Well, it worked once," Danny explained, referring to our summer sauerkraut-for-bubble gum exchange that we had arranged with the German POWs. This transaction was the first of a series of events that ultimately led to the POW escape.

I shook my head and focused on my package. The parcel was about the size of a carton of cigarettes that I had seen people purchase at Pete's Grocery-Liquor-Hardware. Just as Mr. Long had claimed, it was addressed to Master Jase Addison. Sure enough, the return address spelled out Uncle Van's name and the same APO number that Aunt Maude used to send letters to him. And it was postmarked with the words, *Victory Mail.* When I shook it, nothing moved, but it was heavy so there was obviously something inside. I was stumped. I turned to Danny. "I wonder what this is. I have no idea. Do you?"

Danny smirked and shook *his* head for a change.

What provoked that reaction to my question? I wondered, but I didn't stop long enough to figure it out.

I tore off the wrapping and ripped open the box. Out tumbled a menacing German dagger, nearly a foot in length. It was housed in an elegant sheath finished in highly polished black enamel with an SS insignia composed of twin jagged lightning bolts inscribed in embedded silver. The dagger's handle was decorated with heavy silver renderings of stylized Nazi eagles and swastikas. I had seen these figures in photographs taken at Nuremburg during the Nazi's first national assembly back in the early 1930s, before the world learned that Hitler and his henchmen were murderous monsters.

Holding the sheath in my left hand, I grasped the woven grip of golden cord with my right and carefully extracted the dagger. The blade was beautifully etched with SS symbols and haughty-looking eagles. As I gently touched one of the twin cutting edges with my finger, I quickly learned that it was razor sharp. This was not a toy!

"Boy! This is swell! I would have never guessed. Would you?" I asked rhetorically.

"I awredy did! That day at the Woolworth lunch counter where Aunt Maude works. She let us know that Uncle Van was bringing you a war souvenir."

"Oh, my gosh! I remember now. But how did you know what it was?" Danny gave me another smirk, even more pronounced than his first. I had completely forgotten about that conversation at Woolworths. Danny was right. That day back in June, he had *assured* both Aunt Maude and me that Uncle Van's souvenir was going to be an SS dagger.

"I wonder why he mailed it instead of waiting and giving it to me when he got home," I pondered aloud.

"Because I wrote and asked him to send it. So we could take it to show Miss Sparks when school starts," Danny explained matter-of-factly.

"Oh!" was all I could muster. "Thanks, Danny."

"Let's put the dagger under your mattress and then go for a swim," he ordered. Then he turned and walked into our house without looking back.

SINCE WE HAD MET earlier that summer, Danny and I had only gone swimming at three places. Of these, the only one officially authorized by our parents was the public pool in Trumble Park. For very different reasons, the other two sites were strictly off limits.

Our first illegal dip had been at the Riverton City Waterworks, a majestic building located on the banks of the Chippewa River at the north end of our neighborhood. Naturally our parents were unaware of this aquatic indiscretion. On a warm Saturday morning in June, we had used the shower in the waterworks locker room to wash our filthy clothing following our accidental splash landing into an icky pothole in our neighborhood swamp.

While our laundry drip-dried, we killed a little time by taking a soothing swim in the pool containing the city's water supply. But we were caught in the act by Gentleman Jim, one of our neighborhood bums at the time. He made us promise that we would never again swim in our city's drinking water. Because we would never break a promise to him, that was our last dip at the waterworks.

Our second illicit dip occurred in the same area of the neighborhood. Just west of the waterworks, the city had built a footbridge to provide its employees easy access to the city's wells that were sunk in the flat plain across the river from the main building.

The simple bridge consisted of a band of wooden slats, lashed together and suspended from two parallel, loosely strung cables that were less than four feet apart. Because of its construction, the neighborhood boys saw the bridge as an extremely long hammock, swaying in the breeze above the tempting waters of the river. An ideal diving platform!

The neighborhood parents saw the bridge as a dangerous, attractive nuisance that would, they agreed, ultimately result in the early death of one or more of us boys. We were *strongly advised* never to go near that bridge unless we wanted to end our young lives by drowning or having our necks broken by diving into the shallow waters below.

Our parents were right of course, but strong parental restrictions only increased the swinging bridge's allure. After being outlawed, illegal use of the bridge by otherwise obedient boys intensified and continued unabated for years. Some years later, city officials finally ended this reign of defiance by tearing down the tempting, old bridge.

When Danny moved to our neighborhood, as you would expect, I felt obligated to introduce him to this beloved summer-time diversion. Danny, generally known for his brazen behavior, at times surprised me. During our first unlawful bridge dip, the unpredictable bridge suddenly upended my new friend and dropped him unceremoniously into the cold waters of the Chippewa. His splashdown was both ungraceful and, I suspect, quite painful. After considerable flailing of arms, spitting, and sputtering, Danny stumbled out of the river and wrapped himself in his warm towel. In a shivering voice, he then declared, "Swinging bridges are boring. Let's not come here again. Promise?"

Since Danny and I would never break a promise to each other, that was our last splashdown from the swinging bridge.

WE STORED THE SS dagger under my mattress, adding to the growing collection of valuable objects that Danny insisted on inventorying each time he entered my bedroom. As I held up a corner of the mattress, Ebenezer S. Danny counted his treasures.

- √ Two very full marble bags — just waiting for the opening of marble season, the first day of school.
- √ Danny's awesome samurai sword — a war souvenir from his admiring uncle who confiscated it from a fallen Japanese soldier on Guadalcanal.
- √ An official Nazi postal service book — evidence gathered by FSG members during the investigation of suspected Nazi spy, Hans Zeyer.
- √ The SS dagger — of course.
- √ A pair of shiny cap guns and abundant supply of caps — gently extorted by Danny from the Woolworth store manager who bought Danny's goodwill after my friend suffered a nineteen-stitch wound caused by a deadly Woolworth lawn sprinkler.
- √ The tiny silver key to my Treasure Chest bank — the repository for my other boyhood treasures and my spare cash.

I made a mental note to find a relocation site for the pointier pieces. Sleeping on top of this collection every night was becoming downright uncomfortable.

After his count was complete, Danny nodded his approval. I lowered the mattress and quickly smoothed the covers.

Then I asked, "Wanta use my old suit again?"

"Yep!"

I handed my last year's model to Danny. Though tight on me, it fit him perfectly. After slipping on our identical, newly-acquired black sneakers, we grabbed two bath towels from the narrow linen closet in my family's only bathroom.

Danny always insisted on the lime green one with the pink flamingo. He called it his *ostrich towel.* At first, I thought he was joking, but I came to learn that ornithology and Danny were on two different planets.

As we headed for the front door, with Danny in the lead as usual, he glanced back into my bedroom. Suddenly he stopped. He leaned into the room for a closer look. He had been in my room dozens of times.

What had captured his attention this time?

"Jase, what are those two boxes?"

"They're Aunt Maude's."

He scowled at me. "But what *are* they?"

"Well, that one's a bassinette," I informed him, pointing to the wicker baby bed in the corner. "And that one on my dresser is a bathinette."

"Why does she have two of the same things?"

"They're not the same. This one's for baths and the other's for sleeping."

"Then why are they both called *brass-o-net?*"

"This one is a BATH-o-net. That other one is a BASS-o-net!" I explained, converting the names to his format. "One is for BATH-ing and the other is for —."

My head was spinning. *Why DID they call it a bassinette? They should have called it a sleep-o-net. Or a bed-o-net!*

Danny let me off the hook by coming right to the point. "But what's she going to do with them?"

"She needs them for the baby!"

"Whose baby?"

Sometimes he could be so obtuse! "It's HER baby! Aunt Maude is going to have a baby!"

That stopped him. He glanced around the room quickly, presumably trying to pick up other clues he may have missed. Immediately his face turned red. I believe he was at a loss for words.

I rather enjoyed observing this rare phenomenon. After swallowing hard, he attempted an intelligent follow-up question, largely to break the silence and to remove himself from the hot seat. But he blew it.

"Does she know?"

It was my turn to scoff and frown. Danny looked, first at his shoes briefly, then at me pleadingly. He knew he had muffed it. So I showed him some mercy. "The baby's coming in September, sometime after school starts. We're all excited about it. I'm going to have a new little cousin and a new roommate too."

"Will it be a boy or a girl?" he asked, whiffing his third pitch in a row.

"We'll find out!" I teased, hoping to help Danny recover his dignity.

"Gee! It's goin' to be crowded in here," he observed as he surveyed the cramped bedroom. "Where will the baby sleep? Did you tell me?"

"In this bassinette," I explained. "For a while. Then in my old crib. That'll make it really crowded in here."

He smiled broadly and nodded his head.

Aunt Maude will certainly be relieved to know that she has Danny's approval.

Danny turned and led us toward the front door. I was pleased to be under way at last. As we bounded down the front steps, my unpredictable friend remarked, "But I still wonder why they call both boxes *brass-o-nets.*"

I was pleased that Danny had taken the lead. From that position, he couldn't see me clap my hand over my mouth to stifle the guffaw that I knew was on its way.

TRUMBLE PARK WAS A long two miles from our neighborhood, but attractions along the way made it an extremely enjoyable trip. On our way to and from Hamilton School, we often walked this route just for the fun of it.

The first attraction, the Good Mission Church, stood on the corner of Forrest Street and New Albany Avenue. We heard Edith Squires, the minister's wife, banging out a boogie-woogie version of *Rock of Ages* on her upright piano. Buddy Roe Bibs was sitting on the back porch rubbing his eyes after sleeping off a bit of celebrating. He would soon don his trustee badge and assume his duties, helping the Squires' son Keith in the kitchen.

Right across New Albany from the Good Mission, Pete was sweeping the sidewalk in front of his store.

"Good mornin', Pete," we hollered in unison.

"Gooda morning-ah, boyz! You-sa be gooda today! Okay?" His standard greeting to Danny and me always warmed our hearts. We considered Pete and Mrs. Pete to be our friends. And every neighborhood boy and girl felt the same.

As we made our way down Milford Street, we passed the construction site of the new house for the Matlock family. On temporary loan from the nearby canning factory, the same squad of German POWs that rescued Mrs. Matlock from the flaming house in June was now helping to rebuild the structure. Mrs. Matlock had given Danny and me credit for sizing up her plight and running to fetch the POWs in time to save her life.

She also gave us credit for convincing the *Riverton Daily Press* to print a retraction of their claim that the fire had started as a result of Mrs. Matlock's smoking in bed. We knew for a fact that Mrs. Matlock never smoked or drank alcohol for that matter. After all, we had witnessed the passing steam locomotive shower the roof of the Matlock house with smoldering cinders. That was how the fire actually started.

"Hi, Otto!" we yelled.

Otto grinned broadly and waved from the roof where his squad was laying shingles. "Gut morgen, boyz!"

Otto Klump was our favorite POW. Initially our warm feelings had to do with his access to bubble gum, a scarce wartime commodity for us boys. Not even Pete could get his hands on bubble gum.

But the PX at Camp Riverton, where the POWs were interned, had a plentiful supply that Otto could purchase at prewar prices. POWs could buy personal items using *canteen coupons* that they earned working in the factories and farms in our community. Danny and I had struck a standing deal with Otto to swap jars of sauerkraut from our family's supply for valuable packages of bubble gum. Everyone agreed it was a win-win proposition.

At the end of Milford Street, we crossed the railroad tracks just east of the canning factory. Then we saw it! Paradise lay just ahead. The Riverton City Dump! Not only was the dump a source of *good junk* as Danny called it, but it was also an exciting place to spend the day pawing for prizes. I knew Mom wasn't particularly partial to *Eaux de Dump.* But, to Danny and me, the fragrance was better than the finest perfume money could buy.

After breaking away from the dump, we continued down Trumble Street right into Trumble Park. As we walked toward the pool, I inventoried the park's many forms of amusement. Picnic areas. Swing sets. Horseshoe pits. Ball diamonds. A creek filled with fish. And, of course, a public swimming pool.

Years later, Riverton boys who were home from college would assemble in the park on Thanksgiving morning for our annual touch football game. The grassy expanse adjacent to the parking lot made an ideal field. On one unforgettable occasion, I threw a jolting cross-body block on Eugene Thompson. The poor fellow had anticipated scoring a touchdown and then going home to enjoy his mother's turkey dinner. Instead, he spent the day in the emergency room, being fitted with a cast for his broken collarbone.

I felt very sorry for old Eugene until Danny reminded me of my blockee's wartime transgression. "Silk marble bag — broken collarbone," he reasoned, weighing these two events by moving his open palms up and down in front of my face. "Sounds like retributive justice to me."

Danny must have been right because, since then, my conscience hasn't bothered me a bit.

I wonder if Eugene's collarbone still bothers him on rainy days.

During that summer of 1944, Trumble Park was particularly appealing to us on Wednesdays when Miss Sparks, our soon-to-be sixth-grade teacher, served as substitute lifeguard at the pool. Knowing that she would be my teacher, I had never been more enthusiastic about the opening of school. I simply couldn't imagine anyone who wouldn't want to be with her every day, even if she insisted on completed homework assignments.

Danny was totally smitten with Miss Sparks as well. Who could blame him? She was a beauty, and so very nice to us boys. The sweet anticipation of seeing her at the pool was almost more than either of us could bear. But today wasn't Wednesday, so Danny's urge to go swimming was an odd one, even for Danny.

When we arrived at the pool, we waited in line to wash our feet in the strong disinfectant designed to kill any organism lurking there. After our astringent footbath, we waited to spread our toes.

"All of them. WIDE!" ordered the assistant lifeguard.

The control freak in question was an acne-spotted teenager who was feeling his oats after expelling a sobbing five-year-old. The little boy had apparently exhibited enough of a crack between two tiny toes to be deemed an athlete's foot menace to us all. The patient angrily disagreed with Dr. Pimple's diagnosis, but he got the boot anyway.

"How could he have anything contagious between his toes after stepping into that bucket of bleach?" I asked Danny.

"Fungi may live through such a bath because they are a particularly virulent form of life," he answered medicinally.

Since I didn't have a comeback for that, I held my peace. Danny had obviously boned up on swimming-pool hygiene to impress Miss Sparks.

That day most of the bathers were preschoolers whose mothers came to sunbathe. The chairs surrounding the shallow end of the pool including the baby-polluted wading pool were full, but the other end was sparsely populated. Danny suggested, "Let's go down to the deep end. There's nobody there."

"Wanta go in, Danny?"

"No. Let's jus' sit for a while. I wanna ask you somethin'."

"Okay, shoot!" I replied, slipping onto a sun-warmed chaise.

Danny didn't sit. Looking down on me, he spoke softly, "You ever been to church camp before?"

"No. Why?"

Danny didn't answer, but I thought I knew what was on his mind. Going to church camp had not been his idea. The decision had been made for both of us by Grandma Compton. She meant well, but sometimes her religious fervor got in the way of her common sense. Her camp *gift* fell into that category.

Don't get me wrong. Danny and Grandma were enthusiastic members of a mutual admiration society. When they first met, it was love at first sight. That was fantastic as far as I was concerned. Grandma was the greatest!

The common bond between Grandma and Danny was their love of the same four-letter word. F-O-O-D! Grandpa Compton was convinced that Danny played *host* to a *host* of tapeworms. Grandma placed her faith in the *just-a-growing-boy* theory. I could agree with either side of the argument. Regardless of who was right, I had never met anyone his age who ate more food, and more often, than Danny.

Another one of Grandma's biases came into play when she bestowed this gift on us. Reverend Claude Johnson whom she admired had volunteered to help close Camp Harmony for the season. He would take us with him, thus saving precious gasoline ration points for our family. As a minister, his gasoline supply was unlimited, freeing him to cruise the county in pursuit of sinners.

Grandma and Grandpa Compton enjoyed a warm relationship with Reverend Johnson and his wife Rose. In fact, the Johnsons had lived at the Compton farm for a time before the Barrington Church of Christ found them a place of their own. Grandma attended church regularly, especially if she knew Reverend Johnson would be preaching.

Other members of Grandma's family were not enthusiastic churchgoers. Along with her daughters Marie and Maude, my mother and aunt, Grandpa was another one of her failures to convert, convince, or cajole into going to church.

But she accepted their decisions and seldom imposed her strong Christian beliefs on others. Instead, she settled for taking on special projects like making sure that Danny and I got to church camp. Frankly I was looking forward to it. But I suspected that my new best friend didn't share my enthusiasm.

Two weeks earlier, Grandma announced that we boys, *men* as she called us, were owed a share of the wheat harvest proceeds because we had provided so much help on threshing day. Technically she was correct. I had driven a team of horses, and Danny had *helped* in the kitchen. However, being true to my policy of never taking money for working on the farm, I immediately refused her offer.

Danny's standards were a little more liberal. He happily informed her that, if I didn't want my share, he might know a needy ten-year-old who could use a *couple of extra bucks*. So we compromised. No cash would change hands, thus preserving my high standard. But Grandma would pay the eight dollars for each of us to attend camp for a week.

But, since then, I sensed something had changed with Danny. We were heading off to camp in two days, and he clearly wasn't comfortable with some aspect of that reality. I probed a bit further.

"Danny, is there something bothering you about going to camp? Do you want to talk to me about it? Or to Grandma Compton?"

He didn't answer at first. He shuffled his feet and, with a pathetic look, asked, "I just wanted to know, how many meals will we get while we're there?"

I might have known.

2 | REAPING THE PROFITS

SATURDAYS WERE SLEEP-IN MORNINGS FOR MOST adults in our blue-collar neighborhood. Those who did work Saturday shifts took care to leave for work quietly. Even the area dogs relaxed their bark-at-anything-that-moves policy to catch a few extra winks and dream about the wily cottontails that populated our part of town.

But this morning was an exception, at least at our house. Not long after sunrise, I awoke to the sound of Aunt Maude yawning and stretching her way to the bathroom. "Oh, Jase. Sorry. Didn't mean to wake you," she apologized when she saw me sit up in bed.

"That's okay, Aunt Maude. I wanta get my things together for camp anyway."

We were not the first ones up. The smell of freshly brewed coffee and the clinking of dishes floated our way from the kitchen. I slipped on my clothes and headed in that direction.

"Up before breakfast, eh?"

"Very funny, Danny!"

Danny had appropriated Grandpa Compton's standard morning greeting since his first visit to the farm. When Grandpa said it, I always laughed. Lately when Danny said it, I was tempted to respond with a pop to his lolly.

"Morning, Son. Ready for camp?" Mom asked with a smile on her face.

"You bet! Just got to pack."

"Brought the duffel bags," Danny declared. "Mine's all packed. I'll show you how to pack yours."

Danny turned his attention back to his tall stack of pancakes.

"Jase, do you want some pancakes too?"

"Sounds excellent, Mom. Do we have any more blueberry syrup?"

"Nope!" slurped Danny. "Try some sugar and cinnamon."

At times, having Danny as a frequent early-morning visitor was burdensome. However, I *was* grateful that he no longer felt compelled to follow the normal *come-out call* protocol, dictating how we boys summoned our friends from their houses. His call was deafening. It was hard to imagine how a relatively slight boy like Danny could generate such a megasound. It woke neighbors blocks away and had begun to loosen the wallpaper in my bedroom.

Like the rest of the neighbors, we never locked our doors. So, when Danny arrived, he just came inside and made himself at home in our kitchen. I'll bet that's why he knew we were out of blueberry syrup.

What am I saying? Wasn't the sticky purple-blue ring around Danny's mouth evidence enough?

"Where's Dad, Mom?"

"He's out in his shed getting an early start on some sewing-machine repair jobs. He's trying to catch up with the backlog from when he worked all that overtime at Burkes last week."

The Norden bombsight was one of the most closely guarded secrets of the U.S. military during World War II. The Burke Factory made the *brain* of the bombsight. Its analog computer was assembled from gyros, motors, and gears that were manufactured to the highest degree of precision that only Riverton craftsmen could produce. Like many of his fellow tool and die makers, my father was deferred from military service because of his war-critical skills.

The bombsight could calculate the precise second at which bombs had to be dropped from high altitudes to hit their targets. Its accuracy was astonishing. From a B-17 flying at an altitude of 21,000 feet, almost four miles above the earth, a bomb hit no more than a hundred feet from its target. Using this deadly bombsight, the American bomber crippled the Nazi war machine.

The secrecy accorded the bombsight was extensive. The devices were not loaded into the aircraft until after the crews were aboard. And the bombsight was not uncovered and made ready for use until after the bomber was airborne. During the war, forty-five thousand bombardiers were trained to use the Norden bombsight. Those men were required to protect its secrecy, with their lives if necessary, by swearing under oath to the following:

The Bombardier's Oath

Mindful of the secret trust about to be placed in me by my Commander in Chief, the President of the United States, by whose direction I was chosen for bombardier training — and mindful of the fact that I am to become guardian of one of my country's most priceless military assets, the American bombsight — I do here, in the presence of Almighty God, swear by the Bombardier's Code of Honor to keep inviolate the secrecy of any and all confidential information revealed to me and, further, to uphold the honor and integrity of the Army Air Forces, if need be, with my life itself.

On August 6, 1945, the bombardier in the B-29 *Enola Gay* used the Norden bombsight to drop the atomic bomb, *Little Boy,* from 31,000 feet above Hiroshima. Japan agreed to an unconditional surrender shortly thereafter.

My father was also the area's very best sewing-machine repairman. He operated his demanding side business during evenings and on weekends when he wasn't working at Burkes.

Over the years, his willingness to take time away from us and spend it on his business greatly improved the economic well-being of our family. My mother also helped in the business. She was the very best sewing teacher in the county. In fact, she worked part-time teaching those skills to the POWs out at Camp Riverton. Our whole family supported her role in the war effort.

Mom set my plate of hot pancakes in front of me. "Here you are, Jase."

"Good morning, everybody," Aunt Maude said as she entered the kitchen. "Looks like the whole team's here for breakfast this morning." She gave Danny a robust rub on the top of his Tigers cap.

"Mahw. Ann Mahwd," Danny mumbled through his pancakes.

"Who's that out back with John so early in the morning?" Aunt Maude asked my mother.

Mom stood up and looked out the screen door. "My gosh! It's Junior! He's just gotten home after being released from Walter Reed."

"Junior!" I yelled. "Hurry up, Danny. We gotta get outside."

Junior Shurtleif was one of my heroes. He was the only son of our friends and neighbors, Lars and Emma Shurtleif, who lived across Forrest Street from us. Mr. Shurtleif served as our neighborhood air-raid warden. Mrs. Shurtleif was an operator with the Riverton Central Telephone Company where she had worked with Uncle Van before the war.

After Pearl Harbor, Junior had been one of the first young men in our neighborhood to enlist in the army. He advanced quickly as his battlefield experience accumulated and his leadership skills were recognized.

During the fighting in Sicily, he was given a battlefield commission for his brave and intelligent job of leading his platoon to victory over a superior German force. Unfortunately he was seriously wounded at Monte Cassino in Italy. Knowing that he was unable to walk, he ordered his men to fall back behind Allied lines while he covered their withdrawal with a Browning Automatic

Rifle. After expending his last round of ammunition and being hampered by his wounds, he was taken prisoner by a crack unit of Nazi SS. Fortunately, within hours, his men rescued him and saved his life.

His most serious wound ultimately led to the amputation of the lower part of his right leg. As he recuperated in Walter Reed Army Hospital outside of Washington, DC, he learned to walk again on an artificial leg. Recently we read that, until the army could find a suitable new assignment for him, he had been ordered to an interim desk job down at Camp Custer, only a few hours drive from Riverton.

I knew the details of Junior's army career from overhearing Mr. Shurtleif proudly report his son's progress while he and Dad sat on our back porch smoking their pipes. I had read the accounts of his brave action at Monte Cassino for which he was awarded the Silver Star. Yep, to the boys of our neighborhood, Captain Lars "Junior" Shurtleif was a genuine war hero.

"Look who's here, folks," Dad hollered through the screen door. "It's Junior!"

We had all been so busy concentrating on finishing our breakfast that we hadn't heard them come up the back steps. There he stood, straight and tall. His uniform fit him perfectly. His chest was covered with service ribbons. What an awesome sight! But I couldn't help looking at his legs. Hidden by his trousers, both looked quite normal to me.

"Junior! Well, for the love of Mike! Welcome home! It's so nice to see you. How about a cup of coffee?" Mom offered warmly.

"Sounds perfect, Marie. Oops! I mean *Mrs. Addison.*"

"Cut that out. *Marie* will be just fine, thank you. Besides you've done a bit of growing since I took that splinter out of your —. Oh, well, we don't have to go into that right now, do we?" she teased with another smile.

"Marie it is then, provided you never mention that splinter again."

Before I was old enough to remember, Mom had offered to keep young Junior while the Shurtleifs attended a funeral in

Detroit. Junior found that the sloping basement doors beside our back porch made an excellent makeshift slide. After several painless trips down the slide, a very nasty sliver penetrated several layers of clothing and lodged in his tender backside. Nurse Mom insisted that the sliver must come out. Right now!

The operation was simple, lasting only a few minutes. But the story took on a life of its own. I heard it told and retold, always followed by a hearty round of laughter. By the time Junior reached adolescence, he was not fond of being the *butt* of that particular joke. Mercifully Mom had filed it away until this morning.

After we were settled in on the back porch, Dad said, "You'll never guess what Junior's next duty station is going to be." We all looked at each other, shook our heads, and then turned back to Dad. "Camp Riverton! That's what! He's going to be Colonel Butler's new second-in-command. How about that?"

This was really fabulous news! There were three Gold Stars hanging in the windows of Forrest Street homes. All honored Junior's former playmates. But plenty of fathers, brothers, and sons were still at risk, including Uncle Van. At least Junior was home alive. Alive and a famous hero to boot!

Aunt Maude had always teased him. "Tell us what you've been up to lately, Junior," Aunt Maude urged with a straight face.

After about a second of silence, Junior burst into laughter. We all joined him. All, that is, except Danny who stared at us like we had lost our minds. Junior quickly explained, "It's Danny, isn't it?"

Danny nodded and gazed at him with saucer-size eyes. Junior reached out, grabbed Danny's hand, and gave it a vigorous shake. Danny shook back and shot him a winning smile.

"Maude was teasing me about the flattering coverage of my — ahem — military career in the *Riverton Daily Press*. She knows what a modest guy I am so she was just trying to get my goat."

"Oh, right. Modesty is Junior's long suit," Aunt Maude huffed, laying it on thick. Then she broke into laughter herself.

Turning serious, Junior looked at her and predicted, "Maude, I imagine Van's on your mind all the time. From what I hear, he's a fine soldier, and he's no fool either. He knows how to look out for himself and his men. There's still a lot of fighting to do. But I'm optimistic about Van. Before you know it, he'll be sitting right here on this porch, safe and sound. You'll see."

"Thanks, Junior. Comin' from you — well. It means a lot," Maude assured him as she reached out and patted his arm. "In any case, I'm sure delighted you're home."

Junior smiled. Then he turned to Danny and me. "So you boys are in the bait business, huh?"

"Not anymore," Danny informed him. "Homer Jensen is back home from the Marines. He was wounded in his very first battle, the invasion of Guam. He got a medal. Then he was disgorged."

"Discharged!" I corrected, louder than I had intended.

Danny didn't seem to notice. He looked at Junior and added, "Homer Jensen and Mr. Lyle, Homer Lyle, are back in the bait business together. So Jase and I are retired. I suggested they call the business 'Homer Homer Bait.' They're still thinking about it."

"Well, it's too bad your worm careers had to end. I know my folks enjoyed night crawling around the backyard with everybody. Got any other business plans?"

Never to be discouraged, Danny confided, "We're thinking about the banking business right now." That one brought down the house. After I stopped laughing, I wondered where we would buy our vault.

We all looked out into the backyard as silence briefly descended on the conversation. I noticed that Mrs. Mikas' plums looked ripe. I remembered how the gooey sap sticks to your hands when you pick plums. I made a note to warn Danny ahead of time.

Junior broke the silence. "In this war, not all the heroes are serving on the front. I understand from Colonel Butler that you two boys did a heck of a job outsmarting a couple of bad apples by the names of Reitter and Baden, right?"

Suddenly my cheeks felt hot. I was blushing. For Junior, a true war hero, to put us in his category was more than even my strong ego could bear. But Danny didn't miss a beat. "Yep! They stole our sauerkraut at the canning factory. So we didn't get our bubble gum for a while. But then we caught 'em out at Granville Park with the Libby sisters. The judge sent the Libbys to prison. Reitter and Baden are Nazi rats. But there are good apple POWs too, like Otto Klump. He and his squad rescued Mrs. Matlock after Jase went to get them from the canning factory. That's how we got to be heroes, a couple of times, I guess. Nope, we aren't even in the army yet."

"When you're old enough to enlist, I'd sure like to have Jase and you in my outfit, Danny."

It was Danny's turn to blush.

DANNY DEMONSTRATED HIS PACKING skills by picking up my underwear drawer and dumping its contents into one of his father's duffel bags. Mr. Tucker, a onetime Navy *lifer,* was medically discharged after receiving career-ending wounds at Pearl Harbor.

"Danny, I think we're supposed to fold it neatly. And then put it in the bag."

"Nope, that's with suitcases. Not duffel bags. My dad taught me how."

I shrugged my shoulders and upended my sock drawer into the large bag. I knew there was no arguing with a salty veteran like Danny.

"Do you want to take your ostrich towel, Danny?"

"I awready packed it."

"Are you sure? I hung it on the clothesline after our swim yesterday. I left it out all night to dry."

"I came by and picked it up last night. After everybody was asleep."

I was flabbergasted. "Did you happen to find anything else you needed to pack while you were here?"

"Yep. Some of Aunt Maude's oatmeal cookies. I took most of them so we wouldn't get hungry on our way to camp."

I changed the subject by lifting my mattress to retrieve the key to my bank. "The camp packing list says to bring some spending money. How much are you taking?"

"Seven cents."

"Wow! That much, huh?"

"I figured we could earn some more when we got there."

"How're we gonna do that?"

Danny scooped up the two fully loaded marble bags. He put a bag to each side of his face and smiled. He looked like a chipmunk with his cheek pouches full of hickory nuts. "Marbles!" was his answer.

"How are we —?" I stammered. But I stopped myself.

Experience had taught me that sometimes *not knowing* was often preferable to *knowing* when it came to Danny and his inscrutable answers. So I returned to my packing. It only took a few minutes to finish. I rechecked the list of suggested items before we dragged my bag out to the front room. Because of its bulk, Mr. Tucker had delivered Danny's in the family's old Dodge station wagon. He had propped it up in the corner of our front room near the door. Then he headed for the back porch to chat with Dad and Junior.

"Grandma thought she'd be here by midmorning," I reminded my friend.

Danny flashed a broad smile. We both knew what was in store for us. Grandma was regarded as the family's fastest and most reckless driver. No one dared join her as she launched low-altitude flights in her dashing, green Hudson Terraplane. No one that is, except Danny and me. It was a thrill-a-second experience and we relished it.

Suddenly we heard a scream of brakes and scraping of gravel from the street, culminating with a loud *toot, de toot, toot!* "It's Grandma!" yelled Danny, rushing out the door.

Before I could join him, I heard Dad call from the back porch. "Jase, can you come out here, please?"

"Okay!"

When I arrived, the demeanor of Mr. Tucker, Junior, and Dad surprised me. They appeared to be quite concerned about something. For an instant, I feared that I might have done something wrong.

"What is it, Dad?"

"You need to hear what Junior just reported."

"Jase, the two POWs that you helped capture have threatened to get even with Danny," Junior announced soberly. "They've been boasting to their fellow POWs about what they'll do with him, if they get a chance."

As his message soaked in, a chill worked its way down my spine. I knew that Reitter and Baden were bad apples, but I didn't think they would try to harm us. "But why just Danny? Why not me too?" I asked.

"Not sure. It may have something to do with Danny's — how should I put it? His *style*. Apparently they think he's a little *cocky.*"

They got that right.

Then Mr. Tucker affirmed, "Boy! They got that right." We all smiled at each other. The chill lifted from my spine and curiosity took over.

"Anyway," Junior continued, "Colonel Butler and I have decided to remove them from Otto's squad at the canning factory and send them away from Riverton. That'll make it impossible, or at least very difficult, for them to get back here to our neighborhood and carry out their threats."

"Where will they be working?"

"Don't know yet. But, by the time you boys are home from camp, we hope to have them situated in a remote corner of the county. Permanently assigned to one of our detachments, working on one of the large farms. Or at a pea vinery, sawmill, or the like."

"Does Danny know about this?" I asked, looking at Dad.

"No, Son, he doesn't. We didn't want him to be afraid. But Junior and I thought it was best to let Danny's parents and you know. Just to be on the alert. It sounds like the problem will be fixed by the time you're home from camp. But I still wouldn't say anything to Danny about this, okay?"

We all shook hands on the deal. Then we left the porch to greet Grandma. Mr. Tucker and Dad carried our duffel bags to the trunk of the Terraplane while Grandma welcomed Junior home with one of her patented bear hugs.

"Are you sure you won't stay for lunch, Mom?" my mother asked.

"No, we gotta get out to the farm and get that load of wheat over to the elevator before five. I got a little something made up for me and the boys to nibble on during our wagon trip. We'll be fine."

Danny's eyes sparkled at that news. "Terrific!" he whispered.

I was sure of one thing. Within an hour or two, we could expect a rolling banquet.

"Well, at least let me give you some of Maude's oatmeal cookies. She made a giant batch yesterday so there's plenty to share."

I glanced at Danny whose eyes had rolled upward as if he were examining the limbs of the box elder tree above us. I pinched him. He gave me a dirty look. Then he looked Mom right in the eye. And fibbed.

"Don't think there're any left. Aunt Maude probably took 'em to work!"

"Geez!" I wheezed under my breath.

Whenever Danny was in a tight spot, he employed a creative exit strategy that frequently included one of his whoppers.

"What Danny means is that we've packed them for camp. Sorry, Mom," I confessed for my sticky-fingered colleague.

He thanked me by shaking his finger at me, as if I were the culprit.

"Oh, that's a relief," announced Grandma, coming to the rescue. "In a pinch, we can always break open one of those duffel bags."

After a warm round of hugs and goodbyes, Danny and I piled into the dusty Terraplane and braced ourselves for takeoff. Grandma revved her engines, popped the clutch, and roared down Forrest Street in a cloud of swirling gravel dust. As we squealed around the corner at New Albany, the only person I could see clearly in our wake was Junior Shurtleif. He was standing in the middle of Forrest Street, shaking his head in disbelief.

That was just before Grandma hit the afterburners. As we lifted off New Albany and cleared the treetops, she adjusted her flying goggles and tossed her long silk scarf over her shoulder. The wind caught the scarf and snapped it like a bullwhip.

Flying with Grandma may have been risky, but there was nothing like it in terms of sheer excitement. At least that's what a pair of giggling admirers thought at that very moment. As we came to our heading, Danny looked at me and grinned. I replied by blinking my eyes at him, twice.

"In this war, not all the heroes are serving on the front!" he screamed as Riverton disappeared over the horizon.

WE VEERED INTO THE circular driveway and screeched to a halt behind the wagon parked next to the granary. Harnessed and standing in front of the wagon, Gene and Teddy snorted, stretched their necks, and shook their heads to welcome us. This sleek pair of chestnuts was Grandpa's light team. They were more spirited and faster than Jim and Fannie, the older heavier team.

"Hi, Grandpa!" I yelled as I leaped from the car.

"Howdy, boys! 'Lo, Maw!"

My old friend Mick, the bouncy fox terrier, leaped into the air, *yapping* like he had something important to tell us. His welcome earned him a vigorous chin rub. Waving a few fingers at Grandpa, Danny smiled broadly, adjusted his Tigers cap, and rested his hands on his hips.

Grandpa stood just inside the granary's wide-open sliding doors. He was sweeping the leftovers from his grain-loading operation out onto the driveway where jostling chickens, mostly Plymouth Rocks, were fighting for every kernel.

"Dad, how'd the new loader work?" Grandma asked.

"Dandy! That Old Nate's a genius."

Nate Craddock owned the farm that adjoined my grandparents' place. Old Nate was an artist with a welding torch, but he wasn't much of a farmer. So Grandpa worked Old Nate's farm for him and they split the profits equally. Old Nate contributed his valuable mechanical and carpentry skills, *free gratis,* as Grandpa put it.

Old Nate had crafted a widemouthed hopper out of lightweight angle iron and pine boards. The hopper hung from a light block and tackle mounted on the granary ceiling. The hopper could be fastened, flush and tight, against any of the grain bins that lined the granary walls.

The ingenious device enabled Grandpa to download large quantities of grain from high bins into the wagon below using gravity, instead of the old method, one shovelful at a time. Grandpa merely secured the hopper against the bin and pulled up the top slat. The grain fell, first into the hopper, then down a long canvas tube, about a foot in diameter, and into the waiting wagon. It saved hours of backbreaking work.

"Where's that old buzzard?" Grandma asked.

"Maw, when he saw you comin', he hightailed it outta here afore you could catch him wearin' his old duds. Haw! Haw!"

"Dad, you mean to tell me he's still wearing that grimy green set of work clothes?"

"Green? I'll be darned. Are you sure? They looked kinda charcoal-colored to me."

"What am I going to do with that old —." She didn't finish but merely sputtered to a conclusion.

The battle between Grandma and Old Nate had been waged lovingly for the better part of a decade. Nate was another one of Grandma's *special projects.* He was a bachelor who, over the years, had lost interest in his personal appearance and hygiene. Grandma took it upon herself to clean up his act and dress him in untattered outfits.

And so the war of wits continued. Sometimes Grandma would win. Other times Old Nate wiggled away. In either case, the conflict fascinated Danny and me. Not being too clean ourselves,

Old Nate was our sentimental favorite in the battle. But backing Grandma was more likely to pay off, in the form of ice cream and other goodies that she bestowed on her allies in the Nate campaign.

I grabbed hold of the front rack and pulled myself up to see the contents of the wagon box. The rounded load of wheat was a beautiful gold-orange color that signified its ripeness. I reached down and lifted a handful to my nose. It still exuded that fresh odor of harvest that I so loved. I tossed the handful back on the load and turned to Grandpa for instructions.

"Okay, Jase. You're free to take off whenever you want. You know the route. I'd take Henry Road, if I's you. Less traffic on it than Riverton Road. You just take it on over to the state highway. When you get there jog a mile north and turn west again right on into Granville. You remember the way, don't cha?"

"Don't worry, Grandpa. I know just how to get there. Grandma and I've driven it lots of times."

Boy! That was the truth. One of Grandma's frequent ice cream stops was the gas station and general store at the corner of Granville Road and the state highway. We'd beat a path to that door at least once a week whenever I stayed at the farm.

"Maw, you know what to do when you get there, don't cha?"

"Yes, Dad. We've been over it a number of times. I have my co-op identification card. And you showed me how to fill out the paperwork. And I know how to deposit the check in our account at the Granville bank. So don't you worry about a thing. Just take a nap or listen to a baseball game. It won't be long before we're back with that big deposit receipt."

"Okay, okay. You better shove off if you wanta git home afore dark. Jase, better top off the team now. Then you can fill them up again over at the elevator afore coming home. Hand 'em a few handsful of wheat before you off-load, okay?"

"You bet, Grandpa."

Danny could barely contain himself. I could tell he was bursting to say something. As I brought the horses to a stop at the watering tank next to the cow barn, he let loose. "Are you really gonna drive the horses?"

"Sure! Why not?" I responded nonchalantly, attempting to hide my bursting pride.

"Why doesn't Grandpa drive 'em? Or Grandma? I don't get it!"

"Grandpa isn't supposed to drive on the highways. Remember how I told you about his losing sight in his gray eye? The accident at the foundry. He's blind in that eye and he doesn't have insurance."

"But what about Grandma then?"

"Grandma's a pretty decent horse driver when she's just gotta go back and forth in the field. When you're doing that, the horses pretty much drive themselves. That's not real hard. But, when you're driving horses out on the roads, especially with cars whizzing by, it's a lot harder. Besides you know how she drives her car."

"Oh, yeah! Now I get it. I think I'd rather have you drive the horses, Jase."

His words were music to my ears. Besides a few cousins, not many people my age knew about my horse-driving skill. And, of course, Danny's approval meant the most.

"Jase, how long you been drivin' horses?"

I couldn't honestly answer him because I had started at such a young age. As I got older, Grandpa depended more and more on me to work with the horses at the farm. Although he never came right out and said it, I thought my ability and availability to drive for him during the summers were why he kept two teams of horses. Not many farmers had two teams. Under normal circumstances, it would have been considered an extravagance. But with two drivers working the farm, it made sense.

However, Grandpa didn't always feel this way. In fact, had it not been for the typically nasty Michigan winter weather, Gene and Teddy might have been working for another Chippewa County farmer. Before you can fully appreciate the circumstances, you have to know something about our street in Riverton.

JUST BEYOND THE COTTONWOOD tree, Forrest Street takes a nosedive, sloping rapidly downward past the swamp and ending at the Chippewa River. Never plowed in winter, the street surface is quite treacherous for cars but excellent for sledding. One false move and a car could skid over the shoulder and into the swamp, an unfortunate event because towing fees were high. Moreover, few tow-truck drivers were eager to take on the risky job of pulling a car from the swamp.

Each winter, a few Forrest Street drivers who *should know better* were among those who paid an unexpected visit to the swamp. As a matter-of-fact, we experienced our first, and fortunately our last, such visit during the winter of 1940.

One particularly cold Thursday morning in mid-December, Sergeant Jeff Tolna, our neighbor and Riverton police officer, convinced Dad to take a vacation day so they could try their luck ice fishing on the Chippewa River near the end of our street. Appreciative of Jeff's suggestion and needing time off from his usual state of work-induced exhaustion, Dad offered to cart the fishing equipment, kerosene heater, and windscreens down to the river in our Chevrolet.

On their way home for supper, about halfway up our hill, Dad sneezed. Yes, sneezed. At least, that's his story. He always tells it the same way, so it must be true. The Chevrolet ended up balanced precariously over the edge of our street with its nose down in the swamp and its rear bumper high in the air.

They tried to jack up the front of the car, but even on this frigid day, the base of the jack sank into the yet unfrozen swampy muck. After an hour of unsuccessful attempts to free the car, the two frozen men slipped and slid back to our house to break the bad news. While the frosty fishermen sat next to the hot woodstove in our front room, plotting their next move, Grandpa and Grandma Compton arrived with bad news of their own. They had spent the day at the Riverton Livestock Yard. After a disappointing livestock auction, they stopped for a short visit before heading back to the farm.

Earlier in the fall, Grandpa had acquired Jim and Fannie, a dappled white and a sorrel, both giant Belgians. He needed the new heavyweights to provide increased power for the bottomland plowing along the creek on the north end of the farm and for fitting Old Nate's hardened, clay-ridden fields. Even though he was extremely fond of Gene and Teddy, the more flexible and faster lightweight workhorses, he began to realize that a farm with only one farmer could not afford the luxury of two teams. After considerable deliberation, Grandpa decided to sell Gene and Teddy, his pair of young, perfectly matched chestnut workhorses, to avoid the expense of feeding two teams over the winter.

Every Thursday, potential buyers assembled at the stockyards and commenced their prebidding ritual of poking, prodding, and pinching the broad assortment of beef and dairy cattle, butcher and breeder pigs, wool and mutton sheep, and workhorses hauled in by sellers from farms in the Riverton area.

In November, before bad weather set in, Grandpa had made arrangements to board the team at the stockyards. This arrangement eliminated the need for hauling them back and forth to the stockyards and enabled potential buyers to inspect the chestnut team well before auction day.

But this particular Thursday had not been a good day because of the foul weather and the proximity to Christmas. Bidders, especially for lightweight workhorses, were few and far between. The auctioneer and Grandpa had agreed beforehand on a reasonable starting price for the team. But Grandpa didn't receive a single bid above the minimum. So back into the boarding barn they went for another week.

Upon hearing the fishermen's sad story, Grandpa suggested a solution. He had wanted to exercise the chestnuts before returning home anyway. And he was certain he could round up the necessary harnesses and rigging at the boarding barn to outfit his team to rescue Dad's stranded Chevy. As a matter-of-fact, he remembered seeing an old stone boat, a flat wooden carrier resembling an oversized door that could be towed to transport the team's driver more easily over the snowy mile-and-a-half run to the swamp.

With the solution in hand, Dad and Grandpa piled into Grandma's Terraplane and headed for the stockyards. Dad drove because of Grandpa's bad eye. By agreement, Jeff headed back to the Tolna house to round up his family and a stock of Polish delicacies to add to the spread that Grandma and Mom would put together in anticipation of a successful rescue.

In less than an hour, the handsome chestnut horses, shaking their borrowed harnesses and blowing their steamy breath high into the frosty evening air, pranced down Forrest Street. Behind them were two figures, one balanced expertly with the reins in his hands and the other hanging on for dear life as the stone boat bounced over snow banks and wheel ruts in the street.

Upon arriving at the abandoned Chevy, Grandpa unhitched the team from the stone boat and, using a chain that he borrowed at the stockyards, secured the team to the car's rear bumper. Then, responding to Grandpa's gentle urgings, Gene and Teddy effortlessly lifted the car out of the swampy mire. When all four wheels were solidly back on earth again, Grandpa unhitched his spunky team and rehooked them to the stone boat.

Dad jumped into the car. The Chevy started immediately. Not wasting a minute, Grandpa snapped the reins and the team headed back up Forrest Street, followed by Dad in the Chevy. This procession continued by our house and on to the stockyards.

Grandpa drove the team slowly to cool them down, both physically and mentally. The horses seemed to know that they had saved the day. They strutted in a cocky cadence all the way back to their place of lodging. Once there, Grandpa curried their haunches, necks, and backs vigorously and rubbed down each one with a coarse horse blanket. Finally he treated them each to an extra ration of fine oats and scratched their ears affectionately before turning off the barn lights.

When Dad and Grandpa arrived home, the celebration began. What a feast! Funny thing though, freshly caught fish were not on the menu that evening.

As a result of this experience, Grandpa decided he couldn't part with Gene and Teddy. So that next spring and for many springs thereafter, two teams of spirited workhorses were enjoyed by the farm's sole farmer and one grateful, apprentice horseman named Jase Addison.

APPARENTLY DANNY HAD ACCEPTED my explanation for driving the horses that day because he abruptly changed subjects. "Do we have time for a snack before we leave for the escalator?"

I didn't correct his pronunciation. Instead, I gave him an assignment that I thought would appeal to him. "Why don't you help Grandma load the picnic lunch? Then we can leave for the elevator right after I hitch up the horses."

"Okay, I will!" he shouted as he turned and ran toward the kitchen. But then he stopped. "Jase, do you have that insurance so you can drive on highways?"

His question caught me by surprise. "Nope!"

With that, Danny sped off toward the house. Evidently there were visions of picnic goodies dancing in his head. I wondered if he'd even heard my answer.

Danny, my friend, you asked an excellent question. I'm going to check on that answer with Grandpa, right after we get back from Granville.

But that could wait. This was going to be my longest and most important trip. And I didn't want to miss it.

Gene and Teddy were drinking deeply. Seeming to sense that something exciting was about to happen, they shivered, stomped, and snorted. Nothing enthuses a *work*horse more than the prospect of *work*.

After Grandma and Danny finished preparing our feast, Grandma used the king-size scoop shovel from the granary to level the wheat. Then the two of them spread the tarpaulin over the load and placed several blankets on top of that. Finally right in the center, Grandma had spread her red and white checkerboard tablecloth. And, on top of that, the plates, silverware, and dish after dish of delicious smelling food!

I stepped to my driver's position high on the front rack above the wagon bed. "Gitty up! Haw over there, Gene! Haw, Teddy!" I ordered as we rolled slowly past the house and out the driveway.

"This wagon looks like my dining-room table at Christmas time!" Grandma exclaimed.

Grandpa waved goodbye as we pulled onto the road.

"Merry Christmas, Grandpa!" Danny yelled, chomping down on his first chicken leg.

WITH GENE AND TEDDY on the job, we were making excellent time. About an hour-and-a-half into our trip, Grandma suggested we pull off the road so I could join her and Danny for dinner. I sensed a trace of urgency in her voice.

"I'll just pull into Granville Park, Grandma."

"Wonderful idea!"

Once we entered the park, I halted the team under a tall elm tree just off Granville Road. I tied off the reins and climbed down from the front rack to the wagon bed. It didn't take long to figure out why Grandma wanted to stop. Danny had already put a considerable dent in the available food supply. I grimaced and looked at Grandma who responded by closing her eyes and shaking her head.

"Good thing I stopped, eh, Danny?"

"Maleff mum shlluff," he answered.

I grabbed the last chicken leg before it was sucked into the human food processor. "How far do you think it is into Granville, Grandma?"

"Not more than two miles, I'd say."

As I quickly finished my dinner, I surveyed the park. About two months earlier, Danny and I had shared an interesting adventure not far from where we'd stopped.

"Hey, Danny, do you recognize this place?"

He swung his glance from picnic table, to swing set, and back to sandbox. Then he looked at me and shook his head. Grandma gave him a hint. "Isn't this where you two boys became local heroes this past June?"

It was just a mile or so north, at the other end of the park, where Danny and I had stumbled upon Reitter and Baden. There the POW escapees had spent the night with several bottles of wine and their two accomplices, our neighbors, the Libby sisters.

As the *Riverton Daily Press* couched it, we had used our "wits and courage to capture the foursome." Actually we weren't alone in the effort. We did have just a little help from a dozen Riverton Police officers, the sheriff and every one of his deputies, a squad of Military Police from Camp Riverton, and even Dad.

"But," Danny carefully explained to me, "if they need town heroes, it might as well be us."

"Wonder if there are any POWs here today?" Danny asked wistfully.

"Naw, just a buncha Boy Scouts, I bet."

While Danny helped Grandma stow the picnic remains in the basket, I scooped up a Tigers capful of wheat for Teddy and jumped off the wagon. After giving Teddy her treat, I tossed my cap to Danny and asked him to scoop me another serving for Gene. But he threw my cap back to me. For reasons I didn't understand, he insisted that I use *his* Tigers cap this time. I did so just to humor him.

Granville was abuzz with activity. Businesses were doing a brisk trade that afternoon. The crowded streets and stores belied the town's true population that stood at less than a hundred souls. But the farm families in the area were extremely loyal shoppers, especially the frugal Dutch and Amish. In their cases, the loyalty was not exactly by choice. Their only conveyance, horse and buggy, made a drive to Riverton, ten miles to the south, nearly an all day round trip. The many black buggies tied to the hitching rail at the general store indicated the loyalists were shopping in numbers today.

"We're passing over the spot where you boys saw the movie in the street." Grandma reminded us. During the summer to lure shoppers to town, Granville showed free movies on Monday, Wednesday, and Thursday evenings when the stores were open. The town budget could only afford old B movies, mainly westerns. This delighted Danny and me to no end.

"Yeah! And where I beat the pants off that old Mayor Simmons," Danny bragged. Danny had made quite a name for himself the last time we visited Granville by besting the town's champion in the *walnut shell-hidden pea* game.

Traffic in the tiny downtown area was so heavy that we came to a standstill. While I waited for it to clear, I twisted around to join Danny and Grandma's conversation.

"Now you boys know I didn't approve of that gambling game. Shame on Grandpa for letting you play. And I'm still not sure why Reverend Johnson joined in. But, I suppose, it was for a good cause, wasn't it?" Grandma rationalized.

"Cause? What was the cause, Grandma?" I asked. "I forget."

"Why, it was the Church of Christ camp fund. Don't you remember?"

"I remember, Grandma. When we get up to camp, Jase and I are goin' to add to that fund. Aren't we, Jase?" Danny asked, winking at me.

I was lost until Danny screwed his thumb and forefinger into his deadly marble-shooting position. I frowned at Danny and shook my head. Fortunately Grandma was lost too. And she stayed that way.

Lord, what if she knew that Danny planned to outmarble, for money, all those innocent church kids at camp? But, on the other hand, according to Danny, it would be for a good cause.

With that little bit of rationalization of my own, I inched us forward toward the waiting line of wagons at the Granville Co-op elevator. Grandma reached into her purse and extracted her co-op identification card. Danny continued his imaginary marble game by flicking his fingers in midair.

What a pro!

GRAIN ELEVATORS WERE ONCE a common sight in the farm country around Riverton. Elevators were built in nearly every town situated on a branch of the railroad network that covered the region. The purpose of the grain elevator was to receive, store, and ship grain to market. The grains grown in our part of the country were principally wheat, oats, and corn.

Many elevators, like the one in Granville, were owned and operated by farm cooperatives. Similar cooperatives or mutual companies were formed by farmers to operate dairies, purchase large, expensive farm equipment like threshers, and insure farmers from risks of fire and wind damage. The Granville elevator was designed for simplicity and speed, especially in the process of receiving grain.

The first stop for each wagon was the scale. After the horses were unhitched, the grain and wagon were weighed together. Then the wagon was emptied and, finally, the empty wagon was weighed again. The difference, of course, was the weight of the grain. Then the horses were rehitched to the empty wagon, and the wagon left the elevator. And that's all there was to it.

Emptying the wagon was done quickly. As the wagon was parked on the scale, a hydraulic lift raised the front end of the wagon. The wagon's boot gate was opened and the grain flowed from the back of the wagon into a hopper. As the grain flowed from the wagon, a sample was collected and used to grade the load. Grading consisted of measuring the grain's moisture content, kernel size and quality, and dockage, which is the amount of undesirable material in the grain.

The market price, grade, and weight of grain combined to determine the total payment due the farmer. After the grain was dumped and graded, the grain was then lifted by a conveyor belt to the top of the elevator for distribution into one of the dozen vertical storage bins comprising the tall tower structure. There Grandpa's wheat would be mixed with the wheat of other farmers. The entire procedure was performed by skilled elevator workmen in no time flat.

Waiting in line was often the most time-consuming part of the elevator visit. When we joined the line, there were a dozen wagons ahead of us. We would be in Granville for some time. Grandma and Danny rolled up the table cloth and blankets that had been covering the tarpaulin. But, when Grandma began to roll up the tarpaulin, one of the elevator men hollered at her to leave it for them. She waved her appreciation and hopped down from the wagon.

"Jase, will you be okay here by yourself? I need to go to the office to complete the paperwork. And, while I'm here, I want to check on things over at the cemetery. After that, Danny and I need to do a little shopping."

Danny's face lighted up at that news.

All of Grandma's ancestors were buried in the small cemetery beside the Granville Church of Christ. She enjoyed returning to her hometown church, especially when Reverend Johnson was preaching there. This was one of the churches on his circuit. She always took advantage of her church visits to check the graves of her grandparents, parents, aunts, and uncles. Sometimes she placed bouquets of fresh flowers on their graves, clipped the grass with her lawn trimming shears, or shined the tombstones with a ball of tissue from her huge leather purse.

Grandma was a firm believer in the tissue-and-spit method of cleaning. I know from personal experience that this practice was particularly well-suited for scrubbing the faces of young boys.

"I'll bet the Granville Ice Cream Parlor will be one of your stops, right Grandma?" I teased.

"You bet!" Danny answered for her.

"I'll be fine, Grandma. Have fun, Danny."

"I should be back before you're unloaded, Jase," Grandma speculated.

"Don't worry about it. I know just what to do. I'll unhitch the team and water 'em down while the wheat is emptied and graded. Then I'll hitch 'em up again and drive over to the office."

I watched a vast flock of English sparrows lift and circle for no apparent reason, only to land again and resume pecking at spilt grain, their main source of food. Even though the wait was a long one, time seemed to pass quickly. When the unloading process was completed, I headed for the office as I had promised Grandma.

"Now there's a familiar face! One of the heroes of Riverton, I presume. Who knew you were such a skilled horseman? I been watching you out of the office window there. I'm very impressed. How are you, my young man?" It was Mayor George Simmons, the master of the walnut shell and pea.

"Hello, Mayor Simmons."

"This is the first time I've seen you since the Matlock fund-raiser at the Good Mission Church. Wasn't that a marvelous time? I been trying to think of something like that for Granville. If I come up with something, I'll ask you to be my chairman. Boy, that would be something, wouldn't it?"

Mayor Simmons was the quintessential politician. Talk, of the sweet and smooth variety, was his stock-in-trade. Nonetheless, he was a most likeable man. And he had contributed his considerable shell game talents to help us raise funds to rebuild the Matlock house.

"Come to think of it, I've never seen you without your sidekick. Where is that little sharpster Danny?"

"Here I am!" Around the corner of the office building, came Danny with Grandma in tow. He was just finishing his ice cream by licking the long drips from his forearm. Grandma still had a ways to go on her cone.

"Whew! Danny insisted that we run back to be on time. Well, hello, Mr. Mayor!"

"'Lo, Jane. How you been? Where's Bill? I miss him at my games on movie nights."

"He's home, Mayor. He got in trouble by playing your game last time he was here, so he's been on restriction. Couldn't leave his room for thirty days unless he was going out to work in the field or do his chores. See the trouble you caused him?"

"You're pulling my leg, Jane. I don't believe one word of it."

"Just ask these boys!" Grandma looked at her watch and added, "I've got to get my check so I get to the bank before it closes."

Grandma was only gone a second. Coming down the steps
with the check in her hand, she suggested, "We might as well drive
the wagon over to the bank. It's on our way out of town."

We said our goodbyes to the mayor who bestowed an
additional layer or two of flattery on us as a going-away present.

"Boy, he sure can talk," Danny declared.

"Look who's talkin' about talkin'," I teased. Danny looked at
me and smiled.

We boarded the wagon and set off for the Granville Farmers
Bank. While Grandma went inside, Danny and I rolled up the
tarpaulin and blankets to form a makeshift sofa up against the
front rack. Grandma emerged, waving two white envelopes. "Here
it is, boys! Your share of the profits as promised," she vowed
opening her purse. "I'll keep them in here until we get home.
Remember, you're to give these to Reverend Johnson so he can pay
your camp dues. Or whatever it's called. Okay?"

We both nodded our heads.

I still felt a little uncomfortable about taking Grandpa and
Grandma's money. Sometimes they were too generous for people
of modest means. My mother had described the tough times they
had faced during the early 1930s after Grandpa's eye injury at the
foundry. He was out of work for years.

Unemployment was commonplace during the Depression.
That was bad enough. But, when the Riverton First National Bank
closed its doors, the Compton family savings disappeared with the
bank. Too proud to allow his family to go on relief, Grandpa
became a farmer again.

I had learned about the bank closing when I asked my parents
why Grandma had so many bank accounts. On my various jaunts
with her around the county, I could name at least four banks where
I had seen her deposit or withdraw money. I guess they weren't
taking any chances on losing all of it if a single bank failed.
Spreading their savings around was preferable to keeping it in their
mattress.

Incredibly, years later, Danny and I earned some spending
money one summer working for Mr. Arthur, Vice President of the

Riverton Second National Bank. The Second National had acquired the meager remains of the First National after the bankruptcy judge declared the defunct bank officially dead. Among those remains were dozens of bankers' boxes stuffed with ledgers, account records, and correspondence. After twenty years, the bankruptcy court order allowed for the old records to be destroyed.

Our job was to bring those boxes from the dank basement to the street level using the dilapidated old elevator. A pair of heavy steel doors flapped wide open as the elevator surfaced through a hole in the sidewalk next to the curb. Then we loaded the musty, mildew-ridden records into Mr. Arthur's trailer attached to his family car and drove the load to the Riverton City Dump for disposal.

But we couldn't just leave the records there. We had to burn each and every page, individually, to ensure that each private, albeit ancient, record was completely destroyed. Because most of those pages were made of very fine, cloth-woven paper, dampened by years of storage in the basement, they were extremely resistant to fire.

We spent days at the dump. The work was hot and dirty. And we each inhaled enough rotten smoke to give an elephant emphysema. We wore the oldest clothes we could find. All of our soiled tee shirts were too far gone to make the cut on laundry day. In fact, they were in such bad shape that they didn't even qualify for the ragbag. So we buried them in the alley with the garbage.

At both of our houses, the Saturday-night-only bath rule was waived for those days we worked at the dump. Our family members couldn't tolerate the amount of concentrated dump odor that we brought back with us each day. Once we were out of the heat and smoke, we didn't mind the odor. After all, combing the dump for buried treasure had been a major pastime for us as kids.

Remarkably, among the thousands of sheets of paper that I burned were the records for Grandma and Grandpa Compton's savings account whose balance had disappeared along with the balances of hundreds of other Riverton depositors. I couldn't bring myself to tell them what I had seen. My respect for their pride and privacy compelled me to lock this secret in my heart. I didn't even tell Danny. Now that I think of it, this was the only iota of my life that I failed to share with him.

I continued to mull over Grandma and Grandpa's unusual banking habits as we rumbled past Granville Park toward home. The setting sun behind me cast an orange glow on the road ahead. We'd be home at just about dark I estimated. Lost in my thoughts, I hadn't realized that the conversation from my travel mates had quietly subsided and then disappeared altogether.

I looked down from my perch to see Danny snuggled up next to Grandma on the improvised sofa. Grandma had her arm around his shoulders. Both of them appeared to be dozing.

"Good night, Grandma." Nothing.

"Good night, Danny." Nothing.

Good night, Jase. I'm proud of you!

And you know what? I was.

3 NORTHWARD HO!

WHEN I ENTERED THE KITCHEN, GRANDMA AND Danny were weighing the pros and cons of Grandma's plan-of-the-day. Con-man Danny was about to prevail.

"I don't really feel like going to church today, Grandma. Can't Jase and I just stay here with Grandpa? Please!" he begged. "Pul-leese!"

As usual, Danny had his way. Grandma was an easy mark for the Old Sharpster.

But Danny's no-church position surprised me, almost as much as it disappointed Grandma. Back in Riverton, Danny and I had established a reputation for taking in as many as four church services on a single Sunday. So why he chose to miss the opportunity on this particular Sunday was a mystery to me.

Now, instead of Grandma turning us over after the service at the Barrington Church of Christ, Reverend Johnson would have to follow her back to the farm. This new plan would require him to drive south for three miles before turning around and driving north again over those very same roads.

As we watched the Terraplane roar out of the driveway and fishtail north on Barrington Road, Danny turned to me. "Whattaya want to do?"

"Let's go see what Grandpa's doing. He's probably in the granary."

Just as we pushed open the wide granary door, a startled mouse leaped to the ground, barely missing Danny's left sneaker. Then it scurried to safety under the adjacent corncrib.

"Yow! Holy Cow! Geez!" Danny screamed, stomping and waving his arms. "What was that? A badger?"

"It was only a little mouse, Danny. It won't hurt you. But we don't want any mice in the granary, so I better check the traps. Come on, I'll show you how I do it."

Each year, Grandpa selected seed for the next spring's planting from the best of his harvest, including wheat, oats, corn, and beans. He preserved this valuable seed in specially tagged burlap bags that hung on pegs in the driest area of the granary. The most serious threat to his seed, and to the rest of the harvest stored there, came from ravenous mice and rats. Those pests never gave up their constant fight to gain access to what they considered their personal food supply.

Grandpa's first line of defense against those furry foes was the Compton cat brigade, commanded by Old Lucy, the dowager orange. She had earned her stripes by producing a litter of eight to twelve young recruits, every few months during the nineteen years of her exceptionally long life. Lucy established her headquarters in the cow barn behind the old cultivator and under the pile of straw that Grandpa had placed there for her use as a birthing place.

Old Lucy and her kittens stayed close to Grandpa in hopes of catching, quite literally, an occasional treat from him as he sat on his milking stool. An accurately aimed, arching stream of warm cow's milk was their occasional payoff. Even more rarely, they enjoyed a few milk-sodden slices of dry bread that Grandpa smuggled from Grandma's pantry.

Those kittens, fortunate enough not to be eaten by skunks, weasels, possums, foxes, and cannibalistic roving tomcats, followed Lucy's incomparable example and quickly became skilled mousers. When the summer weather brought abundant harvests, the mouse population boomed and the number of cats reached two dozen or more.

But winter made for difficult *mousing*. The cat brigade, like their prey, spent most of the day curled up under the straw trying to stay warm. During those hard times Grandpa's charity, in the form of table scraps and scarce milk, peaked. The strongest cats including Lucy always survived to mouse again the next spring.

Mice were most likely to be found lurking near the granary, one of the two corncribs, the back shed, the chicken coops, or the pigpen. Veteran mousers, like Lucy, ranged even farther, stalking prey in such unlikely places as the dump in the corner of the woods in spring, around the edges of Grandma's vegetable garden during summer, and at the base of corn shocks and wheat sheaves in the fields in fall.

Because Grandpa did not want to depend solely on cats to protect his precious seeds for the next spring planting, he wisely deployed an inner defense perimeter around his seed bags. This mouse-sized armored division consisted of a ring of ten sturdy wood and steel spring-operated mousetraps. A small number of casualties in the granary trap line was a good sign. This meant that the granary was relatively mouse-tight.

One of my jobs was to check the granary traps. First, I secured a small pinch of cheese from the kitchen. Rebaiting all ten traps required no more than a quarter teaspoon of cheese.

"A mere smear of cheese is plenty. Just a whiff of cheddar will bring 'um from forty miles," Grandpa used to say.

Some of the traps were located on the cross beams above the bins. To tend these, I needed both hands for crawling up the bin slats to reach them. So I always stuck the lump of baiting cheese behind my right ear before the climb.

When I caught a mouse, I opened the trap and released the dead villain to the granary floor below. Then I smeared the bait flange with cheese, reset the trap, and carefully put it back, exactly where I had found it.

Grandpa always told me, "Where there's one mouse, there're always a thousand more."

Once I'd smeared, reset, and replaced all my traps, I carried my catch by the tail to the cow barn and placed it in Lucy's rusty pie tin that Grandpa used for his occasional bread-and-milk treats.

Then I hollered, "Lucy!"

I was always amazed when the whole brigade would appear from nowhere.

"Danny, the traps are all baited and set, so we can go. But, first, let's make some wheat gum."

"How do you make a wheat *gun?*"

"Gum! Like chewing gum. Grandpa gave me his recipe."

Homemade Wheat Gum

Assemble these ingredients:

- 2 cups wheat — the fresher the better, preferably straight from the field on threshing day.
- 2 quarts spit — and an experienced spitter to go with it. Store spit in spitter until required.
- 2 tons patience — rarely found in boys, fresh from town.

Place a small handful of freshly harvested wheat in your mouth. Chew vigorously without swallowing. As wheat becomes a sticky dough ball, spit frequently to remove tiny bits of hull and excessive saliva from your mouth. When wheat ball is reduced to a manageable size, add another portion of wheat. Repeat as often as necessary to produce an optimum sized wad, one that is not quite large enough to choke you. Continue chewing and spitting for approximately twenty minutes.

Yield: One small glob of smooth wheat gum for a satisfying chew.

Danny was an excellent student. He mastered the art of wheat gum creation on his very first attempt. I attributed his success to his experience as a world-class spitter and the power of his word-strengthened jaw.

"Let's check the cow barn. Maybe Grandpa's there."

Chewing and spitting, we made our way toward the barn. We skinned-the-cat over the frigid water pipe leading from the milk-house well to the watering trough and popped open the side door. Having just left the bright morning sunshine, it took a few seconds for our eyes to adjust to the darkness.

"Hey, boys! I'm over here," Grandpa called.

He was lifting a heavy pail of ground feed from a wooden barrel that served as the cow-barn feed bin. By the fullness of the barrel, I surmised that he had ground fresh wheat from the recent harvest as a treat for the cows.

"Jase, I was just about to take this out to the herd, but now you can save me some steps. Do ya mind?"

Did I mind?

I'd do anything Grandpa asked, just to please him. And the more I did, the more competent I became. His trust in my ability to learn was paying off for both of us. I was gaining self-confidence and developing a strong work ethic, and he was benefiting from the help I provided.

From my back pocket, I extracted my red and white farm hanky and wrapped it around the bail of the heavy feed pail. My hands were not as calloused as Grandpa's, so this wrap made my grip more comfortable. This time of year, the cows were pastured in the apple orchard. The distance to the orchard gate was at least a hundred yards from the cow barn. Just to show off for Danny, I was determined to carry the feed pail without stopping.

With Danny leading the way, even though he wasn't sure where he was going, we took a shortcut across the wide yard that spread from the barn area to the house. At the Leghorn chicken coop, we veered right and headed straight for the orchard.

As we approached the gate, I noticed Sarah off in the distance. Because cows can detect odors up to five miles away, she had caught my scent and was hightailing toward us. I set the pail down and rubbed the palm of my carrying hand.

Then Danny noticed Sarah too. "Boy, that white cow sure must be hungry. Look at her run!"

"Naw, she's just glad to see me."

I opened the gate, entered the orchard, and dumped the feed into the long trough next to the water barrel. Danny followed timidly, taking care not to step in any of the fresh cow pies that dotted the area near the gate. With Bessie in the lead, the rest of the herd slowly ambled our way.

Sarah, a three-year-old Holstein and the largest cow in the dairy herd, arrived a full five minutes before her sisters. She greeted me with a huge slurping lick with her sandpaper tongue and backed me into the gate with her playful head butts. Finally I gave in and began to scratch the underside of her chin. She stopped moving all together and purred like a kitten.

From experience, I knew this would quiet her, but I also knew she wouldn't want me to stop. Leaving her was going to be difficult this time because we were both on the same side of the fence.

Danny noticed Sarah's twisted jawline. "What's wrong with her face?"

"Her jaw was broken when she was a calf."

Mesmerized, Danny watched me stroke my giant pet. "Why does she let you do that? Do cows always act like that?"

"She thinks I'm her mother."

Sarah and I had bonded the day she was born. She was the first calf of a young heifer that was not keen on motherhood. In fact, when the calf attempted to nurse, the indignant mother kicked the calf in the face, snapping the jawbone. In excruciating pain, the calf let out a deafening scream and ran in circles.

When Grandpa and I finally cornered her, I held her down while he examined the break. His decision came quickly. "We need to put her down, Jase. She'll never be able to feed with that jaw."

"But, Grandpa, couldn't we tie it up and let it heal? I could feed her."

"I don't know, Jase. I hate to see an animal suffer. I think we should put her out of her misery. Don't you?"

This was the first time that I can remember disagreeing with Grandpa. I don't know why I wanted to rescue the poor animal. Maybe it had something to do with her unusual coloring. The calf was completely white except for a black *handprint* over one eye. Perhaps my unwillingness to give up on Sarah impressed Grandpa. He changed his mind.

After painting the jaw with disinfectant, applying a wide bandage, and binding the jaw tightly, we placed the calf in a special "box" that we built to restrict her movement. From an old catsup bottle capped with the thumb of a rubber glove, Sarah consumed quart after quart of milk, taken from her mother by Grandpa or me. Within a few months, although crooked and swollen, her jaw was fully healed. And Sarah and I were forever attached.

"Danny, let's see if we can get Sarah interested in some ground feed before it's all gone."

I shared my plan with Danny who reluctantly agreed to do his part. After filling his Tigers cap with feed, he opened the gate and slipped outside. Leaving the gate cracked to facilitate my quick escape, he took up position behind me on the other side of the fence. While continuing to scratch Sarah's throat, I reached over my shoulder, grabbed a handful of freshly ground feed, and stuck it under Sarah's pink nose. Immediately she began to lick my hand.

"Okay, Danny. Now you feed her while I slip out through the gate."

"Oh, okay," he whimpered with fear in his eyes.

The minute Danny began to feed Sarah I could see a change in both of them. First of all, Sarah remained still, even though no one was scratching her chin. But the biggest change was in Danny. As Sarah lapped up the last of her snack, Danny began to purr just like Sarah. The amorous cow was mesmerized. She never noticed that I left her to join Danny on his side of the fence. Instead, she chewed her cud and gazed fondly at Danny as he scratched her chin. I left the two of them purring softly and headed for the cow barn.

Do you suppose a cow can bond with two human beings?

Before an answer came to me, I noticed the dusty rooster tail of the Terraplane roaring southward on Barrington Road toward the farm. It reminded me of the time earlier that summer when I had seen Grandma run Aubrey Kirby, the RFD mailman, off the road and into the ditch. Grandma kept on going, skidded into the driveway, and bounced into the garage, unaware of the mailman's plight. You will be relieved to know that Mr. Kirby was unhurt, and there wasn't much damage to his car. But Grandma's mailbox was totally destroyed. This was the kind of occurrence that I was careful not to relate to Mom who already had her doubts about my riding so much with Grandma.

But what did it all matter? We'd soon be on our way to camp!

REVEREND JOHNSON PULLED INTO the driveway a full ten minutes after Grandma had landed and taxied the Terraplane into its hangar. By this time, Danny and I were standing next to our duffel bags on the porch steps.

"What took you so long, Claude?" Grandpa asked with a grin.

Reverend Johnson and Grandpa were fully aware of Grandma's driving style. And they joked about it often.

"Must be something wrong with my engine. It'll only do eighty!"

Grandpa guffawed and slapped his co-conspirator on the back.

"Now, now! You men cut that out! I had to hurry home to put the picnic supper together for your trip. Didn't want to hold you up. You got a long drive ahead of you. Besides, any minute now, the rest of the family's gonna show up for Sunday dinner!" Grandma rationalized. "Danny, put this in the backseat and keep it upright. I don't want your iced tea to spill."

We opened the spacious trunk of Reverend Johnson's dusty black Ford sedan. Our two duffel bags joined his old leather valise, a rusty pair of jumper cables, tire iron and pump, jack, and a well-worn spare tire. The picnic basket plus a sealed cardboard box went in the backseat with Danny. For some reason, he chose to sit there rather than his preferred position, up front, astraddle the gearshift lever.

"What's in the box, Grandma?" I asked.

"Oh, just some emergency supplies. These weren't on the camp packing list, but I thought you might need them. Oh, I put that jar of wheat in there like you asked, Jase."

"Whatcha goin' ta do with that? Feed the church birds up at camp?" Grandpa asked.

"Nope! To make wheat gum," Danny replied, propelling a practice spit out the car window.

Opening the box, he began to inventory its contents aloud. "Wheat gum jar. Shoe strings. Compass. Screwdriver. Horehound drops. Candy bars —"

I might have known.

"— Sen Sens. Black cough syrup. Ugh! Writing paper and stamps. Rubber bands. Bottle of ass-burns —."

As we rolled out of the driveway, Mick bounced up and down like a rubber ball. Grandma waved weakly, wiped an eye with the corner of her apron, and then disappeared inside. Grandpa smiled and gave us a two-armed wave, sending us off in grand style.

When we turned west on Henry Road, I suddenly remembered the two white envelopes. "Danny! Do you have the envelopes with the camp money?"

He answered by inventorying the last of the emergency supplies. "— two white envelopes. One for Jase and one for Danny. And that's it!" He tossed them over the front seat.

I caught them and breathed a sigh of relief. "These are for you, Reverend Johnson! Eight dollars in each for the camp fees."

"Just put them there on the dashboard. I'll put the money in my wallet when we stop for gas."

After we'd settled into the drive, Reverend Johnson regaled us with stories about when he and his wife Rose lived with Grandpa and Grandma. He particularly enjoyed the times when he and

Grandpa listened to Tigers games on the big console radio in the front room next to the kitchen door.

"I do that with Grandpa."

"Me too," Danny chimed from the backseat.

Reverend Johnson glanced at me and smiled.

"It's about a three-and-a-half, or maybe, four-hour drive. We'll stop for gas when we're about halfway there, around four o'clock. We can open that picnic basket then, okay?"

Bam!

I heard the basket lid slam shut.

"Um, okay," Danny muttered guiltily.

"Then, I figure, we'll drive for a couple more hours to get there before seven. You boys'll have to check in late. But afternoon on the first day is free time anyway. We'll be there in plenty of time for vespers."

"I like vespers," Danny informed us.

"What are they, Danny?" I asked, setting my trap.

"Mrs. Mikas baked me some and I ate them all. I like her Hungarian sugar cookies too."

At that, Reverend Johnson's stomach jiggled but, to his credit, he didn't quite laugh out loud.

"RJ, how much longer until lunch?" Danny asked innocently.

RJ!

Reverend Johnson looked at me and shrugged. Thanks to Danny, *RJ* entered our vocabulary.

"Like I said, a couple more hours."

"Oh!" Danny replied forlornly.

RJ quickly changed the subject. "Rose and I came up to camp last month to supplement the staff for a few days during the peak of the season. We arrived about nine o'clock in the evening. As we got out of the car, we heard men's voices singing loudly from the dining hall. It was most unusual."

"Why? Aren't you allowed to sing at church camp?" Danny asked.

"Oh, no. That's not it. These weren't campers. These were grown men, singing in German!"

"Sounds like POWs," I speculated.

The army had established a German POW branch camp in Harmony State Park, the large forest preserve just to the west of Camp Harmony. The POWs were brought to the park that summer to cut in fire lanes and clear underbrush to prevent forest fires.

Most people are amazed to learn that thousands of POWs lived and worked in America during the war. Counting some 5,000 Japanese, 50,000 Italians, and 375,000 Germans, there were over 400,000 POWs interned across the country. In fact, only four, out of the 48 states back then, did *not* have POW camps. Sadly, for many reasons, this intriguing chapter of history has been neglected.

The terms of the Geneva Convention allowed POWs to be used as workers in non-defense jobs such as farming, food processing, and forestry. Employers, including government agencies, contracted directly with the army and paid the local going rate for labor, ranging from forty to sixty cents an hour, depending on the type of work. Of the money they earned for the army, the POWs were only given eighty cents a day. The rest of the money was used to pay for housing the POWs and financing the war.

POWs were paid in canteen coupons that they used to purchase razor blades, stationery, and other personal items in the POW camp stores. Some stores even sold beer and wine. What the POWs didn't spend, they could save and take home with them after their repatriation.

The International Red Cross administered a program to enable POWs, Germans in this country and Americans in Germany, to earn college credit by taking courses taught by local college professors. Nicolas Katzenbach, U.S. Attorney General in the Johnson administration, earned much of his Princeton under-graduate degree as an American POW in Germany during the war. During his captivity, he also participated in the events that inspired the World War II POW movie, *The Great Escape*.

Because Camp Harmony had a nearby kitchen staff and dining facility, the army contracted with the camp to provide the POWs with two sit-down meals each day, breakfast and supper. The camp

cooks packed hearty sack lunches for their noon meal. In
gratitude, the army officially named the POW camp, *Camp
Harmony Two.*

"The POWs eat their breakfast before and their supper after the
campers. The Camp Director, Reverend Thomas, allows them to
sing during the period after *Vespers* and before *Taps*. Boy-oh-boy, do
they ever sing. They're teaching our camp choir director a thing or
two about harmonies."

"Harmony Two brings harmonies to Harmony One. We got
POWs all over Riverton. Now we got 'em at church camp too.
Jeez!" Danny observed with more than a hint of sarcasm.

"Danny, I thought you liked POWs. Like Otto's men. They
sure like you," I reminded him.

"Not all of them!"

"Oh, you mean Reitter and Baden?"

"Yeah! They wanta get even with me for capturing them."

I noted that Danny had taken sole credit for the capture. But,
more importantly, how had Danny learned the secret that I had
pledged yesterday not to reveal to him? Before I could ask, RJ beat
me to the punch.

"This sounds very serious. How do you know it's true,
Danny?"

"Otto told me that Reitter and Baden wanted to grab me and
cut off my ears. And he warned me that they were *dead* serious
about it."

Instantly I imagined Danny without his large, round ears.
How would he hold up his glasses? I wondered before regaining
my senses.

"When did Otto tell you that?" I asked incredulously.

"Last week."

"Why didn't you tell me?"

"I didn't want you to be — to be afraid."

I turned around and looked at Danny. He shrugged his
shoulders and smiled at me warmly.

"I wonder if the army folks at Camp Riverton know about
this," RJ asked rhetorically.

"Yes, they do. Junior told Mr. Tucker, Dad, and me, just yesterday morning on our back porch. The two POWs are going to be moved from the canning factory. Far away, so they can't hurt Danny."

"Why didn't you tell me?" Danny asked just as incredulously.

"I didn't want you to be afraid either."

There was silence for a minute or two.

Then RJ said it all. "Jase and Danny, I want to tell you something very important. Not many people in this world share a friendship like yours. Thank you for making it possible for me to observe and learn from it."

"Thank you, RJ," I responded.

"You're welcome, RJ," my best friend replied. "How much longer do you think it is now?"

THE OLD BAY GAS Station and General Store had evidently been RJ's planned midtrip stop from the start. We stepped out of the car and stretched.

"Nice to be Up North, isn't it, boys?"

I never quite knew where *Up North* was, but I could tell we were there. Somewhere behind us we had crossed over that invisible line. Now the air was cleaner. It smelled like pine needles, winterberries, and wet leaves. Though the temperature was cooler, the sun seemed warmer and brighter. My cares vanished and I felt exhilarated.

Yes, we were definitely Up North.

While RJ topped off the tank, Danny and I removed Grandma's basket and headed for the picnic table that stood under a majestic weeping willow, undulating gracefully as the gentle breeze caressed its yellow-green, grasslike branches. We laid out our supper on Grandma's prized red and white checked tablecloth. Then we waited patiently for RJ while the gas station owner washed the windshield and then checked the oil and the air pressure of each tire including the spare.

The warm afternoon sun brought swarms of obtrusive yellow jackets that seemed as excited about our picnic as Danny. We shooed them away as best we could.

When RJ joined us, we hungrily tackled the sumptuous meal. Grandma had really outdone herself today. Chicken, pork chops, still-warm mashed potatoes and gravy, biscuits, butter, honey, strawberry jam, sweet corn, tomatoes, cold iced tea, and three kinds of desserts. Apple pie, chocolate cake, and ginger snaps.

As the last crumb was consumed, I felt absolutely stuffed. "Boy! That was certainly worth the wait. Right, Danny?"

"Melsh oba toofah da," Danny replied succinctly as he put away the last pork chop.

After we finished eating, we sat quietly for a few minutes watching a pair of phoebes flitting between the willow tree and the eaves of the twin outhouses standing behind the gas station. "Why do all outhouses have moons on their doors?" I wondered aloud.

"Because sometimes you have to use them at night," Danny stated emphatically.

"But what's that got to do with it? They're not electric lights!"

"Still keeps people from gettin' scared."

This conversation was going nowhere!

"Oh, I almost forgot about your envelopes!" RJ took the two white envelopes from his pants pocket and tore open the first one. "I'll transfer this money to my wallet. Takes up less space. When we arrive, I'll pay your fees, okay?"

"Yep!" we both agreed.

"What's this?" RJ exclaimed, pulling a crisp, new ten-dollar bill from Danny's envelope.

"Wow! Let's open mine!" I urged. The same result. "Why did Grandma give us ten dollars? She told us that she was only giving us eight dollars for the wheat. Camp only costs eight. Right, RJ?"

RJ nodded his head, looking as confused as I was.

"I know! She gave us two dollars for spending money. I knew she would!" Danny insisted.

"Did you tell her you only had seven cents for spending money?" He nodded his head. "Geez! Danny, you're something else!" He gave me another nod.

We dumped our trash in the large barrel next to the gas pumps. The picnic basket, much lighter now, was returned to the backseat.

But, before we got in, RJ suggested, "Anybody want to use the facilities again before we get under way? It's another couple of hours before we get there."

Danny and I shook our heads and piled into the car. Once under way, we serenaded ourselves with a dozen renditions of our favorite song, *My Old Kentucky Home,* all with subtle variations that I am sure RJ truly appreciated. But we soon tired of singing and fell silent. Then Danny decided to entertain us by reading, aloud, a series of small signs as we passed them.

Do you love me? Or do you not? You told me once. But I forgot. Burma Shave!

That got a rise out of RJ and me, so Danny proceeded to read *every* sign we passed.

Pineview Motor Inn. Cabins from $3. Hot Water. No Meals. No Dogs. No Kids. Welcome!

White River Trading Post. Souvenirs and Postcards. Snacks. Groceries. Kerosene. Fishing and Hunting Licenses. Fishing Tackle. Post Office. Gas. Oil. Water. Free Air.

You get the picture.

But soon the hum of the road, Danny's droning on, and the fullness of my stomach caused me to drop out and give in to my need for a siesta. I fell asleep for what seemed like only an instant. In reality, I had oozed into twenty full minutes of luxurious, deep sleep.

Bam! Flop! Flop! Flop! Flop!

The car veered toward the shoulder of the road, and RJ brought us to a quick stop.

"What was that, RJ?"

"A blowout! Doggone it! I should have had him patch that spare!"

"Who?"

"Aw, the man that waited on me at the Old Bay. He found a nail in the spare and asked if I wanted him to patch it for us while we ate. But I declined. Doggone it!" This was the closest thing to swearing that I had ever heard from RJ.

"What'll we do?"

"I'll have to patch it myself, I guess. Let's take a look at the front tire to see if it's damaged any."

We piled out of the car and walked to the blown-out tire. RJ ran his hand over it, inspecting thoroughly for tears or bulges. "The tire looks okay but I bet that tube is shot. I better patch the tube in the spare. It's new. No patches, until now that is."

RJ retrieved the spare tire, jack, tire iron, tire pump, and the tire patching kit from the trunk. He set the emergency brake, found a flat rock, and set the jack on it. He removed the hubcap and loosened the lug nuts. Then he jacked up the car. When the tire cleared the ground, he removed the nuts and placed them in the hubcap and then pulled the wheel off the axle.

Using the tire iron, he removed the spare tire's inner tube. The nail had made a neat, clean hole. He buffed the area around the puncture with a piece of rough sandpaper from the patching kit. Then he applied a small dollop of rubber cement. With his cleanest finger, he smoothed the cement over the area. Finally he peeled the foil from a large patch and pressed it onto the inner tube and held it there with his fingers for a minute.

"Would you hand me that pump, Danny?" RJ asked. Danny picked up the tire iron.

"The other thing," I coached.

RJ tested the newly patched tube and declared it fit. Within minutes, we were back on the road. I felt the tension in my shoulders slowly melt away.

Seeming to sense the need for therapeutic small talk, Danny asked, "RJ, where will we sleep when we get to camp?"

"We'll stay in *Judea*, the boys' dormitory, up on the hill overlooking the camp. I'll bunk in the counselors' area on the first floor. But I imagine you boys will be on the second floor —

because we're arriving late. Most people prefer the first floor, especially in the warmer months. It's cooler than the second."

"Did you and Mrs. Johnson stay in the counselors' area last time you were there?" I asked, trying to join in.

"Oh, no. She stayed in *Galilee* down near the lake. That's the girls' dorm."

"Girls!"

"Girls!"

Simultaneously Danny and I reacted negatively to this news.

"No, not girls!" pleaded Danny whose older sister Queenie was at times the bane of his existence.

I completely agreed with my friend. Girls had no place on an adventure like this one. This indeed was terrible news.

"We don't have to do stuff with girls, do we?" Danny asked hopefully.

"Yes, I'm afraid you do. You'll share a number of activities with them. Church services. Choir practices. Swimming. Boating. Canoeing. Handicrafts and hikes. And you'll eat all your meals together in the same dining hall. It'll be a valuable experience for you, interacting with members of the opposite sex."

I had never heard any adult use the word, *sex,* let alone a minister. First, it was *doggone it!* Now this. I was beginning to feel a little queasy.

"We gotta *eat* with 'em too! Darn, I'd rather eat with the POWs," Danny affirmed.

While this conversation was not going well for RJ, it wasn't doing much for me either. The thought of spending an entire week, trapped in the same camp with a bunch of girls from Galilee did not set well. My stomach was doing flip-flops. Maybe I could use a vesper or two.

Reading my mind, Danny asked, "RJ, is it too late to go back home?"

4 CAMP HARMONY

WE TURNED OFF THE MAIN HIGHWAY ONTO A dusty dirt road and immediately passed under a pine log archway. Spindly birch branches nailed to the structure spelled out *CAMP HARMONY*.

"We made it!" I announced excitedly.

"It's still another mile or two through the woods," RJ replied.

We crept along slowly to minimize the dust that, nonetheless, rose in billows around us. The late afternoon light had plunged the thick pine forests on either side of the road into an eerie near darkness. RJ turned on his headlights. The only sound I heard was the melodious mixture of my sleeping friend's heavy breathing and the humming of the Ford's engine.

Soon the dark forest gave way to rolling fields of grass. After taking the right-hand fork in the road, we circled upward toward a large, stark white cinder-block building. A small sign informed us that we were on the *Road to Judea*.

Parents and boys about our age were strolling down the hill toward Lake Harmony. The shoreline was dotted with a collection of similar white structures including the dining hall, auditorium, camp store, handicraft center, chapel, and, of course, the girls' dormitory. I assumed that a *Road to Galilee* was down there someplace.

As RJ had predicted, it was almost seven o'clock when we came to a stop in the Judea parking lot. Danny awoke with a bang.

"Hey! Cut it out!" he yelled, startling us. "That's my canoe. Get your own!"

"Danny, we're here. At camp," I whispered, not wanting to startle him.

"Okay! What's next?" he mumbled, signaling his successful reentry from dreamland.

We carried our bags and emergency-supplies box into Judea and set them down in the middle of the dormitory lobby. Comfortable-looking, black leather chairs lined the perimeter. A large rack against the wall near the entrance held religious magazines and pamphlets. Bibles were stacked on small tables interspersed among the chairs. Evidently campers were encouraged to read and, perhaps, meditate there. And there were plenty of Bibles for those who may have *forgotten* to bring one.

The camp registration table stood right in front of us. A large sign hanging on the wall read, *Welcome to Harmony!*

"Where is everybody?" Danny asked. "I want to see my room."

"I don't see Shepherd Bob," RJ observed. "He'll probably be back soon."

"*Shepherd* Bob!" Danny sniggered, repeating the name several times. "Is that his real name?"

"No, he just likes to think of himself as a shepherd. A leader of his flock. Let's see. Yep, you boys are assigned to Shepherd Bob's group all right," RJ confirmed, checking the typewritten sheets taped to the table.

Danny wrinkled his nose and asked, "We've gotta be *sheep* all week? Geez, RJ."

"Well — I —," stammered RJ.

Suddenly the missing shepherd bounced into the lobby. Short and moon-faced, he appeared to be about sixteen.

"Welcome! Welcome! Just showing some new *sheep* — I mean campers — to their quarters. Who do we have here, Reverend Johnson?"

His uniform was as elaborate as it was odd. Our leader wore sturdy brown hiking boots with khaki knee-length stockings, khaki shorts, a khaki web belt, and a khaki short-sleeved shirt. The tails of his khaki neckerchief dangled through a wooden slide carved into the shape of a cross. Another wooden cross was pinned, front-and-center, on the khaki campaign cap perched on his overly large head.

Shepherd Bob looked like a safari guide who had mistakenly stumbled into Judea on his way to a big game hunt. Not the best kind of first impression.

"I bet I know the color of his underwear," Danny whispered to me.

My bet was that our overgrown Boy Scout would soon learn how fast Danny could say *Baa Bye* to the weird sheephood idea.

"Hello, boys. I'm Shepherd Bob. You two young sheep will be in my flock this week. Won't that be *wooly, wooly* good?"

"Pleased to meet you," I replied, feeling my face redden with embarrassment for the poor fellow.

Danny wasn't quite as polite.

"Down, Shep! And I *wooly* mean it," Danny declared, mimicking his khaki-clad victim.

Shep!

I liked it. And, as poor Shep would soon learn, so did the other boys in his flock. All week long, his would-be sheep competed with each other to come up with the cleverest use of his canine nickname.

"Here comes Sheepdog Bob! Here, Shep! Sit, Shep! Roll over, Shep! Fetch, Shep! Wanta go for a walk, Shep? Go get your leash! Attaboy!"

His sheep were vicious. *Wooly* vicious.

But I have to admit that Shep's registration process was efficient. He quickly collected our fees and gave us each a receipt. Then he provided us with a copy of the daily schedule that he explained fully *and* succinctly.

CAMP HARMONY DAILY SCHEDULE

6:00 AM	REVEILLE/SHOWERS
6:30 AM	INDIVIDUAL MEDITATION
7:30 AM	BREAKFAST
8:30 AM	BIBLE STUDY
10:00 AM	HANDICRAFTS
11:30 AM	LUNCH
12:30 PM	QUIET HOUR
1:30 PM	SPORTS
3:30 PM	AQUATICS*
5:30 PM	DINNER
6:30 PM	VESPERS**
9:30 PM	TAPS

FRIDAY ONLY:

* BAPTISM SERVICE
** FAREWELL SONGFEST

And the whole process took less than five minutes.

After agreeing to meet back in the lobby in fifteen minutes, RJ headed for the counselors' area. And we set out to find our quarters and unpack our duffel bags. After that we were going to our first vesper service. When Danny heard that news, he licked his lips.

On the way upstairs, Danny asked Shep, "Can I have a room overlooking the lake?"

"What do you think we're running here? A five-star hotel? Boy, this isn't the Ritz. This is a dormitory. There *are* no private rooms. I'm *wooly, wooly* sorry, Your Highness!"

Danny didn't respond. I had seen him in similar situations. He was biding his time and keeping his powder dry. When we reached the top of the stairs, Shep opened the door and waved us in.

He was right.

The second floor was one large, sparsely furnished room. Metal frame, double-decker bunk beds lined the walls of the dormitory. Small and plain casement windows between each bed had no curtains or blinds. Two metal footlockers were provided for each bunk bed, one at the foot and the other against the wall under the window. A long row of austere steel tables with linoleum-covered tops spanned the length of the room. Each table was equipped with four metal folding chairs.

"Can we have that one?" Danny asked, pointing to the end of the dorm farthest from the lake.

"Which one?" Shep asked, looking in the direction of Danny's point.

"There! In the corner!"

Glancing at his clipboard, Shep confirmed, "Okay, Your Highness, you got it."

"When do we get *our* uniforms?" Danny asked.

Evidently Danny thought we'd been shanghaied and pressed into military service. Our dorm furnishings did resemble the army boot camps we'd seen in war movies at the Grafton Theater.

"Huh?" replied Shep, failing to decipher His Highness' strange inquiry.

"Your uniform! Don't we all get one?"

"Wha —. No! I'm the only one at Camp Harmony who wears a uniform."

Danny smirked and looked at me.

"No uniforms! What kind of a church camp is this anyway?"

THE FINAL WEEK WAS the least popular one in the summer schedule. With the early onset of fall, cool temperatures were almost a certainty, especially since the camp was located in the upper half of the Lower Peninsula. Campers found it difficult to enjoy aquatic activities when howling winds raised white caps on the icy waters of the lake. In addition, the dormitories and other buildings were not heated. With the start of school close at hand, parents were reluctant to expose their children to the risk of earaches, sore throats, or flu.

Although Grandma was overly cautious about many things, worrying about Danny and me catching cold was not one of them. She knew that we came from hardy stock. Members of our families were seldom sick. Besides she wanted us at camp when her minister RJ would be there to look out for us.

But Danny and I decided that this was a fabulous week to be at camp. First of all, we were both extremely eager for school to begin. But that wouldn't happen until the Monday following Labor Day. So being away from Riverton, in this new setting, provided an ideal diversion.

Second, it was immediately evident that the counselors were afflicted with a serious case of short-timer's attitude. They were far less gung ho than earlier in the summer when they were really obnoxious. A camp run by overcontrollers was no place for freedom lovers like Danny and me.

Third, the camp population had shrunk to about half its normal level. We didn't have to wait in line for activities. We also had more privacy. Our sleeping arrangements were a superb example. Danny's choice of bunk beds was ideal. Those campers who checked in early had chosen bunks on the first floor. Most campers on the second floor had selected bunks at the end of the dorm nearest the lake. Our corner *bedroom* was a good sixty feet from anyone. Now we could both have a bottom bunk and still be close enough to chat about the day's activities without disturbing anyone or being overheard.

On that first night, we were lying in our bunks doing exactly that. "Danny, wasn't it strange to hear POW singing, way up here in the north woods?"

"Reminded me of Otto's crew. Same songs, I bet."

"Did you like *Vespers?*"

"Nah, who wants to sit around a campfire with a bunch of girls? Besides it was just like church. I came up here to get away from church for a while."

"But this is a *church* camp!" No response.

From the direction of the lake, the sound of a bugler playing *Taps* floated into the dormitory. It was ghostly, but soothing. Lights all over the camp, including those in Judea, were extinguished, one by one, as duty counselors made their rounds. Suddenly we were immersed in blackness. Outside, the winds howled. Strong gusts pounded against the glass of our bare windows.

To take my mind off these frightening surroundings, I asked, "Danny, are you going to meditate in the morning?"

"We have to! It's on the camp schedule. Everyday!"

Danny sounded a bit like Shep to me. *Down, Danny!*

But he was right. The daily routine called for *Individual Meditation* during the period after *Reveille/Showers* and before *Breakfast*. Campers were to find a personal *quiet place* to provide an optimal setting for their spiritual activity. Some campers sat under the tall trees that lined the shore of the lake. Others sought the solitude of the forest surrounding the camp. Still others chose large rocks in the creek that meandered through the meadow. I had my eye on the grassy area behind the softball backstop that we had passed as we had entered camp. I wondered where Danny was heading. I was pretty certain that it wasn't the Harmony Chapel.

"Jase, do you know how to meditate?"

"Nope! You?"

"Nah."

Crack! Boom! Bang! Boom!

Bam-Bam!

Boom! Crack! Crack! Boom!

Jagged lightning slashed across the blackened skies and, unimpeded by shades or blinds, decorated the dorm walls with swaths of eerie blue-white light. Deafening thunder exploded around us. Again and again! The hairs on my arms and at the nape of my neck stood on end. Wave after wave of sonic explosions and blinding light bombarded us.

Judea was under siege and the storm warriors were winning.

Through a sliver of silence I heard Danny gasp. The lightning enabled me to see him sitting up in bed with his hands clapped over his sizeable ears.

"You — *Crack!* — afraid?" I yelled.

"Shoulda found out — *Crack!* — how to — *Boom!* — before coming!" he yelled back.

"How to *what?*"

Bam! Ka-boom!

"Meditate!!!"

He had that right!

DANNY AND I QUICKLY fell into the camp routine. Despite our tendency to avoid structure, especially when imposed by adults, we found the predictability of the daily schedule comforting.

The variety of offerings suited us as well. Because our interests and tastes differed, we seldom saw each other during the day. But we did meet at mealtimes in the dining hall. There we were assigned to a long table with the rest of Shep's puppies, whom we found to be excessively boring for the most part. Naturally we capped each day with our nightly debriefing that often extended well beyond *Taps,* especially when our experiences were particularly noteworthy.

By that fateful Thursday, we had memorized the schedule that was thumbtacked to the wall between our bunks. I suspected that Danny was skipping *Individual Meditation.* But where he went and what he did during that period was still a mystery. Once I asked him about it. Silly me!

"Danny, where do you go to meditate — in the mornings?"

He knew that my quiet place was behind the backstop.

"My *quiet place* is a very quiet place, especially, in the *morning.*"

What?

I didn't ask a second time.

After his first experience with *Vespers,* Danny chose not to attend any more *churchie-girlie* events, as he referred to them. Personally I came to enjoy sitting on the beach at the campfire watching the sunset. Candidly I didn't mind sharing the experience with the gals from Galilee.

Danny declared that he preferred *to vesper to himself.* Whatever that meant.

But, out of respect for RJ, he agreed to attend *Bible Study* taught by Reverend Thomas. Almost immediately a conflict erupted when Danny offered his own, alternative interpretations of the scriptures.

For example, he insisted that Cain had invented sugar. And he'd done so, just as soon as he was Able. And Moses invented roses. Lot invented real estate. And Gomorrah was the capital of Ireland. These goodies brought a few laughs from his fans, like me, but only served to heighten the tension between him and Reverend Thomas.

But, thanks to the intervention of RJ, a compromise was struck. During class, Danny was allowed to sit at a table in the back of the auditorium and pursue his newest handicraft interest, basket weaving. In return, Danny agreed to desist from offering further Biblical interpretations. Before agreeing to the deal, Danny exacted another promise. Reverend Thomas had to agree not to offer suggestions or opinions related to Danny's basketry. Thanks to this truce, the rest of us actually learned something about the Bible.

For my sports activity, I chose softball. Danny opted for archery, a strange choice since he was the only boy in the class. Soon his motive was revealed. One day Miss Hood, the archery instructor, loudly accused Danny of deliberately shooting at his classmates. The exchange was so dramatic that we softball players called a time-out so we could enjoy watching the nearby brouhaha.

"Danny, do *not* shoot at other people's targets, especially when they are retrieving their arrows. It's too dangerous."

No response.

"Don't give me that innocent look. I know you're doing it on purpose. You may think it's funny but it's very dangerous. Look at poor Martha. She's in tears. Is that the Christian way to treat a fellow camper?"

Mumble.

"I heard that! Don't you use that language with me! Shame on you, young man! Wait 'til Shepherd Bob hears about this! You'll be sorry."

At the mention of Shep's name, the two teams of softball players spontaneously broke into a chorus of dog noises.

"Woof! Woof! Bow wow! OOOOOOooooo! Yelp! Yelp!"

Danny turned our way, doffed his Tigers cap, and bowed from the waist. We cheered at the top of our lungs. Miss Hood lost it. Suddenly she turned and ran toward us, shaking her fists and screaming like a banshee.

When our young counselor/umpire saw her coming, he yelled, "Game's over, boys! Run for your lives!"

And run we did!

As we scattered to the four winds, Miss Hood rushed at us like a cheetah trying to nab dinner from a herd of leaping and bounding impalas. We left her standing, frustrated, on the pitcher's mound while we loped back to the lake to prepare for *Aquatics.*

By the time I reached the boathouse, my sides were aching from excessive laughing and running. Somehow Danny had arrived a few seconds ahead of me. Since daytime temperatures had fallen, we had opted for activities atop the water, rather than in it.

Because we had become rather proficient canoeists, our instructor assigned us our own personal canoe, a sleek red number, which we stored upside down on the beach near the dock. Our paddles and float cushions, conveniently stored under the canoe, allowed us to launch quickly. The offshore breeze was brisk.

"Kinda windy today, guys. Be careful out there," admonished the instructor.

Undeterred, we prepared to launch. We flipped the canoe over, carried it to the shoreline, and slid it into the water. Danny held the bow while I returned to fetch the paddles and cushions. While Danny crawled out to his place in the stern, I steadied the canoe between my knees, using the official crossed-arms grip. When he was situated, as he was taught, Danny shoved his paddle downward into the sand. Looping his fingers around the paddle, he grasped the gunnel to hold the canoe in place.

"Okay, I got it! Hop in!" he instructed.

I released the bow and was about to do just that. Suddenly a freakish gust of wind roared down the beach, pivoted the canoe around Danny's sunken paddle, and propelled him out into the lake. Danny paddled furiously, attempting to turn around, but the wind was simply too strong. The canoe shot like an arrow toward the opposite shore.

"Danny! Use your J-stroke," I hollered. "Paddle harder!"

But it was to no avail. No matter how hard Danny tried, he was unable to bring the bow around into the wind.

"Don't worry. We'll come get you!"

He stopped flailing and looked over his shoulder at me. Panic filled his eyes. He waved weakly and went back to fighting the wind. I turned around to ask for help from our instructor, but he seemed to have disappeared. I ran toward the boathouse and looked inside. He was nowhere to be found.

"Hi, Jase. How's it going?"

"RJ! You've got to help me! It's Danny!" I screamed. "He's caught in the wind. It's pushing him across the lake. Come quick!"

We ran toward the lake together. "Oh, Dear God! Where's your instructor?"

"Jase, why is Danny out there alone?" shouted the instructor, running toward us with a cup of coffee from the camp kitchen. "You know the rules!"

RJ took command. "Launch the punt and get out on that lake before Danny panics and does something stupid."

"No can do. I'm painting it — I —."

"Who cares about that? Get the oars and get out on that lake!"

"No oar locks! I took 'em off to paint it. It's the end of the season."

The three of us stood helplessly watching the strong wind blow Danny and his canoe farther and farther out into the lake. "Let's call the sheriff's office. They've got a rescue boat," the instructor suggested.

From the telephone in the camp office, RJ spoke to the sheriff who assured us that he was on the case. There was nothing more that we could do so we headed for the dining hall. As we entered, we bumped into a muscular army MP sergeant.

"Howdy, Reverend. I was hopin' ta see you. Just in talkin' ta the cook about tomorrow night's *Farewell Songfest*. Our guys are all ready. Believe me! It'll be a terrific show."

Then the friendly soldier turned his attention to me. "Now who's this?"

"Sergeant Saunders, meet Jase Addison. He's one of the two Riverton boys I mentioned. They're well-acquainted with POWs."

"So you're one of the town heroes, eh? I understand you've met some good uns and some bad uns. Pleased ta meet cha," he said, extending an enormous paw.

"I gotta get back ta Harmony Two and pick up my crew for supper. See ya two tamorrah night then." Off he jogged to his jeep, parked next to the dining hall.

"RJ, are the POWs going to be in the *Farewell Songfest?*"

"That was my idea. All summer the POWs have serenaded the staff from a distance every evening. I thought including them in this last *Farewell Songfest* would be a fine way to say goodbye to them and their army guards. Sergeant Saunders let us know that the POWs and his guys are very enthusiastic about it. And they should add a lot to the show."

After supper, RJ and I wandered back to the office to see if there was any news from the sheriff. No news. I was worried about Danny's safety. It was getting dark. The wind had stiffened and the temperature was falling. We hurried back to Judea to get our jackets for *Vespers*. After the service, we returned to the camp office. Still no news.

"Jase, there's not a thing we can do here. They'll tell us when they hear something. Let's go back to Judea. We can wait in the lobby."

We sat in a pair of leather chairs nearest the door. Soon it would be time for *Taps,* so RJ asked the duty counselor to keep the lobby lighted. We prepared for a long vigil. Others joined us. Before long the lobby was teeming with campers and counselors. Somebody suggested singing camp songs. Under the circumstances, I wasn't wild about the idea, but I went along anyway. After all twelve verses of *Green Grow the Rushes-Ho,* the singing suddenly stopped, whether out of respect or boredom I wasn't certain. But I welcomed the quiet.

Bam! Bam!

At the sound of car doors slamming, I leaped to my feet and ran outside. The rotating dome light on the sheriff's patrol car flooded the windy, dark night with eerie red and white light. Danny stood next to the car, wearing an oversized sheepskin coat with the insignia of the sheriff's office over his heart.

"So long, Danny. Nice knowin' ya. Go on inside now. Your friends have been waiting a long time. Tell 'em where we found ya." When Danny began to remove the heavy coat, the sheriff held up his hand. "You keep that on until you get warm. I'll swing by in the morning to collect it. Night, Danny!"

Danny waved at the sheriff's car as it disappeared over the hill. Then he turned, looked me in the eye, and smiled.

"Where have you been?"

"At a seafood buffet! Hmmm. Delicious!"

"What?"

"I was rescued by a seafood restaurant on the other side of the lake."

"Why didn't you call the camp? Or the sheriff?"

"The owner and his wife *begged* me to eat first. I was starved. So I did."

I looked at RJ and he looked at me. We put our arms around Danny and walked back into the lobby. The curious campers surrounded Danny, patted him on the back, and stroked his sheepskin coat. Danny, put his thumbs under the wooly lapels and quipped, "Don't tell Shep about this. He'll wanta shear me." That brought down the house.

After *Taps,* as we lay in the silent darkness, a thousand questions raced through my mind. But I only asked one. "Were you scared, Danny?"

"Yep!"

"Me too."

"Night, Jase."

"Good night, Danny."

A good night indeed!

THE REPETITIVE NATURE OF the daily routine had an unexpected effect on me. Unconsciously I had begun to feel that camp would last forever. So, when I realized we had reached Friday, the last full day of camp, I reacted, first with disbelief, then with sadness.

Moving from event to event, I said farewell to new friends with whom I had shared fellowship, learning experiences, and fun times. We exchanged addresses and made sincere promises to write. Promises that I wasn't certain would be kept.

Danny seemed a little sad as well. On the other hand, we were both excited about the two special events planned for the day. Instead of *Aquatics,* we could look forward to the *Baptism Service.* And *Vespers* would be replaced by the *Farewell Songfest,* featuring a special appearance by *The Harmony Two Chorale.*

At lunch, RJ asked us if we had ever seen a baptism. Danny and I looked at each other and nodded. Because we frequently attended multiple church services on Sundays, we were familiar with different baptismal styles, ranging from *few-drops-on-head* to *total-immersion.* Danny and I preferred the latter. We believed that the wetter you got, the greater the likelihood of washing away all those sins. It was just common sense.

"But have you ever seen a baptism done in a lake?" He had us there. In addition to having their sins washed away, today's baptizees were certain to experience chattering teeth and blue lips. Lake Harmony was frigid. "Why don't you sit with me on the bleachers? That way we'll have an unobstructed view."

"Who's gonna be baptized today, RJ?" I asked.

"Usually there are a couple dozen people. Church of Christ members from town. Maybe a POW or two. One of the army guys. Camp staff members. And, of course, campers."

"Campers! Really?"

"I didn't see the list, but maybe so!"

Out of the blue, Danny informed us, "Sheep don't go under water. It makes their wool stink."

"Danny!"

"I meant to say *shrink.*"

That afternoon brought our last softball game. I would miss playing with two full teams. At home, we sometimes had to settle for three or four players on a side. And having an impartial counselor-umpire was preferable to somebody's older sister, like Queenie.

We normally played ball right up to the end of the period. But, on this last day, we stopped early to say goodbye. We milled around the infield, shaking hands, slapping backs, and spitting. I glanced over at the archery class.

Miss Hood and all the girls were standing in a long line waiting to say goodbye to Danny. One by one, each girl hugged him and patted his Tigers cap. While he acted shy and embarrassed, he didn't fool me. He was enjoying every minute of it. Imagine my thinking that Danny had signed up for archery just to shoot girls!

Not wanting to be late for the ceremony, I left Danny still savoring his hug line. By the time I arrived, Reverend Thomas was standing in the lake, up to his knees in water. Apparently the cold didn't bother him. Or, perhaps, he was putting on a brave face for those about to join him there. I climbed the bleachers and took my place next to RJ.

"Where's Danny, Jase?"

"He may be a little late." When I informed him of Danny's going-away present from his archery classmates, RJ guffawed.

Then Reverend Thomas explained the origin of baptism, how important it was to Christians, and the seriousness of the decision to be baptized. His sermonette lasted longer than I expected. Even on dry land, I was a little chilly. And he was standing in ice water! When he finished, he nodded his head toward the boathouse behind us.

The twenty people waiting there formed a long line and marched toward the lake. We weren't able to see them until they had passed our bleachers. They were dressed in white choir robes. We couldn't see their faces but by their heights most appeared to be adults or at least teenagers. There were, however, three shorter candidates at the head of the line. Presumably these were campers, just as RJ had predicted. In any case, they were to be baptized first.

Stopping at the water's edge, they faced Reverend Thomas. He smiled and summoned the first in line. With excessive ceremony, the boy extended his arms forward like a sleepwalker and moved with exaggerated steps through the deepening water toward the waiting minister. A wave of snickers rolled through the audience.

At long last, the boy reached Reverend Thomas who bent over, put his arm around the boy's shoulders, and whispered in his ear. I assumed that the boy was receiving a personal blessing from the Good Reverend. But this *blessing* seemed to go on forever. And it was a two-way blessing with the boy doing much of the whispering. Everyone in the bleachers craned their necks and cupped their ears, attempting to catch a snippet of the blessed exchange occurring before them.

Finally the whispering stopped. The two nodded at each other and shook hands. Then Reverend Thomas placed one hand on the boy's back. And, with his other hand, he pushed the boy's face under water and then jerked him upright. The boy sputtered and spit. Abruptly, without so much as a thank you, he turned and ran for shore. As he splashed his way toward us, he reached under his robe and pulled something from his pants pocket.

A crumpled Tigers cap!

RJ groaned, "What am I going to tell his parents? They told me he'd already been baptized at St. Thomas Catholic Church."

"Maybe Danny thought that *Reverend Thomas* has something to do with *St. Thomas —,*" I speculated wildly.

RJ looked at me and then put his face in his hands.

Danny sloshed up the bleachers, waving his arms wildly and smiling from ear-to-ear. He gave us each a wet hug and excitedly delivered his news.

"Guess what? I'm a Baptist!!!"

WE DECIDED TO PACK our duffel bags before supper and the big show. RJ wanted to leave immediately after breakfast. He had some church business to attend to back in Riverton before his Sunday services. Now that camp was coming to an end, Danny and I were looking forward to getting home. We also had some business to take care of before school started.

"Hey! What's this?" I held up the empty jar that had held the wheat earmarked for gum-making at camp. "We were supposed to make some wheat gum with this. Where'd it go?"

A sheepish look spread over Danny's face.

"Don't tell me. You got a little hungry and ate our wheat, right?"

He smiled and nodded. I shook my head and changed the subject.

"Look what we forgot to do!" I observed, holding up my marbles bag. "I hid these in my footlocker the night we arrived. That seems like a hundred years ago."

"We didn't forget."

"But you said we were going to win some money playing marbles."

"Baptists are never supposed to gamble. Besides Grandma Compton gave us two dollars spending money. And we've still got it."

"Danny, I hate to break it to you, but you're *not* a Baptist. You and I don't belong to *any* church. Baptist is a type of church. You know, like the First Baptist Church in Riverton."

"But I got baptized, so I'm a Baptist, right?"

"No. You're just *baptized.* You gotta join the Baptist Church to be a Baptist. Besides I don't think you want to be a Baptist. You couldn't smoke or drink beer. Or dance. Or use swear words — or —."

"We don't do any of those things, anyway, so why don't we just be Baptists. I'm already baptized, so I'm ready."

"So you want to give up gambling — with marbles — right?"

That stopped him in his tracks. He pondered my comment for a while and then suggested, "Let's not join any church. Let's just keep going to all of them like we do now, okay?"

Amazing! With only one week of church camp under our belts, Danny and I were able to hold an intelligent conversation on the nuances of religious affiliation. At eight bucks apiece, Camp Harmony had turned out to be a valuable investment.

"You finished packing, Danny? I want to get seats up front for the *Songfest.*"

As we walked down the hill, I asked, "Danny, when we first got here you told me that you didn't want to go to *Vespers* because it was too *churchie* and too *girlie.* Then you sign up for archery with all those girls. And then you get baptized. That's pretty *churchie* if you ask me. I don't understand."

"Someday, you will!" he promised with a wink and a sly grin.

"Yeah, I'll bet!"

Danny shrugged his shoulders and whistled *Under the Double Eagle.* I picked up the tune and forgave my friend's inscrutable ways. We stomp-marched down the hill and into the dining hall.

"Hey, boys! Why don't you sit up front with me tonight?" RJ offered.

The MP guards and the German POWs usually ate during the time we were at *Vespers.* But tonight, because they were participating in the *Farewell Songfest,* they ate with us. With the low camper population, half the tables were empty, so it worked out just right. The main course was deep-fried Lake Michigan whitefish, lightly battered, just the way I like it. We ate heartily.

But Danny was curious about something. "RJ, does Camp Harmony always serve fish on Fridays? We had tuna fish sandwiches for lunch today, and we're having whitefish for supper."

"Ha! You're a keen observer, Danny. Andy Ebert, the camp cook, is a devout Roman Catholic. He insists on a menu that will allow him to follow his church's observances. So he imposes this practice on all of us. No exceptions. But we don't object. He's too talented a cook to disagree with, wouldn't you say?"

Danny smiled. "I'll bet he makes exceptions once in a while."

Why did I think Danny was right?

As soon as the tables were cleared and the noise of banging dishes and cookware from the kitchen had subsided, Reverend Thomas took the floor.

"I want to welcome all of you to the traditional Friday night entertainment, our *Farewell Songfest.* Tonight is very special. We are celebrating both the conclusion of another wonderful week of camp and the end of a very successful year for Camp Harmony. In my opinion, 1944 was our best year ever. I'd like to introduce the members of our staff who made it all possible. But first I'd like to say —."

His introduction droned on for about fifteen minutes.

"Psst! RJ," Danny whispered. "Are ministers paid by the word?" Danny had heard Grandpa Compton use that line during a friendly spat with Grandma. RJ smiled. Danny grinned smugly.

"The first half of tonight's musical program will be under that able direction of Miss Hood, Camp Choir Director. Miss Hood, front-and-center, please."

"Danny! I thought she was just the archery instructor," I whispered, as Miss Hood walked on stage.

"Archery is just a *collateral* duty for her."

What on earth does collateral mean? I wonder where Danny heard that one.

Front-and-center meant that Miss Hood was standing about ten feet from Danny. She was clearly pleased to see the former menace from her archery class. Smiling at Danny, she blew him a kiss. That brought a chorus of *cat calls* from Shep's kennel. In typical fashion, Danny stood, grabbed his Tigers cap from his pocket and waved to the crowd. As if on clue, the German POWs waved hats of their own and broke into a wild German marching song that halted abruptly after about thirty seconds.

The power of their blended voices stunned Miss Hood, but she recovered quickly.

"Thank you, gentlemen. Your voices are indeed magnificent. I look forward to your program and more of your splendid music. But right now I would like to introduce the Camp Harmony Choir."

Two dozen staff and campers marched forward and stood on the small stage behind Miss Hood.

"For those of you who are new, I would like to explain how our *Farewell Songfest* works. The choir will sing a number of Camp Harmony favorites. The lyrics are on your song sheets. We invite you to sing along with us."

With that, she threw back her shoulders and launched her half of the show that consisted of these old favorites:

- *Three Blind Mice* (A round)
- *John Jacob Jingle Heimer Schmidt*
- *The Bear Went Over the Mountain*
- *Clementine*
- *The Animal Fair*
- *Alouette* (Another round)
- *Johnny Verbeck*
- *Do Your Ears Hang Low*
- *Ezekiel's Wheel*

And finally, as a special treat for Reverend Thomas, *Praise the Lord and Pass the Ammunition.*

It's no wonder that Reverend Thomas was ecstatic about this popular World War II song written by Frank Loesser in 1942. According to the lyrics, the song is based on the wartime heroics of a certain navy chaplain. During the Japanese sneak attack on Pearl Harbor, low-flying Japanese Zeros knocked out an American ship's gun station by killing its crew. Laying aside his Bible, the chaplain manned the antiaircraft gun and continued firing at the attacking Zeros. His only prayer was for sufficient ammunition to keep on fighting.

No one was ever sure whether this incident had actually happened. Witnesses claimed to have seen at least three different chaplains on three different ships act in a manner described by the song's lyrics. Which of those is the Real McCoy is anyone's guess. Regardless, the song was extremely popular, selling over three million copies in record and sheet music forms.

Unheard of today, the song's creator donated all of his royalties from the sale of the song to the Navy Relief Society. The song was so popular that the Office of War Information limited the number of times it could be played over the radio to six times daily so the public wouldn't tire of it.

Miss Hood's program was a rousing success. Everyone in the dining room, including Danny and me, belted out each and every song with the choir keeping us on key. Following Danny's example, Miss Hood bowed from the waist and left the stage to a standing ovation. The German POWs stood and gave her a cheer that nearly brought down the rafters. Her face turned a deep crimson.

Reverend Thomas resumed his role as Master of Ceremonies. "Thank you, Miss Hood. Well done! Members of the choir and everyone who joined in with so much enthusiasm. Thank you. Thank you. The second half of tonight's musical program will be under that able direction of Sergeant Saunders of the United States Army. Sergeant, front-and-center, please."

I was amazed that Sergeant Saunders was the choir leader. He looked more like a heavyweight boxer. But, as I soon learned, he was very talented.

"Thank you, ladies and gentlemen. Our format will differ slightly from the first half of tonight's show. Naturally much of our program will be in German, so we don't expect you to sing along.

But, in case some of you speak German or are just brave, we've placed sheets with the lyrics on your tables."

The list of their songs was shorter. I only recognized the last two.

- *Es War Ein Edelweiss*
- *Jawoll, das Stimmt.*
- *Gold und Silber*
- *Die Ganze Kompanie*
- *Lilli Marlene*
- *Onward Christian Soldiers*
- *God Bless America*

"The last two songs are in English. So please sing with us then. The POWs will use their best English on those two as well. Oh, yes. We have a guest vocalist for the last song.

"You'll notice that many of our selections tonight are marching songs. These are especially important to German soldiers. Because no one calls cadence when they march, they must rely on the tempo of the music to keep in step."

No wonder POWs are always singing!

The sergeant nodded at the POWs. Immediately they stood up and formed a tight rank in the back of the dining hall. Then they marched silently to the stage, clicked their heels, and bowed. We all applauded. Suddenly the hall resounded with stirring music. Their strong German voices blended in flawless harmony as they moved from selection to selection. Some pieces were marches. Others, like *Lili Marlene,* were sad love ballads.

Before singing *Onward Christian Soldiers,* Sergeant Saunders invited us to stand. When we began, the towering sound filled the dining hall. The accented words emanating from the Germans added a curious dimension to the familiar hymn. It was breathtaking.

After we stopped patting ourselves on the backs and had quieted down, Sergeant Saunders returned to center stage. We girded ourselves emotionally for the singing of *God Bless America.*

"Before we begin our final selection, our guest vocalist will sing the first verse and chorus. Then we invite everyone to join in. Now it is my privilege to introduce a very talented young man. Danny Tucker. Come on up, Danny."

I couldn't believe my ears! Danny scurried to the stage. No one said a word. We were astonished. Then, to the utter amazement of all, Danny sang *God Bless America,* a cappella, in the purest voice that I had ever heard. Even when we joined him on the second verse, I could still hear Danny's powerful voice soaring above the others. I had heard Danny sing before on those occasions when we belted out *My Old Kentucky Home* or *Dutch Land Goober Olives,* but his voice never sounded like this. I was stunned!

Afterwards everyone in the dining hall shook Danny's hand. What a way to end the show! And my wondrous week at camp with Danny!

AS WE LAY IN bed that last night, I told Danny, "Now I understand why you skipped *Vespers.* You were practicing with the Harmony Two Chorale, weren't you?"

"Remember, I said you'd understand."

"But the POWs couldn't sing until after Vespers. What did you do until then?"

"Had supper with them."

"I suppose you had breakfast with them too."

"Yep! That was my quiet place. The dining hall."

"Next I suppose you'll tell me that you had lunch with them too."

"Sure! Mr. Ebert, the cook, made me a sack lunch just like the POWs. Except he always made my sandwiches with ham, even on Friday."

"So I guess your Catholic baptism didn't take, huh?"

"Night, Jase."

"Good night, Danny. Oh, I almost forgot. You have an amazing voice!"

"I know."

5 THE CONTEST

"YOU BOYS HAVEN'T MOVED AN INCH SINCE breakfast. Have you run out of things to do? Only four days left 'til schools starts. Times a wastin'."

Mom was right. Here it was, Thursday morning. We were sprawled out on the back porch, racking our brains for something more to do between now and *The Big Day*. On the way home from camp, we laid out what we thought was an ambitious plan. But we had raced through those events and activities in record time. Now we languished in lethargy.

"Got any ideas, Danny?"

"Nope!"

"I don't have any either. Got have any suggestions, Mom?"

"You could pull weeds in the Victory Garden."

I could tell from Danny's mumble that this was definitely not a good idea. So I responded, "Oh, Mom, I just did that yesterday."

"How about washing the windows in Dad's shed then?"

"Gee, Mrs. A." Danny didn't mumble this time.

I came to the rescue, "Maybe we missed something, Danny. Let's look at the list again."

Danny lifted the bill of his Tigers cap that covered his eyes. I pulled the worn list from my pocket and held it so he could see.

Danny & Jase - Do Before School List

√ Search for Treasures — City Dump
√ Get Cold Drink — Waterworks
√ Dry Sweaty Shirts — Foundry Roof
√ Swim — Miss Sparks —Trumble Park
√ Ride All Day — City Buses
√ Pick/Eat Plums — Mrs. Mikas
√ Read New Comics — Pete's Store
√ Check on Building Progress — Matlock House
√ Say Hi to Otto & POWs — Canning Factory
√ Say Hi to Waitresses — Chop Suey Diner
√ Say Hi to Gentleman Jim
√ Visit — Homer and Homer Worms
√ Buy School Supplies — Woolworths
√ Break Up Old Sewing Machines — Dad's Shed
√ Dig New Garbage Pit — Addison Alley
√ Visit Sammy & Sonny — New Matlock Twins
√ Watch for Enemy Airplanes — Box Elder Tree
√ Count Our Money — Jase's Room
√ Move Toads — From Basement to Victory Garden

We were out of ideas for filling our time when, out of the blue, Danny suggested, "Let's build a secret FSG *underground* camp."

"Why would we want an underground camp?"

"So we can use it this winter. I know where we can get roofing for it."

He explained that his father had just reroofed part of the Tucker garage. So two perfectly good sections of discarded corrugated metal roofing were stacked there, awaiting removal by Bohunk Joe, the neighborhood bum and operator of a pushcart recycling service, on his next collection day.

"Fantastic! But, Danny, how are we going to haul them to our campsite?"

"Let's borrow Sherm's old wagon. It'll work fine." We headed for Sherm's and an uninterrupted morning of heavy construction.

Danny and I were no ordinary construction team. We were Navy Seabees under fire from Jap snipers and malicious malaria-laden mosquitoes, carving an airstrip out of the jungles on Bougainville. Naturally we were armed. Danny packed his samurai sword and I, my genuine SS dagger. Of course, we both carried deadly jackknives, kept razor sharp by frequent application of my father's whetstone and light motor oil sharpening technique.

Of all the building projects we would undertake over the years, the FSG underground camp proved to be our masterpiece. There was a reason for our success. Before breaking ground, we did our planning. Our first consideration was the site itself. The location had to be secret to keep out nosy neighbors, yet close to important things like the Addison kitchen for food, Dad's shed for tools, and Pete's for candy bars and pop.

The first site we considered was the Addison alley. But we dropped that option after considering the prospect of spending hours underground surrounded by all the fermenting garbage that was buried there in the family garbage pits that I was personally responsible for digging. The area behind Mr. Reilly's chicken coop was nixed because of another potential odor problem. In the end, we chose the prairie grass-covered slope just down the hill from the pen of Wolfgang, Hans Zeyer's German shepherd.

Next we focused on building materials. The cast-iron treadle frames from junked sewing-machine cabinets would make ideal roof supports. And Danny's discovery of the roofing material was a stroke of luck. It saved us days of dump scrounging. Finally we agreed that we had to construct the camp without being observed.

We assembled the materials and tools at the building site. We laid Danny's stiff metal sheets side by side on the grass to make a pattern. The hole we were about to dig would be an eight-foot by six-foot rectangle. Using Dad's best garden shovel, I carefully cut away the sod and set each chunk aside for replacement later. We shoveled the rich black humus into Sherm's wagon, hauled it down the hill, and dumped it into the dried up potholes in the swamp.

The soft dirt was relatively easy to dig, so we made excellent progress.

We left a foot-wide ledge around the excavation's perimeter, about three feet below ground level. There we planted several cast-iron sewing-machine bases for roof supports. The leftover ledge space would be used for seating FSG members. We pulled the roof sections over the hole and aligned them with the supports.

After covering the roof with a layer of humus, we carefully replanted the sod. After sweeping away any telltale humus from around the building site and straightening the trodden grasses, we stood back to examine our work. Even from a short distance, it was impossible to tell the roof of our camp from the rest of the grassy slope.

Convinced that we were safe from detection from above, we wiggled down through the narrow entranceway and took our seats on the ledge. As we dangled our feet and smiled at each other, the morning sun poked its rays down through our front door. Still we required more light. Candles would do. We also needed more materials to complete the inside finish work. Drawers, shelves, a lockbox, and hooks and hangers for swords, daggers, and other deadly weapons.

Danny suggested we deploy diamondback rattlers as *Watch Snakes* and post a sign at the entrance to warn intruders. I wasn't sure where we would acquire these deadly desert critters or why sharing our underground camp with poisonous snakes was an acceptable idea, so I didn't comment.

"Jase, we need some shelves in here."

We loaded our digging tools into Sherm's wagon and headed for Dad's shed to borrow a pair of hammers, a wad of finishing nails, and his flashlight. We loaded an assortment of sewing-machine cabinet drawers and other promising pieces. Our spirits restored, we marched to Danny's quick-paced version of *Under the Double Eagle* on our way back to the FSG subterranean hideout.

After an hour of hard finish work, we paused to admire our accomplishments in the glow of Dad's fading flashlight. There were shelves galore and hooks for hanging our belongings. We even had a secret safe, the former home of a set of outdated sewing-machine attachments. The brightly painted box, about half the size of a normal cigar box, was made of sturdy metal. We buried it in the far corner of our underground meeting place. There it would await its new purpose, secret storage for FSG dues and, hopefully, other revenues.

Danny leaned against the cool dirt wall and observed, "We sure could use some curtains down here."

"Curtains? Why curtains?"

"Then we could open them up and let in some light."

"But we don't have any windows. We're underground!" I reminded him.

"That's what I mean. We need windows," Danny asserted unflinchingly.

I ignored Danny's proposal and suggested we return the borrowed hammers and flashlight before Dad needed them. I also made a mental note to replace Dad's flashlight batteries from future FSG revenues, should they materialize. Before leaving, we paused to admire our *cellar house*. You would have never known it was there.

When we arrived home, we washed the black humus from our hands and arms at the spigot under my bedroom window. Next we replaced Dad's tools and restacked the leftover materials behind the shed. Danny's sword and my dagger were restowed under my mattress. I noticed that my bed was beginning to look pretty lumpy, but I doubted that anyone would notice.

We returned to the front porch and stared into the street. After a while, I asked, "Want to go back to our underground camp?"

"No. It's too cold down there."

"Then how are we supposed to use it as a winter camp when it's too cold even before school starts?"

"Maybe we can use it next summer, okay?"

I didn't really have any better suggestion. "Okay."

And that's how our day was going when we were rescued.

Toot, de toot, toot! Bam!

I recognized the Terraplane horn instantly. It was Grandma Compton. "Whoo hoo! Anybody home? It's Thursday! Who wants to go to the stockyards?"

"Jase! We're saved!"

Officially, the Riverton Livestock Yard was only open for business on Thursdays, but what a day it was. Farmers, breeders, and packers for miles around came to the big auction to buy and sell cattle, pigs, sheep, and horses, as well as to socialize with each other.

Outside in the parking lot, dozens of produce vendors sold seasonal fruits and vegetables to the farm women and housewives of Riverton. Crowds swarmed the vendor area creating a carnival-like atmosphere that always fascinated Danny and me. Women chatted with friends, neighbors, and relatives, catching up on the news that was not always good, owing to the mounting war casualties since Normandy.

We had established ourselves as volunteer stock boys and cashiers for a small number of vendors who competed for our services because of our popularity with their customers. We endeared ourselves to the women shoppers by refusing to accept gratuities out of respect for those serving overseas.

The vendors, eager for us to work for them, promised free lunches at the popular café nestled in the rafters above the auction ring. At the end of the day, they paid us with overflowing baskets of delectable leftover produce that they delivered, along with us, to the front doors of our grateful families.

"Marie, is it all right to take these boys with me?"

"Is it all right? They're at loose ends. You're more than welcome to them."

"Do you need anything? Berries? Corn? Anything?"

"Don't think so, Ma. Mrs. Petrov has kept me well-supplied. She's had a bumper crop in most things this year. Her garden is real fertile and she's such a hard worker."

Mrs. Petrov, the Russian woman, who lived at the end of Forrest Street, maintained a garden covering more than two acres of rich bottomland. Each spring, the garden was re-nourished when the Chippewa River left its banks and turned our neighborhood into waterfront property. With a moderate amount of work, the garden produced many times the needs of the Petrov family. So she sold the surplus harvest at bargain prices to her neighbors.

The mention of Mrs. Petrov brought to mind an incident that occurred in Mrs. Mikas' front yard earlier in the summer. Danny and I had witnessed a brutal beating that the brawny Mrs. Petrov had inflicted on Hans Zeyer, a formerly suspected Nazi spy. Fortunately Hans and Mrs. Hans were now respected friends of all the families in the neighborhood including the Petrovs.

"Okay then. Come on, boys. I'm in the market for some raspberries, and you've got influence with that little Italian man who sells 'em."

We piled into the Terraplane for a short, but invigorating, hop. Grandma soared over Pete's Grocery-Liquor-Hardware Store then leveled off briefly before plunging into a breathtaking nosedive that culminated in a dusty four-point landing in the stockyards parking lot. We skidded to a halt just a short distance from the vendor area.

"Wow! That was magnificent!" exclaimed Danny.

"Hey, boys! Wanta work for me? Looky here atta da mush melons I gotta today. Plenty for yer folks. And who's dat, your Granny? Some for her too. They gotta tasty chilidog special today. I'm buyin'. Howsa 'bout it, boys? Come on, helpa me out."

"Don't work for that skinflint. I'll buy two lunches. One now and one before you go home. And I got peanuts to nibble on while we work. Let's do business, huh, boys? You can be cashier, Jase."

This was all very flattering, but we weren't interested that day. We were focusing on Mr. Soldani who offered the best berries on the lot.

"Hiya, boysa! Howsa camp? I really missa you helpa. But I know yousa gotta school comina up, so I gotta wait 'til nexa summer, right? Unless yousa canna helpa me today. Mornina, Mizza Compatone. Whatcha needa today? I gotta plenty dee-liciousa reda razaberry. Tasta soma."

From a wooden quart berry box, he sprinkled a generous portion into each of our outstretched palms. He was right. His berries were indeed *dee-liciousa.*

"Oooooow! They're delicious, Mr. Soldani. How much are they?" asked Grandma, without noticing the sign that clearly spelled out all his prices.

From experience, Danny and I knew that Mr. Soldani didn't negotiate. Because he offered his produce at a fair price, his customers knew not to ask him to settle for less. "Mizza Compatone, thesa berry sella atta fifteena cent a quarta," he declared, pointing to the sign.

"Oh, of course, Mr. Soldani. Beg your pardon. I didn't see your sign. That's a fair price. I'll take ten. No, make that fifteen quarts, please. I'm making jam today."

"Nowa, justa a minuta, Mizza Compatone. Thesa berry sella fo fifteena cent. Buta fo you —." Then he leaned forward and whispered in Grandma's ear, "Zata, okay?"

Grandma's eyes popped open and she broke into a wide grin. "Are you sure, Mr. Soldani?"

He answered by putting his hand over his heart and nodded soberly. Danny and I knew that we had witnessed an extraordinary event. A discount from the Fixed Price King!

Grandma shook his hand. "Thank you. You are most generous."

His response to Grandma's thanks was directed at Danny and me. "Soldani seesa you nexa summar. Righta, boys?"

We shook his hand in agreement. He was already one of our favorites without the inducement of a price break. But it *was* a nice gift for Grandma, I rationalized.

"Oh, maybe yousa helpa me. I needa sweeta corn! And tomato. I'ma almosta solda outta. No tima drive back to my farma fo restocka dem. Iz der anybodies in youra neighborhoud dat coulda helpa me outta?"

"Mrs. Petrov, maybe," I offered. "We could check, right now. Couldn't we, Grandma?"

"Sure we can! We'll drive over there now, Mr. Soldani. Then we'll come right back and tell you what we've learned. We can load the berries then. Come on, boys. Hop in the car! Let's hurry."

Hurry! I thought. *If Grandma hurries anymore, she'll break the sound barrier.*

We lifted off and, seconds later, landed at Mrs. Petrov's house. It was an awe-inspiring flight.

"Afternoon, Anna. We need your help." Grandma described Mr. Soldani's predicament.

As Grandma spoke, Mrs. Petrov began to nod and smile.

"Sure, I gotz plenty doze cornz and tomatz. Butz, day mush be pecked. Kahn you boyz, help me peck? You peck. I pay."

"Boys, looks like you got a job! I'll go back and tell Mr. Soldani his problem is solved. You get the tomatoes and corn picked and put up in baskets. I'll tell him to pick it up in his truck. Say, in an hour, okay?"

Mrs. Petrov nodded in agreement.

"But, Grandma. Who'll sell his produce when Mr. Soldani comes over here?"

"I will. I know his prices like the back of my hand!"

"Well, I'll be dipped in sugar!" Danny added.

By the time Mr. Soldani pulled up in his truck, we had assembled a dozen bushels each of succulent red tomatoes and tender sweet corn, the best the Petrov garden had to offer. Danny and I had picked about half the harvest. Mrs. Petrov had shown us how to do it right by picking all the rest in record time. She was a dynamo. We loaded the truck quickly.

Mr. Soldani and Mrs. Petrov agreed on a price without a quibble. Mr. Soldani counted out the bills and handed the money to her. She promptly peeled off two crisp dollar bills and handed one to Danny and the other to me. It was too much for the little work we'd done, but we didn't say no.

"You peck. I pay," she repeated.

"We're rich!" Danny yelled as he jumped up and gave Mrs. P a big peck on the cheek. Danny's affectionate gesture caught her off guard. She stammered, her face turning bright red.

Forever considerate, Danny explained.

"You pay. I peck!"

WE WATCHED GRANDMA POP her clutch and stomp on the gas. Before the dust settled in the parking lot, she had soared over New Albany Avenue, cut in her afterburners, and punched a hole in Mach 2. In no time, she was out of sight.

"She's gone, Jase! Let's go see Mr. Kolarik."

After taking time to help Mr. Soldani, Grandma was running late. We knew she was eager to get home and put up her raspberries. So, to save her time, Danny and I offered to walk home from the stockyards. Besides we needed to check on the feasibility of Danny's fascinating idea. We had Grandma's approval. The only other person needed to implement the plan lived right next door to the stockyard.

The Riverton Public Schools maintained a large fleet of school buses that plied the country roads of Chippewa County each morning, collecting the sons and daughters of farm families and depositing them on the steps of schools in Riverton. Mr. Kolarik, a retired shop teacher, took pride in driving the cleanest, shiniest, and best-maintained bus in the fleet. We walked up the driveway and joined him under the shade of the towering Dutch elm tree that stood next to his house. He was waxing his bus and humming happily. The start of school was a Big Day for him too.

"Afternoon, Mr. K."

"Hello, Danny. Hi, Jase. You boys all ready for school?"

"Only thing left is church. Then we'll be ready."

"Danny, sixth grade isn't that tough. I don't think you'll need divine intervention to succeed."

"*Divine Invention?* Naw, we don't go to that church. We go to the First Methods, the Mission, and the Church of Christ. Oh! Did you know we went to church camp? Now I'm a Baptist."

Mr. K frowned, shook his head, and returned to his waxing without commenting on Danny's assertion. He was a very wise man.

"So what can I do for you, boys?"

We laid out our idea. When we were finished, Mr. K thought about it for a minute and then declared. "You got yourself a deal! We'll give her a trial run, just like you said."

We shook hands on it.

"Danny, you got an alarm clock?"

"Don't need one. I got a sister."

Once again, the wise Mr. K didn't ask. "How about you, Jase?"

"Danny gets me up every morning."

"Well, okay then. See you boys early Monday morning at six o'clock sharp."

As we turned down Forrest Street, I thought about our day. "Remember this morning, Danny? We had no idea what to do today, but it turned out to be a pretty interesting one."

As we approached the front porch, Dad's car pulled into the driveway. I hadn't realized it was already time for him to return from work.

"Hi, boys! Have a productive day?" Dad asked us as he picked up the afternoon *Riverton Daily Press*.

Our list of accomplishments impressed him. Mom got us off her porch steps. Grandma got raspberries at a price that no one would believe. Mr. Soldani got sweet corn and tomatoes for his customers, not to mention our promise to help him the following summer. Mrs. Petrov got rid of surplus corn and tomatoes, for a nice profit. She was also the fortunate recipient of an unexpected smooch from an admiring younger gentleman. Mr. Kolarik got two new passengers for his school bus and an offer he couldn't refuse. But, because Dad wasn't a member of FSG, we didn't mention the secret underground camp.

And both Danny and I were a dollar richer. Our windfall suddenly opened options that we hadn't counted on, even hours before. A whole dollar would provide enticing additions to our list of preschool time killers.

"Danny, did you really give Mrs. Petrov a kiss? Boy, from what I hear about you at camp and now this, you're becoming a regular Ramon Navarro," Dad teased.

Now it was time for Danny's cheeks to turn red.

"Have you read the paper yet, John?" asked Junior Shurtleif as he crossed the street and headed our way.

"No, not yet. What's the war news?"

Danny and I were intrigued by what he reported. Our week at camp and the tempo of our schedule since we returned had prevented us from keeping abreast of the rapidly changing news from the war.

"Well, looks like the Russians are really putting pressure on Germany's eastern front. They moved into Bucharest last week. Then they signed a ceasefire with Finland, a former Nazi puppet state. Of course, the French retook Paris. That was largely a symbolic victory to bolster the morale of the occupied French citizens. Not that it was a piece of cake in the doing. Van will undoubtedly attest to that when he returns.

"But the big news is what's happened elsewhere in Europe. The Allies, mainly Americans and Brits, have now taken Verdun, Dieppe, Rouen, Antwerp, and Brussels, just to mention a few.

"Also the Americans are expected to reach the Siegfried Line within a week or two. By pushing the Germans to the east, away from the English Channel, the V-1s are no longer falling on English cities. They're beyond the range of those nasty Buzz Bombs. Of course, the German bombers no longer run missions over England. They got their fill during the so-called Battle of Britain. Thanks to the British Spitfires and their pilots."

Most military aviation experts agree that the most effective fighter planes of the World War II European Theater were the German Messerschmitt 109E, the British Supermarine Spitfire 11A, the German Focke-Wulf FW 190, and the American P-51 Mustang.

The Messerschmitt and the Spitfire fought tooth and nail during the Battle of Britain. And, if the British hadn't led in the development of early warning radar, the outcome might have been different. The more advanced FW 190 and P-51 most certainly played decisive roles in the air war over Europe during the latter stages of the war. In the Pacific Theater, the Japanese star was the Mitsubishi A6M Zero. In addition to the P-51 Mustang, the American stars were the Lockheed P-38 Lightning and the Chance Vought F4U Corsair.

Since being honored to keynote the annual meeting of the U.S. Army Air Force 25th Bomb Group Association, I have studied the contributions of another British combat aircraft that deserves considerable credit for services performed in the European Theater. The unsung hero is the British DeHavilland DH-98 Mosquito.

The *Mossie* was perhaps the most versatile aircraft of World War II. The aircraft admirably performed its original purpose as a two-seat, unarmed bomber. Because of its sound fundamental design, the aircraft performed even better in a diverse range of specialized roles.

During three years of service as night fighters, Mossies managed to down 600 enemy aircraft and destroy another 600 flying bombs, the German V-1 Buzz Bombs. Most impressively, the 25th BG used the Mossie to great effect for photo and weather reconnaissance. When in a jam, the recon-configured Mossies evaded Messerschmitt 109Es by simply outrunning them. The Germans couldn't best the Mossie's top speeds that resulted from its most unusual attribute, a super-light, all-wood construction.

Dad and Junior continued their exchange of news about the war. "Boy, that's wonderful news about the European Theater, Junior. How about the Pacific?" Dad asked. "I haven't heard anything since we retook Guam and the Marianas."

"News from the Pacific Theater is harder to come by. Having a front line stretching hundreds of miles over hostile waters makes it more difficult for the press to observe our progress there. I can't tell you all I know, but I have a feeling that we'll soon be reading about B-29 raids from Guam hitting targets deep behind the Jap lines."

"Sounds like payback time for Pearl, Junior."

"Yep. Won't that be sweet?"

"Here comes Aunt Maude, Dad."

Aunt Maude stepped off the bus, crossed New Albany Avenue, and headed our way. When she reached us, she asked, "Good evening, gentlemen. Can a lady join this club? Or is it for men only?"

"Join in, Aunt Maude. We were just talking about the war?"

"Jase, I might have guessed. Probably because the Tigers aren't doing that well."

Aunt Maude wasn't really much of a baseball fan. She was just guessing. Actually 1944 was a pretty good year for the Tigers. Pitcher Hal Newhouser would win the first of his back-to-back MVP nods that year. Of course, in 1945 the Tigers would win the World Series from Chicago in seven games.

"Heard anything from Van lately?" Junior inquired.

"By now he's probably left Paris for *destinations unknown.* That means he's east of Paris, somewhere on the Allied front. He tells me his job is building telephone booths for generals. I guess he thinks I don't know what he really does and how close to the action he is all the time."

"That sounds like Van," Dad confirmed.

"Well, if you have a minute, I'll update everybody on Reitter and Baden. Earlier this week, we transferred them out of Otto Klump's work squad. They've been posted to a remote site where they'll seldom see anything but hard work, let alone pretty female coworkers or opportunities to carry out threats against Danny."

"Junior, that's a relief. Did you tell the Tuckers?"

"I stopped by there just before coming home, John. Naturally they're relieved."

"I'll sorta miss 'em," Danny offered, surprising us all. "Those two keep me from forgetting that the Nazis are still our enemies. Otto and the other POWs don't."

We all nodded in agreement. With so many friendly German POWs in our midst, sometimes it was hard to remember that Germans were still killing Americans in Europe. And thanks to Reitter and Baden, the Libby sisters were serving long prison sentences. Danny had an excellent point, all right.

"Jase, just in case, let's go up to our air-raid post for a while, okay?"

"Okay," I agreed, while trying to connect the dots inside Danny's brain.

"Oh, boy! I'm thankful you mentioned that, Danny. Here's the latest deck of spotter cards from my father. He really appreciates your helping him with his air-raid warden duties," Junior said as he removed the deck of spotter cards from his pocket and handed them to me.

"Wow! Tell him thanks for us, Junior."

After about ten minutes, Danny lost interest in scanning the skies over Riverton. Normally I had more stamina for patriotic labor but the sun was setting. It was getting a little cool. Besides my stomach had been growling for about an hour. But since neither of us wanted to be the one to say *Uncle,* we killed time by examining our new deck of cards.

Aircraft spotter cards were a precious commodity in our neighborhood. Besides Danny and me, only one other boy had a deck. Like regular playing cards, the spotter cards were packaged in a small cardboard box. The front of the box was imprinted with a war poster featuring a pair of smiling American airmen, parachutes over their shoulders, jogging across the runway toward their brand-new B-29.

The poster caption read:

THE MEN WHO FLY 'EM SAY:
"WE'VE GOT THE AXIS' NUMBER NOW ... B-29!"

This same poster was also printed on the front of each spotter playing card inside the box. There were the usual four suits with thirteen cards per suit. The thirteen American warplanes were spades. British, hearts. German, diamonds. Finally the Japanese were clubs. The card number and suit were printed in black and red.

The back of the card also depicted the port side, overhead, and belly views of a single warplane, as well as the nationality, model number, and nickname. Those elements were printed in stark black. For example, the ace of spades was:

U.S. Bomber
B-25 "Mitchell"

Most importantly, the back of the card box carried a *personal* message to Danny and me that read:

June 1943

Training Division
Bureau of Aeronautics
Navy Department
Washington, DC

This special deck of spotter playing cards has been prepared to assist you in learning the characteristics of friendly and enemy aircraft. While the primary purpose of these cards is to show you how one type of airplane may be distinguished from another, we have, by adding regular playing card indexes, created a combination: entertaining and educational.

Danny and I never used the deck for entertainment. Our use was strictly air-raid prevention and we took our jobs very seriously. Another message, printed on the *Joker* of the deck, was a sobering reminder of the serious nature of our assignment:

This document contains information affecting the national defense of the United States, within the meaning of the Espionage Act, as amended. The transmission or revelation of its contents to an unauthorized person is prohibited by law.

Who could play gin rummy with the Espionage Act looking over your shoulder?

"What's wrong with the Germans? Their airplane names are dumb, like Messerschmitt 109 or Heinkel 111."

"Danny, we use model numbers, too, like F-4F and P-38."

"Yeah, but we give them other names, too, like F-4F *Wildcat* and P-38 *Lightning.*"

"What difference does it make?"

"Well, say you're a soldier in a foxhole, right? And a guy yells, 'Watch out! Here comes a Heinkel!' Then, a couple of minutes later, some other guy yells, 'Watch out! Here comes a Wildcat!' "

He leaned into my face.

"Be honest, Jase. Which one's gonna scare *you* the most?"

No wonder Germany lost the war!

THE NEXT MORNING I was awakened by the low drone of my friend's voice. When I entered the kitchen, Mom, Dad, and Aunt Maude were staring at Danny who stood before them gripping one of Mom's wooden spoons with both hands.

"What's going on?" I asked as I took my place at the table.

"We're getting a lesson on how to paddle a canoe properly," Mom explained.

I scowled at Danny who answered with his sheepish grin.

"Better be off to work," Dad announced, seizing the opportunity to duck out. "Thanks, Danny. That was very informative."

Dad scooped up his hat and lunch pail and hurried to the car.

"Hi, Sam," we heard him shout as our milk man placed two quart bottles of whole milk on the front porch.

Then Aunt Maude asked, "Only three more days until school, huh? What's on the agenda today?"

"Marbles!" Danny informed her.

That was news to me but it made perfect sense.

"Gotta practice before school starts. Bring your marbles, Danny?"

With some difficulty, he extracted his huge marble bag, a red-green-yellow argyle sock, from his back pocket. I was surprised that I hadn't noticed the bulge before. He handed the bag to Aunt Maude.

"My goodness! This bag must weigh two pounds. May I look inside?"

Danny nodded. I knew what she would see, marbles of all kinds. Black ones. Red ones. Blue ones. Striped ones. Speckled ones. Cat's eyes. Tiger's eyes. Steelies. Agates. And gigantic boulders. As Aunt Maude inspected Danny's treasure, I heard the glass marbles *clicking* against each other. I loved that sound.

In our neighborhood, marbles were the coin of the realm. They provided us boys with a versatile medium of exchange. We traded them. We bought things from each other with them. Like currency, marbles had denominations. One aggie equaled five regular marbles. One boulder equaled two aggies. And so on.

Because of their value, certain boys were known to *hock* (steal) marbles from others. Those who attended schools other than ours, like St. Thomas Catholic School, were particularly vulnerable. There were even cases where marbles were kidnapped and ransomed back, usually to younger boys whose parents had just bought them their first marbles.

We gambled with our marbles in games of chance. It was not unusual for a boy to lose two hundred marbles in an hour playing with sharks like Danny and me. We played pot marbles. Pinkies. Aggie poker. And shooter. We loved our marble games!

Every boy in our neighborhood had his stash of marbles. Keeping it safe was a top priority, especially if you were preoccupied with other important duties such as scanning the skies to protect your neighborhood from enemy air raids.

Marble bags were used to impress or intimidate other players. Most were constructed from rawhide, finished leather, or fine cloth. Your initials or your nickname, as in my case, had to be embossed or embroidered on your bag. Of course, some bags garnered strong sentimental value, particularly those that brought good luck or showed off real well.

Eugene Thompson's mother stitched his quart-sized marble bag from a pure white silk fabric. Even my own bag, the former nesting place of a New Home buttonhole attachment, was made from luxurious royal purple velvet with braided gold pull-strings. Naturally there was Danny's exquisite argyle sock.

Incidentally, Eugene only used his dazzling silk bag a few times. Once Danny and I made it clear to him that his was, not only a sissy bag, but also unpatriotic, he donated it, without his mother's knowledge, to the American Red Cross Rags-for-War Drive.

It was only fitting, we informed him afterwards, because his silk bag represented a clear violation of the War Materials Act and may very well have deprived some unfortunate P-38 pilot of a full-sized parachute, absolutely essential when bailing out of his burning fighter plane over an island in the Pacific.

Marbles in the old neighborhood were a predictor of life after Forrest Street. Some marble magnates, like Danny and me, would succeed in business. Others, who regularly employed the hocking and extortion methods, would develop expertise in posting bail. And boys with sissy bags often suffered broken collarbones later in life.

My marble bag was safely ensconced under my mattress, right below my pillow. Nobody in the world knew it was there. Naturally Aunt Maude, Mom, and Danny didn't count.

"When you get tired of playing marbles, here's another fun project for you. A chance to win a valuable prize," Mom informed us without looking up from yesterday's *Riverton Daily Press.*

She was perusing it, one last time, before placing it in the stack for Bohunk Joe.

"We really don't need any marbles practice, Jase." Danny had read my mind. "Tell us more, Mrs. A. We're feeling lucky."

Mom spread the *Riverton Daily Press* across the kitchen table.

"There!" she said, pointing a finger at a page that was covered with hundreds of tiny numbers. "Read the little box in the corner."

**IF YOU CAN COUNT,
YOU CAN WIN A VALUABLE PRIZE!**

**Add up all the numbers on this page and submit
your grand total to our manager
before 6:00 PM on Friday, September 8, 1944.
The contest entrant coming closest to the
actual grand total will be our winner.
The name of the winner will be announced one hour
after the contest closing time shown above.**

**RIVERTON FURNITURE STORE
115 WEST MAIN STREET
RIVERTON, MICHIGAN
TELEPHONE 1210**

"Do you have some scissors we can borrow?" Danny asked Mom.

"Scissors? Sure but what are you —?"

Danny interrupted Mom before she finished her question. "Divide and conquer!"

Using Mom's scissors, Danny cut the full-page ad in half, taking care to preserve each number by cutting around it. Then he cut each half in half. And then again. And again, a fourth time. When finished, he had sixteen small squares of paper, each having a manageable quantity of numbers. With a pencil from the kitchen drawer, he lightly numbered the back of each square from *1* to *16*.

Using a sheet from my new school tablet, he listed the number of each square and drew a line next to it. Here we would enter the total count for that square. Finally under the column of square totals, he drew a long line and labeled it *Grand Total*.

When he finished, he turned to us and asked, "Who wants a square?"

"I'm afraid you boys are on your own. I'm going to take the bus downtown with Aunt Maude when she goes to work in a few minutes. She wants me to look at some patterns at Woolworths. Then I'm going to do some fabric shopping. Besides you want to do this by yourselves so you won't have to share that valuable prize with us ladies, right?"

"Right!" Danny agreed. "Valuable prizes are hard to share."

I wasn't quite sure what that meant but I didn't object. After all, we had all day. And there were two of us. How much time could it take to add up the numbers on sixteen squares of paper? We were about to find out.

We decided on a process for checking our arithmetic. Each of us would calculate the total for each of the sixteen squares. If our sums agreed, we would post that number on the totals sheet. If not, the two of us, working together, would add the numbers a third time. And additional times, if necessary, until we agreed.

We started the process at nine o'clock in the morning. By noon, we had only agreed on the totals of four squares. We were tired and hungry, but we decided to press on until we had completed at least twelve squares.

By three o'clock, we had reached our goal. Allowing ourselves time for a quick bite, we each wolfed down four slices of bread wrapped around cinnamon-covered dill pickles, washed down with cold milk. Our lunch hour lasted about three minutes.

As we were working on our last square, I heard Dad pull into the driveway. When he walked into the kitchen, I quickly explained what we were doing. He shook his head in amazement and went off to look for the afternoon paper.

We had each calculated the sum of the last square about six times without coming up with the same number. Fatigue was dulling our senses. And I felt tension in my shoulders. Finally Danny offered *1,113!*

"Bingo!" I responded. "That's what I just got!"

We had agreed on all sixteen squares. Now to add up the sixteen numbers and arrive at the Grand Total. We used the same process as before. Each of us calculated the sum of the sixteen numbers. Then we compared our results.

"*16,021!*" I announced.

"Nuts! *16,044!*"

We were almost out of patience. Just then, Mom and Aunt Maude came through the front door.

"My gosh! You're still at it. You only have a half-hour to get your entry to the store."

"I can give them a lift. It'll only take ten minutes to get there. Let's wait outside. Give them some quiet so they can finish up."

"*16,044!*"

"Bingo! Bingo! Beeeeeeeengo!" Danny screamed.

We ran out the backdoor and around the house to the driveway. Mom and Aunt Maude were in the back seat. Dad was behind the wheel. The car was idling eagerly. The instant the door closed, Dad hit the gas. The spinning wheels shot gravel into our backyard. We raced up Forrest Street to New Albany and squealed around the corner. Dad drove like a maniac, faster than I had ever seen him drive.

"Just like Grandma Compton!" Danny yelped. Mom moaned from the backseat. She was always concerned for our safety when we flew with Grandma. We skidded to a halt in front of Riverton Furniture. Danny pushed open the front door. We dashed into the store.

"Holy crow! You boys made it with only two minutes to spare," the manager confirmed, looking at his pocket watch. "Just put your Grand Total and your names on this entry form. Then we'll slip it into this box!"

We hurriedly filled out the entry form, inscribing both our names and what we just *knew* was the correct total. *16,044.*

"You're the last entrants. We'll announce the winner at seven o'clock on the dot. Come on back and see who wins. And thanks for choosing Riverton Furniture!"

"Thanks for choosing our number!" Danny retorted.

The embarrassed manager smiled nervously, lifted the box stuffed with entry forms, and disappeared through a door marked

Private Office. Dad was double-parked in front, so we scurried back to the car.

"Where to, sirs?" Dad asked, imitating a cab driver.

"Moore's Ice Cream Parlor, driver. And get a move on!" answered Aunt Maude. "I'm starved! And supper's on me tonight."

"Hurrah!" yelled Danny.

I couldn't have agreed more. We were all famished. The nervous tension that filled the air as the deadline approached and the anticipatory anxiety as seven o'clock drew near combined to stimulate everyone's appetite. When the bill came, I knew it would take a big bite out of Aunt Maude's weekly paycheck, but she didn't seem to mind. We thanked her profusely and left the restaurant.

"Why don't we walk over to the store? We have time," Dad suggested.

"Tremendous idea! I'm stuffed and could use the exercise," Mom agreed.

Riverton stores were open on Friday nights so the streets were crawling with shoppers.

When we arrived at Riverton Furniture, a small crowd was milling in the street. The store itself was packed with curious people of all sorts, browsing through couches and easy chairs, just killing time, waiting for the big announcement.

At one minute before seven, the manager, carrying the entry form box, emerged from the store. He placed the box on the sidewalk and stepped up onto a wooden chair so that those in the back could see him. Those inside poured out to join the rest of us on the street.

"Folks, thank you for coming down tonight. I'm the manager here at Riverton Furniture. I want you all to know that we really appreciate your business. Oh, Miss James, I almost forgot, would you please go back to my office and bring out the Grand Prize?"

The petite young woman smiled and returned to the store.

Pulling three completed entry forms from his coat pocket, the manager continued his speech from atop his chair.

"We are pleased as punch to have had over six hundred entrants for our add-up-the-numbers contest. Among them, we had three entries that came very close. I know how much work went into entering this contest, so I will read the names and numbers of the third and second place entrants before announcing our first place winner."

Miss James returned with the Grand Prize, a box wrapped in white paper and tied with a bright red ribbon. "Look at that beautiful package. Wonder what's inside? We'll all know in just a few minutes!"

The crowd cheered and clapped.

"Okay, folks! Okay! I know you're eager to get on with your shopping, so here's the third closest entry. The sum was *16,133*. Submitted by Mrs. Edna Parrish. You here, Mrs. Parrish?"

We all looked around for a hand to pop up, but apparently number three wasn't present. The crowd moaned and looked impatiently at the manager.

"The second closest number is *16,099*. Submitted by Howard Smithers from Owosso. You here, Mr. Smithers?"

Mr. Smithers was a no-show too.

"People from Owosso don't know how to drive after dark," a red-nosed joker called from the crowd. Four or five people roared with laughter. The manager and the rest of us ignored the bore.

"Okay, folks! Okay! Here we are! Get that big prize ready, Miss James. Unfortunately the prize-winning entry also failed to hit the actual total. But the entry was very close. Only off by *43* points."

"You forgot something!" Danny hollered. People around him stepped back and stared as if he had horns growing from his Tigers cap. That included his best friend from Forrest Street.

The manager ignored this second heckler, just as he had the first. He simply continued. "The actual count was *16,001!* The entry coming the closest to our count was —."

"*16,044!* And that's the right number! Your count's wrong!"

This time, the manager rose to Danny's bait. But he did it with class. "Now wait just a second here, young man. I have a feeling I know who you are."

The crowd immediately fell silent. You could hear a feather drop.

"Are you Master Jase Addison *or* are you Master Daniel Tucker?" Not waiting for Danny's answer, he announced, "Ladies and gentlemen! I give you our Grand Prize winners, with an entry of *16,044!*"

The crowd roared and closed in on Danny and me. People shook our hands or slapped us on our backs. Our entourage from Forrest Street grinned from ear-to-ear and gave each of us a hug.

"Let the boys come on up, folks. Make way. Bring two chairs for the boys to stand on, would you please, Miss James?"

Even though we were standing on chairs, we were barely visible above the crowd. So we stood on our toes to wave at Dad, Mom, and Aunt Maude who were wildly clapping like everyone else.

The manager raised his arms to silence the crowd. "You're Danny, right? Okay, Danny, now your number was off by *43* points. Isn't that right?"

"Nope!"

"Now that's the third time you've said that. I'd better let you explain yourself. Our accountants went over those numbers again and again. Where did we go wrong, Danny?"

"You forgot the numbers in the little box in the corner, the contest instructions box."

"I don't remember any numbers being printed in that box. Just words. Instructions, like you said before."

"What about the deadline time? And the date? Street number? And that phone number? They're numbers, aren't they?"

The manager seemed puzzled. He looked at Danny, then at me, and finally at his assistant. "Help me out here, Miss James. Is it possible that Danny's right?"

Miss James nodded and replied, "The accountants tallied the page before we placed the instructions box in the advertisement. Don't you remember?"

The manager shook his head, "You are absolutely right, Miss James. And you are too, Danny. Just how much did we miss it by?"

"Only *43* points, sir. Your count was *16,001* plus *43* is *16,044.* That was our entry."

The crowd broke into a roar. As usual, Danny bowed from the waist, nearly falling off his chair in the process.

"Well, I'll be dipped in sugar!" declared the manager.

"Yes, you sure will," Danny agreed.

"Well, we at Riverton Furniture are big enough to admit when we make a mistake. And we made a big one. No doubt about that. Yes, sir. But there's one thing we are sure about. This is a fine Grand Prize. How about opening it so we can all see what's inside, Danny?"

"No, thank you, sir. We'll open it later at home, but we'll let you know what's in the box tomorrow. We'll be coming downtown to go to the movies." With that Danny hopped down from his chair and snatched the prize away from an astonished Miss James. The crowd was dumbfounded. After applauding one last time, people began to drift away. Soon the pedestrian traffic was back to normal.

As Dad pulled his car to the curb, Danny turned to the manager, "Do you like selling furniture more than you liked being in the army?"

"Wha — I wasn't in the army. I have — er — flat feet. Eh! Eh!"

"When I saw the name painted on your door, I thought you were in the army."

"What name?"

"Private Office!"

General Danny strikes again.

"DANNY, WHY DIDN'T YOU want to open the box at the store?" I asked as we pulled into the Tucker driveway.

"I wanted my family to be there."

"Oh, I see. Then let's open the box inside. That way everybody can watch."

We piled out of the car, and Danny carried our prize up the Tucker walk. As soon as the door was open, Danny yelled inside, "Hey, everybody, come quick. See what we won!"

Mr. and Mrs. Tucker were sitting in the front room reading the paper. I could hear Chub and Queenie thumping down the stairs from the attic room that served as the kids' bedroom.

"Who won what?" Queenie wanted to know, immediately! She was two years older than Danny and always seemed to manage to get her way.

"We did! Jase and me. A contest at Riverton Furniture. We were first place out of six thousand entries!" Danny bragged proudly, if not quite accurately.

"Just lucky, I bet! Anybody coulda won. No big thing."

I didn't want to disagree with Queenie directly. That could be dangerous. So I explained to Mr. and Mrs. Tucker how Danny had devised the *divide and conquer* method of counting the many numbers printed in the ad. And how we had worked all day to come up with our prize-winning total. Finally how Danny's process had produced a number that was more accurate than that of Riverton Furniture's management and accountants.

They congratulated both of us. Queenie hummed quietly and leafed through the movie magazine that, evidently, she had been reading when we arrived. Chub was still in the doghouse for removing all the wrappers from the family's large stock of assorted food cans stored in their basement. He had learned to keep a low profile.

Without our noticing, he quietly began to remove the ribbon from the box that Danny had placed on the coffee table. But Mrs. Tucker caught him in the act.

"Let Jase and Danny unwrap that, Chub. It's their prize."

"You can open it, Jase," Danny offered.

I quickly untied the bow, removed the wrapping paper, and opened the box. There it was! Our magnificent Grand Prize. An RCA portable radio handsomely encased in walnut and plastic. We were speechless.

"Wow! Look how small it is," Dad observed.

"Let's give her a test run," suggested Mr. Tucker, uncoiling the cord.

Mrs. Tucker unplugged the lamp from the outlet next to the davenport.

"There we are. Plug it in here."

Immediately a light on the front of the radio flashed on. We gasped in surprise and delight. The radio squealed as Danny turned the tuning knob. Then, suddenly, the room was filled with sound.

"This is WLAC, coming your way from Nashville, Tennessee. Welcome to our show ..."

We couldn't believe our ears! Nashville, Tennessee! "It's from overseas!!!" yelled Chub.

"No, it's not, either," corrected Queenie who had suddenly taken a great interest in our prize. "Let's take it up to our bedroom. That way we can listen to it while we do our homework."

"No!" Chub yelled. "I want it in the basement so I can hear it when I'm playing."

"Now hush!" scolded Mrs. Tucker. "This is Jase and Danny's prize. They'll decide where it goes. Not you two."

"We can share it, Danny. You keep it for a week. Then bring it over to my house."

"Do it!" ordered Queenie.

"Nope! The radio goes to Jase's house and that's where it's going to stay, all the time. And that's final!"

"Just because you've been baptized twice, you think you know everything!"

Both Mr. and Mrs. Tucker glowered at Queenie. Evidently this was not a subject they wanted to discuss in public.

Despite vehement objections from Dad, Mom, Aunt Maude, and me, Danny was firm. The radio went back in the box and into the car. As Queenie pouted, the rest of the Tucker family waved goodbye. When Danny came out to say good night, he revealed his motive for wanting me to keep the radio.

"I hate Big Band music!"

"You could listen to something else then."

He shook his head in disagreement. "Queenie *loves* Big Band music!"

He didn't have to say another word.

6 WEEKEND DIVERSIONS

"LET'S GO SEE THE RADIO," I SUGGESTED AS SOON AS Danny arrived the next morning. "But be quiet. Aunt Maude's still asleep."

We crept into my bedroom where, sure enough, my roommate was sleeping soundly. Danny tiptoed to the small table under my window that overlooked Mrs. Mikas' plum trees and sat down quietly. He stared at the prize radio. Then he stroked it gently and murmured his admiration.

Finally he turned and whispered, "Get your dollar and let's go!"

Our new dollars were burning holes in our pockets. Ordinarily, following the admonitions of President Roosevelt to sacrifice for the war effort, Danny and I were frugal savers. Dutifully we purchased war savings stamps from our teacher at school. We pasted them into special booklets. When full, one of these could be converted to a war bond. Because this was our last weekend before buckling down to the new school year, we decided to splurge. Besides we hadn't seen a movie in ages.

Our plan was to spend all day Saturday and all day Sunday at the movies. Because of the schedule change on Sundays, we could take in six different full-length films, two serials, two newsreels, and four cartoons. All in a single weekend!

And the cost? Eleven cents for the double feature at the Grafton Theater and a whopping fifteen cents for the classy single feature at the Chippewa. Of course, this didn't include our nickel bus fares and refreshments.

Normally Sunday afternoons were spent at the farm. But Grandma had decided it was time to drive north to visit Uncle Raymond, Aunt Betsy, and my cousins Tommy and Teddy. Uncle Raymond had just finished building an addition to their house and was eager for his parents, Grandma and Grandpa Compton, to see it. So we were free for the weekend and movies were a super way to make time fly.

We cleared the house and headed for the bus stop. That morning, we had plenty of time to walk to town, but we were in the bucks so we chose to ride in style. The Chippewa Trails Bus Line was our preferred mode of transportation on that bright day. Besides taking the bus would allow us to arrive downtown before the Grafton opened. Mr. Dykstra, the theater manager, just might let us help set up for the first show. This usually involved a lot of sweeping and emptying of trash barrels, but sometimes he even let us replenish the shelves displaying highly desirable movie candy including Milk Duds, Jujyfruits, Raisinets, and Necco Wafers in the tiny lobby snack bar. What a treat!

As we sat on the bus-stop bench, I recalculated our budget for the weekend's entertainment. "Let's see. Four bus fares each day at a nickel apiece is twenty cents. Times two days is forty cents. Then four tickets for the single feature at the Chippewa at fifteen cents. That's sixty cents."

"Plus four more for the double features at the Grafton for eleven cents each. That's forty-four cents," Danny added. Then he picked up a twig and scratched the numbers in the dirt at our feet. "Forty plus sixty. Plus forty-four. Equals a dollar forty-four. That's what we figured yesterday. So we have fifty-six cents to spend on candy and popcorn, if you still want to."

"Fifty-six cents is a lot even for two days."

"Jase, we could just buy nickel bags of popcorn. Then use what's left over to buy savings stamps from Miss Sparks when school starts."

"Not a bad idea!"

I was relieved that Danny felt the same way I did. I wanted to make a good impression on Miss Sparks. I hoped she would rank frugality at the top of her list of virtues. Besides, even if she favored some other virtue, I didn't want to take a chance, especially on the first day of school.

"Look! Here comes Bohunk Joe. I bet he's got a delivery of dented cans for Edith," Danny speculated. "But who's that with him? I know it isn't Gentleman Jim. Not anymore."

For years, Bohunk Joe and Gentleman Jim served together as our neighborhood bums, a respected position in our part of town. Our bums kept us humble and charitable even after the booming defense factories brought economic recovery following the Depression.

Each Saturday, Jim had delivered a burlap bag or two of canned food to Edith Squires, the minister's wife and chief organizer at the Good Mission Church. The Mission, as everyone called it, was home to passing hobos, local bums, and other poor souls, each of whom was a potential convert in the eyes of Reverend Squires.

While the food inside was perfectly safe to eat, the cans couldn't be sold because of the dents. So the foremen down at the Chippewa Canning Corporation donated them to various worthy causes, including Jim and Joe who shared their bounty with the Mission.

But, during the trial of the Libby sisters, Gentleman Jim had cleaned himself up and offered dramatic testimony as a character witness for the young women. Harry Chambers, the Libby sisters' attorney, convinced his old friend Jim to reapply for his former job. And this fall he would reassume his position as history teacher and football coach at Riverton High School.

"Holy Smokes, Danny! It's Bibs! And they're not driving in a straight line."

Bohunk Joe's pushcart followed a zigzag course as he and Buddy Roe Bib Overalls headed our way. They were obviously still feeling the influence of last evening's refreshments. Undoubtedly their wine of choice was a fortified red from Pete's store, located directly across from the bus stop where we sat.

"Bibs better not let the Reverend or Edith see him in that condition. He'll lose his trustee job again," Danny predicted.

"Whatcha got in the cart, Mr. Joe?" I asked as they pulled up beside us.

Joe didn't seem to hear my question, so Bibs answered for him. "Carps! Lotsh of carp for the Mission kission. I mean *kischen!*"

The pushcart was filled to the brim with twenty or more large fish, still alive and flopping helplessly in the morning sun.

"Where'd you catch 'em?" I asked, wondering how they could possibly amass such an impressive mess of fish, especially in their condition.

"Shhhhhhh!" Joe hissed with a finger to his lips. "Mza jool tzak." When Bohunk Joe was *under the influence,* his ability to speak English left with his equilibrium. But, despite this small handicap, he attempted to tell us his secret. "Mza jool tzak e jool, prezit," he declared, elaborating on his first answer.

Not wanting to be impolite, we nodded, pretending to understand. That pleased him. He smiled broadly and began to dance a little jig on the sidewalk. We looked for help from Bibs who leaned our way, placed his mammoth arms around our shoulders, and whispered loudly, "Built ah carp trap lash night. And diss moring it was fool of fishhh. We got lots more carps at Joe's. But dohn't tell nobahdy, espec-lee Sargent Tolna."

Fish traps on the Chippewa River were strictly illegal, unless you happened to be a Chippewa Indian. By treaty, much to the chagrin of Michigan sports fishermen, those Indians were permitted to take fish, year-round, using any method they could devise.

Just then Edith poked her head out the front door of the Mission. "Buddy Roe Bib Overalls! Come here! I need to talk to you!"

Edith seldom addressed a Mission resident by his full formal name. But when she did, he'd better watch out. Edith was a tough taskmaster and not a bit patient with those who consumed alcohol, especially among the Mission trustees. Old Bibs was in for it. It was clear that Bibs and Edith were engaged in a heated discussion on the front porch, but none of us could hear their words. Suddenly the exchange ended.

Bibs waved to us, motioning his fishing partner to wheel the pushcart around back to the kitchen entrance. He tapped himself on the chest, pointed inside, and then disappeared through the door. We all got his meaning. He would go through the Mission and meet Bohunk Joe out back.

But, when Joe attempted to pivot his carp laden pushcart toward his target, he slipped and fell on the sidewalk. Danny looked at me. I nodded. We each grabbed a handle and slowly turned the cart toward its destination. By the time Joe recovered from his slip, we were well on our way. When we rounded the corner of the wide back porch, Edith and Bibs were waiting for us. "Good morning, boys," Edith said, finally acknowledging our presence. "How have you been?"

We formed a bucket brigade, using carp instead of buckets, and passed the entire load of heavy fish up the back steps, across the porch, and onto the wide counter that ran the length of the kitchen. "You boys like to clean fish?" Edith asked, with a welcoming smile.

Danny's glance divulged how he wanted to answer her question. We both turned and answered simultaneously, "You bet!"

Danny and I rolled up our sleeves and grabbed fish scalers.

"Don't forget to remove the mud line," Edith reminded us on her way out of the kitchen.

Keith Squires stopped his preparations for lunch and observed, "Boy, I've never seen so many big fish. How many are there?"

Twenty carp — and two suckers!

HAVING COMPLETED OUR CARP cleaning duties, we were sitting on the bus-stop bench anxiously awaiting the next bus. Our practice of leaving very early for appointments usually compensated for neither of us owning a watch. But, because of our carp diversion, we were concerned about the time. I saw the bus coming our way up New Albany Avenue.

"Think we'll be there before the show starts?" Danny asked nervously.

"Here it comes. If it's the 11:30 bus, we'll make it okay."

"Hey, you guys! Wait for me!"

Danny and I turned to see Sherman Tolna, holding up his baggy pants and running our way. He waved at us and emitted a gushy giggle. At age six, Sherm the Worm was the youngest member of the Forrest Street Guards, organized at the height of the Hans Zeyer investigation. FSG had been inactive since we discovered, to our embarrassment, that we had hounded an innocent man.

"Where are you going, Sherman?" I sneered. I wasn't quite sure why abusing my snotty-nosed neighbor was so gratifying to me.

"Grafton! To see the noon show. I got a quarter for helping Mrs. Zeyer butcher chickens. I plucked. Where you guys going?"

"None of your business, shrimp!" Danny snapped. He and Sherman were not the best of buddies, even though we three were FSG fraternity brothers.

"I get to ride the bus by myself! You guys taking the bus?"

"No, Vermin, we just like to wave at it when it goes by," Danny growled. "That's why we're standing here."

"I don't get it," Sherman confessed.

We were saved by the bus. We hopped on, deposited our nickel fares, and sat in the seat we prized, just across from the driver. Running parallel to the aisle, this was the only seat like it in the bus. Without being invited, Sherman squeezed in beside us and smiled impishly.

Can't we shake this little rat?

"Morning, Mr. Smalley," Danny and I chanted.

"Howdy, boys. What's new?"

"We're going to the movies," I answered. When Danny elbowed me, I realized my mistake.

"Oh, boy! Can I come with you then?" Sherm chortled.

Danny ignored him and asked, "Mr. Smiley, is this the 11:30 bus?"

"Yep! And we're right on time."

"Mr. *Smalley*, did you hear about Danny's solo at Camp Harmony?" I asked, providing Danny with the driver's correct name.

Mr. and Mrs. Smalley were members of the First Methodist choir. Danny and I attended their church often because of the superb musical programs. Of course, Danny had an admirer among the church members, his former foe, Miss Elizabeth Bundy. I liked Mel Carmody, the friendly usher. Of course, both of us were fond of Mel's wife Anne who was the Sunday school registrar and provider of the best church snacks in town.

"Well, Danny, you'll have to try out for our choir. We could use a fine, young voice like yours. Why don't we talk about it tomorrow after church?"

"Are we going to church tomorrow, Danny?"

"Can't think of a better use for some of that fifty-six cents."

Then Danny turned and saw a car pulling onto New Albany from a side street about two blocks ahead. "Watch ou —!"

He caught himself before he let the warning fly. Danny had nearly driven Mr. Smalley crazy with his driving tips over the course of the summer. Recently Aunt Maude had joined us for a bus ride downtown. Afterwards she took Danny aside and *suggested* that he knock it off, for the sake of Mr. Smalley's mental health and the safety of his passengers. Danny promised to refrain from offering further *help*. But it was difficult for him to hold his tongue. Today was no exception.

"Sorry, Mr. Smalley," he apologized, getting the name right this time.

Mr. Smalley smiled at him. "Then I'll see you at church in the morning, right?"

"I'll bet you don't know what's showin' at the Grafton!" interrupted Sherm.

"Of course, we do," I retorted. "Why would we be going if we didn't know what was on?"

I was bluffing. Danny and I had neglected to check the listings in yesterday's paper. Only it didn't matter. We knew it would be a cowboy double feature, a serial, and one or two cartoons. This was the Grafton's standard fare every day of the week. We looked forward to being surprised by the offerings today.

"No, you don't! You don't know. You don't know and I do! You don't knooooow!" Sherm was losing it and incurring our wrath in the process.

As usual, his bouncing loosened a slug of mucus that oozed out of his nose and, with a quick wipe, onto the sleeve of his summer jacket. I noticed that Sherm's sleeves needed chipping. In recent weeks, the thick, glassy coating had become so heavy that he walked with his arms hanging down, reminding me of Mighty Joe Young.

"Okay, smarty pants! Tell us what's playin'. I dare ya!" Danny hissed.

"One's ah Hot Gilson. And tha other's ah Tex Rider."

"You mean *Hoot Gibson* and *Tex Ritter?*"

"That's what I said! I bet you don't know who's in the serial, either!"

He was right of course. Most serials ran for eight or ten episodes and it had been months since we had seen one. But, if you had to bet your life, it would be either Lash LaRue or The Durango Kid.

"Lash LaRue!"

"No! No! No! It's Derange-do Kid!"

Talk about a deranged dodo!

"Durango, dummy!" Danny spat.

Feeling sorry for the abused underdog, Mr. Smalley lent his support. "That Hoot Gibson's a dandy one. *Cavalcade of the West* it's called. Then there's *Tex Rides with the Boy Scouts.* Not so good. But okay."

Without knowing the first thing about the Grafton offerings, Danny and I now possessed the stars' names and their movies' titles, plus a comprehensive review of each. And I was certain that we had extracted this information without revealing any hint of ignorance on our part.

Maybe we should reactivate FSG and get back in the counterintelligence game while we're hot!

"We're here, boys. Enjoy the show!" our friendly driver announced as the bus door opened with a hiss.

We tumbled out at the downtown bus terminal, said adieu to Mr. Smalley, and made a beeline for the Grafton. Sherm tagged along behind us like a puppy dog. We ignored him as best we could. As we rounded West Main Street, we saw that the line was long. But we soon had our tickets and slipped inside the lobby.

The smell of popcorn made my mouth water. "Want some popcorn now, Jase?"

"Yes, I do!" answered little Sherman, still sticking to us like a leech.

"You got enough money, Sherm? Or were you planning to borrow from us?"

"I got four pennies and a dime. Change from my quarter. Is that enough for popcorn and the bus?"

"Yes!" Danny answered impatiently. "Here give me your dime! I'll get three nickel bags."

"But I don't want to spend my dime on three nickel bags."

"Sherman, when are you going to learn arithmetic?"

"Do I have to?"

"No, stay a dope! But just don't say another word. Do you want one nickel bag and a nickel's change or not?"

Sherm turned to me for guidance. I nodded, so he nodded at Danny. This was a taxing process. We needed to claim our seats. And fast! "Hurry, Danny! Let's get some seats down front."

The first row of seats, down in front on the main level, were the most popular with us boys. However, they required us to slouch back and view the screen at an upward angle. If we were lucky enough to get one, the honor of landing that seat more than made up for the stiff neck and bleary eyes we suffered from sitting for four hours in that awkward position.

We got our popcorn and trotted up to the ticket taker who informed us that the only empty seats were in the balcony. That was dreadful news. Because of their great distance from the screen, about seventy long feet, balcony seats were the least popular with the boys of Riverton.

Typically the balcony was only occupied by the few adults who were brave enough to attend weekend matinees. Those wise people chose not to mix with the noisy tangle of boys down front. Besides being more peaceful in the balcony, it was much safer. No gum in the hair. No drinks spilled on your clothes. And no danger of being splattered when a boy ate too much junk food and then, without warning, decided to start over, if you get my drift.

During the war, Riverton was home to many Mexican and Jamaican farm laborers. They worked in great numbers alongside German POWs from Camp Riverton in the fields around Chippewa County. Shipments of sugar from South America and the Caribbean were curtailed by the presence of German U-boats. So America replaced cane sugar with beet sugar, much of which was grown on Michigan farms including those around Riverton. Those farms required workers to plant, weed, and harvest beets by hand. And local farmers preferred Mexicans — men, women, and children — for these tasks.

The Riverton Sugar Beet Company also used Mexicans to process the beets. The resultant white sugar was shipped to markets all around the country. Those migrant workers lived in a cluster of wooden shanties that had been hastily constructed beside the railroad tracks on the grounds of the sugar beet factory.

On weekends, the Spanish-speaking Mexicans sought entertainment. The shoot-'em-ups at the Grafton were relatively easy to follow, so they paid their eleven cents like us boys and joined us. For some reason, the Mexican families all chose to sit in the balcony. Whether because of an unwritten theater rule or because of their own preferences, the dark-skinned Jamaicans stayed away. There were no other black families in Riverton, so the Jamaicans' absence did not seem unusual to us.

"Let's grab those three in the front row so we can put our feet up on the railing," Danny ordered, leading the way.

We filed in and sat down. The previews were just finishing. By the time Hoot and his boys hit the screen, I noticed that Sherm had developed an interest in the young Mexican woman directly behind him. Sherm was not subtle. He had turned around in his seat and was staring at her. To her credit, she was apparently ignoring the intrusive worm. I didn't think this unusual since Sherm wasn't as worldly as Danny and I. We had seen a lot of Mexicans at the Grafton. So I focused on the movie and forgot about Sherm.

As usual, Hoot made quick work of rounding up his *owl hoots,* depositing them in his *hoosegow,* and riding off into the sunset with his *sidekicks.* When the serial started, we discovered it was our lucky day. This was the last in the series of ten Durango Kid heart-stopping episodes. In a mere fifteen minutes, The Kid rounded up his *varmints,* many of whom looked like the *owl hoots* that Hoot had just corralled, deposited them in what looked like Hoot's *hoosegow,* and rode off into a familiar-looking sunset with a bunch of Hoot's *sidekicks.*

Was it déjà vu? Or low movie budgets at work?

I glanced at Sherm who was still mesmerized by the woman behind him. I decided to take a look for myself. Typical of Mexican mothers at the Grafton, the woman was nursing a tiny brown baby that clung to her breast, busily finishing lunch. The woman smiled at me. Her bright teeth flashed against her weather-tanned face. I smiled back. Then I gently turned Sherm around by the shoulders. He awoke from his trance and stared at me.

"Watch the cartoon, Sherman," I whispered.

"Okay," he whispered back and lost himself in an exciting adventure of *Felix the Cat.*

Danny gave me a wink and a smile. I gave him the rest of my popcorn.

AFTER THE TEX RITTER show, we left the Grafton, contented by a full afternoon of cowboy entertainment. Feeling a bit charitable toward Sherman, we decided to walk him to the bus station and wait long enough to ensure that he got on the right bus and was safely on his way home.

"Mr. Smalley was right," I observed as we strolled along. "I don't think they had Boy Scouts in the Old West. That seemed strange, if you ask me!"

"I'd rather see just cowboys and Indians," Danny admitted.

"I like Indians!" Sherm yelped with far too much enthusiasm.

"Got your bus fare?" Sherm nodded yes. "Okay, hop on the bus then," Danny ordered, patting him on the head.

"Bye, Jase. Danny. Thanks for taking me to the movies. It was fun! I'm goin' to tell Mrs. Zeyer what I did with my quarter. She laughs when I tell her things. She's from Germany but she's not a Nazi. Mr. Hans isn't either. He's nice. He lets me play with his puppets. Hey! You guys wanta play again tomorrow? Why don't we —?"

Mercifully the bus door hissed shut and soon Sherm was out of sight. We stood there on the sidewalk alone and quiet, absent our mascot. At first, I felt a tremor of sadness. Then a sense of relief passed over me. Peace settled over downtown Riverton.

As we strolled under the maple and elm trees along the street, I noticed that the leaves had begun to change color. Some had already fallen to the sidewalk below. It was hard to believe that soon we'd be raking and burning leaves. How I loved fall!

"Let's go in early and get some better seats this time," I suggested.

Located on East Main Street, the Chippewa Theater was only two blocks away. We loped along wondering what was showing. Whatever it was, we knew we were in for a classy, first run movie. The Chippewa also updated its patrons on the war with informative newsreels. Of course, the cartoons shown there were current, unlike the antiques at the Grafton. And everyone enjoyed the *follow-the-bouncing-ball* sing-along. These benefits more than made up for the Chippewa's obvious shortcomings:

- Single features, rather than double
- No serials
- A single cartoon
- Never any cowboy movies, unless you count
  The Ox-Bow Incident
- Sky-high ticket prices (Fifteen Cents!)

We read the marquee from a distance. *Since You Went Away.* Neither of us had heard of it. "Sounds like another dog movie," Danny surmised.

"Oh, you mean like *Lassie Come Home?* Yeah, you're probably right."

When we arrived at the theater, we hurried to the glass case beside the ticket window and studied the *Feature of the Day* movie poster. Danny read down through the cast.

Claudette Colbert. She was one of my mother's favorites. Danny admitted he liked her too. **Jennifer Jones.** Danny wondered if she were related to Spike Jones. I didn't know. But I noted that there was no mention of *City Slickers* so we couldn't be sure. **Joseph Cotton.** We remembered him from that eerie Orson Wells movie whose name always escaped us. **Shirley Temple.** That's good news. Can't go wrong with a kids' movie! But where's the dog? **Monty Woolley.** There he was.

"Ever heard of a *woolley,* Danny?"

"*Monty?* Let's see. I think it's a Royal Canadian police dog."

"Okay then! Let's get our tickets!"

We each plunked down fifteen cents, grabbed our tickets, and entered the theater. The ticket takers and ushers wore tightly tailored navy-blue uniforms with two rows of brass buttons running down their chests. Their trousers had a wide gold stripe extending from the waist to the pant cuff. And, on their shoulders, they wore nifty epaulets of braided golden cord. They always reminded me of the tiny, wooden-soldier ornaments that we hung on our Christmas tree.

We stuffed the torn half of our tickets into our pockets and entered the opulent lower lobby. Our feet sunk into the rich red carpeting as we ambled toward the snack bar. Danny ordered two more nickel bags of popcorn. Here they each cost a dime. After all, the Chippewa was a very ritzy place.

"Where you wanta sit, Danny?"

Stuffing a gigantic handful of popcorn into his mouth, he pointed up the stairs with his nose.

"The balcony! Terrific!"

We strolled up the wide carpeted stairway leading to the loge. The gradual rise made the climb a comfortable one, even for older patrons. No mandatory elevator back in those days. Giant sand-filled urns, placed at frequent intervals, encouraged smokers to dispose of their cigarettes and cigars and to tap out their pipes before taking their seats.

Several couples occupied the comfortable red velvet settees that lined the loge. The men in suits and ties balanced felt hats on their knees. The women in tailored suits and fine dresses wore tiny hats and high heels. No Mexican women here!

Those people were waiting for the current show to end before entering the balcony. This was one practice that Danny and I seldom followed. We loved movies, all parts of them, including beginnings, middles, and ends. And we didn't much care in what order. So, as usual, we decided to take our seats immediately.

Just past the tall restroom doors, made of heavy brass and difficult to open, a short flight of stairs led upward from the loge to the balcony. At the top of the stairs, we were intercepted by an officious usher. His badge of authority was the black flashlight. By flashing it at our feet and raising his hand, he ordered us to halt.

"Still be a few more minutes before the next show starts. We're just showing the ending. Wouldn't want to spoil the show for you," he whispered, much more politely than I had expected.

Danny swallowed his popcorn and responded, "We don't mind. We're planning to see it more than once anyway. Besides endings are the best part."

The usher was confused by Danny's logic. Frankly so was I, but I didn't let on.

"Okay," conceded the usher. "But please be quiet. Where do you want to sit?"

Using his flashlight as little as possible, he led us downward to the first row of seats. We were nearly in the center of the expansive balcony. We took our seats and settled in. I looked forward to the end of the show when the house lights would come up, illuminating the ornate furnishings of the old Chippewa. I loved this place.

We focused our attention on *Since You Went Away.* There she was. Claudette Colbert. And we recognized Joseph Cotton right away. But that younger actress with dark hair. She didn't resemble old Spike. But, by process of elimination, we concluded that she must be Jennifer Jones. There was another woman who looked a lot like Shirley Temple, but much older. We theorized that it must be Shirley's mom, Mrs. Temple. But where was the dog? Then we saw him. A big old, wrinkled bulldog. So *that's* a Monty Woolley! So much for our knowledge of dog breeds.

Everybody in the balcony seemed to be sniffling. People were blotting their eyes with hankies. We didn't get it.

"Geez! The dog's back home, safe and sound, for cripes sake. What's everybody cryin' about?" Danny whispered, not too softly.

"Shhhhhh!" came at us from all directions.

I didn't know about Danny, but I was looking forward to seeing what *beginning* and *middle* could possible make so many people sniffle at this innocuous ending.

"Maybe it's a science fiction movie, Danny," I whispered, softly this time.

"I think you got it. Check out that weird-looking *woolley!*"

AS IT TURNED OUT, *Since You Went Away* was neither a lost dog nor a science fiction story. Depicting life on the home front, this movie was typical of the films produced in America during World War II.

Hollywood was an unabashed supporter of the war effort. Top movie makers considered it their patriotic duty to support their country with, not only their own time and money, but their studio's filmmaking expertise and resources. Countless movie executives took commissions in the armed forces or became *Dollar a Year Men* in Washington to help organize and implement the American counterpart to Germany's pervasive and effective propaganda program orchestrated by Joseph Goebbels, one of Hitler's top henchmen.

Famous movie stars like James Stewart, Clark Gable, and Henry Fonda put their film careers on hold and, like millions of other Americans, volunteered for military service. John Wayne, Errol Flynn, Gary Cooper, and others, who did not serve in the military during the war, nonetheless, contributed by taking on film roles as brave war heroes.

During those years, Danny and I tried our best to see every war movie shown in Riverton. The Grafton specialized in low-budget war films that were long on action and short on acting, not unlike the cowboy movies that we saw there. In fact, some movie studios shot both genres on the same set. It was perplexing to see Nazi soldiers being rounded up in the shadow of that big boulder from which Gene Autry had rescued dozens of panic-stricken ladies by jumping onto their runaway buckboards. But we didn't complain. During the war, we all had to sacrifice.

The upscale Chippewa presented many films that were either Oscar winners or runners-up, such as *Sergeant York, Mrs. Miniver, Casablanca, The Human Comedy, Watch on the Rhine*, and, yes, *Since You Went Away.*

At the conclusion of the ending that we didn't understand, the house lights came up and the mammoth red velvet curtain closed in front of the screen. Those around us put away their hankies, pretending they hadn't needed them, and exited the balcony.

Danny propped his feet on the shiny brass rail, folded his hands on his stomach, and closed his eyes. This was his normal posture during intermissions. As always, I spent a moment admiring the elaborately decorated ceiling, the gold leaf trim on the box seats overlooking the theater stage and orchestra pit, and the plush upholstery of our seats. Then I also closed my eyes and drifted away to dreamland.

"Ladies and gent —," The loud voice brought me back to reality. "Ladies and gentlemen. My name is Mike Hannifin, manager of the Chippewa Theater. Tonight it's my pleasure to introduce our feature movie, *Since You Went Away.* As you may know, the film was honored with a number of Academy Award nominations including Best Picture, Best Actress for Claudette Colbert, Best Supporting Actress for Jennifer Jones, and Best Supporting Actor for Monty Woolley."

"A *woolley* is an actor?" Danny exclaimed. "Then who's that wrinkled dog?"

"I know you will enjoy this poignant portrayal of a wife who, with her two daughters, is coping with the absence of her husband who is away, serving his country at war. I'm sure you'll see similarities to families, perhaps even your own, right here in Riverton."

I looked around the crowded balcony where people were already extracting handkerchiefs from their purses or pockets. "Glad we saw the ending first," I whispered to Danny.

"Me too. Didn't bring a hankie."

The manager then explained his *real* purpose for being on stage. "While most of us are optimistic about the war's outcome, we still have a long way to go. And the country needs each of us to continue to do our part. Specifically we need to help President Roosevelt and our military leaders by buying War Bonds."

Danny and I had heard this speech many times before.

"To assist you in fulfilling your patriotic duty, an officer from the Riverton Second National Bank will be in the lobby during the intermission. He will help you with the necessary paperwork, collect your contribution, and issue your War Bond, right on the spot."

After thanking us, the manager waved at the projectionist to start the show. The curtain slowly opened as the theater lights dimmed. Knowing the ending helped us navigate through the seemingly endless movie. Counting the manager's bond pitch, the newsreel, previews, cartoon, and feature, the show lasted well over three hours.

When the curtain finally closed, Danny leaped up and announced, "We gotta go to church tomorrow. Let's go!"

AFTER OUR BATHS, AUNT Maude and I listened to my new radio. We tuned in an exciting episode of *The Whistler* coming right into our bedroom from downtown Chicago. The signal was as clear as a bell. When the murderer got what was coming to him, I turned off the radio and lamp. I stretched out on my lumpy mattress and reviewed the day's events. All in all, it had been a fine one.

"What movies did you see, Jase?"

I related how we met up with Sherman Tolna and what we had seen at the Grafton. I really didn't want to mention *Since You Went Away.*

"What was showing at the Chippewa?"

Reluctantly I reminded her.

"Oh, that's right. Was it sad?"

"Yes, most people cried."

"With Uncle Van gone, I think I woulda cried too."

I wondered why Danny and I hadn't cried. As I was thinking about that, tears suddenly filled my eyes. I choked back a sob.

"That's okay, Jase."

And it was.

"PLEASE REMOVE YOUR HATS here in the sanctity of the Good Mission Church auditorium. No smoking or chewing during the service. No drinking anywhere on Mission property at any time."

Danny and I had heard Reverend Squires lay out his Righteous Regulations dozens of times. But this time was different.

"All bottles and trash must be removed from the front porch before —. What? Do you have a question Buddy Roe Red Skivvies?"

Reverend Squires called everybody *Buddy Roe*. And, if he didn't know a person's name, he often added words that described something about that person. In this case, *Red Skivvies* described the union suit, visible through the holes in the elbows of the hand-raiser's tattered blue flannel shirt.

"Speakin' of bottles, I gotta report a thief!" replied Red.

"I did not steal your dang bottle!" declared another overnight guest defensively.

"Where was this bottle at the time it was stolen?" Reverend Squires inquired, cupping a hand behind his ear.

"In the dormitory, next to my shoes!" hollered Red, becoming more agitated by the second.

"Is that where you found it, Buddy Roe Butch Haircut?"

"Nope! 'Cuz you don't allow no bottles of alkeehol up there. So how could I?" Butch affirmed, demonstrating his newly acquired knowledge of the house rules.

"What about that?" Reverend Squires asked Red.

"Like he sez. I didn't have no bottle in the dormitory. Nope, not me. Cancel that theft report, Rev'r'd."

Danny looked at me and wrinkled up his nose. "What a waste of time!" he whispered.

Reverend Squires seemed disappointed. Both sinners had given him the slip. But, putting it aside, he resumed the service.

"Buddy Roe Danny and Buddy Roe Jase are our trustees today. Boys, will you kindly pass out the Worship Agenda, as usual? And then assist with serving the meal, if you please. I think Keith's ready in the kitchen."

Pausing now and then to inhale the intoxicating fumes of the purple ink, we passed out the mimeographed sheets to the fifteen attendees, seated at the hand-me-down tables and chairs.

Then we went into the kitchen where Keith had heaped immense quantities of this morning's breakfast onto the serving dishes for each table. The Squires believed that serving meals family style would bring civility into the lives of their unruly guests. Danny and I believed that it brought a lot of cheating on the part of the Buddy Roe who grabbed the serving dish first.

We anticipated some version of the carp that we had laboriously cleaned yesterday, but we were disappointed. This morning's fare was pancakes and syrup, no butter or oleo-margarine, but plenty of catsup from a large dented can, courtesy of the canning factory. No gefilte fish and bagels here!

We also placed a large aluminum pitcher of the morning beverage on each table. Edith called her concoction *fruit punch*. The Buddy Roes called it *SW*, their secret code for *Swamp Water*. As if they could keep a secret from Edith.

While we served breakfast, Edith treated us to a jaunty collection of spirituals on her piano. In addition to being Mission Manager, Edith headed the music department. No one played religious rhythms to a ragtime beat better than Edith.

As everyone dug in, Reverend Squires began his service. He stood behind the shaky podium and addressed his munching congregation. "I think I better change the subject of my sermon this morning. Let's talk about the Seventh Commandment. Who knows what that Commandment says?"

"*Thou Shalt Not Steal!*" Danny yelled.

"Right you are, Buddy Roe Danny!" declared the Reverend, surprised but, nonetheless, impressed by his young protégé.

BR Danny's correct answer astounded me almost as much as the Buddy Roes who stared at him in disbelief. But, when the news of the new sermon topic finally sank in, several of them put their hands over their eyes and groaned. Apparently they had heard this sermon before. Danny and I sank into our chairs and waited for the collection.

After about an hour's worth of podium pounding and pontificating, Reverend Squires abruptly stopped. Evidently he'd run out of steam. Several Buddy Roes breathed audible sighs of relief.

On a nod from Reverend Squires, we rose and retrieved the collection plates from the chair next to the piano. The plates whizzed around the room with nary a contribution except from

Danny and me. In step with Edith's ragtime beat, we marched the plates to the podium. Looking down, Reverend Squires saw our pair of Petrov dimes. He patted us on the back and smiled broadly. We hustled back to our chairs and prepared to depart. But then I remembered that the verbose minister's benedictions sometimes took as long as his sermons. Here is where he got in his last licks before losing his audience. This morning was no exception.

He concluded with this admonishment. "When you steal from each other, you're stealing pieces of your mother's soul. Each time you break a Commandment, her time in heaven is foreshortened. So, for her sake, knock it off! Got it?"

"Got it!" Danny repeated as we zipped out the back door.

We crossed New Albany, angling westward in the direction of the First Methodist Church. But suddenly Danny veered to port and headed for the large trash barrel in front of Pete's store.

There he stopped. "I gotta get rid of something."

He dug into his pocket and pulled out a nearly full pint of Pete's fortified red wine. The words *Red's — Hands Off* were scribbled across the label. Unceremoniously he dropped it into the trash.

"Where'd you get that, Danny?"

"Out of Buddy Roe Butch Haircut's back pocket when we were serving breakfast. This'll teach him to break the Seventh Commandment."

"Yeah, but you broke it too, Danny!"

"You're right! Let's hurry to church before my mother's soul hears about it."

THE FIRST METHODIST WAS rapidly becoming our church of choice. There were many understandable reasons for this. Although not the wealthiest congregation in Riverton, during the 1920s, the tithing Methodists had constructed a splendid house of worship using the finest building materials money could buy. The pure white wooden structure was crowned with a dazzling steeple that caught people's attention and attracted new members, especially from among the younger families in our part of town.

The church's interior, finished in the same austere lines as its exterior, appealed to those austere people who worshiped there. Yes, those clean-living Methodists were a far cry from the wine-loving Buddy Roes that stumbled in and out of grace at the Good Mission Church each weekend.

Owing to Danny's unpleasant first encounter with Miss Elizabeth Bundy, our acceptance into the fellowship of Methodists had taken some time to be fully realized. But, happily, Miss Bundy could now be counted among Danny's most admiring fans. And, as his best friend, I shared in his good fortune.

We had both taken an immediate liking to the young minister, Reverend Noble, whose funny bone was particularly vulnerable to Danny's antics. As I mentioned earlier, our feelings about the Carmodys weighed heavily in our positive assessment of the church. Of course, there was also the exceptional church choir whose membership included Mr. and Mrs. Smalley.

Mel Carmody, the friendly usher, met us at the door. "Welcome, boys! What brings you here this morning? I bet you gotta repent before school starts tomorrow, right?"

"Danny does!" I quipped, attempting to be funny. But remembering Mrs. Tucker's soul, I immediately regretted my remark.

"Then I'd better seat you right down front so you don't miss a word of the sermon. Besides, Danny, someone wants to see you. There, in the second row." He escorted us to our seats. "Morning, Miss Bundy. Will you keep an eye on these two scalawags during the service for me?"

"Well, for crying all night, it's Danny and Jase. We haven't seen much of each other lately. I hope you boys haven't been up to no good. Where *have* you been?" she asked, gently removing Danny's Tigers cap and placing it beside her in the pew.

"Jase and I went to church camp! We had to vesper a lot. Our counselor was a sheepdog. I was rescued by a seafood restaurant. I sang ah lotta songs with Germans. I almost shot a girl — I mean — *some* girls with arrows. But most important, I'm a Baptist!"

"You're a what?"

Danny was saved by the bell. More precisely, by the organ, announcing the beginning of the service. I was relieved that it was now in the capable hands of the first-stringer, not that high-school summer substitute who definitely needed more lessons. Before turning her full attention to the service, Miss Bundy gently patted the back of Danny's hand to let him know he was off the hook, at least for now.

As usual, the choir was exhilarating. But, for the first time, I noticed that its members were all adults. I wondered how Danny, despite his exceptional voice, would fit in. Unbeknownst to me that very question had been the subject of a heated debate between the members of Danny's Methodist fan club and the church's talented choir director, Mrs. Oakley.

As expected, Reverend Noble's sermon was particularly uplifting that morning. With the coming of fall, his subject was Death. That is to say, he talked about the natural cycles of life here on earth. And, if we lived sin-free lives, he promised we could look forward to a joyful eternity *after we transcended,* as he put it.

I was thoroughly pleased with his sermon, especially the *decaying* part. It entered my mind to ask Danny which, if any, Commandment covered *Thou Shalt Not Decay* or something along those lines. But he was pretty busy shooting off his usual barrage of *Amens,* so I didn't interrupt him.

Ostentatiously we plunked down our Petrov dimes in the shiny brass collection plate and prepared for our departure. We were anticipating a quick getaway when Miss Bundy spoiled our plan.

"Danny, could you possibly spare a few minutes of your time? I spoke with Mr. Smalley, and we would like you to do something for us," she whispered in her sweetest voice.

Without responding, he nervously picked up his Tigers cap and placed it on his head. Miss Bundy smiled at him and removed it again.

I knew what was bothering him. He was torn between his intense desire to please Miss Bundy and the demands of the schedule we had agreed to earlier that morning. Our movie-watching agenda included both films at the Grafton and the single feature at the Chippewa. The schedule was tight because tomorrow would be the first day of school. We needed to be in bed early!

Before leaving my house, we had checked the new listings for both theaters. We were in for a dynamite afternoon and evening! For starters, the Grafton offered the first of ten episodes of a *Flash Gordon* serial that promised breathtaking adventures in outer space. We were thrilled by the prospect of hurtling through the galaxy in Flash's rocket ship. However, we hoped that the movie producer had upgraded the props a bit.

Last time, the rocket ship bore a striking resemblance to the cardboard barrel in which our school janitor received his yearly supply of sweeping compound. In fairness, I should say that Flash's barrel had been meticulously covered with shiny tinfoil, presumably, to ward off the sun's deadly rays. And it appeared to be propelled by *real* steam, from some stagehand's tea kettle, we surmised.

The double feature would lead off with Roy Rogers and Dale Evans in *The Yellow Rose of Texas*. Neither of us had seen this new release. The second movie featured Ken Maynard in *Avenging Waters*. Even though we'd both seen it five or six times, we were eager to watch it again. Undeniably, this film was nothing short of a cowboy classic.

On deck at the Chippewa was a movie that had won a slew of Academy Awards. *Going My Way* (Best Picture) starred Bing Crosby (Best Actor), Ingrid Bergman (Best Actress), and Barry Fitzgerald (Best Supporting Actor). But Danny and I couldn't imagine a Bing Crosby film without Bob Hope!

We were both ambivalent about Ingrid Bergman after she dumped poor old Humphrey Bogart at the airport in *Casablanca*. But, having seen her image in the Chippewa advertisement for *Going My Way*, our animosity toward her had subsided. Neither of us felt comfortable holding a grudge against a nun, especially a pretty one like Ingrid.

Barry Fitzgerald was problematic. I couldn't remember who he was. But Danny insisted that we had seen the splendid actor in another Oscar-deserving performance as Johnny Mack Brown's sidekick in *Rogue of the Range*. Danny knew his cowboy stars so, naturally, I bowed to his expertise.

We agreed completely on one thing. With a cowboy star as famous as Barry Fitzgerald playing a key role, this movie would be a sellout. To grab a first-rate seat, we would have to arrive very early. But I certainly didn't mind. I loved endings.

"Let's go downstairs, boys," Miss Bundy suggested. "This shouldn't take too long."

"Okay," we both agreed, caving in to the most strong-willed, little old lady that we had ever met.

"There you are! Good! Good!" said Mr. Smalley. "I want you to meet some folks. Danny and Jase, this is Mrs. Oakley, our church choir director. I think you know Mrs. Smalley, Mr. and Mrs. Carmody, and, of course, Miss Bundy."

Danny and I were accustomed to greeting adults using one of two methods. We either wiggled our fingers at them or gave them a short, bend-at-the-elbow, open-hand wave. We greeted Mrs. Oakley and the others using the latter method.

Suddenly I was struck by a sickening revelation. We had just rendered the same halfhearted Nazi salute that we had seen Adolph Hitler use on countless occasions in newsreels. I made a mental note to confront this serious gaffe with Danny next time we were alone. From now on, we'd stick to finger wiggling.

"Danny, I've heard about your stunning performance at Camp Harmony. And a few of us have — er — um — *persuaded* Mrs. Oakley to give you an audition to try out for our choir."

"Okay, but we gotta leave soon," Danny declared tersely, checking his imaginary wristwatch. "Gotta important engagement."

Immediately Mrs. Smalley sat down at the piano used for choir practices on Wednesday evenings. She folded her hands and nodded at us, indicating that she was ready for action.

"I understand you know some patriotic songs, Danny. But we're a church choir. Do you know any religious ones?" asked Mrs. Oakley.

Danny turned to Mrs. Smalley, "Do you know *Ave Maria?*"

She nodded and turned toward her keyboard. "Ready? Key of G if you please, Mrs. S. Ah one and ah two and ah three —."

I won't attempt to describe what we heard that morning. Suffice it to say, it was fortunate that Miss Bundy had several wads of tissue in her huge leather purse. Six sobbing adults were almost too much for this young sidekick to endure. When Danny finished, his audience was astounded. They shook their heads and dried their eyes.

Finally Mrs. Oakley declared, "Mr. Smalley, you were absolutely right! We must have this talented young man in our choir. Thank you for moving me off the dime. Thank you, one and all." Then she turned to Danny. "You have a beautiful voice. It would be an honor for me to work with you in the coming year. Will you join our choir, Danny?"

"You bet, Mrs. Oak-leaf!"

Then he turned on his heels and ran toward the stairs, yelling over his shoulder, "Hurry, Jase! Tomorrow's the first day of school!"

"TOMORROW'S THE BIG DAY! You must be excited!"

"I really am, Aunt Maude. I thought tomorrow would never get here."

"You and Danny sure have kept yourselves busy lately. Today you went to church, twice. Then you saw three movies, including *Going My Way!* Your mother and I haven't even seen that one. Did Bing Crosby sing any songs?"

"Yes, he did. And some other people too. But my very favorite was the boys' choir singing *Ave Maria.*"

"That's a beautiful song."

"Very beautiful, Aunt Maude."

"Good night, Jase."

"Night, Aunt Maude."

Night, Danny. Mrs. Oak-leaf. Miss Sparks. Lash. And —.

7 SCHOOL DAYS

MY ALARM CLOCK SHOOK MY SHOULDER AT precisely four o'clock in the morning when, in the midst of a delicious dream, I was baking Hungarian sugar cookies with Mrs. Mikas. Cracking open my eyes, I discovered Danny, standing in the semidarkness, grinning at me.

"Do you know what time it is?" I whispered.

"Yep, grab your savings-stamp money and let's go! I packed you a special lunch," he whispered back.

My stomach rumbled at the thought. No telling what *special lunch* meant to Danny.

"It's cool outside. Better take your new jacket. Com'on, hurry. We'll be late."

I dressed quickly and went to the bathroom where I splashed cold water on my face and brushed my hair. Then I squeezed a small dollop of toothpaste onto an index finger and rubbed the chalky stuff over my teeth. After rinsing my mouth from the tap, I wet my toothbrush thoroughly so no one would know.

When I reached the kitchen, Danny was standing on the back porch with two brown lunch bags bulging with surprises. In the porch light, I could see that he was dressed exactly as we had agreed. Brand-new blue jeans, long-sleeve tee shirt, with maroon and dirty yellow stripes in his case, Tigers cap, and brand-new black sneakers with white sweat socks. And, of course, our jackets.

For stocking Texaco motor oil, the distributor gave Mr. Tucker a macho Texaco jacket that had been confiscated by Danny. Mine, a handsome Massey-Harris number, was given to Grandpa as an inducement to purchase one of that company's Model 101R tractors. "Couldn't that travelin' salesman tell I wasn't in the market for an $800 tractor when I awredy got two perfectly fine teams of workhorses? Some people are just thick."

Thick or thin, Danny and I had two macho jackets that would be the envy of Hamilton School. What if they were a little baggy? We'd grow into them in a few years. The important thing was to be suave and sophisticated.

"Do you think we'll need our marbles?" I asked, wanting to be prepared for any opportunity to relieve some poor sucker of his stash.

"How are we going to play on the bus?"

He had me there. Our new conveyance to school would require some getting used to. But the adventures it promised more than compensated for the inconvenience of not having our marbles at the ready. With double handfuls of Aunt Maude's oatmeal cookies, we bounced down the steps and launched *The Big Day.*

"You excited, Jase? Me too." Danny knew me so well that he now answered his questions to me before I could.

But what were best friends for anyway?

When we arrived at Mr. Kolarik's house, the giant yellow school bus was still asleep under the elm tree. Even in the dark it shone like a new penny. There was a faint light in an upstairs window, probably the bedroom.

"Fantastic! Mr. K's up. Maybe we can convince him to leave early. Or maybe he'll invite us in for breakfast!"

Danny had a way of turning awkward situations into eating opportunities. I didn't really mind. Despite having just consumed a pound or so of cookies, I could stand a little breakfast.

"What are you boys doing out there? Gosh, it isn't even five o'clock yet. Did your sister go off early, Danny? Well, ya better come on in here. I was just going to fix some coffee. And maybe some toast and jam. Like some, boys?"

The bus driver held the kitchen door open and we popped inside. This was the first time we had been inside his house. It smelled just like Mrs. Mikas' house, an absolutely mouth-watering combination of stewed onions, garlic, cooking oil, tomatoes, and cinnamon.

After knocking off a large mug of coffee and four or five slices of toast, we leaned back in our chairs and looked at Mr. Kolarik. He sensed we expected him to say something, so he did.

"Now you're sure you checked this with Mrs. Compton, your grandmother. Right? I figure your idea's going to save me at least two miles a day. That's ten miles a week and about four hundred miles a year. A real savings of gasoline!

"I've been driving that route for two years since I retired, and I drove past there all those times. I swear it never entered my mind until you two boys came along to suggest it. I'm going to tell the superintendent about it. Yes, sir. It's real important in wartime to find creative ways to cut back on gasoline consumption."

I'd never seen Mr. Kolarik so talkative. Maybe it was his three giant mugs of coffee that wound him up.

"And all you boys want is to ride along and be dropped off with the junior high kids, huh? You sure must like riding buses."

He was certainly right about that. For a nickel fare and unlimited free transfers, Danny and I had spent much of our summer touring the streets of Riverton over the many routes covered by Chippewa Trails buses. We loved every minute of it. But with the coming of school, how could we find the time for our touring hobby? Riding the school bus was a perfect solution. Besides we'd probably be awarded the Medal of Honor for saving scarce war materiel at the rate of two-miles worth of gasoline a day.

Mr. Kolarik's junior high and high school pickups were concentrated in Barrington Township about ten miles northeast of Riverton. The first leg of his route was an empty run through New Albany, the Chippewa County seat, and on out into farm country. After he hit Riverton Road, his progress slowed as he zigzagged from farm to farm picking up cleanly scrubbed students in brand-new school clothes, eager to start the new school year.

"Hey, Mr. Kolarik, who are these runts? Where'd you pick up these hobos? Are these kids yours, Mr. Kolarik? You didn't tell us. Are these midgets or are they just shrimpy kids?" The barrage of questions and snide comments, especially from the high schoolers, went on and on.

The two Donaldson girls who lived just south of Grandma's house were the last pickups. When they were aboard, Mr. Kolarik continued north on Barrington Road as usual. But, instead of continuing the additional half mile to Henry Road and turning around there, he unexpectedly slowed and turned into the Compton circular driveway.

"Why are you turning here? Who lives here? Why are you changing your route?"

When Grandma emerged from the house, carrying a large tray of cookies and other goodies, the noise finally subsided.

"Open the door, Mr. Kolarik. I have some fresh coffee for you and I don't want it to get cold. Any of you kids like a cookie or a brownie? Don't tell your parents I fed you sweets after you brushed your teeth."

The students crushed forward, completely surrounding the unexpected Mrs. Claus. Grandma emptied her tray in seconds, patted us on the shoulders, and hopped off the bus. As she waved goodbye, the bus load of munchers cheered at the tops of their lungs. The bus completed the circular drive, turned left onto Barrington Road, and headed south toward Riverton.

"Yep, being able to turn around in the Compton circular driveway will save me at least two miles a day. And I get a coffee refill to boot. But I still don't understand. Why would you boys want to get up two hours early just to ride this bus?"

"Look out for that car pulling into the road on the left, Mr. K," Danny warned.

"What — oh — okay, Danny. Thanks for the help. I better watch the road."

"That won't be necessary, sir," Danny assured him, as he leaned over the driver's right shoulder. "I'll keep an eye on it for you."

"HOW COME YOU GUYS were on the school bus?" Butch Matlock asked as we entered Hamilton School and headed toward Miss Sparks' classroom.

Butch and I had not been particularly close friends. But, after his family's house was destroyed by fire, the Matlocks accepted Mrs. Libby's invitation to live with her until their house was rebuilt. Butch was now my neighbor, living on Forrest Street just past the cottonwood tree. I hoped we would become closer friends.

For some reason, Butch was speaking very softly for a Matlock. Perhaps living with Mrs. Libby had eliminated the Matlocks' need for loud voices when speaking to each other. But, despite his soft words, Butch was an imposing figure. He was at least a head taller than Danny and me and extremely muscular for a sixth grader. Even counting the junior high students, Butch was definitely the tallest, strongest, and heaviest student at Hamilton School.

"Since we got up early, we decided to catch a ride with Mr. Kolarik. He wanted us to show him how to cut his route in half so he wouldn't burn so much gasoline. So we did! That's why he gave us a ride to school. We might do it again tomorrow. Right, Jase? You wanta come along? Mr. K likes us at his house by five o'clock so he can fix breakfast for us."

Danny's tendency to fib had surfaced early in this explanation. But the rendition clearly impressed Butch who was nodding his head excitedly as we entered the classroom.

After stowing our lunch bags in the bank of cubby holes in the back of the room, we took our seats according to the seating chart posted on the bulletin board just inside the door. Danny and I were only a few desks apart. I turned around to check out the feasibility of passing notes or whispering to my friend.

We had decided against hanging our macho jackets in the cloak room. We wanted everybody to see them first, especially Miss Sparks. Just as we settled in our seats, she entered the room. "Good morning, class. Welcome back to school."

We answered her brightly. "Good morning, Miss Sparks!" She looked gorgeous in her new yellow and brown plaid dress. Danny and Butch were staring at her through glassy eyes.

I guess I have some competition this year. Better be on my toes.

Suddenly Danny raised his hand. "Yes, Danny, what is it?"

"This year, do we have to read the Bible, Miss Sparks? Jase and I go to three churches every Sunday. And we just got back from church camp. Lots of Bible classes there. And girls too. Besides I'm a Baptist now. So do we have to? Huh, Miss Sparks?"

"Why, Danny, I am so happy for you. Sounds like you had an interesting summer. But, yes, I'm afraid that we will follow the same routine this year. We'll start each morning with a Bible reading and then we'll say the Lord's Prayer followed by the Pledge of Allegiance. Speaking of summer, today we're all going tell each other *What I did this summer.* Danny, maybe you can tell us about church camp. Or some other adventure. Okay?"

With that, she gave him one of her million-dollar smiles. He shrank back into his seat and gave her a very un-Danny-like response, a wimpy nod.

The poor sucker's got it bad!

A glance at Butch confirmed that he too was lost among the pink clouds. The boys from the neighborhood were definitely losing their grip.

After finishing the morning rituals, we each introduced ourselves for the benefit of the new students, a pair of twin boys named Edgar and Seth Cowherd. As if their first names weren't bad enough, their last name triggered an eruption of guffaws and jeers from the boys in the room. But disorder quickly vanished when Miss Sparks frowned slightly. She let it pass and continued.

"We have a few more items of business before we move on to your reports. In the compartment under your seats, you should have six books. English. Arithmetic. Science. Health. Reading. And geography. Please check to make sure you have them all."

Shuffle, shuffle, bam.

"Any missing books? No? Fantastic! Next, please give one of these notices to your parents. They tell your folks about the cost of some things that you will need this school year including lunch milk and your Weekly Reader. I hope you'll all subscribe.

"It also informs your parents how we here at Hamilton will support the war effort by selling savings stamps, packing Red Cross boxes for our soldiers at the front, and gathering milkweed pods and cattails to be used in life preservers for the U.S. Navy. I hope you all know where those milkweeds and cattails are growing. Our sailors need your help. Okay! Are there any questions?"

Prior to World War II, navy life jackets were filled with kapok, the white, fluffy fiber that surrounds the seeds of the kapok or ceiba tree. Since kapok fiber was buoyant and water resistant, it was ideal for flotation devices and padding. Because of the nature of the tree's special resins, the fiber was also non-flammable.

When the war began, ninety percent of America's kapok was imported from the Dutch East Indies. When those islands fell to the Japanese, the primary kapok supply was cut off and a replacement was sought. At this time, a Chicago company had begun using cattail cotton as stuffing for furniture cushions and baseballs. So the Navy decided to investigate using cattail and then milkweed pod cotton as an alternative to kapok.

Tests showed that life jackets stuffed with those substitutes maintained their buoyancy, even after being submerged in water for more than a hundred hours. School children throughout the country became the primary harvesters of milkweed pods and cattails, suddenly valuable commodities. Then the navy had its ersatz kapok. Actually the idea of using cattails was not an original one. In colonial days, several Native American tribes used cattail fluff to line moccasins and papoose boards. Later pioneers used this down to stuff quilts and dolls.

Those high-quality and inexpensive alternatives were recognized for their attributes for only a brief period. When the war ended, kapok again became the stuffing of choice and, sadly, cattails and milkweed returned to their former status as *weeds*.

Danny raised his hand again. "Jase and I spent the summer together, so can we give our report together? Okay, Jase?" He looked at me and then answered for both Miss Sparks and me. "That will be fine," he declared and took his seat.

Miss Sparks was surprised by Danny's unusual *request for permission*. Nothing from Danny surprised me anymore. Well, almost nothing. "Yes, Danny. Jase. That will be fine. You *may* give your reports together. Since you are so anxious to tell us about your summer, why don't you go first?"

I gave Danny a dirty look and he smiled as usual. He pointed at the front of the room. Obviously he wanted me to start without him. *How did I get myself into this?* I thought as I heard myself saying, "Wheat *thrashing* day at the farm was —."

I can't remember the words I used that day. But threshing days were among my most cherished memories of the farm, despite the seeming chaos and the deafening noise of machinery. The chugging steam engine. The clattering threshing machine. The flapping drive belt. The banging grain separators. The scraping shaking sieves. The screaming elevator lifting golden wheat into granary bins. The whining blower shooting straw through the air. The squealing wagon wheels rolling into the dry hot yard.

The clamor of forty farmers, loading and unloading, laughing and hollering. The twang of pitchforks feeding the voracious thresher. The coughs of unloaders, choking on swirling dust and wheat chaff. The cackling and laughing of farm women preparing the sumptuous midday meal. The cheering and giggling of wildly joyful children. The barking of dogs at their heels. The screaming of hawks overhead, circling above homeless mice in the fields.

Yes, all of this was what I loved about threshing day!

Each July and August, the Chippewa Grange leased a threshing machine and steam engine for use in harvesting the grain crops of its members. Over a week's span of time, the farmers, accompanied by their large families, assembled at the first farm, completed the harvest there, and then moved on to the next until everyone's grain was safely stored in their granaries.

The women brought an endless variety of food on broad serving platters and in large bowls. In the backyard, long tables were improvised from old doors, sheets of plywood, and planks that were laid out between sawhorses. The tables were covered with cloths of assorted fabrics and laid with plates, silverware, and glasses.

No food was put out until the operator of the steam engine blew his whistle, signaling the start of the dinner hour at just past eleven in the morning. When the whistle sounded, all threshing activity suddenly stopped. The dust settled and peace momentarily descended on the farm.

The farmers formed a long line at the washing station, a low bench covered with washbasins, bars of Lava and Lifebuoy, washcloths, towels, and combs and brushes. Removing his cap to wash a grimy face, each man displayed a curved line of demarcation between his suntanned face and stark white forehead. And, with rolled up shirtsleeves, each revealed a similar line on his forearms.

The owner of the farm took his seat at the head of the table. On his right, the operator of the threshing machine and steam engine joined him. Then the other farmers sat down and waited patiently for the meal to begin. When the women served the abundant food, another form of chaos erupted as the ravenous farmers, many just growing boys, stacked their plates high. When the last crumb of pie, cake, or cookie had disappeared, the farmers retired to the cool shade of a nearby tree. As soon as their heads hit the grass, many fell into a sound sleep. Again peace fell over the farm. But chaos resumed once more when the steam engine whistle summoned the farmers back to work.

"Thank you, Jase. That must have been an exciting experience. Danny, do you have something to add?"

Danny stood up and strolled to the front of the class.

Gazing fondly at Miss Sparks, he began, "You heard Jase mention *straw.* Most people who live in town don't know the difference between *hay* and *straw.* They think it's the same stuff.

But I learned the difference this summer at Jase's farm where Grandma Compton cooks lots of good food."

He strayed from his subject for a second but quickly regained his momentum.

"Straw is all the dried stalks of grain, like wheat and oats, left over after thrashing. This yellow-brown stuff makes super beds for cows, pigs, horses, cats, dogs, and birds. Animals don't eat straw because it isn't very tasty. When you use straw, your animals don't eat their beds. You can also use straw to fill the gutters, those long ditches behind the cows. Straw soaks up all that stuff there that you don't want in your barn. Then you can throw the whole mess out on the *mature* pile.

"Hay is different than straw. It's kinda grayish-green, and it's got wholesome things to eat, like grass and leg-irons."

I shook my head.

"Like grass and *legumes,* I meant to say. Lots of different grasses grow in Chippewa County. Timothy is one kind. It's named for one of the disciples in the Bible who liked to eat hay. He owned a bunch of horses. That's why horses really like Timothy hay. Any questions?"

Surprisingly, there was one small hand raised by a freckled-face girl who seemed to be enamored with Danny. "What's a legume?"

"It's a breed of chicken."

"Oh, thank you," replied the girl mistily.

Danny frowned at me and took his seat.

SUMMER REPORTS CONTINUED ALL morning and into the afternoon. When recess finally arrived, we had listened to every imaginable way a sixth grader could have spent the summer. We endured exhaustive descriptions of summer camps, family reunions, uncles coming home on furlough, building dollhouses (Yuck!), trips to the library, and learning to sew or knit.

Just what we boys needed!

We were ready for a change of scenery and some fresh air. When the recess bell rang, as usual, the elementary girls ran out of the building but stopped just outside the door. Using the cement steps and sidewalks close to the building, they broke into a furious flurry of playing jacks, skipping rope, bouncing balls, and hopscotching. At the north end of the playground, the junior high boys gathered around the gym teacher to review the rules of touch football.

Making our way through all the girl activity, we elementary boys soon assembled at the ball diamond to choose sides for soccer-baseball. This game, our invention from the year before, was played exactly like baseball but without bats or baseballs.

The *pitcher* rolled a soccer ball to the *batter* who attempted to get on base by kicking the ball through the infield. This was no easy feat because our ball was a heavy, partially deflated, scuffed leather sphere about the size of a regulation basketball. As a result, this lifeless ball was seldom lifted into the outfield by a solid kick.

Most batters got on base by way of an error, usually a younger infielder muffing a ground ball. Ironically those of us, having athletic ability and enough sheer power to get off a decent kick, did so at our peril. Striking a fast-rolling, leather cannonball with a fast-moving toe is a very painful way to win the adulation of teammates. But there was nothing sweeter than limp-running your way to first base with everybody cheering you on.

Danny appointed Butch Matlock and himself as team captains. After winning the coin toss, Danny made an excellent first choice by selecting me. Then Butch picked the former owner of a certain silk marble bag, Eugene Thompson, a first-rate athlete with whom I would play sports all through school.

To everyone's amazement, Danny used his second choice to pick Sherman Tolna. A sputtering Sherm left his fellow underclassmen and bounced his way to our side of the field. I was nearly overcome with dismay.

Danny patted my shoulder and whispered, "Just wait and see. It'll be fine."

I didn't share his confidence.

Having won the toss, our team took the field first. Butch appointed himself lead-off *batter/kicker* and Danny appointed me *pitcher/roller.* On my first pitch, Butch launched a stupendous kick.

Wham!

The soccer ball shot through the air and hit our first baseman square in the stomach. He tumbled over backwards but somehow managed to hold onto the ball. Then he lurched forward and landed right on top of the bag. Gasping for air, he rightly proclaimed that Butch was *out.*

We all cheered for the brave first basemen who responded by throwing up in the first-base coach's box. After his replacement was in position, we got through the rest of the inning without Butch's team scoring.

Sherm was our lead-off hitter, and his first at bat made it into the record book. He was the only batter in soccer-baseball history to strike out. He whiffed all three of Butch's pitches despite the fact that Butch was deliberately rolling the ball to ensure that it hit Sherm's foot.

When Sherm fell to the ground having missed his third pitch in a row, Danny turned to me and declared, "See, I told you it would be all right."

Huh?

The rest of our side grounded out. The contest continued without either side scoring. Just before the recess bell sounded, Butch took the plate.

Danny, positioned deep in center field, was actually closer to the older boys' touch football game than our game. With all my strength, I wound up and pitched my fast roll to the Mighty Butch. He creamed it. The ball sailed over my head and bounced into center field. Danny froze as the ball shot past him and onto the football field. Then he turned and dashed after the ball which had begun to lose speed.

David Thorndike, the toughest boy in eighth grade, had just eluded a last defender and was running full speed for the winning touchdown. The collision occurred at the fifty yard line. Danny was catapulted into the air but miraculously landed on his feet.

David was not so fortunate. His nose plowed a small ditch from the fifty yard line to the forty-eight. With blood dripping from his nose, he staggered to his feet. When his eyes came into focus, without warning, he charged at Danny like a mad bull, swearing a blue streak.

Blowing his whistle frantically, the gym teacher ran toward what would surely be the end of poor Danny. Every boy on the playground raced at top speed toward the scene of the impending murder. But Danny was spared.

"I'll get you, twerp! Just you wait!" David screamed as the gym teacher dragged him off to the showers. "I'll tear you apart!"

"Yeah! You and whose army?" Danny yelled. "You couldn't punch your way out of a wet paper bag, you loudmouth, you."

The rest of our first day of school was a blur. I couldn't stop thinking about Danny and his horrible mistake. What rolled off his quick tongue usually made people laugh, but this was no laughing matter. I was terrified about what might await us after school.

My head cleared just in time to hear Miss Sparks' good news. "Well, we've heard what everyone did this past summer — and you all did a fine job. Tomorrow we'll begin our regular schedule. Remember now, bring your milk money. And, first thing after the Pledge of Allegiance, you'll have an opportunity to buy savings stamps. See you in the morning!"

Surprisingly, Queenie was waiting for us as we left our classroom. She hugged Danny. He put his arm around her waist as she led him out the door. Butch and I followed them, in silence, down Hamilton Street toward home. Every twenty feet or so, I glanced over my shoulder, half expecting to find David, bearing down on us.

After crossing the Grand Trunk railroad tracks, Queenie steered us onto the path that led to the canning factory. "They have a million crates of new apples in the yard," she advised.

Area farmers unloaded their harvests of seasonal fruits and vegetables in the assembly yard. From there, factory workers moved the produce inside where it was processed into cans of wholesome food. When harvests were heavy, even by running three shifts, the canning factory just couldn't stay ahead of deliveries, so the produce remained in the yard, sometimes for days.

During this period, it was ripe pickings for us neighborhood boys and girls. Fortunately the canning factory management didn't seem to mind as long as we only took a modest amount, preferably one serving per snitcher.

After we each selected a luscious red apple from the inventory, we sat down next to the towering stack of brimming apple crates. We wiped our apples on our shirts and took our first juicy bites.

We chewed contentedly for several minutes before I asked Queenie, "Did you hear what happened to Danny today?" I was sure she knew about it or she wouldn't be here with us. Seeing her as a loving and devoted sister was new to me. By golly, I liked it.

"Everyone in junior high is talking about it. David Thorndike is not a nice person. He lives in a dingy house on the other side of the school. He has an older brother Bobby. Nobody knows much about his parents. He's always picking fights with the other boys. They're all afraid of him. That's why I —."

She stopped and looked at Danny. "Says, when he turns sixteen, he's gonna quit school and join the navy. Good riddance."

"Hello, twerp!" I choked and looked up to see David Thorndike standing above us with his hands on his hips. "We got some unfinished business, wise guy."

In the blink of an eye, Queenie jumped up and threw herself at the giant eighth grader. He reeled backwards, throwing up his hands to protect his face from her sharp nails. She slashed at him with both hands. He managed to shove her back and she fell to the ground.

I was stunned. Butch was not. He stood up, took a deep breath, and waded in. Both combatants appeared to be about the same size. Butch grabbed his adversary around the waist in a powerful bear hug. The muscles in Butch's arms rippled and bulged. David tried desperately to break the hold but to no avail. Finally the defeated bully yelled, "Uncle! Uncle! I give up!" and slumped limply.

Butch slowly let go. The former champion of Hamilton School now lay on the ground in a pathetic heap. Butch pushed him over with a toe and bellowed, **"YOU GO NEAR DANNY AGAIN AND I'LL GIVE YOU ANOTHER WHIPPIN'. YOU UNDERSTAND?"**

His mega-voice returned just in time. David shuddered, whimpered, and nodded his head. Queenie added her two cents worth. "And you'll have me to deal with too!" With that, she reached into her purse and extracted a giant bottle of Blue Waltz perfume and dumped its contents over David's head. The odor was nauseating. "Explain that to your buddies in gym class tomorrow."

Leaving the sobbing and stinking bully in a heap, the four of us locked arms and skipped across the assembly yard. When we reached Forrest Street, we stopped. Danny and Queenie patted Butch's back and thanked him again. Butch turned red, lowered his head, and clicked his heel plates on the sidewalk. We watched as Danny and Queenie, locked arm-in-arm, headed for the Tucker house.

Looking over his shoulder, Danny informed us, "I coulda taken that guy, you know?"

"WELL, BOYS, HOW WAS your first week of school?" Mom's question was the first time anyone had spoken in at least ten minutes.

All of us at the breakfast table, including Danny, still seemed half asleep. On this Saturday morning, with no strict timetable pressuring us, we stared into space and picked at our breakfast. Dad lowered his newspaper to hear our report.

Danny spoke for both of us. "We played lots of soccer-baseball. I tackled a bully, and then Butch Matlock squeezed him until he was an uncle. Queenie and Butch joined FSG for saving somebody's life. (That was news to me.) We rode the school bus every morning, but Mr. Kolarik thinks he can drive by himself from now on. We took our Woolworth cap guns to school to show the class. I dropped a big rock on a box of caps to show how a bomb works. Miss Sparks had to tell the principal what happened.

"We practiced penmanship, but we could only use one sheet of paper because of the war shortage. So we wrote our sentences back and forth, then up and down, on the front and back. We bought savings stamps. Not quite enough for a war bond yet. Sherm ate so much paste during art class that he threw up. When we packed Red Cross boxes, we ran out of tooth brushes so some soldiers will have to share. We won 143 marbles. And a little freckled-face girl stabbed me with her pencil."

He pulled up his pants leg to show us the gray-blue wound on his knee. "Let's see. I guess that's about it."

"Well, I'd say you had quite a week. What is *FSG* though?"

Danny answered Aunt Maude by placing an index finger on his lips and shaking his head. He was fond of telling people that *Loose Lips Sink Ships,* especially when he didn't know the answer.

"Oh, I see here in the paper that Tom Dewey's going to be in Riverton this coming week. Whataya know?"

Thomas E. Dewey was a native of nearby Owosso, Michigan. He had also graduated from the University of Michigan that I hoped to attend someday. After law school at Columbia University, he entered private practice with a topnotch New York law firm. After a few years, he was recruited by the U.S. Department of Justice to tackle the crime bosses who ruled the underworld of New York. After four years, he was named United States Attorney for the Southern District of New York. Decades later, this same post would be filled by a tough young lawyer named Rudolph Giuliani who would continue Dewey's battle against organized crime by bringing down a key kingpin named John Gotti.

As the Special Prosecutor for Organized Crime, Dewey toppled many top criminals including the mobster known as Dutch Schultz. Because of his reputation as an honest hard-working man, he easily won his first election for Governor of the State of New York, a position that he held from 1943 until 1955.

In the summer of 1944, he accepted his party's nomination as Republican candidate for President of the United States. Since his opponent was Franklin Delano Roosevelt, his chances for winning were slim. But it was a great honor to be nominated, and members of both parties in our part of Michigan claimed him as their native son.

"This has been quite a week for our boys in Europe," Dad reported, turning back to his newspaper. "The U.S. Army finally reached the Siegfried Line near Aachen, Germany. In fact, on the 10th of September, less than a week ago, a patrol crossed the frontier and set foot on German soil for the first time since the First World War. How about that?"

"Dad, what exactly is the Siegfried Line? And where's Aachen?"

"The Siegfried Line is Hitler's west wall. It's a defensive belt of fortifications along the German border. There are mutually-supporting pillboxes. That means they're positioned to cover each other. Bunkers, command and observation posts, and anti-tank obstacles, called Dragon's Teeth. This menacing wall is also completely camouflaged by heavy woods and covered with thick brush that's grown since the line was built before the war. With these kinds of fortifications, it's not gonna be easy to cross into Germany. No, sir! Nothing easy about it."

He opened the paper and showed us a map. "There's Aachen, a German city located where the borders of Belgium, Holland, and Germany all come together. See it right there?"

We stood over the newspaper looking at the map. Suddenly Aunt Maude moaned, bent over, and fell back into her chair. She gave us a funny look and whispered, "I think it's time. Better get me to the hospital. The bag's all packed, in the bedroom."

Without a word, Mom and Dad sprang into action, leaving Danny and me alone with the expectant mother. Just in the past month, I had noticed that Aunt Maude's tummy had practically doubled in size. But, with all that was happening, I must have put the projected mid-September delivery date out of my mind.

Aunt Maude steadied herself between Dad and Mom as she walked toward the car that Dad had pulled around front. Mom was carrying the suitcase. Danny and I followed them to the car. When the car was loaded, Mom turned to me and said, "When we get to the hospital, we'll call Mrs. Henry and ask her to run over and tell Grandma what's going on. But there's no telling whether

Ma's home or not. On a Saturday morning, she just might be on her way into town. Why don't you boys stay here in case she shows up?"

Mom was right. Grandma pulled up about twenty minutes after Dad sped off to the hospital. Mrs. Henry, who had the only telephone within miles of the Compton farm, would make a trip in vain. Of course, it wouldn't be the first time owing to the unpredictable habits of my peripatetic grandmother. But, at least, Grandpa would hear what was happening from Mrs. Henry. I quickly explained the situation to Grandma.

"Oh, laws!" she responded. "I had a feeling that today might be the day. I could tell just by looking at her that it would be soon. Always comes when you're least expecting it. Doesn't it, Jase?"

I hadn't the faintest idea. Aside from my own, this was my first direct experience with childbirth. So far, I hadn't exactly mastered the subject. And Danny was really in the dark. In fact, he was amazingly quiet. He hadn't uttered a word since his summary of our week at school.

Grandma also sensed that something was going on with my friend. "Danny, cat got your tongue?"

He looked at her quizzically, stuck out his tongue, and shook his head. I was pleased to see that the old Danny was back.

"Well, we better be on our way. We don't want that new baby to beat us to the hospital, now, do we?"

As it turned out, there was no rush. No rush at all. We spent the entire day at the hospital waiting for my new cousin to make an appearance. By late afternoon, Grandma was fit to be tied. She paced back and forth in the waiting room, wringing her hankie.

"Ma, you need to get out of here. Take a break. Go to a movie or something. Doctor Moran says that he's not sure when this will happen. Why don't you take the boys out for a bite to eat and then take in a movie? John and I'll go back down to the cafeteria for our supper. Really you should."

Rick's Grill wasn't fancy, but it had some of the finest food in town. Serving sizes were colossal and prices were, well, downright cheap. Located next door to the main bus station, Rick's was a combination grill, drugstore, and travel shop. In fact, there was a double glass door between Rick's and the passenger waiting room. Those waiting for buses to Flint, Saginaw, or Detroit could browse through magazines, postcards, playing cards, and stationery in the *Travel Needs* area of Rick's. Local bus riders found the drugstore a convenient place to pick up prescriptions. But the food at Rick's was its most attractive feature as far as I was concerned.

For a late Saturday afternoon, there were surprisingly few restaurant patrons. Instead of sitting at the soda fountain where Danny and I usually sat, we chose one of the four comfortable booths, each having its own jukebox. Since the five jukeboxes at the fountain served fifteen stools, we felt very fortunate. Danny hit Grandma up for two nickels. He played the same song with each nickel, *Boogie Woogie Bugle Boy.*

When the waitress arrived, we all ordered the hamburger deluxe with a chocolate milk shake. Heaven! Their burgers melted in your mouth, a major improvement over the fare at the hospital cafeteria. For some reason, we all were hungrier than usual. So we each ordered another deluxe delectable. After Grandma had paid our check, we slurped the last drops from the bottom of the paper cones inside the milk-shake holders. Not wanting to miss an atom, Danny even licked the outside of his straw.

"Well, boys, what next? A movie?"

"Nope! Football. Riverton High's opening game is tonight. You know that Gentleman Jim is the new coach, right? We should all go to the game. Shouldn't we, Grandma Compton?" I swear Danny fluttered his eyelashes at Grandma.

Danny and I had talked about this game for several days, but Aunt Maude's impending motherhood removed any possibility of Dad's taking us that night. However, here we were with a card-carrying adult, required for our admission to the stadium. All we had to do was to talk Grandma into it.

"Well, I've never been to a football contest before. Where's it played? And when does it start? How much does it cost? Do either of you know how it works? I haven't the faintest idea what to look for."

Danny took charge of filling Grandma's football information gap. "Riverton High is playing Owosso High tonight. The football *game* starts at seven o'clock at Waters Field. You know, where the stadium is. The tickets cost a quarter for adults and ten cents for children. That's about forty-five cents. Our coach is Charles James Comstock who used to be a bum by the name of Gentleman Jim. Now he's a football coach. And a history teacher. And our friend. And a *former* bum."

That just about covered it, but it was obvious that Grandma had not yet fully embraced Danny's idea. So he delivered the coup de grace. "They sell popcorn, pop, and hot dogs at the stadium too."

In the early 1930s, Waters Field had been constructed by the city to encourage community involvement and support of its school athletic programs. Consisting of the football field, practice fields, track facilities, and, of course, a football stadium, the ten-acre facility was built by the same architect who had designed the University of Michigan Stadium in Ann Arbor. But instead of surrounding the football field on all sides with over 100,000 screaming fans, the Waters Field stadium only surrounded the field on one side with just over two thousand screaming fans. Modest bleachers were constructed on the opposite side for fans of the visiting team.

Before the game, Grandma insisted on going by the hospital. She returned to the car, relieved to know that we would be back in plenty of time. The doctor had ordered her to go and enjoy herself. The bounce in her step indicated that she had taken his advice. Grandma was going to her first football game.

Since we were early, we had our choice of seats, but Grandma was extremely fussy. She didn't want to be up high. Too easy to get the *vapors* up there. Whatever that meant. She didn't want to be too low. Too easy to see disturbing things if a player were hurt. Didn't like the north end. Too noisy with people milling around the refreshment stand. Didn't like the south end. Too near the river. She didn't swim. Finally we selected three seats, right on the fifty yard line, about halfway up or halfway down, depending on your viewpoint.

As soon as we were seated, the stadium began to fill around us. We heard the drums of the Riverton High band marching toward us from the high school. You could feel the excitement in the air. Both teams were on the field doing their pregame warm-ups. We saw Jim, wearing a school jacket, baseball cap with a big *R,* and neatly pressed trousers. His entire wardrobe was a tasteful mixture of blue and gold, Riverton High's school colors.

"If this is a Riverton High School game, why is the county's name on that sign down there by those big clothes poles?" Grandma asked.

Next to the goal posts on the river end of the field stood a scoreboard to record the scores of *Chippewas* and *Opponents.* After the *clothes poles* remark, I knew we were in for a long night. But Danny evidently saw Grandma's ignorance of the game as an opportunity to endear himself to her.

"*Chippewas* is the Riverton team's nickname. The Owosso team's nickname is the *Trojans,* like the Greek wooden horse guys. There's lots of Greeks in Owosso. Lots of Englishmen too. But *English* doesn't work too well as a nickname. It's better as a *class* name. Like *English class,* you know? And those aren't clothes poles, they're flag poles. See those little flags tied to the tops? They tell everybody which way the wind is blowing."

I was relieved to know that Grandma was in the hands of a real football authority. Danny didn't stop there. "See that little brown ball down there. That's a football. When the game starts, they'll play keep-away with that. If you got the ball, you run around the field so all the other guys can't whack you. If you don't have it, you get to whack anybody you want. Those men in black and white shirts are the umpires. When somebody whacks somebody the wrong way, the umpires throw rocks at them. Their rocks are tied to hankies, so they can find their rocks later and hit somebody else with them." Danny sure knew his football, all right.

I had read in the sports section that Owosso had a strong team this year. Riverton was definitely the underdog. But, when the gun sounded at halftime, the game was scoreless. At least both defenses had played well.

"It's over, boys! That was fun. Let's get back to the hospital." Danny had apparently forgotten to mention quarters and halves.

"Not yet, Grandma Compton, they have to go inside to take a shower and cool down for a few minutes, but they'll be back out. They'll start playing again, right after we get back from buying our hot dogs and popcorn."

Not wanting to be responsible for delaying the start of the second half, Grandma hustled us down to the refreshment stand. Funny how things like this always seemed to work out just right for Danny.

When we reached the ground, I peered into the tunnel that ran under the stadium. To my delight, I saw Jim Comstock talking to Chuck Nichols, our reporter friend who had given us exceptional coverage during the fund-raising campaign for the Matlocks. He spied me and waved. Jim followed his lead and then beckoned to me.

"Grandma, Coach Comstock wants to talk to me. I'll be right back."

Normally Danny's curiosity would have compelled him to join me. But, after all, he *was* in line for hot dogs and popcorn. He waved at Jim and then continued his explanation of the finer points of the game. Grandma was engrossed. As I entered the tunnel, I heard Danny telling Grandma about the penalty for *unnecessary rudeness.*

"Jase! Good to see you. Where's Danny? Oh, there he is with your grandmother. I can't believe she's here at the game! Well, good for her. Listen, I gotta get back inside. But one of the team members told me your family rushed to the hospital this morning. Is everybody okay?"

When I told him about Aunt Maude, he was greatly relieved.

"Boy, that's good news. Give her my best and tell her I'll come visit her next week after she's feeling better. I want to see that little cousin of yours. But right now, I really should get back inside.

"Oh, Jase. One day next week I want to bring someone by your house. He's come a long way to see Danny and you. But I gotta go now. Give my best to everybody. See you later!" As he ran for the locker room, I waved and wished him luck.

I rejoined Grandma and Danny who were walking toward me with their arms full. "We got you something, Jase. Now you won't be hungry."

Since our enormous supper at Rick's, I hadn't suffered a single hunger pang. But, not wanting to be a spoilsport, I gratefully accepted my share. I was a bit concerned about Grandma's spending too much on us boys. On those rare occasions when Grandma's absence required Grandpa to prepare his meals, he always fixed himself a big bowl of milk and bread. I imagined him at home that evening pushing the big chunks of bread, torn just the way he liked them, down into the bowl of milk with the back of his spoon. The way Grandma was going through the cash, he'd be eating many more milk and bread meals in the future.

By the time we reached our seats, the teams were back on the field. The offenses finally came to life. After a hard-fought second half, the gun sounded, and we found ourselves celebrating a slim, come-from-behind victory. This time the score was *14-13* in Riverton's favor. Given what I read in the paper about the likely outcome, I was thrilled with the job done by Riverton's new coach.

With the game behind us, I suddenly remembered Aunt Maude. Apparently Grandma had the same thought. "Come on. Let's hurry to the car and get on up to the hospital. I don't want to miss anything."

Grandma drove cautiously, not wanting to be delayed by having to explain to a policeman why she was flying through the streets at Mach 2 on a football Saturday night. She slowed down to a measly Mach 1. Still we touched down at the hospital in no time flat.

Despite having a rather *husky* frame, as people called it back then, Grandma demonstrated how to run, really fast. We literally flew up the front walk, through the door, and down the corridor to the waiting area where we saw the doctor talking to Mom and Dad.

"Doctor Moran was about to give us the news! Go ahead, Doctor."

"Okay, John. Glad you're all here. It was a long and difficult labor. But Maude has given birth to a son who, I have on good authority, will be named *John Jason Harrison* in honor of some relatives I think you all know. Discounting the exhaustion factor, mother and baby are doing exceptionally well. And that's it in a nutshell."

Grandma and Mom pressed him for details that I didn't think mattered much like his exact weight, his length, and his precise time of birth. *If baby humans are anything like baby cows or pigs, they grow so fast that those statistics would be obsolete by now. Especially if Aunt Maude is —.* I thought of the pretty Mexican mother at the Grafton and felt embarrassed for having connected the two thoughts.

The doctor congratulated us all. And we all thanked him. I was excited that soon I would have a new roommate who, according to the doctor, was born with a shock of fluffy black hair. I could hardly wait to see him. The conversation trickled out, owing to an *exhaustion factor* of our own. So we stood quietly, lost in our own thoughts for what seemed like an eternity.

Then Grandma broke the silence. "My gosh! Jase, I completely forgot to ask you. Why did Jim Comstock want to see you during that half-intermission-time period or whatever it's called?"

Dad was beside himself. "You went to the game? And you spoke to Jim Comstock at halftime? Wasn't he busy coaching the Riverton team? I can't believe my ears. Grandma Compton at a football game! What's going to happen next?" Dad shook his head. Then he remembered to ask, "For goodness sakes, who won anyway?"

I told Dad about the game including the final score. He was ecstatic! I explained that Jim had heard about our rushing to the hospital. And how relieved he was when I told him about Aunt Maude and the baby. And how surprised and pleased he was to see Grandma at the game. That made Grandma blush. She revealed that she always liked Jim. *Who didn't?*

"But the strangest part of our conversation was that some day next week he wants to bring someone by to meet Danny and me. Someone who's traveling a long way to see us. I have no idea who he's talking about."

Everyone was as baffled as I was. Everyone, except Danny that is. "I know who it is!"

"Who?" we all chimed.

"Why, Thomas E. Dewey, of course!"

AFTER SCHOOL, THE ENTIRE membership of the Forrest Street Guards, including the two new recruits, assembled under the cottonwood tree for the initiation ceremony.

"Yeah, but why do we need FSG now that Hans Zeyer is an okay guy?"

This was the fifth time Queenie had interrupted the secret oath. Even Sherm seemed annoyed and his standards weren't that high. Butch was quietly compliant. Since Queenie was his sister, Danny had a distinct conflict of interest. So he wasn't saying a word either.

I pressed on. "— so I do solemnly swear that I will never reveal the secrets of FSG." I knew Queenie was about to ask what those secrets were. I quickly closed the deal before she could object. "So help me, God!"

"I do!" swore Butch.

"Oh, I guess I do too." Queenie exhaled, studying her nails. "Now can we go listen to the radio?"

My warm feelings for Queenie were beginning to cool. In exchange for her agreement to join FSG, she had insisted on full access to the prize radio. Without thinking, I agreed. But Danny was adamant that the radio stay in my room. How Queenie could have full access in a room filled with Aunt Maude, little Johnnie, two *brass-o-nets,* and me remained a mystery. I gathered that Queenie was confident of a compromise when she asked, "Does Aunt Maude like Big Band music, Jase?"

"Look, you guys!" Sherm squealed, pointing down Forrest Street. "Two black lemon-scenes in front of Jase's house!" We gaped at the mammoth Cadillac limousines that had come to a stop under our box elder tree. The FSG meeting quickly adjourned and we galloped toward my house. Dad and Mom were standing on the porch as Jim Comstock introduced them to several men in dark suits.

"Here they are now! Governor, please allow me to present Jase Addison and Danny Tucker. Boys, this is Governor Thomas E. Dewey. He's visiting Riverton as part of his Presidential campaign." Jim introduced the other members of the governor's entourage. Then he introduced Queenie, Butch, and Sherm. We all shook hands. I recognized one of the gentlemen as Mr. Richard Church, owner and publisher of the *Riverton Daily Press*. But the only person I really knew was Chuck Nichols who gave us a big hello.

"Boys, I am honored to meet you. A number of people down in Washington have informed me of your heroics in capturing two escaped POWs and about your hard work to raise funds for a family who lost their home in a fire. I believe that was your family. Wasn't it, Butch?" Butch Matlock scuffed his heel plates and stared at his belt buckle.

I immediately liked the man.

"Two of them in particular asked me to stop by and give you their personal thanks. So I am pleased to deliver personal notes from both J. Edgar Hoover and from my able opponent, Franklin D. Roosevelt, our President. Here you are, boys. Congratulations!"

By this time all our neighbors were out in the street witnessing, what had to be, the biggest event in our neighborhood's history. While Governor Dewey chatted with Mom and Dad, Chuck Nichols looked at his watch and cleared his throat.

"Boys, I have to leave now. I'm scheduled to be on the evening news at WRDP in a few minutes, so I have to get on over to the studio. If you haven't observed a radio show being broadcast before, perhaps your folks will allow me to take you boys along." The Governor turned to Mom and she nodded her agreement. "Okay, then, let's go. Come on, boys. You can ride with Mr. Nichols, Coach Comstock, and me."

On the way to the studio, we learned that Jim and *Tom* had been fraternity brothers at the University of Michigan. Another member of their fraternity was Harry Chambers, the Libby sisters' attorney and the man who convinced Jim to rehabilitate himself. "Small world, hey, boys?" observed our new friend *Tom*.

Owned and operated by the *Riverton Daily Press,* WRDP was brand-new. Since its first day on the air, everyone in the county had become avid listeners. Although the signal could only be heard in the homes and cars within thirty miles of the transmitter, we listeners thought that WRDP had finally put Riverton on the map. The programming was mainly local. News, housekeeping tips, and polka music were the station's most popular offerings. But, whatever the program content, WRDP's loyal fans stayed tuned.

Since the station had been on the air, Chuck Nichols had assumed the role of radio newsman. His pleasant voice was ideal for the job. Besides he was a knowledgeable reporter and was well-respected in the community. "Ladies and gentleman, it is my distinct honor and privilege to introduce the Governor of the State of New York and Michigan native son, the candidate for the Presidency —."

Governor Dewey spoke into the microphone without a hint of nervousness. Public speaking, either in person or over the air, was one of his long suits. He talked about the issues that lay ahead for our country. Yes, we were still engaged in a war whose outcome was not altogether certain. But we must nonetheless prepare ourselves for the complex problems that would face America and the world when the war did come to a victorious conclusion. We needed new leadership with a fresh vision for those difficult times ahead. His convincing rhetoric was beginning to shake my long-standing loyal support for our neighborhood's hero FDR.

His concluding remarks surprised everyone. "We have in the studio two young Rivertonians whom you folks listening out there already know and admire. But here's something you don't know. Just an hour ago, I delivered two personal notes of congratulations and gratitude to these young men from none other than J. Edgar Hoover and Franklin Delano Roosevelt. Yes, you heard me right. The Director of the FBI and my loyal opponent, the President of the United States. Come on in here, boys!"

Jim shoved us through the door. "Rivertonians, I'd like to introduce Jase Addison and Danny Tucker. Your local heroes and personal friends of mine. Danny. Jase. Say hello to the folks."

Two weak "Hellos" were all we could muster.

"Boys, don't mean to put you on the spot. But who do you support for President?"

I was speechless. But not Danny. "Governor, I would like to support you."

"That's very kind of you, Danny. Thank you."

"But *you* didn't write me a note."

8 HUNTING SEASON

ON SUNDAY AFTERNOONS, ALL FOUR OF GRANDMA and Grandpa Compton's children and their families *came out home* for a visit. Of course, those serving in the armed forces were temporarily excused, but all others were expected.

My cousins and I played in the barns, fields, creeks, and woods until we were dog-tired. The women gathered in the kitchen and served an ongoing buffet as they *pieced* and gossiped. In warm weather, the men assembled under the maple tree for their sessions with Grandpa. But in cold weather, they collected around the dining-room table to smoke and talk or to play setback.

"Hard to believe that hunting season opens in just a week," Grandpa declared. The other card players grunted, acknowledging his point without breaking their concentration.

Setback was not very complicated, but it did require careful thinking to conceive and implement a winning strategy. Only the adult men and grandsons with good card sense were allowed to play. I qualified when I was eight.

"High! Low! Jack!" Grandpa shouted, slapping his cards down on the table. "And the Game!" Groans erupted. Nobody could beat him.

Losing another game to Grandpa stimulated my appetite. I wandered into the kitchen where Danny was sitting in Grandpa's rocking chair holding little Johnnie. He was surrounded by Grandma, Mom, and my aunts who were admiring the new baby. Danny acted as if he, not Johnnie, were the center of attention.

"What smells so good?"

Those magic words signaled Grandma and her kitchen crew that a new customer had arrived. Immediately I was whisked into a chair and presented with the full array of choices. Performance at Grandma's table was measured by how much you consumed. Requests for second and third helpings were highly praised. Certain gestures such as loosening your belt or unbuttoning your trousers brought appreciative smiles from the women. Even an occasional burp was interpreted as a sign of appreciation.

"Thanks, Grandma. That looks tasty." I knew better than to ask what it was.

The Compton farm fare was predominately meat and potatoes. Lots of meat! At the beginning of the week, Grandma oven-roasted sizeable quantities of meat. Then she created meal-sized portions on several serving platters that she stored on the closed shelf of her perpetually warm woodstove. During the week, she reheated each portion, usually by frying it in pork lard.

Owing to leftovers and new additions, each serving platter evolved into a mysterious combination of pork, beef, chicken, goose, guinea hen, duck, or squab. During hunting season, October through February, the prolific harvest of wild game added pheasant, rabbit, squirrel, partridge, wild goose and duck, venison, and even black bear to her warming platters. All meat looked alike, dark brown pieces swimming in melted fat. In short, by appearance, you never knew what you were selecting. And, by taste, it was usually difficult to discern what you were eating.

Year-round there were lots of potatoes! Sometimes boiled and mashed but usually thickly sliced and fried. Freshly dug potatoes were considered inedible until they aged over the winter in the dark root cellar under the kitchen. By spring, after you spent hours removing the sprouts, they were deemed to be edible. Potato peels, considered unfit for human consumption, were fed to the pigs. Consequently I was an adult before I ever experienced the delicate flavor of a baked new potato and its flavorful skin.

Summers seldom brought much in the way of variety. On occasion, we had sweet corn and tomatoes fresh from the garden. But usually those vegetables, as well as white beans, peas, string beans, carrots, and beets, were not served fresh. Instead, they were canned immediately after harvest. Vegetables, whether served in summer or winter, had been home-canned the summer before. Salads were nonexistent unless you counted the small samplings of white and red radishes, green and red bell peppers, green onions, and lettuce. Those vegetables were only eaten fresh because they didn't can well. Oddly enough, lime Jell-O *did* pass for salad!

Occasionally fresh apples, pears, plums, cherries, and peaches, produced in abundance at the farm, made it to the table before being converted into applesauce, pies, jellies, and jams. Even black and red raspberries, strawberries, and gooseberries from the garden and blackberries from the woods were whisked into canning jars before they could make an appearance at the supper table.

I was lost in my thoughts and dishes of Grandma's cooking when I heard her remark, "Danny, you're really good with the baby. You must be a terrific help to Aunt Maude, right?" That's all Danny needed.

Immediately Doctor Tucker commenced his standard lecture, *The Proper Care and Feeding of Babies.* I had heard it about fourteen times in the past two weeks. When he delivered it to our class at school, the boys thought he was daft, but the girls were mesmerized. The little freckled-face girl apologized for stabbing him in the knee and asked if he gave private lessons or words to that effect. Forever the professional, Dr. T declared that the answer was no, not at the present time. Because that could change, he suggested she check periodically with his *nurse,* referring to me.

Danny's baby care program had three major components. "You gotta have lots of *food.* That's milk, right? Lots of *diapers.* If you have lots of food, you need lots of them! And you need lots of *soap and water.* Working with diapers is a messy job, especially at first."

His baby cleanliness philosophy was similar to his baptism philosophy, the more water the better. "You fill the brass-o-net to the brim with warm water. Check it with your elbow. Add soap and drop in the baby. Some of the water might spill out. But that's okay 'cause you got lots of diapers to soak it up. A baby needs lots of water, especially its lower end."

Dr. T wouldn't answer questions on feeding the baby, explaining that this section of his lecture was *still under development.* But he promised, just as soon as Sam, our milkman, began delivering Johnnie's meals, instead of Aunt Maude, he would alter his policy. I was relieved by this decision.

Since I passed the boy-am-I-stuffed test, I was free. Looking for any excuse to get some fresh air, I told Danny that we needed to check the granary mouse traps. Putting a dab of cheddar behind our ears, we exited the kitchen and headed outside. Before we reached the granary, Danny whom I respected for his knowledge of fine cuisine asked the *$64 Question.* "How come your family overcooks everything?"

Mass meat-cooking practices were common among early farm families who only had root cellars or springhouses for refrigeration. Even in later times, small home iceboxes or electric refrigerators seldom offered sufficient storage for sizeable quantities of uncooked meat. Grandma, like her farm neighbors, followed the common sense rule that it was much safer to store meat after it was cooked, especially in the summertime.

After butchering a large animal, like a pig or cow, most meat, not immediately consumed, was processed into a form more easily and safely stored, such as smoked ham, bacon, and sausages or canned beef, *bully beef* as our family called it. Any remaining fresh meat was given to family and friends or taken to the local meat locker.

After World War II, tractors and motor trucks along with ample supplies of gasoline to propel them became available again, making transportation of animals less time-consuming than with horse and wagon. So in-town meat lockers soon took over the butchering, cutting, packaging, freezing, and storing of meat for farmers. With an abundance of beef and pork cuts in her locker, Grandma could bestow frozen gifts on us all year long.

My family's practice of converting wholesome, fresh foods into less palatable, although more enduring, forms was rationalized by habit *(We've always done it that way!)*, lack of refrigerated storage *(If we didn't, the produce would spoil!),* and taste preferences *(I'll take canned peas over fresh any day!).*

At the heart of it was their unadulterated Puritan ethic. To enjoy fresh strawberries was considered wasteful and self-indulgent. Such an act of immediate gratification would not only divert perfectly good strawberries away from their natural fate as jam, but also lessen our family's preparedness for potential worldwide famine or another Depression. Besides we were at war!

"Jase, I have another question. How come your family never eats real vegetables?"

I equivocated, giving him an incomplete answer. "They don't want things to spoil. I guess they're afraid of germs. You know, making themselves sick."

"Then they ought to use more soap and water!"

The learned Dr. T had spoken.

ON THE TWO DAYS following our Sunday at the farm, Danny and I had no school. Riverton teachers were off to East Lansing for a teachers' institute at Michigan State College. Grandpa asked us to help him prepare the farm for the opening of hunting season that next Sunday. I wasn't sure how useful we would be, but we volunteered to stay on because, well, who doesn't like being needed?

With chores and breakfast behind us, we lingered at the kitchen table so Grandpa could brief us on our duties. He showed us the signs that had to be posted. These signs, made of stiff, red paperboard, were about the size of a sheet of tablet paper and had large, bold, black lettering that read:

NO HUNTING

WITHOUT PERMIT

Obtain Permit from: _____

On each sign, Grandpa used his carpenter's pencil to etch his name and address in bold block letters. The signs looked impressive.

"This postin' business is new for Barrington Township farmers this year. Never needed it before. In the past, hunters, even the ones you didn't know, were respectful of your property. Came to the door, first, for permission to hunt the farm. Never did any harm except to rooster pheasants.

"But, owin' to wartime meat rationin' coupled with the bumper crops of pheasants lately, farmers 'round here been gettin' large gangs of hunters from as far away as Detroit. They trample corn and soybeans still in the fields. Shoot anything. Cocks, hens, and even your chickens. Strew beer bottles and trash all over. Knock down fences and posts. Well, it just isn't right. So, now, we got huntin' by permit only."

"Where we gonna put these signs, Grandpa?"

"The county game warden said to post the perimeter of the property. Maybe a couple hundred paces apart, especially along the roads. Not so close on the boundaries with other farms. Because I'm workin' Nate's place, I'm postin' his farm too. Each farm gets four permits. Nate gave me his. So people'll come here to get 'em and he won't be bothered."

"Will we tack 'em on fence posts? Some are pretty spindly, old and rotten in places, especially back in the woods. And there's only that rail fence between your woods and the Donaldson's."

"The warden suggested tackin' 'em on five-foot stakes, two-by-twos. Then they'll be high enough to see over the underbrush growin' along some fencerows. If the signs don't get rain-soaked and ruined, we can reuse 'em next year. Save us time. When the season's over, just pull 'em up and store 'em in the barn."

"What'll we do for stakes? There's a few two-by-twos in that pile between the garage and the horse barn but not many."

"I still got a positive balance in my account over at Hagen's so Elmer's makin 'em up for us to have this mornin'. He came by here on Friday, takin' Old Nate another load of lumber. Nate's buildin' a new outhouse, for company he says. We'll just hitch the team to the wagon, load the sledge, hammers, and nails — er, maybe tacks — carpet tacks might work. Pick up the stakes then start at the south end of the farm and work our way north. We'll finish up over at Nate's. Somebody can tack 'em while somebody else drives 'em into the ground. We should be done afore the noon meal."

Like many farmers in the area, Elmer Hagen operated a side business to supplement his farm income. The lumber business was ideal because lumber was generally produced in the winter months when he, like most farmers, had little to do. His reasonable prices for high-quality lumber attracted builders and cabinetmakers from New Albany and Riverton who traveled out to the Hagen Sawmill for terrific values, especially in certain hard to find varieties of wood like hickory and walnut.

But Elmer had a perennial problem. Over the years, as his lumber business grew, his sawmill had consumed every lumber-worthy tree on his farm. So he needed a new source of trees to feed his sawmill, particularly the hardwoods dotting the woods of nearby farms. Farmers also had a problem. They needed lumber and firewood. So a mutually beneficial arrangement was created to meet both needs.

Using their special equipment and timbering expertise, Elmer and his crew harvested trees from the woods of nearby farms. Each tree was appraised according to its specie, age, quality, and size, i.e., potential board feet. This value, in dollars, was then credited to the farmer's account. Trees not suitable for lumber were felled for use as firewood.

When the farmer needed lumber of any kind, he simply purchased it using the credit in his account. No cash was exchanged. Elmer got his trees. The farmer's need for lumber and firewood was met and his woods was thinned at no additional cost. It was a win-win proposition.

The Hagen farm was located two miles south of the Compton farm. Before we had gone a mile, I heard the distinctive sounds of the busy sawmill. The piercing *ping-tap-ping* of the steam engine that powered the mill. The *thump-da-thump* of newly-felled, massive logs as they rolled from wagons onto carriages for their journey into the powerful, spinning saw blade. The deafening *scree-rrrurr-scree* of the giant circular saw as it sliced these logs into lumber. As we pulled into the driveway, I smelled fresh tree sap and the pungent sawdust that billowed from the open building that housed the engine, blades, carriages, pulleys, and belts, all laboring together to produce Hagen's fine grade of lumber.

I steered the team toward the old milk house that served as Elmer's office. I waved at two German POWs, wearing the familiar army fatigues emblazoned with large *PWs*. Elmer had hired the pair to supplement his crew after his two sons enlisted.

Our stakes were neatly stacked against the milk-house wall. While Grandpa went inside to take care of the paperwork, Danny and I loaded them into the wagon. Each was planed smooth to minimize the chance of splinters. One end had been angle-cut, twice, to form a sharp point, designed for easy sinking into the ground. The workmanship displayed by the Hagen workers was always impressive.

When we finished loading, Danny and I went into the office to escape the noise. As we entered, Mr. Hagen was speaking to Grandpa. "Yep, Katz and Jammer get a kick out of my nickname for 'em. They been with me since the POW camp first got here. They're fine fellows. Real hard workers with pleasant dispositions. I trust 'em fully, like members of the family. Shoot, they stay right here in the milk house every night. Take all their meals in the kitchen with me and my wife. Yep, they're fine boys, all right."

He paused to acknowledge our presence. Then he continued. "The two new ones are off cutting trees today. They're just the opposite. Wouldn't trust 'em as far as I could throw 'em. I don't let 'em eat with us. Bring their dinners in sacks put together for 'em by the cook over to the little POW camp at the pea vinery. I won't let 'em stay here after work. They go back to the pea vinery to spend the night. Since they got armed guards at night there, none of 'em gets tempted to make a run for it. These two new guys done that before, you know?"

"What's that, Elmer?" asked Grandpa.

"Made a run for it. They're the ones that ran off with them two Libby sisters. Reitter and Baden! That's their names. Wouldn't trust 'em as far as I could throw 'em. No, sir. Not them two."

Danny's eyes widened. He shuddered and turned to me. "Jase, I'm scared!"

"Grandpa, I think we should go!"

GRANDPA HAD JUST THE right remedy for Danny's concern about the ominous presence of Reitter and Baden. "With huntin' season just around the corner, you oughta learn to shoot a gun, Danny. How'd you like Jase to give you a lesson after we finish postin' the signs?"

Immediately Danny's disposition turned from glum to gleeful. Grinning wildly, he grabbed the nearest hammer and madly pounded the wagon bed. "Careful, son, don't want to smash that trigger finger! Jase, you can use the .22. I bought a new box of shells, long rifles. They're on the ammunition shelf."

I knew exactly where they were. I had spotted them that morning as I poured the milk into the cream separator in the back shed. An array of pegs beside the kitchen door accommodated Grandpa's old 12-gauge shotgun, the .22 caliber, single-shot rifle that I used to take potshots at distant crows, and his heavy canvas hunting coat with the roomy game pocket in the back.

Because of frequent visits by younger grandchildren, those firearms were never returned to their pegs until they had been unloaded and the ammunition stored in the colorful boxes of shotgun and rifle shells on a high shelf above the egg-grading table, far beyond the reach of the youngsters.

Grandpa also owned a handsome .30 caliber, lever-action deer rifle snugly buttoned in its sheepskin cover. But this valuable firearm was hidden under his rock-hard, horsehair mattress in the small front bedroom where he slept when Grandma snored. And where I slept when she didn't.

We posted the first signs along Barrington Road. Then we entered Grandpa's south field that was covered with wheat stubble and low-growing hay, sufficient to hide many a succulent pheasant. This field butted up against the Donaldson cow pasture that was enclosed by an electric fence. Not taking any chances, Grandpa warned Danny that the fence in front of us was electric. And, if he touched it, he would experience a nasty jolt. Danny stepped back and gave the dangerous *hot* strand of barbed wire a wide berth.

As a young boy, like all the Compton grandsons, I was fascinated with electric fences. I was particularly fond of the one running from the barnyard to the woods where the cows spent their summer days grazing and lazing. Receiving jolts from this fence was a rite of passage among us cousins. Whether by accident or by trickery, each of us was obligated, before the age of eight, to take his turn being shocked by that dear old fence.

When a nervous younger cousin failed to volunteer quickly enough, we certified shock-takers resorted to deception. First, we shut off the power to the fence using the switch on the transformer, a large red box mounted on the horse barn.

Grasping the barbed wire fence, we would swear, *See! It doesn't hurt! You try it.*

As soon as the victim grabbed the wire, we switched on the power. Without fail, the fence knocked the younger cousin on his butt. We laughed until we cried at the sight of the victim running back to the house with his hair standing on end! What fun!

As we were finishing the stretch along the pasture, I looked up to see Ralph Donaldson coming across the field toward us. He was a tall, broad-shouldered man, dressed in denim coveralls and a white sleeveless undershirt. He wore this outfit every day, indoors and outdoors, all year-round. There was definitely something different about how his body reacted to hot and cold and, as he had often demonstrated, to electric shock.

"Grandpa, here comes Mr. Donaldson." Grandpa looked at me and wiggled his eye brows. I knew what he was thinking. "I wonder if he'll show Danny his trick."

"What trick?" Danny wanted to know.

"You'll see," Grandpa promised him.

Ralph Donaldson kept walking until he reached the electric fence.

"Mornin', Ralph."

"Mornin', Bill. Master Jase. Who's the new hand?"

"This is Danny Tucker, Ralph. He's a town boy, workin' on becomin' a farmer." Ralph smiled. This was excellent news to him. He leaned forward and placed his sizeable hands on the electric fence, pushed it down, and stepped over it. As he did so, tiny threads of lightning danced around his gold wedding ring and around the brass grommets in his work shoes.

"Pleased to meet you, Danny," he said, offering his once electrically-charged hand. Danny looked at Grandpa and then at me. We were both trying very hard not to laugh.

Danny smiled and grabbed Mr. Donaldson's hand.

"Mr. Donaldson, you just gotta show me how to do that!"

JUST AS GRANDPA PREDICTED, we finished posting Old Nate's farm and made it back home by noon. After watering the horses and turning them loose to graze in the small fenced yard outside the horse barn, we headed inside. Grandma met us on the side porch with good news.

"Dinner's all ready. Just wash your hands and set down."

During dinner, we gave Grandma the bad news about Reitter and Baden. She shivered, reached over, and hugged Danny. "Don't you worry about a thing! They're way off down the road. They don't know you're here. Besides you'll be going home in the morning. Grandpa's got his shotgun handy. And Mick is a dandy watch dog." At the sound of his name, the ever-alert fox terrier rolled over in his box next to the kitchen stove, opened one eye, and yawned.

"Dad, did you say anything to Elmer about those rascals and this youngster?"

Before we left the Hagen farm, Grandpa had talked to Elmer Hagen while Danny and I waited in the wagon. I didn't know what was said and, for Danny's sake, I didn't ask.

"Well, I informed him about the threats to Danny. He didn't like that one bit, but it didn't surprise him. He promised me that he would try to get those two reassigned. Maybe over to the pea vinery. If not, at least have an armed guard assigned to them at the mill. Apparently the army offered a guard, but Elmer decided it wasn't needed. He'd had such good luck with his first pair of POWs, I guess he got a little overconfident. But he'll do what's right. He doesn't trust those bad apples any more than we do."

After dinner, I retrieved the .22 rifle from its pegs in the back shed and grabbed the box of shells. As an experienced gun-handler, I was completely trusted to use firearms at the farm, even at a very young age. Like every red-blooded Michigan boy, my first gun was a Red Ryder BB gun. From there I graduated to a six-shot, bolt-action .22 caliber rifle. My first shotgun was a 4-10, but I never got the hang of it. I missed a lot of pheasants with that gun. So my father bought me a single barrel, 20-gauge shotgun that fit me to a tee and improved my shooting immensely. I still own that gun and I'll never part with it.

Danny talked incessantly as we headed for the shade of the maple tree beside the house, my customary spot for taking potshots at crows. "Can I hold it, please, Jase?" Danny held the rifle as I went through the basics. I showed him how to hold the rifle. Aim. And finally how to squeeze the trigger properly to improve his chances of hitting the target. All through my lesson, I emphasized the safety aspects of firing a gun.

Danny listened intently, appearing to understand and appreciate the seriousness of what I was telling him. To allow him to hear the rifle's report, I took the first shot. I wanted him to be familiar with its sound before he fired his first round. The puff of dust in the distance let me know that my shot hit ten feet to the left of my target, a giant crow scavenging for leftovers in the stubble field across the road.

"Okay! You try now." Danny loaded the rifle carefully. Raised it to his shoulder. Took very careful aim. And fired.

Crack. Ping.

"I hit something! What was it?" he yelled.

"Hold your fire! Hold your fire!" hollered Grandpa as he hurried toward us from the house. "What were you shootin' at?"

"Those crows over there!" Danny pointed at a small flock of crows about thirty degrees to the right of my target crow.

"Well, congratulations, Danny! You just plugged Grandma's mailbox!"

"Yep, I know. That's what I was aiming at," Danny vowed with a sly grin.

Grandpa looked at me and shook his head. Then he headed for the mailbox to inspect the damage.

"I really like hunting season, don't you, Jase?"

Is there a bag limit for mailboxes?

AFTER STORING THE RIFLE in the back shed, we retrieved two leftover sign stakes from the wagon and walked back to the house. Mick was curled up on the porch steps, pretending not to hear us coming.

"Watch this, Danny," I whispered. "Mick! Let's go huntin', boy!"

I raised the stake to my shoulder and mimicked the sound of a discharging shotgun.

Che-um! Che-um!

Mick leaped to his feet, *yapped* excitedly, and ran in circles around us, impressing Danny with his enthusiasm. We set off down the road for the south field where I suspected we'd be successful. Mick ran ahead, returned to *yap* once more, and then ran on ahead again. He repeated this maneuver several times before we reached the field.

"Doesn't he know these aren't real guns?"

"Well, sometimes I use a stick. Other times a corn stalk. Mick loves hunting so much that he's not very fussy."

But that wasn't entirely correct. Mick was extremely fussy when it came to choosing his hunting partners. He refused to hunt for anyone but Grandpa or me. Even my father couldn't entice Mick to join him in the fields. And what a hunter he was! When we reached the south field, the impatient terrier immediately put his nose to the ground and systematically traced wide arcs in front of us, searching for a fresh pheasant scent. "When he finds a pheasant, be ready to run," I warned.

Suddenly Mick *yelped,* lowered his nose, and took off. Danny and I gave chase. Two pheasant hens flushed almost immediately. I *shot* them both.

Che-um! Che-um!

Danny followed suit.

Ba-loom! Ba-loom!

But the frenetic fox terrier continued to run and *yelp.* "It's a rooster!" I yelled.

Cocks are wily. Unlike the hens, they seldom flush early, preferring to outrun a hunter or a dog. But fox terriers are very fast. The most difficult part of hunting with Mick was keeping up with him and his quarry.

"I'll try to head him off!" I angled for the corner nearest the Donaldson cornfield that I figured was the bird's ultimate destination. By running at top speed, I passed Mick. Danny lagged behind, staying on the dog's tail. When I reached the corner, I was only about fifty feet ahead of where I thought the pheasant was probably located. I looped to my left and ran straight at Mick, hoping to flush the bird with a squeeze play.

Whoosh!

The ring-necked beauty kicked up right in front of me and flew over my head toward the corn. Defiantly he serenaded me with his *ca-ca-ca-ca*. But I silenced him with a blast from my stake-gun. Joyously Mick leaped and *yelped*. And leaped again.

"Did you get him?" Danny yelled between pants.

"Yep! Wasn't that fun?"

"Yeah! But how do we get Mick to find us another one?" Danny didn't know it, but Mick was just warming up. We hunted the rest of the afternoon, *bagging* 23 hens and twelve roosters. Not bad for a couple of young hunters and a fox terrier.

We deposited our stake *shotguns* on the lumber pile and hurried into the house.

"Any luck, boys?" I gave Grandpa a detailed scouting report, including locations, counts, and specific descriptions of the pheasants we had flushed, including estimated age, sex, and unusual markings. While I reported, Mick lapped from his water bowl for, what seemed like, five full minutes. Danny helped Grandma prepare supper by inventorying the contents of her refrigerator.

"Boy, that's excellent news, Jase. You boys'll be able to hire out as huntin' guides when the season opens."

"Now who's that coming?" Grandma was standing on her tiptoes, peering out the window over the kitchen sink. "I don't know who it is, but the car's sure beautiful."

"Anybody home?" The voice sounded familiar to me. "Hello, Bill! It's me E.F."

"Hello, E.F.! What brings you out to the country? Haven't seen you since that day at the stockyards. Maw! Put an extra plate on the table. We got company!"

"No, no! I can't stay, Bill. Sure smells good, though. I apologize for dropping in right at supper time. But I was out this way looking over a herd of beef cattle that's for sale and —."

He interrupted himself as he entered the kitchen. "Evenin' Miz Compton. I'm E.F. Graham. I believe we met when Bill and I served on that county fair committee a few years back. How you been?"

"Just fine, Mr. Graham." Turning to us she said, "I believe you know the boys."

Our friendship with Mr. Graham had gotten off to a rocky start. E.F. Graham owned a chain of neighborhood grocery stores in Riverton. Without knowing the details of an incident involving Danny and me and one of his store managers, E.F. Graham had essentially accused us of fibbing. But, thanks to Mom's intervention, he realized his error, apologized, and fully redeemed himself by contributing generously to the Matlock fund-raiser. We now considered him a decent man and good friend.

"Hello, boys. Nice to see you again." After we exchanged pleasantries, Mr. Graham revealed the purpose of his visit.

"Bill, I need to ask you for a favor. This coming weekend, I've got a couple of important Chicago bankers in town for three days of meetings. Initially we planned to meet on Friday and Saturday. Then finish up on Sunday. But you know how Mrs. Graham feels about working on the Sabbath! So we postponed the last day's meeting until Monday. I need some way of entertaining these two gents on Sunday. I racked my brain for days. Then I realized Sunday's the opening of hunting season. I was hoping —."

"They'd be welcome to hunt here on Sunday, E.F."

Mr. Graham smiled from ear-to-ear. Then he got serious again. "I'm aware you and your neighbors in the township are using the permit system this year. Darn fine idea, by the way. But will you have enough permits for the three of us, plus your family?"

Grandpa explained his arrangement with Old Nate. Then he counted the number of hunters he expected. "Well, of course, there's me. But I don't count. Owners don't need permits or huntin' licenses to hunt their own property. Then there's your three. John Addison's bringin' Sam Tucker. And one for our son Raymond, if he decides to drive down. The last two're for Jase and Danny there. It works out just right!"

Danny? Grandma must have found a recipe for fricasseed mailbox.

After thanking Grandpa about five hundred times, Mr. Graham finally departed. Then Danny and I peppered Grandpa with questions about Danny being on the list of hunters. Instead of answering us, he picked up his RFD-delivered, day-old newspaper and sat down in his rocking chair. This was indeed strange behavior for him. I couldn't remember ever being ignored by Grandpa Compton.

I looked to Grandma for help. She seemed upset about something. Finally she let Grandpa know what it was. "Blabbermouth!" she declared.

"Sorry!" was all he said. Then he tried, unsuccessfully, to change the subject. "You boys be sure to have your fathers take you down to Pete's for your hunting licenses."

"Dad! For goodness sakes! You say another word and you'll sleep in the barn tonight!"

After pondering that possibility, Danny offered some sage advice, "Better stay clear of Sarah!"

THE NEXT MORNING, GRANDMA drove us home. As we came to a dusty stop in front of our house, I noticed three people standing under the cottonwood tree. Before I could say anything, Danny beat me to it. "Hey, they can't have an FSG meeting without us!"

The meeting broke up and the three offenders walked our way. Grandma went into the house to say hello to Mom and Aunt Maude and check on little Johnnie. "Welcome home! Was it fun?" Queenie asked us pleasantly. Her unusual demeanor caught me off guard. But I decided to give her the benefit of the doubt when Danny surprised me.

"We had a great time. I shot a gun. And we killed 35 *ring-tailed peasants!* How was your birthday party?"

"Birthday party! I didn't know it was your birthday. How old are you? Who came? What did you get? What games did you play?" I sputtered.

"Yesterday was my thirteenth birthday. With no school, my mother let me have a party. I invited ten people so I got lots of presents. When you come over, I'll show them to you." Queenie was being *sooooooo* nice! I didn't get it. "We played spin the bottle. Pass a life saver on a toothpick. And we played pass the orange under your chin. Do you know that one?"

"We don't play that orange game. I guess it's just for girls."

"Oh, no! The two boys liked it best. Even better than soccer-baseball they said."

"Pass the orange! Spin the bottle! You didn't have two boys there! You had two sissies!" Danny informed her in no uncertain terms. Then he turned around to seek moral support from the FSG *men*. Butch's face turned red as he clicked his heel plates on the sidewalk and stared at his belt buckle. And Sherm, nervously, adjusted the seat of his pants and wiped his nose, four times.

Danny was about to launch his attack on the two *birthday boys* when Queenie started up our walk. "Where are *you* going?" he snapped.

"To Jase's room. Being thirteen, I'm now Johnnie's official baby-sitter. By the way, do you know that Aunt Maude *just loves* Big Band music?"

The Big Game Hunter threw his hands in the air and declared, "FSG's going to the dogs!"

Poodles would be more like it.

We were beside ourselves when Mr. Tucker pulled up in his battered Dodge station wagon.

"I saw you guys go by in Mrs. Compton's Terraplane. So I figured I'd come over before you disappeared somewhere. We gotta go to Pete's to buy your hunting licenses."

I looked at Danny and asked, "Are we the only ones in the dark?"

There was nothing more macho than having a hunting license pinned to the back of your shirt or jacket. Some boys wore it all the time. To school, to play, to church, and naturally to hunt! They even wore it year-round, hunting season or not.

Back in those days, a small-game hunting license entitled you to hunt a wide range of species that fell into two categories, closed-season game and open-season game. Those having closed seasons for a portion of the year were also protected by specific daily and season bag limits. Game falling into this category included pheasant, rabbit, squirrel, quail, grouse, dove, woodcock, and waterfowl. To hunt waterfowl you needed to purchase an additional duck stamp, entitling you to hunt duck, merganser, coot, moorhen, snipe, rail, and Canadian goose. Of course, there was open season and no bag limits on certain undesirable species. Skunk, woodchuck, and crow were definitely in the cross hairs of the hunting license folks.

When we arrived at Pete's, out of Danny's earshot, I asked, "But, Mr. Tucker, Danny doesn't have a gun for hunting pheasants. Why does he need a license?" Mr. Tucker got that same look on his face that Grandpa did just before Grandma called him a blabbermouth. But Sam Tucker was no blabbermouth. He was a *blabbereye*. He winked at me and smiled.

I guess Danny's the only one in the dark now.

When Dad arrived home from work, Danny and his father were sitting on the back porch chatting with Mom, Aunt Maude, and me. Completely updated on Johnnie's every facet, Grandma had left for home. And, mercifully, Queenie had finally sauntered off. Dad opened the conversation that Danny and I had waited twenty-four hours to hear. "Jase, your 4-10 is going to Danny."

I was filled with mixed emotions. I would certainly miss my very first shotgun, but I was delighted that Danny now had a hunting weapon. *But what was I going to use?*

"Your new shotgun is out in the car!" And that's how I became the owner of my 20-gauge shotgun.

"Come on, Danny. Let's go see our new guns!"

As darkness fell over the neighborhood, Danny and I sat silently on the porch steps with our new shotguns over our knees. "Sorry about your new gun, Jase."

"Sorry. What do you mean?"

"Well, my first shot ever was with a 22, right?" I nodded my head. "So I'm sorry that you had to go from a 410 all the way back down to a 20."

"But, Danny, that's —."

"I won't tell anybody."

Oh, Danny. I just knew I could count on your discretion.

THE WEEK BEFORE HUNTING season was pretty much a loss as far as school was concerned. Reentry after any four-day weekend would have required time for the class to settle back into the established routine. But, with nearly every boy in class daydreaming about pheasants, shotguns, and hunting dogs, attention spans were almost as short as teacher patience.

During the remaining three days of that week, Miss Sparks had no trouble identifying those of us whose minds were already in the fields and woods around Riverton. We wore new hunting caps, boots, canvas jackets, and, of course, brilliant red hunting licenses framed in shiny plastic holders pinned to our backs. In an effort to impress certain boys, certain girls accessorized with pheasant feathers all that week.

One morning, poor Danny was sent home after a half dozen 4-10 shells spilled out of his new hunting jacket and rolled across the floor, causing all the girls to scream and flee to the opposite end of the classroom.

However, those of us who were knowledgeable hunters, not just townies trying to look macho, shared a major concern about the season opening. There had been no appreciable rain for two weeks and none in the forecast. The near-drought conditions gave the distinct advantage to the pheasant whose scent would be harder than ever for even the finest hunting dogs to detect. We all crossed our fingers and wished for rain. Despite those last sleepless nights filled with a mixture of warm dreams of hunting success and vivid nightmares of missed shots, opening day finally arrived.

"Jase! Jase, wake up!" Dad whispered. "Get dressed and have some breakfast. The Tuckers will be here any minute. Get your gear together and meet me in the kitchen, okay?"

My gear had been together for days so that was no concern. As I brushed my teeth, I assessed the familiar emotion that I felt on every opening day, an edgy tension born out of my intense desire to shoot well in the presence of Dad and Grandpa. Now Danny and Mr. Tucker were added to my list of people I didn't want to let down. After carrying my gear to the front room, I joined Dad in the kitchen.

"Not even a drop of dew." He had answered me before I asked.

We heard the Tucker station wagon creak to a stop in front of the house. We turned on the front porch light to see our way out to the car. "Morning, Sam. Danny. Are you rarin' to go?"

After we stored our equipment, I crawled into the dark back seat with Danny. "Here, Jase!" he whispered. Then he reached over, pried open my hand, and placed on my palm what felt like a shard of porcelain. "I finally got one."

"Great! Now you're ready!"

Since receiving the gift of my old 4-10 shotgun, Mr. Tucker had put Danny through a two-session, crash course on how to shoot his gun safely and accurately. He borrowed a clay pigeon trap, a device that shot clay disks into the air, so Danny could practice on the bird-like, moving targets. The three of us assembled the rig in the open field near Trumble Park where skeet shooters practiced regularly.

Danny took awhile to master the process. On his first few attempts, he yelled, *Pull!* and pulled his trigger at the same time, even before the pigeon left the trap. To his credit, Mr. Tucker patiently explained that Danny's *ready-fire-aim* approach was not particularly effective. Despite outstanding coaching, that evening the clay pigeon team won 60 to 0. Feeling my presence might not be helping Danny's concentration, I offered to skip the second lesson. Mr. Tucker seemed grateful. It must have worked because Danny *finally got one.*

As we pulled into the farm driveway, a faint glow in the eastern sky announced that dawn would not be long in coming. We stacked our gear next to the porch and went into the kitchen. Grandma greeted us with large mugs of steaming coffee and assorted goodies. Having already eaten, we settled for a fried cake or two. Soon we heard the Graham party pull into the driveway.

"They're right on time," Grandpa advised, checking the kitchen clock over the sink. "John, I thought I would go with them and hunt the south end of the farm. With this dryness, their dogs should do better there in the hayfield. But dry fields never bother Mick. So you, Sam, and the boys can go to the north end. Hunt the creek — I should have said — dry creek on over to Old Nate's and then swing back here, say, midmornin'. Then we can change ends."

As we left the kitchen, Grandpa handed a permit to each of us. "Here's your permits. Keep 'em with you. Stick 'em behind your license in your holder there."

Leaving the porch, we saw Mr. Graham and his two banker associates retrieving their equipment from the trunk of his shiny black Cadillac. Their hunting outfits and guns were first class. From the other vehicle, a wood-paneled station wagon, a gaunt man smoking a pipe attached leashes to a pair of sleek English Setters. At a safe distance, Mick studied his highbrow competition with detached indifference.

Mr. Graham introduced everyone except the man who was tying the hunting dogs to the door handle of his station wagon. "Joe, come over and meet these folks. Folks, this is Joe Morgan, my dog trainer. And over there are my two bird dogs, Ham and Bullet. Not only are they champion show dogs, but they're two mighty fine hunters." Upon hearing that news, Mick uttered a low growl that ended when I touched him with my toe.

"Bill, we want to thank you again for inviting us out to spend opening day with you. How are we going to do this?"

Grandpa outlined his hunting assignments for the day and we set off. With Mick in the lead, our team walked the road north until we reached the bridge over the creek. Dad presented his plan. "Let's hunt the creek over to that cornfield. Jase and I'll take this side and you two take that side. We'll set up differently when we reach the corn." I reminded Dad that Mick had flushed three pheasants from the dry creek bed just days before. "Okay, let's be alert!"

We stepped off the road and began to descend the bank. Suddenly Mick let out a *yelp*, crashed down the bank, and attacked an island of dry rushes in the middle of the creek bed. Two roosters burst into the air. One flew north and the other south.

Bam! Bam!

Mr. Tucker and Dad had downed our first two birds. Danny and I hadn't gotten a shot off.

"Jase! You were dead right. Sam, good shootin'. You got yourself a nice bird there. At this rate, we'll have our bag limit before the sun's hardly up."

When we reached the corn, Dad formulated another plan. "Jase, you walk through the corn at this end. When you get over to the east edge, hurry on up to the north end. Cut 'em off if they try to run across the road up there. Sam, why don't you follow Jase over to the east and walk that edge at my pace? Danny, you walk up this edge, but don't get too far ahead. Keep your eyes open. Those roosters like to double back on the edges. Mick and I'll go up the middle, makin' a lot of noise, to drive 'em to you other fellas, okay?" We had used this plan many times before, especially in fields of dry corn stalks.

Just as I reached my position I heard Mick's *yelping* and seconds later a shot from Mr. Tucker's gun.

Bam!

From the shouts, I knew Mr. Tucker had reached his two rooster bag limit. The hunt resumed and Mick's *yelps* indicated that he was working yet another bird. Suddenly a flock of pheasants lifted out of the center of the cornfield just ahead of Dad. "Hens! All hens! Don't shoot!"

Five minutes later, another bird launched in front of Dad. I heard another shot from Dad's gun.

Bam!

"Missed him! Danny! He's flyin' low! Headin' your way!"

Pop!

Silence.

"Danny did you get him?" Silence. "Sam! Jase! Come take a look at this!"

I ran toward Danny's position. When I broke out of the corn, Mr. Tucker and Dad were looking down on Danny who was admiring the handsome rooster cradled in his arms.

"You did it, Danny!"

"I knew I would!"

Tell it to those 60 winning clay pigeons!

Mick's *yelping* brought us back to reality. Feeling happy for my friend, I turned to run back to my post. I didn't want to miss the chance of getting a bird from the most fruitful part of the field. Rounding the end of the cornfield, I nearly stumbled over a fat rooster. Obviously he was the object of Mick's loud *yapping*. I wasn't sure who was more startled, the pheasant or me. But the rooster lowered his head and dashed back into the corn.

After a particularly passionate series of *yelps*, the bird panicked and took to the air. I raised my new 20-gauge, took aim, and fired. As the bird plummeted to earth, my emotions soared. I'd done it! My first pheasant of the season! This was going to be a good day after all. "Dad! I got one! Dad!"

About an hour later, Dad got his second rooster. With both men at their bag limits, we decided to call it a day. When we entered the driveway, it was about nine o'clock. Much to our surprise, the entire Graham party including Grandpa had beaten us home. The dogs were back in the station wagon. My first thought was that they had reached their bag limits and were calling it a day as well. But, as we got closer, I saw that the trainer had traded in his fancy duds for Grandpa's old overalls and milking jacket. It was a curious scene. Without saying a word, Grandpa turned to us and smiled. Mr. Graham finally let us know what happened.

"I hope you boys had better luck than we did. Not a whiff of a pheasant. I've never seen anything like it. Those champion hunters of mine shuttled back and forth, back and forth, for two hours. Not one scent. Not one point. Nothing! Nothing until — well, Joe won't like me telling this. But Old Ham there did get a scent. And what a scent it was! He came to point over in the wheat stubble next to the woods, just under that old hickory tree. Joe moved in to flush the bird then he — Haw! Haw! Then he — Hee! Hee!"

Mr. Graham couldn't contain himself. Neither could the rest of his party. The bankers and Grandpa joined him. The four of them laughed uncontrollably for five minutes. The only one not laughing was the smug dog trainer who reeked of skunk spray.

When the laughter died down, Mr. Graham asked us how we'd done. We answered him by laying out our six roosters on the grass. "Well, I'll be dogged. Look it there, Joe. Apparently it wasn't too dry for a *champion* fox terrier, was it? You been using that *dry* excuse all day. Now I suggest you get in the car and take those dogs home. And take a bath with lots of vinegar. Or bath salts. You smell something terrible."

Then Mr. Graham turned to Grandpa. "Bill, how'd you like to loan me Old Mick there? I wanta show these Chicago fellas some real Michigan hunting!"

"E.F., he'll only hunt for two people. Jase and me. Why don't I help John and Sam get these birds cleaned? Jase can take you out. He and Danny still need another bird to fill their bag limits. And Mick's as fresh as a daisy."

So off we went. Back to the same fields that had yielded zip for Ham and Bullet. On our way down the lane, I heard Danny reveal the secret of successful hunting to one of the bankers.

"Before opening day, I always practice on *clay pilgrims*. And sometimes mailboxes."

ALL FIVE OF US bagged our limits by midafternoon. Since they hadn't counted on footracing their way through the hunt, the men were dragging. Still full of enthusiasm and energy, Mick was disappointed that we were headed home. Upon reaching the cow barn, I recognized the smell of freshly roasted pheasant wafting our way from the kitchen. I hoped we would arrive before the birds were carved and dispersed among the anonymous meat dishes on the warming shelf.

When we reached the driveway, Mr. Graham and the bankers stored their guns and coats in the Cadillac's enormous trunk. They insisted that their six pheasants go home with Danny and me. We couldn't say no. And E.F. didn't refuse Grandpa's offer of dinner this time either. Danny and I propped my .20 gauge and his 4-10 against the porch and went inside.

The kitchen was overflowing with the makings of a feast including roast pheasant, cornbread dressing, mashed potatoes and gravy, green beans, applesauce, and freshly baked bread. For dessert, several pies were cooling on the window sill. The dining-room table was set for a formal dinner, or at least as formal as dinners ever were at the farm.

"You men go right on in and set down. I'll put dinner out. After everybody's got what they need, I'll join you," Grandma ordered, waving us to the table.

The fresh pheasant was mouth-watering, its succulent dark meat seasoned with a tasty hint of gaminess. We chewed carefully to avoid biting down on the lead shot often embedded in pheasants bagged by shotgun. While Sunday dinners at the farm were always excellent, this one was exceptional. Unlike other Sundays, the rest of the Compton family, knowing it was opening day, had stayed home. So ours was more like one big stag dinner and I loved it. We ate and ate until no one, including Danny, had room for another bite.

It was dark outside before we pushed back our chairs and sat, silently, staring at the center of the table. Finally Mr. Graham broke the silence. "Mrs. Compton, this meal reminds me of our dinners at home when I was growing up. There's something about eating freshly bagged game at the farm. Your cooking is very similar to that of my late mother, bless her soul. It was delicious, all the way around. Thank you so much for having us."

Following the chorus of like compliments showered on Grandma by the Tuckers, the Chicago contingent, and the

Addisons, Danny and I helped her clear the dishes and leftovers from the table. After topping off the coffee cups, the three of us retired to the kitchen to tackle the dirty pots, pans, and dishes.

The men reached for their cigarettes or pipes and conversation about the war filled the air. "Did you hear that the Allies liberated Athens? How about that Rommel, the old Desert Fox himself, committin' suicide? Hear about the Sixth Army invading Leyte? Yep! Gen'rl MacArthur *shall return,* all right."

GENERAL MACARTHUR'S SIMPLE PHASE, *I shall return,* is among the most famous in American history. A genius when it came to using the press to his advantage, the general coined the phrase almost unintentionally. After his harrowing evacuation from the Philippines by Lieutenant John D. Bulkeley, commanding Patrol Torpedo (PT) Boat Squadron Three, MacArthur issued the following statement:

The President of the United States ordered me to break through the Japanese lines and proceed from Corregidor to Australia for the purpose of, as I understand it, organizing the American offensive against Japan, a primary objective of which is the relief of the Philippines. I came through and I shall return.

MacArthur's pledge became the rallying cry of those eager to revenge the egregious atrocities committed by the Japanese against American and Filipino POWs during their forced march from Corregidor, known as the *Bataan Death March.* An army intelligence officer on MacArthur's staff suggested his pledge be printed on packages of cigarettes and companion matchbooks and distributed to the brave American and Filipino guerrillas still fighting the Japanese occupiers. Smuggled in by American submarines and dropped from B-24 Liberator bombers, the cigarettes and matches were accompanied by round mirrored reflectors for signaling aircraft. As an afterthought, a practical sewing kit was also included.

The heroic story of General MacArthur's rescue by Lieutenant Bulkeley was depicted in John Ford's 1945 movie based on William White's best-selling book, *They Were Expendable.* The part of Bulkeley was played by Robert Montgomery and his executive officer, Robert Kelley, was played by John Wayne. For his brave acts, John Bulkeley was awarded the Medal of Honor. He was to become one of the three most highly decorated heroes of World War II. His only peers were army infantryman and future movie star, Audie Murphy, and marine general, Lewis B. "Chesty" Puller.

Before his distinguished navy career ended, Vice Admiral John D. Bulkeley's awards included the Medal of Honor, the Navy Cross, two Distinguished Service Crosses, three Distinguished Service Medals, the Silver Star, the Legion of Merit with the "V" for valor, two Bronze Stars, the French Croix de Guerre, and the Purple Heart. But of all his awards, honors, and war mementoes, the one he held dearest was a dollar bill covered with the autographs of fellow war heroes, world leaders, and movie stars. He kept the bill hidden deep in his wallet and showed it to only a few privileged people. I was honored to have been one of those.

During the Cuban Missile Crisis, Admiral Bulkeley commanded the Naval Base at Guantanamo Bay where he gained worldwide fame for his dramatic face-down of Fidel Castro when the Cuban dictator threatened to cut off drinking water to the base. For this act of defiance, Bulkeley became a hero in the eyes of Cuban emigrants to America who often sought him out to back their plans to overthrow Castro. I personally witnessed a number of these exchanges.

In 1967, he was appointed as President of the Naval Board of Inspection and Survey, a critically important organization of naval officers and civilian engineers responsible for conducting acceptance trials and materiel inspections of all naval ships, submarines, and aircraft. Thanks to a special act of Congress, he served as board president well beyond normal retirement age. In 1987, he retired with fifty-five years of naval service. After his death in 1996, he was honored by the commissioning of the USS Bulkeley, an Arleigh Burke destroyer.

My own last assignment as a naval officer was also with the Board of Inspection and Survey. There I had the honor of serving as Admiral Bulkeley's personal aide and administrative officer. He was one of the most unforgettable people I've ever known, ranking right up there with Danny.

AFTER AN EXCHANGE OF opinions on the progress of the war, predictably, Grandpa suggested a friendly game of setback. He retrieved his lucky deck of cards and began shuffling. "Shall we make it interesting?" one of the bankers asked as Grandpa dealt the first hand.

"Not on the Sabbath, we don't! Hunting is pushing the limit. But gambling, for real money? Not on your life," E.F. declared. "But, Bill, if you've got some chips. Or toothpicks. Or kitchen matches, I think we could add a *little* zest to the game without incurring anyone's wrath."

"No poker chips. Never use 'em. Toothpicks! Don't need 'em with these choppers of mine. But matches we got. Hey, Jase! Could you come here a minute?" he hollered.

When Danny and I entered the smoke-filled room, Grandpa asked me to retrieve the box of kitchen matches from the shelf next to the stove.

"Danny, would you mind doing me a favor?" my father asked. "My tobacco pouch is laying on the dashboard of the station wagon. Would you kindly run out and get it for me?"

As I returned with the matches, I could hear the low rumble of a heavy vehicle pulling into the far end of the driveway. The vehicle chugged to a stop as the driver turned off the engine.

"Now who do you suppose that is?" Grandpa asked, more interested in sorting his cards than hearing an answer to his question. "Probably somebody from Maw's church comin' to see her."

He made no effort to check for himself. "She'll take care of it."

He handed each player a dozen matches and announced, "Penny a match. Everybody, ante up."

Rrrrr-roomem! Roomem! The low hum of a high-performance car engine caught everyone's attention. But it was Mr. Graham's reaction that sent us all running to the side porch. "Hey! That's my Cadillac!"

The sleek black sedan roared out the driveway, leaving clouds of dry dust swirling in the glow of the yard light. Within seconds, we saw the car's headlights approaching the intersection of Henry Road a half-mile away. Suddenly the lights vanished. Extinguished on purpose, no doubt. Soon the sound of the Cadillac's twelve-cylinder engine was lost in the evening air. At first, we just stood there, not believing our eyes.

Then Mr. Graham came to his senses. "Let's go inside and call the sheriff. They took my car! And all our hunting gear! Blazes! Why did I leave those keys in the ignition?"

As we turned toward the house, Grandpa reminded us, "We don't have a telephone! Let's go to the Henry's and use theirs. You better drive, John. Jase, look around to see if anything else's missin' while we're gone."

The two bankers looked at each other and shrugged their shoulders. Since their guns and coats were borrowed, initially at least, they thought they hadn't lost much. With Mr. Tucker's and Dad's gear in the station wagon with the pheasants from the late morning hunt, he was okay too.

Suddenly I thought of my new shotgun. I turned to look at the spot next to the porch where Danny and I had propped our guns. They were gone. "They took our guns too. Danny! They took our guns!" I yelled, not sure where my friend was lurking.

"Danny! Where are you?" Mr. Tucker yelled. He got no answer. "Must be inside." We walked briskly to the porch and entered the kitchen. "Have you seen Danny, Mrs. Compton?"

No one could remember seeing him after he left to retrieve Dad's tobacco pouch from the dashboard. Mr. Tucker's military training snapped into place. Calmly he organized our search party.

"Do you have any flashlights?" There were only two. Grandma was assigned the upstairs and basement of the house. Without a flashlight, the bankers used the yard light to help them check the buildings nearest the house, the two outhouses, and the chicken coops. Mr. Tucker armed with a flashlight took the horse barn and granary. Using the second flashlight, I headed for the cow barn and corncrib.

"Danny! Where are you?" I called. A feeling of panic and desperation gripped my chest. As I approached the barn, my flashlight penetrated the familiar shadow formed by the yard light and the side of the cow barn, a shadow that I suddenly realized was distorted. A chill of fear crept up my spine. I extinguished my flashlight to prevent whatever hid there from easily spotting me. I stopped so my eyes could adjust to the darkness.

Straining to identify the dark shape, I slowly crept forward. I turned my head slightly, taking advantage of the greater light sensitivity of my peripheral vision. When I was within twenty feet of the alien object, I finally recognized what it was.

A truck!

I had nearly forgotten about the sounds of a heavy vehicle that we had heard before all this started. I strained my ears. Not a sound. I took a deep breath and snapped on my flashlight. I gasped. And this was not just *any* truck. On the side of the cab, stark white lettering read:

Hagen Sawmill
Quality Lumber

"It's Reitter and Baden!" I screamed. "They've got Danny!"

9 MISSING DANNY

JUST SECONDS AFTER GRANDPA AND DAD HAD returned from the Henry's, two patrol cars pulled into the driveway. Having responded to an earlier call from Elmer Hagen about his missing truck, Sheriff Connors and a deputy were just starting their fact-finding at the nearby sawmill when the radio dispatcher notified them of the Graham car theft. Because the likely culprits in both cases were the infamous POW pair, the military police at Camp Riverton were also called. The MPs were expected to arrive on the scene at any moment.

Since Mr. Hagen might provide some needed information to the MPs, the sheriff brought him along too. Spotlights, trained on the parked truck, illuminated it sufficiently for Mr. Hagen to confirm that this was indeed his truck. Then the sheriff and the deputy conducted a preliminary inspection of the vehicle. Finding no obvious evidence indicating the whereabouts of the thieves and not wanting to smudge telltale fingerprints, they left the truck and joined us on the front walk.

Grandma had started a giant pot of coffee and placed pies, cakes, and cookies from her coffers on the kitchen table. "It's chilly out there. Why don't you menfolk come inside to conduct your business? Have a cup of fresh coffee and a snack."

The kitchen was soon crowded with nearly a dozen men sipping coffee and sampling Grandma's desserts. At the sound of additional vehicles arriving, I looked out to see Colonel Butler's familiar sedan and three jeeps filled with armed MPs.

Dad and I were well-acquainted with the three men who exited the sedan and entered the kitchen. Captain Junior Shurtleif, deputy commander of Camp Riverton. Sergeant Rick Prella, head of MP guards at the canning factory. Finally Otto Klump, former Luftwaffe lieutenant and leader of the POW squad that until recently had included Reitter and Baden.

Following introductions, we decided, for the sake of comfort, to convene our information exchange in the front room. But not before Grandma provided the new arrivals with mugs of coffee and heaping plates of goodies.

"I think we're all agreed that it's probably Reitter and Baden we're after," the sheriff observed. "So why don't we start from the beginning. How'd they get assigned to the sawmill in the first place?"

With credible assistance from Otto and Sergeant Rick, Junior described the threats made against Danny and the decision to move the two away from the canning factory and close proximity to our neighborhood.

"Mr. Hagen, how'd they work out for you?" Mr. Hagen described the two as completely untrustworthy and added that Danny's reaction to their presence at the sawmill prompted him to request their transfer back to the pea vinery.

"Did they know you requested their transfer?" Unfortunately he told us, they were informed of their impending departure by a loose-lipped sawmill hand who would be fired when he showed up for work the next morning.

"Is there anything else missing from the sawmill?" His face reddened as he reported that the weekend receipts were also missing. In addition to his truck, the fugitives had stolen over two hundred dollars in cash from the sawmill.

"I'm afraid that's not all the cash they have. My two guests and I locked our wallets in the Cadillac's trunk. And they were still there when the car was stolen. We figure they got at least five hundred dollars from us. Of course, our wallets contained our driver's licenses and other forms of identification. And they got our three ration books as well."

The sheriff calmly asked Mr. Graham if that was all. "No, I'm afraid not. They got all our street clothes and shoes, our hunting coats. And most importantly three pump shotguns and several boxes of shells. At least we removed the hunting permits from our license holders and gave them back to Bill before they stole the car."

"They also took Danny and Jase's shotguns," added Dad.

"So what we got here are two desperate Nazis loose in the countryside with a shiny Cadillac sedan. Civilian clothes and coats. Ration books to purchase all the gasoline they'll need. And mebbe seven hundred in cash to pay for it. Five shotguns and ammunition. And poor Danny, to boot. That about it?"

Attempting to add a little levity to the sheriff's sobering summation, Dad added, "No, doggone it! They got my new leather tobacco pouch filled with my best smoking tobacco too."

"Sorry to hear that, John. That'd make me mad too. Well, they got out of here with an impressive inventory of stolen property. But we aren't without resources ourselves. First of all, we already put out an all points bulletin on the Cadillac, the likely thieves, and, of course, the boy. That reminds me, Deputy, would you go out to the car radio and call in an amendment to our APB. Include the clothing, money, ration books, guns and ammunition, and so on." Assuring the sheriff that he had written down everything, the deputy left to put in the call. "As we speak, the Michigan State Troopers are erecting roadblocks encircling the county. That Cadillac is pretty noticeable so I'm optimistic about our chances there.

"Captain, we'll want your Criminal Investigation Division in on the case, as before. They'll want to follow the Cadillac's tire tracks as far as they can. I notice you brought three jeeps and men with you. How about using them to set up road blocks to preserve the Cadillac's tire tracks from being messed up by what little traffic there might be this time of night between here and Henry Road. You can station one here, south of the farm on Barrington Road. The other two up on Henry Road on either side of the intersection with Barrington. Have the other two jeeps drive south then split up and come in on Henry Road from opposite directions, if you follow my meaning."

Captain Shurtleif quickly nodded and then ordered, "Sergeant Prella, please take care of that right away."

"Yes, sir. Consider it done." Sergeant Prella left immediately. Once outside, he barked a set of terse orders to his men. Within seconds, the jeeps roared out of the driveway.

"Thank you, Captain. The POWs would probably have turned onto Henry Road because it's paved, preventing us from tracking them far. But it'd be important to know if they turned east or west on Henry. CID can let us know that.

"CID will also want to go over that truck with a fine-tooth comb. Lift prints as evidence to convict those two after we nab them. We're not dealing with a mere escape here. We're looking at grand theft auto and kidnapping. I'd like to see these rats do some hard prison time, say at Leavenworth. Or better yet get their butts hanged. Oh, excuse me, Missus Compton." Grandma dismissed his comment with a wave of a hand.

"After we leave here, my deputy'll go back to the sawmill to interview the other POWs there. I could use your help, Sergeant Prella. And you too, Lieutenant Klump. Mr. Tucker, we'll need a description of exactly what Danny was wearing and anything he might have had in his pockets, in addition to John's tobacco pouch."

"Sheriff, Colonel Butler stayed at the camp to get the ball rolling. Before we arrived here, he radioed me that the CID boys from Camp Custer will be here by sunup. They're topnotch so we can count on quality help from them. I suggest we establish a command center at your offices in New Albany. We'd do it out at the camp, but you're several miles closer to the crime scene."

"I'll head for New Albany and set that up right away. I'd like Mr. Hagen, Mr. Graham and his guests, and Mr. Tucker to come to my office. We'll take your formal statements there and have them typed up for your signatures." They agreed and gathered their belongings.

Before departing, Sheriff Connors paused, "I want to assure all of you, especially Mr. Tucker, that we will not rest until we've nabbed these Nazis. Not until Danny is safely back home."

For some reason, the grave seriousness of this situation hadn't struck me until that very moment. An immense surge of emotion rose in my chest. I nearly sobbed. Evidently sensing how I felt, Grandma put her arm around my shoulder and drew me close.

"I don't think I'll rest until Danny's safe either," I whispered to her.

She squeezed me tighter.

What would I do without my best friend?

AUNT MAUDE WOKE ME in time for school. Because of what we'd all been through, Mom suggested that I might like to stay home. But nothing sounded worse than sitting around the house thinking of Danny. Even though I'd had a fitful night, I needed to stay busy. School would help me forget, at least for a while.

I didn't feel like eating breakfast, but Mom insisted I have something. I settled for a piece of toast with butter and cinnamon, one of Danny's favorites. Not a wise choice. Each bite reminded me of yesterday's terrible events.

"They're talking about Danny on the morning news!" Aunt Maude hollered from our bedroom as she turned up the volume. Since WRDP was reporting the escape and kidnapping, the story was sure to be in the afternoon paper as well. We went into the bedroom to hear Chuck Nichols' report on Danny.

"— boy is the son of Mr. and Mrs. Sam Tucker of Riverton. The abduction took place last evening at the Compton farm in Barrington Township. The POWs were workers at the Hagen Sawmill located approximately two miles south of the farm on Riverton Road. The Germans made their escape in a stolen black Cadillac sedan belonging to E.F. Graham, owner of the Graham grocery chain here in Riverton. Mr. Graham and a number of business associates were at the farm taking advantage of yesterday's hunting season opener.

"Listeners will recall that Danny Tucker and his friend, Jase Addison, were involved with Reitter and Baden once before. The boys became local heroes for their role in the capture of these two prisoners who, with the assistance of the Libby sisters, escaped while working at the Chippewa Canning Corporation. The Libby sisters are currently serving time at the Women's Federal Prison in Bay City for their role in the escape.

"Since the Lindbergh case, Sheriff Roy Connors reminded us, kidnapping has been a capital crime punishable by death. The sheriff stated that he expects the two escapees to be prosecuted to the full extent of the law, most likely in a military court. The sheriff would not confirm this, but we have it on good authority that the state police have established roadblocks throughout the region. And that the army's Criminal Investigation Division from Camp Custer is assisting in the investigation.

"The sheriff stated that no formal schedule of press briefings will be established. Instead, impromptu briefings will be called when there is something to report. Photographs of the missing boy, the two prisoners, and the Graham Cadillac will appear in this afternoon's *Riverton Daily Press.*"

After we returned to the breakfast table, Dad quipped, "Well, well! You were on the radio again. You're getting to be quite a celebrity, you know?" I knew he was just trying to cheer me up so I smiled and went back to my toast. "When you're ready, how

'bout a ride to school? We can drop off the pheasants on the way."
Neither the Tuckers nor the Addisons were in the mood for a
pheasant dinner, so we decided to donate the eight birds to the
Good Mission Church. "The Buddy Roes will dine in style
tonight!"

"Gut morgen!" Hans Zeyer called as he mounted our back
porch steps. "Vee jest heer on zee radioh about Danny." We invited
him into the kitchen. "Zo sorry, Jase. You muzz be sadz."

"Thank you, Mr. Zeyer. I am sad. And afraid for Danny.
We —." I couldn't finish the sentence.

Mr. Zeyer confessed, "Me alzo." Then he excused himself and
ran to catch his bus that would take him to City Hall where he
worked as Deputy Director of the Riverton Department of Public
Works.

"I imagine a lot of people will say things like that to you. They
know how close you and Danny are. This might be a little hard for
you, but keep in mind that people need to talk about sad things.
They don't mean to make you feel uncomfortable. They're trying
to make themselves feel better," Mom wisely advised. "Remember
the things you said to Mrs. Mikas after she learned that Ivan was
killed in the war?"

I felt a twinge of guilt for feeling so badly about Danny.
Presumably he was still alive. But Mrs. Mikas had lost two sons in
the war. Aunt Maude and I often heard her weeping after we
turned out our lights at night. Hers was one of only three Riverton
homes that displayed two Gold Stars in front windows. War is a
sad business. But I still hoped Danny would be all right.

Buddy Roe Bibs met us at the kitchen door of the Mission. His
eyes were red, not unusual for Bibs at this time of the morning.
But this time was different. "Oh, Jase. I just heard about poor
Danny!" he whimpered, choking back a sob. Without attempting
another word, he helped us carry the pheasants inside. Edith
Squires thanked us and told me that she would be praying for
Danny's safe return.

It went on like this all day. Miss Sparks and every classmate
delivered their personal messages of concern for Danny and best

wishes to me. Millie Zack, the little freckled-face girl, was the most dramatic. Grief-stricken, she collapsed into my arms and showered me with tears. But that's love for you.

It was a relief to walk home with the FSG crew, knowing they no longer felt obligated to talk about Danny. On the other hand, I felt a need to know, "How are your parents taking this, Queenie?"

"My father is fine. But he always is. My mother's taking it very badly. She cried all last night. When I left for school this morning, she was just sitting on the davenport, staring into space. I don't know what she'll be like when I get home."

"Want me to come with you?"

"That'd be nice."

Queenie and I said goodbye to Butch and Sherm and continued on to her house. As we walked up the driveway, the sheriff pulled in behind us. "I've got some news, hopefully good news, to share with the Tuckers."

When we entered the house, Mrs. Tucker was still in her bathrobe, sitting on the davenport. Her eyes were swollen and red. Mr. Tucker was fixing her a cup of tea. Chub was playing checkers with himself at the kitchen table.

"I wanted you to know that the CID boys found a ransom note in the Hagen truck this morning."

"A ransom note!" Mr. Tucker was incredulous. "What next?"

"Yep! It was under the visor on the driver's side. We overlooked it last night in the dark. It was in German so it took awhile to have it translated accurately."

"What kind of a ransom do they want?"

"Well, hold onto your hat. They want fifty thousand dollars in gold and guaranteed safe passage to Spain! They say they will notify us with the plans for a swap. The ransom is for Danny."

We were flabbergasted.

"Sheriff, we don't have that kind of money. What'll we do?"

"Sam, don't you worry about that. First of all, it'll never go that far. We'll nab those scoundrels before anybody seriously considers getting a ransom together. Besides, if it ever comes to that, this is a federal matter. We're at war with Germany and these guys are prisoners of that war. Nobody expects you to foot the bill."

Mr. Tucker looked relieved. Nothing was said for several seconds as we absorbed what the sheriff had told us. Finally Queenie asked, "Why Spain?"

"Technically Spain is a neutral country. But today, Franco's in power because of the help he got from the Nazis during the Spanish Civil War. I guess they think they'll be welcome there. They didn't ask to be sent back to the German army. That might be a hardship on them! After all, they'd have to do some real fighting. Might even expose themselves to real danger. True Nazis to the core, those two are.

"But I want you to know that I consider the note to be a positive sign. As long as Reitter and Baden think they can collect a ransom, Danny is safe."

"Danny is safe —," Mrs. Tucker whispered.

Mr. Tucker thanked the sheriff and shook his hand. Then he patted me on the shoulder. "Thanks for coming, Sheriff. You too, Jase."

"You want a ride home, Jase?" The sheriff asked. "I'd like to tell your folks about the ransom note. Besides I need to ask your father for a favor."

When we pulled up, Dad was just returning from work. After hearing the purpose of the sheriff's visit, Dad suggested we go inside. "Marie! Maude! The sheriff's here. He's got something to tell us."

After delivering the ransom note news, the sheriff summed up Danny's situation more bluntly than he had at the Tuckers. "The good news is that, right now at least, Danny's worth more alive than he is dead to those rascals. But there's some *not so good* news too. Since midnight, dozens of police and army patrol cars have combed the area, searching for that Cadillac. We figured they'd be on the lam. They got everything they need to make a run for it. Big car, guns, money. The works!

"By now, we figured we'd either stumble across them or pick them up at a roadblock. To be candid, we don't have a clue as to their whereabouts. Last night we had a red-hot trail, but it's ice-cold at this point. Either they slipped through a roadblock somehow. Or they're holed up somewhere around here. In either case, with no results we can't inconvenience the public with those roadblocks for too much longer. And stopping every car ties up a lot of police officers who could be following other leads."

"Boy, that's not what I was hoping to hear," Dad agreed.

"And that's not all. Since we have a kidnap-and-ransom situation, our pals from the FBI are pushing their noses into our business. We — meaning the state police, the army CID, and yours truly — want to handle this case ourselves. After all, these Germans are going to end up in an army courtroom. Don't quote me on this, but the FBI is a bunch of glory-seekers. More interested in their press clippings than they are in getting the job done. With all these out-of-town reporters flooding into Riverton, I got enough press troubles. But, if the FBI takes over, I'll be spending half my day behind a podium instead of getting Danny back."

"Wow! How can you prevent the FBI from coming into this?"

"I can't do a thing. But a couple of your friends can. Will you ask them to help me, John?"

"You bet, Sheriff. What friends are you talking about?"

After hearing the sheriff's plan, Dad sprang into action. "Let's go across the street and use the Shurtleif telephone. Two phone calls should get the ball rolling. Then we can hit the road. You want to come along, Jase? You have a vested interest in the outcome of this effort. Danny's your best friend."

An hour later, we were waiting for Harry Chambers in his office. Eager to help, Mr. Chambers was on his way back from the county courthouse in New Albany. Chambers and Chambers was the most prestigious law firm in the area. And Harry Chambers was their finest lawyer. He was also a schoolmate and old friend of my father's.

Another old friend popped through the door. Hello, everybody!" Jim Comstock said. "I just saw Harry parking his car. He'll be here soon." We congratulated Jim on his winning season so far and asked him about the upcoming game with Pontiac. He thought Riverton High would come away with another win. We were all thrilled by the way Jim had turned his life around. He worked hard and deserved his gridiron successes as well.

"Sorry. I'm late! But I didn't want a deputy sheriff pulling me over for speeding on my way to a meeting with the sheriff! Not good form. Nice to see you all. How can I help?"

The sheriff updated Jim and Harry on the case, telling them about the ransom note and the lack of success in their efforts to apprehend the kidnappers. He concluded with the FBI news and asked them for help.

"Sheriff, I'm afraid I have exactly the same impression of the FBI, especially since the Libby sisters' case," Mr. Chambers admitted. "I agree completely with your plan. I think I know who to call to determine the Governor's whereabouts." He pushed a button on his intercom and spoke to his secretary. "— that's right. When you have the number, buzz me, please." He smiled and informed us, "We shouldn't have a long wait."

"Jase, how are you doing without Danny at your side?" Jim asked. "You two have been inseparable since that day I caught you — oops. Better not mention the circumstances of my first meeting Danny. Least, not with the sheriff sitting right here." The thought of Danny and me swimming in the city's water supply made me smile. We'd certainly shared a lot of adventures since he moved to Riverton only a few months earlier.

"I miss him a lot," I confessed.

Just then, the buzzer sounded. Mr. Chambers pressed the button. The secretary's voice announced, "It's Governor Dewey himself on the line. Just pick up your phone."

"Tom! It's you! I was calling to ask your campaign manager to track you down. I didn't think you'd be there. How are you? Only three weeks to go. We're all working hard for you here in Michigan. Look, Tom. I know you're extremely busy so I won't waste time. Have you heard about the POW escape and kidnapping? You did? Good. I thought you might have."

Mr. Chambers nodded his head at us and smiled. "Excellent, Tom! That's why we're calling. A few of your friends are here in the office with me. Brother Jim Comstock. Sheriff Connors. John and Jase Addison. We've just taken a vote and elected you the man to call your pal, J. Edgar Hoover, for us."

He gave Governor Dewey a quick overview of the situation. Then he listened to the Governor's response. He smiled at us and nodded his head. "Delighted you feel that way, Tom. I don't know of another person who would have the courage to ask the Director to stand down. We'll assume that the job is done unless we hear otherwise. Okay, fine. Now I'll let you go. Oh, sure. Just a minute. Jim, Tom wants to talk to you."

"Hello, Tom. Whatcha been up to lately? Ha! Thank you. They're a first-rate bunch of kids. Sorry about that Owosso game. Frankly either team could have won, right down to the final seconds. They're a fine team. Saturday night at Pontiac. That's right. We should take them. But you never know in football. Thanks so much. I — what? Oh, sure. Bye, Tom."

Jim handed the phone to me. "The Governor wants to talk to you, Jase."

I was surprised. "Hello, Governor Dewey."

"Jase, I was very upset to hear what's happened to Danny. You know I'll do everything in my power to help find him and put those Nazis behind bars. I just spoke to a friend of mine at the War Department. He's promised me to beef up the CID support to get this thing resolved. If this dratted election weren't keeping me here, I'd be there running the case myself. One way or the other, I'll be home right after the election. I'll come to see you then. And that's a promise. Let's hope Danny's back home by then. Keep the faith. So long, my good friend."

"Thank you, Governor. Bye."

"Oh, Jase, let me speak to Harry again, please."

I handed the phone back to Mr. Chambers. "Hello, Tom."

He listened and nodded for a brief time. "Right, Tom. I'll tell him. Thank you so much for what you've done. Goodbye, friend."

He hung up the phone and looked at the sheriff. "Sheriff, you won't have to worry about the FBI. And Tom's made arrangements to beef up the CID help for you."

"That's wonderful news!" the sheriff replied, smiling from ear-to-ear. We all agreed.

Out of habit, I thought, *I can hardly wait to tell Danny!*

THE WEEK PASSED SLOWLY. However, one unexpected benefit of Danny's kidnapping was my developing friendship with Queenie. After school on Tuesday, she taught me how to roller-skate. First, she attached her skates to my shoes, securing them by tightening the clamps with her skate key. Then taking both my hands and walking backwards, she helped me keep my balance until I could successfully negotiate the sidewalk without her. Before long, I was whizzing back and forth between the cottonwood and our box elder. Imagine my thinking that roller-skating was for sissies!

Butch and Sherm stayed close as well. After school on Wednesday, even though the rest of us considered ourselves a bit old for it, we went along with Sherm's suggestion to play hide-and-seek. In return, Sherm was subjected to our neighborhood's unique punch-in-the-nose method of selecting that first *It* person. Sherm stood facing the box elder, our hide-and-seek *Base*. Leaning into the tree, he covered his eyes by wrapping his arms around his face.

"Here's the face." On the back of his shirt, Queenie drew a large circle with her rigid index finger.

"Here're two eyes." *Poke! Poke!* She added these to the upper half of the imaginary face.

"Here's the mouth." She slashed a curve under the eyes.

Then she spoke the deadly words, "And here is the nose!"

Our rules called for her to select the person to add a nose. This was accomplished by having the selected person punch Sherm in the middle of his back. Pointing to herself, she hauled off and slugged Sherm with all her might. Once he started breathing again and pinched back his tears, Sherm had to guess who had punched him. If he guessed right, the puncher was *It*. If he guessed wrong,

Sherm was *It*. The strength of the punch left no doubt in his mind. Incorrectly he guessed Butch. So Sherm was *It*.

Next he resumed his eyes-closed position against the base and slowly counted aloud to *100* while the rest of us hid. When he finished, he would open his eyes and commence searching for us. If he spotted one of us, Sherm would run to the base and, while touching the box elder, yell, *"1-2-3 on whomever."* If Sherm were successful, the spottee was *It*.

If Sherm misidentified the hider or if the hider managed to reach the base and yell *Free!* before Sherm reached the base, Sherm was *It* again. This particular game lasted for about a hundred and fifty hours. Or so it seemed to me. During the marathon, Sherm always managed to be *It*. Actually he enjoyed the attention. Fortunately this would be the last time we would play hide-and-seek that year.

For reasons we'd regret, after school on Thursday, we FSG guys agreed to let Queenie teach us all about Big Band music. We gathered in my room for our lesson. Our professor turned on the portable radio and dialed up her precious Big Band show. The announcer informed us that we were to be *treated* to an uninterrupted hour of Glenn Miller hits. Naturally I'd heard of this band leader but I wasn't familiar with his hits. As the music filled the air, Queenie took command.

"Okay, Butch Wax! What's the name of this one?" Butch shrugged his shoulders and gave her a goofy smile.

"Moonlight Serenade, dummy!"

"String of Pearls, moron."

"Chattanooga Choo Choo! It was on the Hit Parade for fourteen weeks. Where have you been? Mars?"

"American Patrol, stupid."

"Pennsylvania 6-5000! The band even yelled out the name of the song, you dodo!"

Apparently none of us had attained the prerequisite level of Big Band expertise before Queenie's lesson. One by one, each of us flunked her quiz. In fairness, I have to admit that I did learn one thing. I gained a complete understanding of Danny's aversion to Big Band music.

By the time school was out on Friday, I was ready for a change. But Queenie was ready for her next workshop. She insisted on teaching us *guys* how to knit. Sherm would normally join any activity with his elders like Danny and me just to be one of the guys. But he surprised even me by immediately vetoing Queenie's idea. He stated emphatically that no self-respecting six-year-old boy would be caught dead with a knitting needle in his hand, or words to that effect. So we were sitting on our front steps searching for a non-knitting alternative when the sheriff saved the day.

"Evening, Sheriff Connors," we all chimed. "Any news about Danny?"

"Well, not exactly. But we've had a breakthrough in the case. Are your folks here?"

We assembled in the front room. Aunt Maude put on a pot of coffee and arranged a plate of her oatmeal cookies. Of course, I couldn't help remembering that they were Danny's favorites.

"I just got back from Frankenmuth. You know, that little German community a few miles south of Saginaw. We were interrogating a man there, a third cousin of Reitter's mother. Name's Martin Mueller. Owns a big dairy farm just outside of town. His branch of the family has been here in America for almost eighty years. But this past summer he learned through family in Germany that Reitter was a POW at Camp Riverton, so he paid him a visit. Thought he owed it to the family, you see?"

"You mean they have visiting hours for POWs? I didn't know that, Sheriff."

"Me neither, John, but actually it's pretty common, especially at POW camps located in areas like Wisconsin and Michigan where lotsa Germans have settled over the years. It's like any other kind of prison in that regard. Once a month or so, we allow visitors for a few hours. They can bring little gifts. Baked goods and personal items like stationery or shaving gear. Real decent of us, right?"

"I guess so."

"Sorry. Didn't mean to get sidetracked. Mr. Mueller visited Reitter, all right. But only once. Thought Reitter was a fanatical

Nazi. Mueller's got a son fighting with the marines in the Pacific, so you can imagine how that went over. Said that Reitter even wanted Mueller to help him escape. Reitter claimed to know some top secret intelligence about what's being manufactured out at Burkes. Mueller had never heard of Burkes, but he told Reitter that everybody in the area knew that secret, so he was just wasting his time. That was a pretty smart move on Mueller's part.

"Apparently Mueller thought it was important enough to mention this conversation to a guard on his way out. Even wrote down the guard's name on a slip of paper that he gave us. Evidently this malarkey was so common with Reitter that the guard didn't bother to report it. He barely remembered talking to Mueller until the CID refreshed his memory. Point is, Mueller's telling the truth."

"But you say he never visited Reitter again, right?"

"That's right, John. But Reitter visited Mueller just last night!"

"That's incredible! How'd he get there in the Cadillac without being spotted?"

"Funny! When I briefed the Tuckers earlier this evening, that's exactly what Sam asked. Here's what Mueller had to say. Reitter and Baden arrived at his farm about an hour after dark last night. But they weren't driving a Cadillac.

"They arrived in what Mueller guessed to be a — 1929 or so — Pontiac sedan probably owned by an old man but driven by Baden. He got a decent look at the car because they talked on the porch. Because Mueller's wife was inside, he didn't want a dangerous man like Reitter in the house. Mueller'd read about the escape and the kidnapping, but he didn't let Reitter know that."

"Did Mueller see who was in the car? Was Danny there?"

"He wasn't sure because it was dark. But presumably Baden was in the driver's seat because Reitter spoke to him in German a number of times. The passenger was sitting on the side away from the porch so Mueller didn't get a real good look at him. But he thought from his posture he was an older man. We assumed that this man owned the car. He also thought he saw some movement in the back seat, but he couldn't swear to it. My bet is that Danny was there with them."

"Then you think they sneaked through a roadblock in that older car."

"That's a definite possibility, especially up around Frankenmuth. Men driving around in old cars and speaking German. Sounds like every other farmer up that way. Many of them, like Mueller, are descendants of families who came here in the mid-1800s, and they still speak German at home.

"Oh, for some reason, this fact struck me funny. According to Mueller's description, Reitter was dressed in Mr. Graham's tweed suit. Won't that be welcome news to old E.F.?" he laughed.

Then he got serious again. "Reitter told him they'd been holed up around Frankenmuth somewhere, waiting for things to cool down some before venturing out to see Mueller. Apparently Reitter had Mueller's address from the prison visit so Reitter knew where to find him.

"But here's the significant thing. Reitter divulged to Mueller that he and his partner had been arguing over what plan to follow. While Reitter didn't come right out and say it, Mueller assumed he was talking about how to handle the ransom. Reitter asked Mueller to help him again, but Mueller refused him. So Reitter announced that they'd drive south down to Port Huron or Detroit. Then cross over into Canada and join up with some other German escapees over there."

"Is that possible?"

"It's possible they want to get to Canada, but there're no escapees to join up with over there. No German in his right mind wants to escape. They got it too good right here. What are they gonna do? Go back to Germany and help out when the Russians, French, and Americans march in? Or hide out in Spain with Franco? But we're not taking any chances. We set up roadblocks on all routes leading to Canada. Even though I doubt they're heading there."

"Where do you think they're going, Sheriff?"

"Nowhere! Not till they get their hands on that ransom. Besides, if they're still arguing about just how to do that, it might be awhile before I hear from them again."

"So you think they're holed up near Frankenmuth then?"

"Nope. Makes more sense to believe they holed up around here some place. That's probably why that Cadillac disappeared so fast."

"Do you think Danny's still all right?" I asked hesitantly.

"What do you think, Jase?"

"I think he's fine," I vowed, without knowing why.

"So do I, Jase. So do I."

Does the sheriff know more than he's telling us?

DURING THE DAYS FOLLOWING the kidnapping, accounts of the crime appeared in newspapers all over the country. The stories emphasized the *desperate* and *dangerous* German POWs and their *poor victim* Danny. When photos of the protagonists hit the wire services, they added a certain degree of credibility to the exaggerated renditions.

As Riverton became the nation's center of attention, reporters by the dozens came to see for themselves. The case offered little in the way of fast-breaking news, so idle reporters decided to *create* some news of their own. As they had done in the Libby case, they knocked on every door in our neighborhood searching for tidbits of gossip to substantiate their outlandish assertions about the POWs and Danny. To make reporters think they weren't home, the Tuckers turned off their lights and hid in the basement.

When brazen reporters insisted on knowing the details behind the Gold Stars hanging in her window, Mrs. Mikas pretended not to understand English, shooing them away with her dust mop. That evening, she wept even longer than usual.

And when they learned that the *victim's* closest friend lived right there in the Addison house on Forrest Street, they hounded us until we could stand no more. Dad suggested we all go hunting.

And Mr. Tucker agreed. Since we had invited Junior Shurtleif as well, I could borrow one of his two shotguns.

Early Saturday morning, we hit the road. Junior rode with the Tuckers, making room for Aunt Maude and me to share our back seat with Johnnie. The WRDP weather report called for early morning fog, clearing as the sun rose. I loved hunting on mornings like this. When we arrived at the farm, Queenie's initial impression was, "They don't have sidewalks! How am I going to skate?"

Chub immediately headed for the kitchen. I recalled his first visit to the farm when he had fallen asleep under the kitchen table. Mick greeted us with an unusual burst of enthusiasm. Since the beginning of hunting season, he had acted younger than his ten dog years.

Grandma took Chub into the front room to show him the *Uncle Wiggily* book that she had recently bought at an auction. The book's colorful illustrations fascinated Queenie.

Mom and the other ladies served a last cup of coffee to us hunters before the sun came up, and we set off for the fields. In a lull in the conversation, a cocky rooster pheasant taunted us with his *ca-ca-ca-ca* cackle. "He's down by the creek or maybe in the lower end of the orchard," Grandpa declared. "Let's hunt the north end of the farm first."

Nothing personal, Mr. Rooster, but we're coming to get you.

Last time, we had walked to the creek by way of the road. This time, we hunted to the creek by way of the orchard. We wanted to cut off that cocky pheasant's route of escape by following the brush-filled ditch that ran between the rows of snow apple trees. It was a perfect plan. As soon as we reached the first tree, Mick *yelped,* and we were off and running.

Because of Junior's recently acquired artificial leg, Dad and I had been concerned about his ability to keep up. But our concerns were unwarranted. He hobbled faster than any of us could run. In fact, he got out ahead of Mick and flushed the escaping rooster.

Bam!

Junior got the first bird of the day, even before the sun had risen above the horizon.

In the cornfield where both Danny and I had bagged our birds on opening day, Grandpa and Mr. Tucker downed the next two roosters. We noticed the number of hens seemed to have diminished. With the onset of hunting season, I suspected they had decided that it wasn't safe to hang around with roosters.

When we reached Henry Road, we paused to sample the fruit of the giant Yellow Delicious apple tree that grew at the edge of the field. No one knew why that tree happened to grow there. Because of its age, most people believed it resulted from an apple core tossed from a horse-drawn carriage traveling along Henry Road. Whatever its origin, at this time of year, we were always thankful for the sweet, yellow fruit that it provided. After finishing his apple, Mr. Tucker asked, "How do you like your new job, Junior?"

"Well, this job is a whole lot different than combat. I guess you could say that about any job. One thing the two have in common is the fine people. I really like working with the officers and men at Camp Riverton. Most have had combat experience and I respect that a lot."

Mr. Tucker nodded his understanding and agreement. "I was in the navy for a number of years before I picked up my shrapnel at Pearl Harbor. So I agree with what you're saying. The toughest thing for me would be to go into an outfit that wasn't squared away, that didn't follow good military order and discipline."

"That was a concern of mine as well. I'd heard stories about laxness at these camps and about the way discipline breaks down as guards get to know the individual POWs. There've been stories about POWs sneaking up and taking rifles from sleeping guards and hiding them as a prank.

"In some camps, lazy guards don't load their rifles because the bullets make their rifles too heavy! Not sure how I feel about this, but some POW camps provide German officers with drivers, cars, and permission to leave the base. Bound only by their word of honor not to escape, they can drive anywhere within a fifty-mile radius of the camp. I have to concede that, so far, not one has broken his word."

"Does that happen at camps in Michigan?"

"No. I think that happens in POW camps somewhere out west."

"Out west? You mean they got German POWs out west? I thought those would be Jap POWs."

"Among the many things I've learned about POWs is the fact that there are POW camps all over the country. In fact, the only states without camps are Montana, North Dakota, Nevada, and Vermont. We only have a few hundred Jap POWs because *Bushido*, their military code of honor, frowns on soldiers who surrender. The Japanese soldiers prefer to commit *hara-kiri*, suicide. So most camps around the country have Germans. But enough about POWs. Let's bag some more birds, okay?"

"Fine idea! Let's follow the fencerow back down toward the woods," Grandpa suggested, picking up his shotgun. "Oughta be a few birds between here and there."

By noon, we all had our bag limits so we headed for home. As we walked through the north hayfield, Grandpa reminded Dad, "John, you remember this spot, don't you?" Then they both laughed. Grandpa shared the story with Junior and Mr. Tucker. "You may not know this, but Jase there is a born horseman. He drives a team better than most men I know."

I could feel my cheeks starting to burn. But I didn't disagree with Grandpa.

"So one evening, when Jase was about seven, we were loadin' hay. Jase was up on the wagon front rack, drivin' the horses. And I was on top of the load mowin' away the hay as it came off the hay loader. By this time, believe it or not, Jase had mastered that job. Anyway John arrived at the house, walked down to the field here, and insisted on takin' the boy's place. He figured he could do a better job than Jase, right? It was against my better judgment, but I went along for the sake of keepin' peace in the family.

"Well, on the *first* pass he left a hundred feet of a windrow on the field. He had to loop back to load it. On the *second* pass, he drifted off course, leavin' more than hundred feet on the field. On the *third* pass, I fired him and replaced him with the best driver in the Addison family, Old Jase there."

Grandpa and Dad burst into laughter. Dad finally managed to say, "I didn't think getting fired was *real* funny at the time. But Bill and I laugh about it every hunting season when we walk through this field. Yes, sir. Jase is one heck of a horseman! A lot better than his dad."

There are some things that I will always remember. One of them was how I felt on that October day in 1944 as we walked back to the house for dinner. Another was squirrel hunting with my father.

When small game hunting season opened, most Chippewa County hunters took to the fields in search of the ringneck pheasant. Often my father and I slipped away for what we both enjoyed almost as much, a sultry afternoon of squirrel hunting. We were most successful when we hunted the stand of tall hickories that grew where Old Nate's and Grandpa's woods touched near the stretch of old rail fence. While decades of neglect had rendered the rail structure ineffective as a fence, it did provide me with a comfortable *easy chair* to rest in while I scanned the trees for signs of the wily fox squirrel.

Most city dwellers do not realize that town squirrels, even of the same species, are much tamer than their country cousins. Unlike walking through Trumble Park where the squirrels were plentiful, I could stroll through Grandpa's woods without seeing hide nor hair of the many fox squirrels that lived there. We knew they were there because their nests, large balls of leaves and twigs, dotted the trees, especially those making up the hickory grove. Why the difference in behavior? I always believed it was because I could legally hunt for squirrels in the country but not in the city. So fox squirrels in Grandpa's woods were a whole lot more wary than those in Trumble Park.

When we entered the woods, the rule of silence was always observed. All communication was conducted by hand signals or mimed words. Creeping toward the hickory grove, we hoped to spot squirrels playing, feeding, or scampering between their favorite trees. We had mastered the stalking technique of walking silently, heel-roll-toe, on the fallen red, yellow, and brown leaves.

Occasionally we were lucky enough to bag our first fox squirrel before settling in for an afternoon of silently watching and waiting.

We assumed our traditional positions on the opposite sides of the grove. I always chose the rail-fence side. These opposing positions defeated the fox squirrel's habitual tactic of scurrying to the sides of limbs and trunks facing away from the sound of an approaching hunter. When we spotted or heard a squirrel, one hunter would create a diversion while the other raised his gun and prepared for a quick shot. The sound of the diversion tricked the squirrel into shifting his position to the side visible to the shooter.

Whether successful in bagging a squirrel or not, the loud discharge of a shotgun caused all the squirrels in the woods to duck for cover. A long, obligatory waiting period then followed before they emerged to resume their normal activities, eating and fraternizing with their friends. So we chose our shots carefully.

But, because of its considerable size and taste, the fox squirrel was well worth the wait. Adult males were nearly two feet in length and weighed as much as two pounds. When fricasseed with rabbit and pheasant, squirrel meat was barely distinguishable from the other richly flavored game animals.

In my book, the most enjoyable part of the hunt was the period between shots. I could look across the grove at Dad, leaning against a hickory tree some fifty yards away. Or scan the yellow canopy for telltale signs of squirrel activity or chatter. Sitting silently consumed at least ninety percent of our time in the woods. This was a time for deep contemplation and occasionally, I admit, deep slumber. It was also a purposeful time of bonding between a boy and his father.

WHEN WE FINISHED DINNER, we pushed back our chairs and had another cup of coffee. "Mrs. Compton that was a fine dinner! When I was overseas, I longed for meals like this. Thank you for having me."

"You're very welcome. Good to have you here, Junior. By the way, I've been meaning to ask, how's the food out at Camp Riverton?"

"Pretty good by army standards. Our quartermaster contracts with local suppliers to provide us with high-quality meat, groceries, and produce. Since our experienced cooks know just how to prepare it, the officers and enlisted men eat well. The POWs also benefit from the food we procure locally. Their food is prepared European style by their own POW cooks.

"The Germans' food preferences seem odd to us. For instance, they don't like butter on their bread. They prefer chopped onions and lard. Shortly after the camp first opened, our cooks offered them sweet corn, but their response was, *Das ist für Schwein!* That's for pigs! But, after their first taste of fresh sweet corn, they changed their minds.

"When they leave for work in the morning, their cooks prepare a sack lunch, or they're issued chits to eat in restaurants near their work. If they're permanently detailed to farms, many times they'll eat at the dinner table with the farmer's family and other workers. Most farmers take a liking to the POWs, especially the more personable and hardworking ones. They give them extra food and special treats like beer and tobacco.

"All in all, POWs eat pretty well, especially compared to those Germans back in Europe whether in the army or on the home front. For the most part, they're quite pleased with their lot."

"We drove by the camp on a Sunday morning last month. I swear I heard hymns being sung. Do you hold church for them there, Junior?"

"Sure do, John. Local churches provide Sunday services for POW camps, sometimes even in German. Prisoners are either transported to churches or, as in our case, local ministers come to the camps. We even have German hymnals for their use. But POWs had to break a bad hymn-singing habit. Back in Germany, Nazi leaders ordered them to substitute the word *Hitler* for the word *God* when they sang hymns. When we stopped that nonsense, most POWs seemed relieved."

"Every now and then, we get glimpses of their Nazi conditioning. When digging drain ditches for the county, some POWs found some Indian arrowheads and asked the guard where they should turn them in. In Nazi Germany, all artifacts like those belong to the state. The guard advised them to keep the arrowheads and show them to their grandchildren. The POWs acted like he'd given them a million bucks."

"One time, we drove by the camp and saw POWs playing kick ball. Others were hittin' a ball with their hands. What were they playin'?" Grandpa asked.

"Soccer. They call it *football*. It's big in Europe. Germans also like to play *fist ball*. Volley ball to us. The YMCA donated the balls and other sports equipment — recreational items too, like books, musical instruments, phonograph records, games, and hobby materials. Even though they're in English, the Germans like the movies we show at the base. Periodically we turn off the projector so their translator can explain what's happening."

"Junior, are there a lot of married POWs out there?" Aunt Maude asked.

"About one in ten is married. Most POWs are in their early twenties. Some are still teenagers. Europeans tend to marry at an older age than Americans. Nonetheless, we do have some budding romances. POWs are allowed to send a single postcard one week and a single short letter the next. Even at this rate, they seem to be able to start and maintain long-distance romances. We've even had a couple of marriages at the camp. We conduct the marriage ceremony on this end and send the paperwork off to Germany through the Red Cross. It's all legal."

"The sheriff informed us that you even have visiting hours out there. That was a new one to me."

"That's right. POWs can see visitors once a month for a one-hour period. You'd be surprised the distances their American relatives will drive to be there for only an hour. That's not much time so some visit their POWs on the farms where they work. Bring them treats that the POWs smuggle back into camp.

"For the most part, the contraband is harmless. Candy, tobacco, and so on. But one of the POW cooks had an old uncle from up around Pinconning who'd visit once a month. After the uncle's visit, the cook always ended up drunk. It took us awhile to figure out that the uncle would hide a bottle in the weeds near the garbage pit before he went through the normal visitor's search. Later, when the cook went out to empty the kitchen garbage, he'd retrieve the bottle and have himself a cocktail party. We soon put an end to that."

"I saw a funny incident the other day. On New Albany Avenue, an army truck loaded with POWs slowed down before turning into the canning factory. A gang of six-year-old boys ran alongside the truck yelling, *Hello, Hitler!* The POWs seemed to get a real kick out of it. They laughed, waved back, and returned the kids' Nazi salutes. I guess not all POWs are like Reitter and Baden, eh?"

After mentioning those names, Mr. Tucker lowered his head and looked at his wife. None of us spoke. "Sorry, Christine."

"That's all right, Sam. I haven't thought about Danny more than a couple of times since we left home. And that's some kind of record for me. Everybody at this table is just as concerned as I am about Danny, especially you, Jase. I know what special friends you've become. And I'm sorry you have to go through this."

"Thank you, Mrs. Tucker. I think of him all the time too."

"Imagine! It happened right here at the farm. Tomorrow a week will have gone by without a word," Grandma reminded us.

"If only I hadn't asked him to go to the station wagon for my tobacco," Dad lamented.

"John, those Nazi brutes just got lucky last Sunday. But their luck will run out, and Danny will be back before we know it."

"Thanks, Junior. I'm sure all of us hope you're right."

I know I certainly did!

10 THE FIRST SNOW

AS I PREPARED FOR SCHOOL ON MONDAY MORNING, I realized that Danny had been missing for over a week. But, instead of being depressed, I decided to be upbeat. With the CID, the state police, and the sheriff's office on the job, the kidnappers were up against a formidable force.

There has to be a break in the case soon!

With an optimistic attitude, I departed for school, whistling the tunes that reminded me of Danny. When we first met, *Under the Double Eagle* became our favorite march. Later, we borrowed *My Old Kentucky Home* from Gentleman Jim Comstock. And, to celebrate our bubble gum-for-sauerkraut deal with Otto, we expropriated Hitler's theme song, *Dutch Land Goober Olives! YA BOLT!*

Filled with warm memories, I stomp-marched past the Matlock's new house singing *Goober Olives.*

"Gut morgen, Jase!" Otto hollered from the front porch. "Yoh happy! Gut noos ahbot Danny, ya?"

"No, not yet. But I'm sure we'll hear something today!"

I don't know why I said that. I guess I just wanted to reinforce my optimism. In any case, I changed the subject. "How's the house coming?"

By smiling and nodding, Otto gave me his *YA BOLT* to my prediction of forthcoming news about Danny. Then he happily informed me that the house was nearly finished. At any moment, the Riverton building inspector would arrive to conduct his final inspection. Otto assured me it would pass with flying colors. Actually he said it would pass with *flowing collars,* the image of which made me smile. Assuming so, the Matlocks would move in on Wednesday.

"That's fantastic news, Otto! I'll tell my folks."

After waving goodbye, I stomped, whistled, and sang my way along the path over the railroad tracks, past the canning factory, and down into the city dump. How I loved taking the scenic route to school!

Greeting me warmly, Miss Sparks and my classmates were especially considerate that morning. I had assured them that they would be the first to know when I received any news, so they stopped asking about Danny. My pleasant mood stayed with me all day, even when I was confronted with the gloomy face of Millie Zack staring at me from the opposite side of the lunch-room table. Leaving her to suffer alone, I joined Butch and Sherm at their table. They were delighted to share my upbeat mood.

We reminded ourselves of the gigantic bag of milkweed pods that we had gathered and turned in the week before. Sherm assured us he was happy for the sailors because, whenever his mother served *kapok,* he always enjoyed the dish. For an instant, I considered that possibility. The Tolna kids' grandparents were emigrants.

Maybe they do eat milkweed fluff in Poland.

But, when Butch winked at me, I came to my senses. Neither of us had the heart to disabuse Sherman of his faulty thinking. I could almost hear the stern reprimand from Sherm's ever-vigilant censor. Nope, Sherman the Vermin would have never gotten away with that one if Danny'd been on duty.

After school, we stopped to see how Otto's final inspection had gone. Butch was excited when Otto delivered the good news. The Matlock house had passed with *flowing collars,* just as he'd predicted. We congratulated him and patted him on the back.

Since Butch was eager to share the news with his family, we thanked Otto and left in a hurry.

"Mrs. Libby wants us to hold an open house on Saturday. Invite all the neighbors," Butch informed us. "You guys'll come. Right, Jase?"

"Sure, we're *neighbors,* aren't we? Besides we're friends. We'll be there!"

"We're FSG members too. FSG members always do things together. Right, you guys?"

As always, Sherm was a bit insecure about his youngest-member status. We nodded our agreement. Sherm's response was, "Yeeeeees! I knew it. I knew it. I knew it. I *am* a member of FSG. Yeeeeees!"

As we crossed New Albany, I noticed the sheriff's car at our house. "Let's hurry!" I insisted, picking up the pace.

Butch continued on to Mrs. Libby's house, his family's temporary residence since the fire. Because his father was a policeman, Sherm explained that he was cleared for police confidential information. As he came inside with me, he reminded me, "My father and your father are old friends, right? Besides I'm a member of FSG, right?"

He was still yammering when we joined Mom, Aunt Maude, and the sheriff on the back porch. After handing the sheriff his cup of coffee, Mom informed us, "The sheriff was about to share some news about the case."

"Thanks, Marie." He took a long sip before getting down to business. "I got a letter from Reitter today, in German, just like the ransom note. So Otto had to translate it for me. Reitter wants to meet with me, alone and unarmed. Well, not exactly alone. Says Otto can come along as interpreter. Wants to meet this Saturday out where the boys discovered the POWs with the Libby sisters at the north end of Granville Park. Says that'll give me time to get the ransom together. He'll tell me where Danny is as soon as he gets his ransom.

"But, to be frank, we don't know whether the boy is unharmed or even alive. Assuming he is, we need to buy time. Sooner or later, they'll make a mistake, and then we'll nab them. For one thing, Reitter'll be followed when he leaves that park. The CID guys are very skilled at that sort of thing."

"What will you tell Reitter when you see him?"

"First, I'll say that the Feds haven't given me clearance to pay the ransom. I need more time. If he buys that, I'll set another appointment for a week or so later. If he doesn't buy it, I'll say that I have to make sure the boy is safe before we pay the ransom. If we can't do that, there's no deal. There're a couple of ways of doing that. Have them put the boy in the hands of a neutral party until the deal is done. But I don't think they'll accept that one. So I'll propose a swap."

"A swap?"

"Yeah, a hostage swap. I'll offer to take Danny's place. I'll become their hostage and they'll release Danny."

"Sheriff! You'd do that?"

"Yes, ma'am, that's my job."

"Do you think they'll agree?"

"No telling. These fellows have very big egos. Holding a sheriff, rather than a ten-year-old boy, might just appeal to them."

"Since the two of them are arguing about things, it will probably take them awhile to agree on my offer, no matter what it is. But the longer we stall them, the better our chances for catching them."

"This all sounds encouraging, Sheriff. Have you let the Tuckers know yet?" Aunt Maude asked.

"Yes. I've told them."

"That's good. They need to know the facts."

"Yes, they do. But they don't need to know about something else that came with the letter."

After looking each of us in the eye, he took us into his confidence, counting on us not to reveal his next piece of information. "They included a small piece of Danny's maroon and yellow shirt, cut into the shape of a human ear. Said that, if they suspect we're stalling, the next letter will contain the real thing."

"Oh, Lord! What's gonna become of Danny?"

THE SHERIFF PROMISED TO tell us what happened with Reitter at Granville Park on Saturday. He suggested that we ask the Tuckers over so he could give all of us his report at the same time. We were eager to share the news with Dad.

When we heard his car door slam, we ran to the front door to meet him. "You just missed the sheriff. Reitter wants to meet with him."

"Tell me everything, Marie." Mom shared all the details with Dad.

The rest of the week dragged by slowly. We were all anxious for Saturday to arrive. We heard nothing from the sheriff. But we really hadn't expected any news. On Wednesday evening, Aunt Maude answered a knock at the front door. It was Mrs. Libby and Jim Comstock.

"Evening, everybody. Just thought we'd come by and tell you about the Matlock open house. Or are we calling it a house-warming party?" Mrs. Libby asked, turning to Jim.

"Whatever sounds best to you, Louise."

"Anyway we're inviting all the neighbors and everyone who took part in the Matlock Building Campaign to come by the new house at two o'clock on Sunday afternoon. Jim and I are providing soft drinks, coffee, and light refreshments. But, if you'd like to bring a little plate of something, it won't go to waste. Perhaps some kind of finger food. Let's see, have I forgotten anything, Jim?"

"No, you did a fine job," Jim replied warmly.

"I'll be there because all FSG members are coming. And I'm a member of FSG." Sherm informed everyone.

The kid's obsessed!

To think, Danny and I made him a member just because he had the newest wagon in the neighborhood.

When Danny returns, I promised myself, *we'll convene an FSG membership committee meeting to consider minimum age requirements. And there'll be no grandfather clause either. Or would that be a 'grandson' clause in Sherm's case?*

We all agreed to come. After saying good night, the couple departed for the Reilly house next door. Sherm insisted he had to go home and tell his mother about the Matlock's *houseworming* party. We all laughed at that one. Dashing out the door, Sherm didn't seem to notice.

Mom and Aunt Maude looked at each other and began to snicker. I assumed they were still tickled by Sherm's antics. Dad looked at me and shrugged his shoulders, "What's so funny, ladies?"

"Funny? Not really *funny*, John. More like *amusing*. Or *charming* or *sweet*."

"You've lost me. Are we talking about Sherm?"

"No, silly! Maude's talking about Louise and Jim."

"What about them?"

"Haven't you noticed? Lately you never see Louise without Jim. Or vice versa!"

"Well, they've known each other for years! The Libbys and the Comstocks shared a duplex back in the days before Jim's wife and babies were —*ah*— passed away. And Gentleman Jim was a character witness at the Libby sisters' trial. Remember, they once saved his life."

It was hard for me to think of Jim Comstock and Louise Libby as anything but friends. For some reason, the image of Millie Zack's freckled face came to mind.

Could Millie's ailment have infected Mrs. Libby as well?

With all we'd been through relating to Jim, Mrs. Libby, and her daughters, the likelihood of romance seemed highly improbable to me. Yet Aunt Maude and Mom, both of whom I respected greatly, were suggesting just that.

Wouldn't it be something if they're right?

"Well, I think we'd better keep your theory under our hats. I'd hate to be wrong about something like that. It'd embarrass them terribly. Besides I think they're just friends."

Father had spoken.

"We shall see!" Mom twittered. She grabbed Aunt Maude's arm and the two of them danced into the kitchen, singing *Don't Sit Under the Apple Tree*.

Right at that moment, they both reminded me of Millie Zack.

"Women!" was all that Dad could say as he sank into his easy chair and reached for the *Riverton Daily Press*. "Did you hear about those suicide bombers attacking our ships around the Philippines? They call themselves kamikazes."

In July 1944, American forces recaptured Saipan, an island in the Mariana chain, enabling American B-29 long-range bombers to reach the main islands of Japan. The Japanese high command predicted that America's next invasion target would be the Philippine Islands because of their strategic location between Japan and the oil fields of Southeast Asia.

To defend the Philippines, the Japanese decided to employ desperate suicide air attacks called *kamikaze,* a term composed of the Japanese word for *god (kami)* and the word for *wind (kaze).* In the 13th century, a typhoon credited with saving the Empire of Japan from a Mongol invasion fleet was named the *Divine Wind* or *Kamikaze.*

When the American invasion of the Philippines began in October 1944, the first Japanese carrier-based fighter-bombers and land-based bombers were configured for suicide attacks. American aircraft carriers were designated as prime targets. During the Battle of Leyte Gulf off the Philippines, seven American carriers and forty other ships were struck by kamikaze attacks. In all, five ships were sunk and twenty-three heavily damaged. And the battle for Okinawa was even fiercer.

By the end of the war, the Japanese had sacrificed nearly five thousand kamikaze pilots. The attacks were responsible for sinking thirty-four American ships and damaging 288 others. All told, the kamikaze attacks accounted for more than eighty percent of the American naval losses during the last phases of the war in the Pacific. Although the effects of the kamikaze attacks were certainly serious, they were not militarily devastating. However, the psychological effects on American sailors were profound, not unlike the effects suffered by the survivors of the suicide attacks on the World Trade Center on September 11, 2001.

"Kamikazes!" Dad declared, "The Japanese High Command must be crazy."

The Nazis aren't exactly the sanest people on earth either.

SATURDAY HAD FINALLY ARRIVED, but having to wait until evening to hear about the sheriff's meeting with Reitter was nerve-racking. Dad found a ready solution for his antsy state. With several repair jobs that needed to be completed before the next week, he went straight from the breakfast table to his shop, a white clapboard shed with a green shingled roof nestled at the top of our lot next to our Victory Garden.

This left Aunt Maude, Mom, and me searching for ways to take our minds off the sheriff's meeting.

"I've got an idea. Why don't the three of us take Johnnie and run out to the farm? Ma's been after us to help her sort out that attic. Jase, you might be able to find a Halloween costume among all that old clothing up there. How about it?"

Twenty minutes later, we were in the car heading for the farm. But, before we had reached the city limits, snow began to fall. And this was not ordinary snow. Each silver-dollar sized flake gracefully drifted to earth, more slowly than usual. The flakes reminded me of the dramatic newsreel footage showing thousands of American paratroopers on D-Day, floating downward into the fields beyond the Nazi fortifications above the beaches of Normandy. The flakes hit our windows like tiny water balloons, melting instantly upon impact.

By the time we reached the farm, the temperature had fallen, causing the snow to stick and even accumulate. Small drifts formed next to fence posts and tree trunks. Aunt Maude wrapped Johnnie tightly in his thick woolen blanket, and we darted into the house.

Grandma's exceedingly warm greeting told us our visit had taken her completely by surprise. She hugged us all and chucked little Johnnie under the chin. "You folks are a sight for sore eyes, you are! What brings you out in the first snow of the year?"

Mom quickly summarized the situation including the sheriff's upcoming meeting at Granville Park and our difficulty with just sitting and waiting to learn the results. We desperately needed a project and her attic was it. Besides Jase could use a Halloween costume. And Maude needed some pumpkins and corn stalks to decorate Jase's classroom for the Halloween Party that she was organizing.

Grandpa joined us in the kitchen. "By gum, it's startin' to 'cumulate. But I bet it stops afore long," he predicted, looking out the window. "Look at that blue sky over toward the Henry's."

"Remember what you always do during the first snow of the year, Dad?"

"Of course, I remember. Jase, let's go bring in the snow apples!"

By the time Grandpa and I had hitched Jim and Fannie to the wagon, the three women were sorting through Grandma's attic treasures. They'd be there for hours. I could trust them to find me a suitable Halloween costume while Grandpa and I conducted men's business in the orchard. We entered through the same gate where Danny and I had been greeted by Sarah only a few weeks earlier.

But today there was no Sarah. By this time of year, she and her sisters had taken refuge in the cow barn for the winter. Between fall and spring, they would only see the sun on particularly warm and pleasant days when Grandpa released them to stroll in the barnyard for a change of pace.

I stopped the wagon under the east branches of the first in the long row of snow apple trees, which stretched from the top of the orchard all the way down to the creek. Grandpa climbed up the rack and stepped into the tree. As he shook each branch that extended over the wagon, dozens of snow apples tumbled from the tree into the soft bed of straw that we had prepared for them before leaving the cow barn. We repeated this procedure at each tree until we reached the creek.

Then I turned Jim and Fannie around and headed back toward the gate, harvesting the west branches on the way. It took over an hour to complete the job. When we finished, the wagon was brimming with snow apples, more than enough to convert into jars of applesauce, slices for apple pies, and filler for our fruit bowls. I reminded myself to ask Grandpa for a bushel of apples for our school party. Bobbing for apples was extremely popular among my classmates, especially at Halloween time.

Arriving back at the cow barn, I pulled the wagon up beside the two sliding doors. We were now parked in exactly the same spot occupied by the Hagen lumber truck on the night of the kidnapping. Grandpa jumped down and opened the barn doors. Using wooden bushel baskets from the stack just inside the barn, we carefully loaded, carried, and dumped bushel after bushel of the pink-red orbs into the three giant, straw-softened bins where they would spend the winter.

When the first layer of apples was down, we spread more fresh straw. Then we laid down another layer, continuing this process until the bins were full. We covered the last layer with straw to finish the job. The entire process had taken us nearly three hours.

The apples left in the wagon filled six bushel baskets. "We'll take three of these over to Old Nate. He doesn't have any teeth, but with that huntin' knife of his he can make these sweet things disappear faster than a bug."

Grandpa pushed Nate's baskets up against the front rack to brace them for the trip. "These'll last him awhile. If he needs more, he can have some from the cow barn supply. We'll take a bushel into the house and send two home with you. How's that sound?"

Before departing for Old Nate's, we pulled up to the walk. Two bushels went into our car trunk and the other went into the kitchen.

I heard Grandpa holler up the stairway to the second floor. "We're off to Nate's to deliver some apples and to bring in that corn over by his barn. I don't want this snow meltin' into it. Gets too wet and heavy."

Grandpa hopped back up onto the wagon and glanced at Mick who was looking forlorn at the prospect of being left at home. "You want to come, Mick. Com 'on! Hop up here," Grandpa ordered patting his thigh.

Immediately Mick squatted down and then sprang into the wagon. I had seen him do this before. And it always amazed me that a relatively tiny fox terrier, no more than a foot or so high at the shoulder, could leap nearly four feet into the air. I suppose, if you want something badly enough, you can do almost anything.

As we pulled into Nate's driveway, we saw tire tracks in the snow. "Looks like Old Nate may have gone off somewhere, Jase. I keep missin' him. Haven't seen him in a couple a weeks."

We continued on up the drive and parked next to Nate's back shed. Not bothering to knock, we off-loaded the apples and left them on the steps. Then Grandpa pointed to the cornfield on the other side of the old horse barn. I drove the team to the spot where Grandpa wanted to start loading.

"Let's take out those rear slats and use 'em as a ramp. Run 'em from the back of the wagon bed to the ground. Make it easier to load."

After we rigged the ramp, Grandpa predicted, "When we knock over these shocks, Mick'll have a ball."

Mick was ready for action. As soon as the first shock was tipped, a dozen mice scampered across the top of the snow in every direction. As quick as a flash, Mick *yelped,* pounced, and nipped. *Yelped,* pounced, and nipped. Until every one of his furry quarry was dispatched.

Excitedly Mick *yelped* and *yelped,* urging us to tip another. But, first, we loaded the tipped shock. Grandpa took the heavy end and I the light. Then we lifted and rolled the corn-laden shock onto the ramp and up into the wagon. We tipped the next shock. *Yelp,* pounce, and nip. We repeated this process until only one last shock remained. Grandpa and I paused to catch our breath before tackling it.

As we leaned against the wagon, Mick's ears shot up. He tensed and stared toward the house. Seeming to hear a familiar sound, he *yelped* and took off. In no time, he had turned the corner of the barn and disappeared from view. Despite the howl of the wind around us, I could still hear his faint *yelping.* "Where do you suppose he's off to, Grandpa?"

"I suspect Old Nate's come home from somewhere. Let's get this last shock up on the wagon and go see for ourselves."

The fortunate mice under the last shock scampered to safety without being subjected to the mouse-eradicating fox terrier. Evidently Mick was on the trail of bigger prey by the name of Old Nate. After loading the last shock, we checked to ensure that the load was balanced. I jumped up on the front rack and grabbed the reins. Grandpa was about to hop up on the wagon, when Mick careened around the corner of the barn and hightailed it our way.

As he approached us at top speed, I could see that he was carrying a dark object in his mouth. I assumed it was a small squirrel or even a rat. Without losing momentum, Mick streaked past Grandpa and leaped onto the wagon. He ran to the rack, reached up with his front paws, and scratched frantically at my ankles. I hopped down from the rack. Mick looked up at my face and dropped his catch at my feet.

"Holy Cow! Holy Cow! It's —."

"What is it, Jase?"

"Dad's tobacco pouch!"

WE FOLLOWED MICK AS he *yelped* his way to Nate's house. As we rounded the barn, we heard Danny's voice, "Help! I'm here. In the basement. Get me out!"

When we reached the house, I went to the tiny broken basement window to reassure my friend while Grandpa rushed inside to unlock the basement door.

"Danny! Are you all right?"

"I'm hungry!"

That didn't surprise me.

"Did Mick give you the tobacco pouch? I heard your voices earlier. I yelled but you must not have heard me. Then you went away. After that I heard Mick barking like crazy. So I broke this little window and yelled and yelled for him. When he came, I gave him the pouch and told him to go to you. I kept repeating your name. Finally he understood and took off with the pouch."

Before I could reply, I heard Grandpa's voice. "I'm over here Grandpa Compton, talking to Jase."

As Danny turned to walk upstairs, I ran to the back door and went inside.

We met in the kitchen where Danny quickly briefed us. "Old Nate's really sick. I made them take him to the hospital. They took his car. The Cadillac's in the horse barn but it doesn't have any gas.

They've been gone about an hour, so they could be back any minute now."

"Jase, run and get the wagon! We gotta get out of here."

After I pulled up beside the back shed, Grandpa helped Danny onto the wagon and then hopped aboard. "Get up here, Mick! Good boy! Okay, Jase, let's go to the Henry's! We gotta call the sheriff!"

The Henry farm was only a quarter of a mile away. We made it in no time. Grandpa leaped from the wagon and ran inside the house. Danny and I just looked at each other and smiled. I had a thousand questions to ask him, but I contented myself with the realization that Danny was safe.

When Grandpa emerged from the house, he gave us our instructions. "While the sheriff sets up an ambush for Reitter and Baden, he wants you boys out of harm's way. So let's get on home! Danny, Mrs. Henry'll call your folks and let them know you're okay."

Two hours later, the sheriff pulled into the driveway. We were all sitting around the kitchen table listening to Danny hum as he consumed plate after plate of Grandma's cooking.

When the sheriff entered the house, his first words were like music to our ears. "Reitter and Baden are in CID custody. And Nate's at the hospital in Riverton. Not out of the woods yet, but under doctor's care."

Then he turned to Grandpa. "Mr. Compton, your suggested ambush point worked out real well. That sharp curve on Henry Road, with the woods blocking the view of the road ahead, was right where we nabbed them. Your idea to bring Otto along was an excellent one too. Thank you."

We all turned to Grandpa who blushed and folded his arms.

"Oh! Before I forget. You won't believe this one. When Reitter saw Otto and me, he was furious because I missed our appointment at Granville Park! While we set up the ambush, evidently, he and Baden went to the park. But I didn't show up! Really made 'em mad."

We joined the sheriff in laughing over that one.

He then turned to Danny. "I'm sure thrilled to see you. Are you all right, son?"

Danny nodded and mumbled, pointing at his full mouth.

"Well, as soon as you're ready, I need to ask you some questions."

Danny took a huge gulp of milk, swallowed hard, and placed his fork and knife on the table. Then he folded his arms and nodded at the sheriff.

"Okay then. Why don't we start right at the beginning? Tell me what happened that night they grabbed you."

"Before I start, I'd like to ask you a question. Why didn't you set up your ambush at Old Nate's?"

"That was my first choice. We could have hidden in the house or perhaps the barns. But Mr. Compton wisely advised against that because of the snow. He thought your tracks might tip them off."

"Good thinking, Grandpa Compton!"

We all looked at Grandpa again. His face was nearly purple.

After I explained how Danny had used Mick and the tobacco pouch to get my attention, everyone turned to admire the canine hero who was lying in his bed next to the kitchen stove. I believe the dog's face turned red as he covered his eyes with his paws. But I might have been mistaken. I didn't have the greatest view.

Then Danny provided a detailed account of his two-week ordeal.

"They grabbed me after I got the pouch from the station wagon. Baden put his hand over my mouth so I couldn't yell. Then they locked me in the trunk of Mr. Graham's Cadillac. I kicked the trunk lid and yelled. But nobody came. That's when they must have snatched our shotguns, Jase's and mine. And then they drove off. It didn't take long to get to Old Nate's.

"They parked the Cadillac in the old horse barn. After they removed the clothes and guns, they never used the Cadillac again. They even siphoned the gas out of it to use in Nate's old Pontiac. Anyway, when they took me inside, Nate was already there in the kitchen, tied to a chair."

"So they were at Nate's before they grabbed you, eh?"

"Nate told me they'd been to his house a couple of weeks before, to deliver lumber from Hagen's. They knew he lived alone and had a car. On the night they got me, while they were tying him up, they were speaking German. But Nate recognized the words *Compton* and *Danny*. So I guess they knew I was at the farm."

"Were you with them when they went to Frankenmuth?"

"Frankenmuth? So that's where we were! No wonder so many people spoke German. We actually went there three times. Twice to buy groceries and beer at a German grocery store and once so Reitter could talk to some farmer he knew. When he got back in the car, he was *very* mad about something. He and Baden started arguing. They argued over everything, it seemed like. That's one reason they took Nate to the hospital."

"How did their arguing result in them taking Nate to the hospital? And, before I forget, I need to know how they treated Nate and you during the two weeks."

Danny answered the second question first. "We ate real well until the last couple of days. They had cash and ration books, including Nate's, to buy lots of good groceries. Baden could cook real well. They even bought soft stuff for Nate. Soups and oatmeal. Because they didn't want him using his knife.

"At first, Baden cut his food up for him, like you do for a little baby. But Reitter got mad and made Baden stop that. Anyway the food was pretty good. And they let me eat all I wanted. But Reitter was real mean. He hit Old Nate a lot. That's how they got me to be quiet in the car. I didn't want Reitter to hurt Nate anymore."

"How did they get through our roadblocks?"

"That was easy for them. Between here and Frankenmuth there's only one, on the main highway between Flint and Saginaw. I read the road signs. Since one of the bankers had a driver's license picture that looked just like Baden, he did all the driving. The four of us always dressed like hunters. We even had four guns with us on every trip. Theirs were loaded. Ours weren't.

"Because so many people who were stopped by the roadblock spoke German, the state police had troopers who spoke German. Baden showed them the driver's license and the banker's hunting license. And Nate's registration. The troopers always waved us through. Coming and going, we always went through the same roadblock. So I think they got to know us a little. Once I heard a German-speaking trooper tell another trooper, in English, that Nate was Baden's uncle."

"I'm glad you mentioned that. I'll tell the state police they'd better tighten their roadblock procedure. Let's get back to Nate going to the hospital."

"Oh, I almost forgot. Well, Reitter hit Nate in the stomach so many times that Nate got sick and weak. For the last few days, he didn't even get out of bed. And I don't think he ate or drank anything, not even any water. Baden seemed to feel sorry for Nate. I know he was really mad at Reitter. He didn't even speak to Reitter during those last three days. So it was pretty easy for me to make them take Nate to the hospital."

"How'd you *make* them do that, Danny?"

"I sang and whistled at them. Real loud. The same songs over and over."

"What songs?"

"My Old Kentucky Home. Under the Double Eagle. And *Dutch Land Goober Olives."*

Danny had committed a war crime.

Torturing the enemy!

BY LATE SATURDAY EVENING, news of Danny's escape from the *Klutches of the Krafty Krauts,* as one Sunday paper headline put it, hit the wire services. Reporters from every corner of America attempted to reach Danny and me. The telephone in Mr. Tucker's garage rang so frequently that he asked the operator not to send a repair team because he was purposely leaving his business phone off the hook.

Those seeking comments from us had to be content with trying to reach us by telegram. Before that Sunday morning, neither of us had ever received a telegram. But, by noon, we had collected over fifty from reporters or news organizations. Most of them requested a collect call from us to enable them to ask *just a few* questions. We decided to discard these.

After the third visit from the Western Union messenger, we arranged to have the telegraph office hold our telegrams. In the long run, we concluded that a dime spent on bus fares to pick up telegrams once a day would be cheaper than multiple messenger visits requiring a nickel tip per visit.

Each of us did receive three telegrams that we quickly agreed to keep forever. In fact, on Monday morning, we would share these with Miss Sparks and our classmates. These telegrams were from a select group of well-wishers including Thomas E. Dewey, J. Edgar Hoover, and FDR himself.

Ah, fame!

Not all reporters were trying to reach us from the far corners of America. Many were already right in Riverton covering the escape and kidnapping. Members of this motley mob knew exactly where we lived and were not a bit shy in their attempts to extract a story from us. But only one reporter made it past Mom and into our kitchen that morning. Because of his new assignment as WRDP's chief, and only, newscaster, Chuck Nichols edited and then delivered the six o'clock news each morning. So he was an early riser.

In fact, he showed up at Danny's house well before the Tuckers were out of bed. "After five o'clock on Sunday mornings," Mr. T informed the early bird, "Danny can always be found at the Addison house."

Quickly apologizing for awakening the couple, the eager reporter headed for Forrest Street.

"Thank you for receiving me so early, Mrs. Addison," Chuck Nichols told Mom as she showed him into the kitchen. "Danny, it's wonderful to see you, and you look no worse for wear. I'm so relieved. And to be rescued by your best friend! You boys live a charmed life. No doubt about it."

"Mr. Nichols, how about a cup of coffee?"

"That'd be swell, Mrs. Addison."

"Boys, the basics of Danny's rescue were covered in the wire service story, but I do have some additional questions for you, if you don't mind."

We agreed to answer all of his questions, but we needed two favors. First, we asked him to cover the Matlock housewarming that would be held that Sunday afternoon. And, second, we asked his advice on handling the other reporters.

"Thanks for letting me know about the Matlocks' party. I've wanted to do a follow-up story on the fund-raiser that you fellas organized this past summer. Their moving into the new house is perfect. I'll be there. And I'd like to bring a photographer. Do you think that would be all right, Jase?"

"When we finish, we can walk down to Mrs. Libby's and ask her. She's the organizer."

"Great idea!"

"She and Gentleman Jim won't be back from church until about ten-thirty."

I didn't ask how in the world Danny could know that. But I believed him. I turned around to catch Mom nodding and smiling at Danny's news. "Wait until Aunt Maude hears about this!"

"Aunt Maude hears about what?" Dad asked, stumbling into the kitchen.

Turning toward Dad, Danny asked, "Did you get your tobacco pouch?"

Dad smiled and pulled the pouch from his pocket.

"Sorry I got it to you so late."

We all laughed.

"What am I going to hear?" called a voice from our bedroom.

After saying hello to Aunt Maude and Dad, the reporter continued. "As to your second concern, I think you boys should hold a long press conference, preferably with the sheriff. I'd be pleased to set that up for you. Get the word out to all reporters in town. I'll call the sheriff's office after we finish to make sure he's available. We could plan to hold it at his office tomorrow after school. Meantime, if you run into an inquisitive reporter, you can simply tell him about the press conference. You'll be delighted to answer his questions there. How's that sound?"

We liked his idea. If the conference were well-attended and lengthy enough, the out-of-town reporters would have their stories and leave town. That would be a relief for us, as well as our neighbors. There was another advantage too. By agreeing not to speak to reporters until late the next day, essentially, we were granting Chuck Nichols an exclusive. He would have written and filed his story hours before the press conference. Given all his favorable and free publicity during the summer, he deserved an exclusive.

Danny and I spent the next two hours answering the reporter's questions. In the middle of the session, he had an interesting idea. "I think it would be ideal to have your Grandfather available to answer questions at the press conference. Think he'd agree to come?"

"Mom, what do you think?"

"Mr. Nichols, we're talking about someone who puts on a one-man trapeze act in the top of his cow barn to entertain his daughters and their children. Whether he'd say yes or no depends on the mood he's in. But I know, if you ask him, he'd be flattered. Besides he was there during the rescue. And he came up with two or three terrific ideas that helped the sheriff trap Reitter and Baden."

"Would you two be available to ride out to his farm with me in the morning?" he asked Aunt Maude and Mom. "Seeing he puts on shows to please you, I'd probably stand a better chance of his saying yes if you were there."

Danny offered some additional advice, "You'd really improve your chances if you offered to pick up Grandpa Compton and take him to the press conference in *your* car."

I'd almost forgotten about Grandpa's fear of flying.

"WHAT TIME IS IT now, Jase?"

The Matlock housewarming was to start at two o'clock. About noon, Danny had begun asking me for the time. This was a bit odd because he was sitting directly beneath our kitchen clock whose loud ticking was a dead giveaway.

But I humored him and read the clock above his head each time he asked. "It's twelve thirty-six."

My previous reading had been twelve thirty-five. I could see that he was bored and distracted. "We could read our telegrams again."

"Nope."

"What do you want to do then?"

"Let's have lunch!"

"We just finished lunch!"

"Was that lunch?"

I didn't answer that one.

"Danny, why don't we just go over to the Matlocks now? Maybe we can help Mrs. Libby."

"Great idea! Let's go."

I told Mom we were going early to help set up. So off we went. When we arrived, Butch was in the backyard using an ice pick to convert a giant block of ice into ice cubes for the soft drinks.

As we approached, he gave us an enormous smile. "Welcome home, Danny! Hi, Jase. Wanna help?"

We scooped up the cubes as they shot from the tip of Butch's pick. With two assistants in place, he picked up the pace. In no time, we finished.

"I got my own room. Wanta see it?"

Neither Danny nor I could make that claim. But, right from the beginning, the Matlock children were promised rooms of their own. Well, that's not quite accurate. Each of the three sets of twins shared a room, and Butch had a small bedroom of his own. He gave us a personal tour of the upstairs, sparing no detail. In the bathroom, we received funny looks from Mr. Matlock, who was standing in his underwear, shaving at the bathroom sink.

In the kitchen, Mrs. Libby and Jim were opening packages of chips and dumping them into bowls. "Danny! It's so good to see you. After church this morning, Chuck Nichols told us all about your rescue. He's doing an article on the Matlocks' new house. Otto and his crew did a beautiful job, didn't they? Oh, Chuck's bringing a photographer with him today. We'll want to get your pictures too. Jim, do you think we bought enough pretzels?"

Judging by how fast she was talking, I could tell Mrs. Libby was excited. Normally she was rather shy and soft-spoken.

"Where's Mrs. Matlock?"

Jim reported that she had taken the newest twins, Sammy and Sonny, to Pete's to purchase paper napkins. "Everybody forgot about napkins. Just got to have napkins." He seemed excited too.

"What can we do to help?"

With all of us working, we were prepared long before the first guests arrived. By half past two, there were so many people in the house that there was hardly room to budge. In addition to plates of food, every guest brought a practical housewarming gift. Because all the Matlocks' possessions had been destroyed by the fire, they needed everything. The range of gifts was extensive.

Hans and Mrs. Hans gave the children a dictionary to help with their spelling. Miss Bundy supplied a giant container of buttons in all sizes, shapes, and colors. Mr. Tucker delivered a case of Texaco motor oil, even though the Matlocks had no car. Dad's gift was a second-hand sewing machine with a year's free service.

Aunt Maude and Mom furnished the bolt of curtain material which they had observed Mrs. Matlock admiring at Woolworths. Sherman bestowed one of his old wagons on the Matlock kids who immediately adjourned to the street to try it out.

Mr. and Mrs. Graham contributed a two hundred dollar gift certificate, redeemable at any Graham Market. With seven children to feed, this would come in handy. Mrs. Mikas brought a flour sifter and a five-pound bag of cookie flour. The Reillys' gift was three dozen eggs. Queenie supplied a nail file for every lady in the Matlock family.

The Carmodys gave them a second-hand vacuum cleaner, still in mint condition. The Squires issued a certificate entitling each of the children to six piano lessons at the hand of Edith. The Shurtleifs furnished flashlights for every floor of the new house.

The POWs carried in case after case of dented cans containing assorted fruits and vegetables. When Chuck Nichols arrived with his photographer, he presented them with a three-year subscription to the *Riverton Daily Press*. And on and on it went. Mr. and Mrs. Matlock were overcome with joy and gratitude. And Louise Libby beamed because the housewarming had been her brainchild.

The photographer must have snapped a hundred photos, only pausing long enough to record the correct names of those whose pictures he'd taken. Chuck Nichols circulated around the house, gathering snippets from which to create his follow-up story on the miraculous restoration of the Matlock family home.

Otto and his crew stood in the backyard receiving slaps on the back for the fine workmanship of the house. Sergeant Prella was there to *guard* them, but he was dressed in civvies and had neglected to bring his tommy gun.

Danny spent the entire afternoon surrounded by his fans, including a certain star-struck, freckled-face girl who, as it turned out, lived right across the street from the Matlocks. He was in his element.

I overheard some of how he described his ordeal for the benefit of his new groupie. "Yes, they tried everything to break me, to get me to talk. In the end, not even their torture succeeded. They were horribly disappointed, but I told them that I was an American. And Americans can take anything dished out by puny Nazis." Or words to that effect.

As the party began to wind down, Chuck Nichols asked Danny and me to step outside. He needed to speak to us in private. We were the only people in the backyard when he delivered a mysterious message.

"Boys, be sure you're home tomorrow night after the press conference. I have it on good authority that about eight o'clock you'll receive a telephone call on the Shurtleif line from someone you know. This call will result in your taking a long trip. Congratulations, boys!"

We begged for more details, but he adamantly refused. Finally we gave up. "He's an American!" Danny explained. "Americans never squeal."

A long trip!

Danny and I were going on a long trip!

11 SHOW BIZ

AT HAMILTON SCHOOL AN EXUBERANT THRONG OF
students surrounded us as soon as we reached the school grounds.
Cheering and rushing toward us, everyone was eager to touch
Danny. If it hadn't been for his bodyguards, namely his fellow FSG
members, the crowd might have smothered him. What a sight!
With some effort, we finally reached our classroom.

Long after the morning bell sounded, Miss Sparks still had not
succeeded in quieting the class. There was far too much excitement
in the air. Finally Danny raised his arms and admonished his classmates to settle down. When silence descended at last, Miss Sparks
thanked him and immediately began the Bible reading. Although
the reverent class was compliantly quiet throughout the morning
rituals, Miss Sparks wisely set aside her scheduled lesson plan.

"Danny, we'd all be interested in hearing about your
kidnapping and escape."

As the class exploded with more cheers and applause, Danny
stood and walked to the front of the room. "Thank you. Thank
you, my classmates and friends. Thank you."

A hush fell over the room.

"Friends, my story begins with and ends with a simple leather
tobacco pouch."

According to Danny, the successful escape was made possible by the quick thinking and brave actions of a humble boy from our class (Danny) who, with help from his best friend (Yours Truly) and a loyal fox terrier (Mick), outsmarted a pack (Two) of sinister Nazi kidnappers.

Moreover, this incredible achievement had not only saved the free world from domination by Hitler's evil henchmen but also sent a strong signal to all Japanese forces in the Pacific. "Watch out! The Yanks are coming!"

Attesting to the magnitude of this feat, Danny read each of our six telegrams, slowly and dramatically, to his awestruck audience. Adding credibility to his performance, he referred to our well-wishers as Tom, Frank, and J. Edward (a.k.a. J. Edgar).

Danny spent the rest of his day, answering detailed questions. What was the dog's name? *Mick.* How did Danny break the tiny basement window? *With Nate's old hoe.* Where are the kidnappers now? *In CID holding cells at Camp Custer.* What did he think about the ransom of fifty thousand in gold? *Surprised it wasn't more.* How many times did he sing *My Old Kentucky Home? 1,456 times.*

This grilling gave Danny an opportunity to rehearse his answers before facing the tough reporters at the press conference arranged for that afternoon by Chuck Nichols. When we left school, I spotted the reporter's car waiting for us at the curb. Grandpa Compton was in the front seat. We exchanged greetings and left for New Albany.

"The sheriff thought it more desirable to meet at the New Albany High School. Their gym has a stage and enough chairs for the large crowd he expects. You boys remember the press conferences this past summer in Riverton. Probably be some of the same reporters there."

The gym was packed. From our table on the stage, we looked down at reporters seated on folding chairs. A single microphone was provided to amplify our voices. After calling the conference to order, Chuck Nichols introduced himself, the sheriff, Grandpa, Danny, and me. He presented a comprehensive review of the escape and kidnapping, referring to initial wire service reports and his own extensive article from that afternoon's *Riverton Daily Press.*

Then the sheriff updated us, "I have just learned that the U.S. Army Judge Advocate General has convened a special military tribunal. Reitter and Baden are charged with a number of crimes including kidnapping and car theft. In cases like this, the proceedings usually move expeditiously. They will be arraigned within the week and their trial will be held at Camp Custer within the month. As you know, conviction could result in sentences including death by hanging or life in prison. For new developments, from here on out, I suggest that you check with the Army PIO. That's the Public Information Office."

Questions came in rapid-fire succession. Most were directed at Danny who handled them adroitly.

Reporters: "Danny, can you tell us why both Reitter and Baden went to the hospital with Nate Craddock? Why didn't one of them stay to keep an eye on you? Why didn't they take you to the hospital with them?"

Danny: "Neither of them wanted to listen to my singing. I planned it that way so I could escape. They were mean, but not too smart. After all, they're Nazis. I'm an American so I never squeal."

Huh?

Reporters: "Danny, why do you think you and Jase received those telegrams from FDR, Governor Dewey, and J. Edgar Hoover? Why would three of our country's leaders and busiest men, take time to send you telegrams? Did it strike you as strange that Dewey and Roosevelt are engaged in a knock-down-and-drag-out political campaign, yet both of them took time to send you guys telegrams?"

Danny: "Owing to reasons of national security, Jase and I cannot answer your questions in this subject area. We're both Americans so you know what that means."

Reporters: "You never squeal, right?"

Danny: "Next question, please."

For me, the high point was when reporters asked the sheriff how he knew where to set up his ambush. When the sheriff told them, Grandpa squirmed in his chair.

When we reached Chuck Nichols' car, he advised, "Mr. Compton, if it's okay with you, I'll take the boys home first. They have an important telephone call this evening."

Grandma's car was parked in front of our house. Grandpa told the reporter that he could just ride on home with her.

"Are you sure? It's no trouble."

Danny felt obligated to offer his opinion.

"Remember, now, Grandpa Compton, you don't have insurance!"

"GRANDMA! WHAT ARE YOU doing here?"

"I was visiting Old Nate at the hospital. Now that he's eating well, he's doing much better. He even got a much needed bath and clean bed clothes. But he's got some broken ribs and some internal injuries. The POWs obviously beat him badly. He'll need to stay there for a while."

Because we were expecting our telephone call, Mom invited Danny to eat supper with us. Now, with Grandma and Grandpa joining us, our kitchen was overcrowded. Aunt Maude, Danny, and I volunteered to eat at the card table in the front room.

"Nate's an unusual case, isn't he?" I heard Mom ask from the kitchen. "Doesn't seem like a typical farmer. Where'd he come from, Pa?"

Grandpa collected his thoughts. Then he related the story of Nate Craddock. Here's what he told us.

Nate Craddock was born just after the Civil War. His father, a trapper and an Indian trader, had settled at the edge of Bear Swamp, the wetlands hugging the Chippewa River up where it turns east and runs for Saginaw Bay. His mother was the daughter of a Chippewa chief who parted with her for a hundred-pound sack of salt, a bone-handled hunting knife, and two quarts of Canadian whisky.

When I was young, Chippewa Indians still inhabited Bear Swamp under the protection of an old fishing-rights treaty. To the consternation of sports fishermen, they plied the river in flat-bottom boats reaping limitless numbers of bass, trout, and pan fish whenever they chose, fishing season or not. And, to the consternation of Lake Huron's commercial fishermen, the Indians employed their twenty-by-twenty drop nets from long birch poles to harvest tons of egg-laden lake mullet, making their early spring dash up the Chippewa River to their spawning grounds.

As a young man, Old Nate abandoned the frontier ways for work at a flourishing machine shop in Ft. Lewis, a small village settled on a patch of high ground in the middle of the swamp. There he became a proficient all-around mechanic. But his specialty was the art of welding, in which he excelled. For forty years, he worked happily at the machine shop. In her eightieth year, his mother quietly departed for the happy hunting grounds. Within weeks, his despondent father joined her there.

When Nate's bachelor uncle learned of his brother's death, he keeled over dead on his cultivator in the middle of his cornfield. So Nate inherited the old family farm down in Chippewa County. Believing himself to be the last living Craddock, he felt duty-bound to try his hand at farming. He said goodbye to Ft. Lewis and headed south to take up his new life. The only significant possessions that he brought with him were his 1929 Pontiac sedan, his collection of personal tools, and a full set of ancient welding equipment.

After selling his uncle's horses, Old Nate used the proceeds, combined with a hefty share of his savings, to purchase a used John Deere tractor. It was huge and very powerful, more than 30 horsepower at the axle. According to the dealer, this 1921 model was *the biggest and heaviest model of the era.* What impressed Old Nate most was its giant pair of crushing, steel lug wheels.

Knowledgeable farmers would not have called Old Nate's forty acres *bad* farmland, but you had to know precisely how to farm *clay.* By some glacial fluke, there was more clay on Old Nate's forty *acres* than in any forty square *miles* of farmland in Chippewa County. Any farmer worth his salt knew if you expected to grow crops in clay-soil fields, you couldn't run back and forth over them with lugged wheels under the world's heaviest tractor. Compressed clay makes extremely fine cookware, but abysmal farmland.

Nate's first spring was a particularly wet one. But a little sticky mud didn't stop him and his monstrous tractor. He was fitting his fields weeks ahead of other farmers who lacked the *advantage* of a heavyweight tractor. By the time his neighbors began their fitting, he had succeeded in compressing and compacting his fields into nothing short of terra-cotta.

While neighbors' crops thrived in the early summer sun, his fields baked into a hardened ceramic on which no seed could germinate. After realizing what he had done, he parked his tractor in the barn for good and entered the house. Sinking into remorse, he only emerged to drive his Pontiac for groceries every week or two.

By the end of his fifth year on the farm, he had been physically transformed by acute arthritis, exacerbated by melancholy and deep despair. He neglected his farm and his personal appearance. His neighbors stayed clear of him. Owing to his ineptness as a farmer, Old Nate became the subject of ridicule. He was the butt of jokes at the county fair and at Grange meetings.

When Grandpa and Grandma Compton became his neighbors, they weren't aware that Old Nate was to be scorned and ridiculed. As far as they were concerned, he was their closest neighbor and an old man who deserved to be treated with civility and respect. Despite his shy ways and depression, he responded to their neighborly overtures. Grandpa agreed to farm Old Nate's forty acres on shares. Using Jim and Fannie, he patiently applied farming expertise and a hundred loads of manure to transform the ceramic fields into productive farmland once again.

During the war years, nitrogen compounds were urgently needed in the manufacture of gunpowder and other explosives. Those compounds were a key ingredient of chemical fertilizer. To reduce the agricultural use of those fertilizers, the U.S. Department of Agriculture urged farmers to practice crop rotation. Rotation called for periodic planting of legumes, including beans and peas, to replace needed nitrogen depleted by other non-legume crops such as wheat, oats, and corn.

Another technique for reducing usage of manufactured fertilizers called on farmers to fertilize the old-fashioned way, by spreading manure. So, after harvest time each year, from fall into winter, Grandpa pursued the ancient practice of preparing his fields for next year's crops utilizing the locally grown variety of fertilizer. He started with the backbreaking work of loading, hauling, and dispersing the mammoth, malodorous manure piles from the barnyard to his nutrient-hungry fields.

For days on end, Grandpa tediously loaded manure, one pitch-fork at a time, into the huge box of the manure spreader. When the spreader was full, Jim and Fannie, the stronger team, were rousted from their naps and harnessed to the foul-smelling load.

As the spreader moved slowly back and forth across the field, the ripened payload was flung high and wide, ultimately reaching every square foot of his famished fields. Manure spreading was the final step in recycling tons of hay, oats, corn, and grasses that had been grazed, chewed, and swallowed by Grandpa's cows and horses over the long course of the preceding year.

During the long winter, the fields, having been fed by the spreader and watered by the autumn rains, rested under a protective blanket of snow. This annual fallow period lasted until May when the returning sun produced Michigan's extraordinarily long days that combined with spring's gusty winds to thaw and dry his fields.

By his own example, Grandpa taught the neighboring farmers not to laugh at Old Nate, but to use the old welder's expertise for their own benefit. While Grandpa skillfully restored Nate's fields, Old Nate artfully restored his neighbors' machinery to good working order with his antiquated welding equipment. For this, his neighbors paid Old Nate with their dollars and gratitude, instead of their ridicule and scorn. There was one exception. Old

Nate refused to take a penny for any welding he ever did for Grandpa Compton.

"And that's how Old Nate became a gentleman farmer after all," Grandpa declared in closing.

GRANDMA AND GRANDPA DECIDED to visit Old Nate again before they left town. But they promised to return to hear the outcome of our eight o'clock call. The sun had set and the air felt damp and chilly. Danny and I zipped up our jackets and anxiously waited on the front porch for our summons to the Shurtleif house. We'd already had a full day, but we were eager to find out about our alleged *long trip* that we'd been promised.

While I was pondering all the possibilities, Danny abruptly broke the silence. "What's that you're humming?"

I didn't know I was humming. So I shrugged my shoulders.

"Well, I'll tell you what it is. It's *Moonlight Serenade!* That's what it is!" he snapped.

I must have looked confused because he explained, "You were humming Glenn Miller's *Moonlight Serenade*. Don't you know what kind of music that is?"

My head was swimming. I didn't remember humming any kind of music. I shook my head. Then suddenly I remembered. *Moonlight Serenade, dummy!* "Queenie made us listen to —."

"I hate Big Band music."

I wonder if they have Big Band filters for portable radios?

"Jase! Danny! Your call, boys. Come on over now," Mr. Shurtleif hollered from his kitchen door.

I picked up the receiver and squeaked, "Hel — hello."

"Jase, this is Governor Dewey. How are you, my boy? I've heard all about your part in Danny's rescue. Well done! Is Danny all right?" Before I could answer, he added, "Better yet, tell him to get on the extension. Mr. Shurtleif said it's in their bedroom, okay?"

We don't have one phone and the Shurtleifs have two! What's this world coming to?

"Danny, this is Governor Dewey! You okay, son?" To his credit, Danny's update on his health and welfare was concise and quick.

"Superb news! I'm delighted you're home safe and sound. Now here's why I'm calling. As you know, I've been pretty busy with this Presidential Election. But, from what I hear, the story of Danny's kidnapping and your role in the rescue, Jase, has captured the imagination of every newspaper chain, radio network, and movie studio in the country.

"Because people know that I'm acquainted with you boys, several entertainment executives have asked me to encourage you to appear on their shows. Frankly I discouraged most of them. They're just not suitable for you. I've informed them, truthfully, that you're not in show business. You have schoolwork and other responsibilities at home. But there is one old friend that I couldn't refuse. Ever hear of Don McNeil's *Breakfast Club?*"

"Wow! Sure we have. Who hasn't?"

"Well, *The Breakfast Club* is a wholesome, all-American show. And Don is a fine gentleman who'll treat you boys with care and respect. He wants you on his show next Monday morning. November 6th, just a week from today."

"Will you be there, Governor?"

"I wish I could. But that's the day before Election Day. So I'm afraid I'll be quite busy campaigning. But you boys should go and enjoy yourselves. Don will put you up for two nights, Saturday and Sunday, at the Allerton Hotel. That's where he hosts the show. Can you find someone to chaperone the trip?"

"Trip to where?"

"Oh, I assumed you knew. The show is broadcast to over three hundred radio stations on the ABC network from Chicago."

"Chicago! Terrific! Thank you, Governor Dewey!" I exclaimed gratefully.

Danny was ecstatic. "Chicago! Jase, we're going to Chicago! I just love California! Thank you, Governor. Thank you!"

Governor Dewey had asked Harry Chambers to make our travel arrangements through his office, so we wouldn't have to worry about any details. The governor promised to listen to the show and to talk with us after the election, if not before. Again we thanked him profusely and wished him luck on November 7th. Danny apologized for intimating on the radio that he wouldn't support the governor just because we had each received a note from FDR.

After all, Danny admitted, the governor *had* sent us both a couple of pretty dandy telegrams. As an afterthought, Danny vowed that he meant to do more for the governor in the past couple of weeks, but it had been difficult to pursue a get-out-the-vote campaign from Old Nate's basement. However, he assured the governor that he had managed to make staunch Republicans out of Old Nate and the two POWs. Then it was Governor Dewey's turn to thank Danny.

After briefing Mr. Shurtleif on our trip and thanking him for hosting the telephone call, we flew across the street to share the news. Danny's family was waiting with my folks. And Grandma had just skidded to a halt under our box elder tree. After Grandpa regained his composure, he joined us in our front room.

"Well?" Queenie demanded. "Where are you going? And when?"

Wanting to stretch out the story and save the best news for last, we gave every detail, emphasizing how much the newspaper chains, radio networks, and even movie studios wanted us. And how Governor Dewey had discouraged all but one.

"Who?" screamed Queenie.

"Don McNeil!" Danny screamed back.

"Don McNeil! *The Breakfast Club* Don McNeil?"

"He's wonderful! And I just love his guests."

"He's been on the air since the mid-1930s. We listen to him every morning."

"Every fifteen minutes, he stops the show and then his audience marches around the breakfast table."

"His show is kinda corny, but it has lots of stars. Music and comedy."

"I like his show, but I get hungry when they talk about all the tasty food they're having."

"Uncle Van hears Don McNeil's show on Armed Forces Radio! Won't he be surprised to hear you boys?"

"Well, I guess everybody approves of the show, but when will you be on?"

We related the details to Dad. Two nights in Chicago. Travel expenses for three. Train fare, taxis, hotel, meal, tips. Special discounts for tours, shows, and shopping. Gifts from the show itself.

"Since you'll miss a day's school, you'd better clear that with Miss Sparks in the morning, okay?"

"Now all we need is a chaperone. Who wants to —?"

"I'd love to go, boys!!!"

Danny and I looked at each other, smiling from ear-to-ear.

"Would you really, Grandma?"

Wow!!!

ON HALLOWEEN DAY, DANNY arrived early. With all that had happened, we had yet to try on the costumes, handpicked for us from Grandma's attic. In fact, we hadn't even opened the large cardboard box in which they came to us from the farm. We stared at the mysterious box on the kitchen table, wondering what it contained.

We were unusually late in selecting our costume, but we were fully prepared in one regard. We could quickly toast the large vinegar-jug cork, which we had found at the farm, on our gas burner. No matter what costume we wore, we could supplement our disguise with burnt cork-applied blackface. However, since all of our friends were likely to do the same thing, the effect would lose its uniqueness. Think of it. FDR. The Cisco Kid. Snow White. Hitler. Santa Claus. And Frankenstein. All in blackface!

"Maybe we should go as Amos and Andy so we don't have to put on blackface," Danny suggested. For some reason, I agreed with his logic.

"Have you opened it yet?" Aunt Maude inquired as she entered the kitchen. "You'll love them!"

Danny and I looked at each other. Shrugged. Then removed the box's cover. Under the tissue paper were layers of shiny black and dingy white fabrics. We yanked on the top layer and out fell an ancient tuxedo-like man's suit. The other garment was a long gown of yellowed silk, complete with ruffles, sequins, and beads. And a veil.

Aunt Maude couldn't contain herself. "Aren't they grand? We'd forgotten all about them. When we were kids, we'd dig them out and play wedding. Your Great Grandma and Grandpa Hope wore them when they were married eighty years ago during the Civil War."

Danny frowned and looked unhappy. I was afraid that Aunt Maude's selection wasn't macho enough for him, but I hoped he wouldn't dismiss the idea out-of-hand. I could see how excited Aunt Maude was about finding them for us.

So I bought some time. "Danny, want to try them on?"

"On one condition!" he asserted. "I get to wear the wedding dress!"

In a matter of minutes, the newlyweds, Jase and Danielle Hope, bounded down the front steps and headed off, arm-in-arm, for another exciting Halloween Party at Hamilton School. For the sake of fabric preservation, Aunt Maude ruled out the use of blackface. But she did allow a small amount of regular makeup. While Danny sported pink lips, I had a black pencil-line mustache. What a handsome couple we made!

Aunt Maude reminded us that she was in charge of the Halloween Party. She'd decorate our classroom while we were at lunch and return at two o'clock with her famous Halloween cupcakes, decorated with yellow-orange, candy-corn teeth and black-brown raisin eyes.

"Hey, you guys! Wait for me!"

Sherm *clopped* our way in what I guessed was a blue-silver Martian suit. He'd covered his blue bunny pajamas with swatches of tinfoil from the Tolna wartime-recycling supply. Each shiny snippet was attached with a generous strip of his father's black electrician's tape. And his flashy silver galoshes added a dramatic flare. I also admired the smelly antennae he had constructed from his earmuffs and used pipe cleaners.

"Can I walk with you guys? We're FSG members, right? You guys goin' trick-a-treatin' tonight? Can I come? I got a big shopping bag from Wool-worts."

Danny simply ignored the ersatz space man and picked up the pace.

"Not so fast, guys, my boots are coming off!"

When we walked into our classroom, almost everyone was in blackface. It was hard to appreciate the wide array of costumes with everyone peering at you through Al Jolson eyes. On the other hand, those of us who'd skipped the cork were stared at only for our costumes. Danny pranced, curtseyed, and fluttered his imaginary fan. Miss Sparks raised her eyebrows. He simply bowed, after that. As usual, I stood by as the bridegroom-in-waiting. With all the excitement, very little in the way of schoolwork was accomplished. Before we broke for lunch, Miss Sparks thanked us for trying and announced that our party would officially start when we returned.

Just as the bell sounded, Aunt Maude walked into our classroom. While we were at lunch, she removed the chains made from black and orange construction paper that we had hung out to dry on the hooks in the boys' cloakroom. Using the long, wooden window opener, she draped our *traditional* paper chains over the blackboard and window frames. In the corners of our room, she arranged a stack of cornstalks surrounded by jack-o'-lanterns that she'd carved the night before. Finally, using the janitor's pail and water from his deep sink, she filled the galvanized tub that would soon contain apples for bobbing.

When we entered the classroom after lunch, the room had been majestically transformed into a Halloween fantasyland. Everyone *ooh'd* and *ah'd*. We wanted nothing more than to follow our normal Halloween pursuits of blackboard eraser tag and bobbing for apples. But, before giving in to pure fun and snacks,

Miss Sparks insisted on first playing a word game. We all groaned. But we soon straightened up and listened when she announced that the winner would receive a two-pound bag of candy corn. With sugar strictly rationed, I suspected this *corn* had spent many seasons in somebody's *sugar granary* before becoming a prize for us palate-challenged sixth-graders. Anything sweet was ecstasy no matter how stale.

Her instructions were simple. "Tear off a fresh sheet of tablet paper. With a fat yellow pencil, preferably one with a sharpened point, print the words, *Halloween Party*, across the top of the paper. At my signal, make a list of words, as many as you can think of, that can be spelled with the letters contained in *Halloween Party*. You have five minutes. When I blow my lifeguard whistle, stop. The person with the most words is the winner. Are you ready? *Go!*"

I loved games like this, and I always did well in them. I was especially gratified to beat all those super-studious girls in my class. Candidly I enjoyed being the subject of all their cold stares. So I lost myself in the challenge of being first.

Halloween. Party. Part. Hall. Low. We. Allow. Art. How. All. Pal. Lap. Tar. Tarp. Want. And so on. When the whistle blew, I quickly counted my words. *125!*

Miss Sparks identified the winner by employing an intriguing process. She began by asking, "How many of you have ten words?"

Naturally everyone in class raised a hand.

"How many have twenty words?" and so on.

When she reached *110 words,* there were only three of us left. Danny, Millie Zack, and me. Because Danny sat a couple of seats behind me, I couldn't see how many words he actually had. But, because Millie sat across from him, I suspected he knew how many she had.

"How many have 120 words?" Still three hands.

"How many have 130 words?" No hands.

"All right, let's go back to 120. How many of you have 121 words?" Two hands. Danny had dropped out.

"How many have over 122?" Two hands.

"Over 123?" I was the only hand and the winner!

The cold stares from the losing girls abated with my offer to share the prize with everyone in class.

While standing in line to bob for apples, Danny and I whispered to each other. "Danny, how many words did you make?"

"Same as you. 125." Miss Sparks had announced to the whole class how many words I had made.

"But why did you drop out at 121?"

"I wanted somebody else to win." Assuming he was talking about me, I thanked him. "You're welcome," he replied with an enigmatic smile.

Later that night, as I lay listening to Johnnie's soft breathing, it would dawn on me that I wasn't the person Danny wanted to win. But I decided never to mention it. Blushing brides always make me nervous.

Aunt Maude returned promptly at two o'clock with her cupcakes. The warm thanks from Miss Sparks were barely audible because of the wild cheering from the class. I was proud of my aunt and for her benefit, I assumed, Miss Sparks asked Danny and me to serve the cider. Miss Sparks was last in line.

When she reached us, Aunt Maude asked, "Have you boys let Miss Sparks know about your trip to Chicago?"

When we told her, she interrupted the class to make the announcement. Another roar of applause went up. Danny and I were on a roll. Miss Sparks wished us luck and promised that she and the class would be listening on Monday morning. Her words created an inexplicable surge of emotion. Finally I concluded it was a mixture of puppy love, pride, and stage fright. I swallowed a huge gulp of cider and it passed.

Normally I would be dragging on the way home from school and looking forward to a peanut-butter sandwich. But both Danny and I, as well as our *close* companion Sherman, were *zinging* with anticipatory excitement. As we snaked through the canning factory assembly yard, Otto and his squad were loading cases of newly harvested apples onto the pallet, hanging from the arms of a forklift truck.

We hollered in unison, "Hi, Otto!"

He waved back and gave us a thumbs-up! It was hard to imagine that, only three days earlier, Otto had played a role in the capture of Danny's kidnappers. Now we're back to normal. As normal as any town can be with nasty Nazis. Friendly POWs. Kidnappers. Ransoms. Army CID investigators. State police roadblocks. Press conferences. Bride and groom costumes.

And best friends like Danny!

TO DANNY AND ME, with the exception of Christmas, Halloween was the most popular holiday of the year. Not only would we amass a full winter's supply of edible treasure, but we would do so unencumbered by normal parental oversight and limitations. Even when Halloween fell on a school night, we could stay out as late as we wanted. And we could solicit goodies anywhere our legs could take us.

Because darkness fell early this time of year, by five o'clock we were out collecting. Porch lights of most houses stayed lighted well past eight. If we hurried, each of us could fill a number of shopping bags with treats before our suppliers cut us off. By *hurry,* I mean we ran at top speed from door to door yelling *trick-or-treat* at the top of our lungs and, I confess, often forgetting to say *thank you.*

Regardless of the neighborhood, Danny and I observed certain collecting courtesies. We always skipped houses where Gold Stars hung in the windows. We didn't want to remind those families that this was yet another holiday to be celebrated without their loved ones.

We also skipped houses without illuminated porch lights. In our neighborhood, those were homes of people too poor even to offer plain popcorn. We bore them no ill will and chased off collectors from other neighborhoods who attempted to *decorate* their windows with a soap bar or candle.

Danny and I weren't soapers or waxers. In the past, we each had expended elbow grease removing those marks from our own windows placed there by collectors who didn't share our families' taste in treats. That isn't to say that we were totally devoid of trickery. Each of us carried a window rattler.

We had created this noisemaker by notching the wooden rims of a large thread spool, wrapping a two-foot length of kite string around the spool, and inserting a spike, a long nail, into the spool hole to act as an axle. Grasping the spike with one hand, holding the notched spool rim against a window, and then yanking the string with the other, created a *brrrrrrrap* that would lift inattentive neighbors out of their easy chairs and propel them to their doors with our treats.

Because ours was a neighborhood of modest means, more desirable treats were available from Riverton's other, more affluent neighborhoods, to the north and west of ours. But ranging out to these *better picking* areas had a downside. During battles in the European Theater, General Patton's tanks often advanced so quickly that they outran their supply lines. Our problem was just the opposite.

Unless we planned our route carefully, we might find ourselves far from home with full shopping bags. That predicament presented us with two undesirable choices. To make more room in our bag, we had to waste valuable collecting time culling and removing as much low-value content as we could see in the dark. Or we had to waste time running home to dump our bags into the main collection bin, a giant cardboard box, in my bedroom.

To avoid this dilemma, Danny and I established a string of secret stashing spots along the route from our neighborhood to the upscale areas of town. When our bags were full, we ran to these spots, stashed our bags, and picked up the new ones that we had hidden there earlier.

But this strategy was dangerous. First, it was infuriating to return to pick up our bags that we'd stashed under a low-hanging bush in the backyard of a spinster only to discover that the neighborhood dogs or raccoons had *treated* themselves to *our treats*. Second, with every kid in town out on the streets, we were likely to have our bags burglarized. Third, we could experience a problem of prosperity. It was no easy feat transporting a dozen or more full shopping bags home in the dark, especially when home was two or three miles away.

Our system was simple. When we finished collecting, we carried our bags to the stash point farthest from home, picked up the two bags there, and carried the four to the next stash point. Then we carried the six bags to the next. Over the years, depending on our age and the weight of bags, this often took more than one trip. We repeated *rolling up* our goodies until we had dumped every bag into our collection bin. Because this operation was performed after eight o'clock or so, there was also the everpresent danger of being accosted by teenage pranksters abuzz with hard cider, roving the countryside in their hot rods in search of windows to wax, pumpkins to smash, or outhouses to tip.

Back then, treats were modest, even in the better parts of town. The standard fare was popcorn, collected by grabbing the biggest handful we could manage from a bowl shoved at us through a front door. Some popcorn portions came individually wrapped in paper napkins. Some came as caramel-coated balls. *Buttered* popcorn ranged in color from stark white to yellow-orange, depending on how much dye the purveyors had mixed into their oleomargarine.

Regardless of color or packaging, most of the popcorn was invariably found at the bottom of our bag in a homogenous mass, serving as cushioning for cookies, candy corn, candied apples, real apples, sticks of chewing gum, peanuts, lollipops, licorice sticks, gum drops, and miniature wax coke bottles filled with colored sugar water.

"I've never seen so many bags of treats," Aunt Maude affirmed as we dumped our last one into the cardboard box. "What on earth will you do with it all?"

Danny responded simply, "Eat it."

Mom couldn't help herself. "Your teeth will fall out!"

"Well, we could give it to Old Nate," Danny reasoned.

"What?"

"He doesn't have any teeth."

Wonder why Mom bit on that one.

DURING THE SUMMER OF 1939, Mr. and Mrs. Henry gave themselves a trip to the New York World's Fair in celebration of their thirtieth wedding anniversary. With the theme of *Building the World of Tomorrow,* the fair was a welcome antidote for the effects of the decade-long Great Depression. The fair's planned opening just happened to coincide with the 150th Anniversary of the U.S. Constitution and of the Inauguration of George Washington in New York.

From their offices high atop the Empire State Building, fair organizers focused on the themes of science and technology as the means of stimulating lasting economic growth and prosperity. They recognized that their success depended on their ability to sell the fair to potential exhibitors, nations and corporations of the world, and then to sell the fair to the American people, their potential paying customers.

To promote the fair internationally, the organizers commissioned Howard Hughes to deliver invitations during one of his famous around-the-world flights. They even convinced the famous aviator to display images of the fair's central structures, the gleaming white Perisphere and Trylon, a large ball and a tall obelisk, on the side of his airplane. By all measures, their first sales objective was achieved. By its grand opening, over sixty countries, including the Soviet Union, and thirty-three states and territories had agreed to participate, making the fair one of the largest in history.

The fair's collection of monuments and exhibition halls was erected on a 1,216-acre tract that had once been an unsightly garbage heap in Flushing Meadows, a section of the Borough of Queens. To secure rights to the site, fair organizers had to promise to turn the rehabilitated site back to the City of New York when the fair was over.

Cleverly the organizers convinced Westinghouse to develop the famous 1939 Time Capsule, a hermetically sealed tube containing millions of pages describing the times on microfilm. The Capsule was not to be opened for 5000 years, in the year 6939 A.D. Presumably by that time, the garbage in which the Capsule was sunk would be a bit more tolerable.

On April 27, 1939, the fair's opening day speaker was Franklin Delano Roosevelt, whose presence was memorialized by the first public broadcast on television, *The Medium of the Future*. Paid attendance on that day was nearly two hundred thousand visitors. The admission fee for adults was 75 cents and for children, 25 cents. But days like this were rare. When the fair closed in October 1939, attendance was well below expectations.

And worse yet, when the fair reopened in May 1940, Europe was embroiled in World War II. Many European exhibitors including the Soviet Union closed their exhibits and returned home to focus on waging war. Even though adult admission fees were lowered to 50 cents, when the fair finally closed for good in October 1940 and despite a paid attendance of 45 million admissions, the fair's revenues were only $48 million, far short of the $160 million invested by its sponsors.

Yet the 1939 World's Fair was hailed as a model for future world's fairs. Its exhibits and the people involved in their design profoundly influenced architecture and industrial design for years into the future. In 1964, the New York World's Fair opened on the same site. Regrettably, this edition was also a money-loser. $60 million this time. Perhaps the garbage had something to do with it.

Nonetheless, the Henrys joined the tens of thousands of early visitors and had a splendid time. They sent all their neighbors, including the Comptons, handsome picture post cards depicting the Perisphere and Trylon. For an anniversary gift, their children had chipped in to purchase a handsome set of leather luggage for the trip. Since their return from New York, the luggage had been stored in their attic. But, when Mrs. Henry got word of our trip, out it came.

Grandma had tied long lengths of red ribbon to the handles of the suitcases, so we could spot them from a distance. Danny didn't think much of her idea. Ribbons were for girls, he had explained. She just shook her head and smiled. There was no more discussion of ribbons.

On Saturday morning, half the neighborhood turned out for our departure from the Grand Trunk depot. Our well-wishers

merged with the throng of men and women in uniform, returning
to their units after hurried, brief furloughs with loved ones. Like
every morning during the war years, the depot's boarding platform
was crowded and busy. Years later, long after the demise of local
passenger train service, this abandoned depot would again attract
those same soldiers and sailors as the meeting hall for Riverton's
chapter of the American Legion.

Well before our scheduled departure time, we all had been
kissed and hugged more than once by every Addison, Harrison
(Aunt Maude and Johnnie), and Tucker family member, including
Queenie!

At the head of our train, the monstrous steam engine *huffed*
and *hissed* impatiently, filling the air with odors of coal smoke,
steam, and lubricating oil. The depot telegraph operator slid open
the window of his tiny office and waved a newly arrived telegram
at the conductor who disembarked, collected the telegram,
checked its addressee, and scurried back to his train.

The station's only redcap stacked the last pieces of checked
luggage on his four-wheel, flatbed wagon. From the open door of
the baggage car, the baggage handler beckoned to the redcap who
immediately grasped the wagon tongue and hauled his load to the
door. As the wagon rolled past us, Danny carefully counted our
three ribbon-tagged bags. Appreciative of his conscientiousness,
Grandma patted him on the back. In no time, the luggage flew off
the wagon and onto the train.

When he finished, the redcap waved at the conductor who
checked his watch one last time and then yelled, "All 'board."

We waved our last goodbyes and hopped onto the train.
Knowing the purpose of our trip, the amiable conductor extended
the VIP treatment. He showed us to our first class compartment
and directed his assistant to stow our bags on the shelf above our
heads. He turned his back as Grandma retrieved the ticket
envelope from Harry Chambers' office that, for safety's sake, she'd
pinned somewhere inside her bodice. After punching each of our
tickets, he returned them, advising her to place them in the hotel
safe when we reached Chicago.

"The Allerton Hotel's only a short taxi ride up from Union Station. We should arrive right on time. Soon the dining car will be serving lunch. Plan to be there early if you want to be served promptly."

Promising to check back with us later, he left us alone to admire our accommodations. "Wow! Look at this little bathroom. And a sink too. What tiny towels! Grandma Compton, can we take a couple of these little bars of soap as souvenirs?"

Danny's question was innocent enough. But he wasn't aware of Grandma's inability to resist *free* souvenirs. The wide mouth of her voluminous, black leather purse immediately swallowed three bars of soap, four packs of matches, and the Grand Trunk ashtray from our compartment.

When we arrived at the dining car, four more packs of matches and another ashtray were consumed by the ravenous purse. After we finished our club sandwiches and chocolate milk, she fondled her silverware and napkin ring longingly. But, before it joined the other souvenirs secreted inside her purse, she noticed my alarmed expression and came to her senses.

So, instead, she settled for the quarter-sandwich that I had left on my plate. "Just a little morsel for someone with the pangs," she explained. Danny agreed by nodding vigorously.

The train route took us west and south through the flat farmland of Michigan's central Lower Peninsula, farmland not unlike that around Riverton. But when the tracks dipped south to pass under Lake Michigan, the topography changed to rolling hills of sandy soil. As our train *rumbled* through northern Indiana and Illinois south of Chicago, we counted hundreds of belching smoke stacks from bustling steel mills.

We saw super-long Great Lakes freighters moored to docks, unloading raw materials (iron ore and coal) and loading finished products (principally steel) destined for manufacturers of the airplanes, tanks, and ships needed in the war effort. At many points along this portion of our journey, the sulfurous gases released by burning coal from the foundries and mills were nearly overwhelming. But we accepted this discomfort as a small price to be paid for winning the war.

"Union Station in twenty minutes! Better get your things together, folks." The conductor had returned as promised. "After we arrive, I'll help you find a redcap who'll take you to your cab, Mrs. Compton. I'll come back just before we pull into the station. Do you have any questions before I go, ma'am?"

"Yes. Forgive me for asking, but what about tips for people on the train? For the redcap? The taxi? And you?" Grandma asked shyly.

"You needn't feel uncomfortable about asking, Mrs. Compton. Not everyone is accustomed to train travel. Generally redcaps are tipped by the bag. A nickel per bag is sufficient. The taxi ride shouldn't be more than thirty cents. So another nickel there. At the hotel, the bellhop should be tipped the same as a redcap. When you eat at a restaurant, a gratuity of ten percent of the check amount is customary. And, in my case, a gratuity is not required. I'm only too happy to be of service to you and the boys."

The redcap put our luggage in the trunk of the taxi and we got in. The cab driver asked our destination. When we told him the Allerton Hotel, he nodded his head. Before we knew it, we were driving north on Michigan Avenue. With our mouths agape, the three of us took in the soaring skyscrapers, car-jammed streets, and throngs of shoppers and sightseers congesting the sidewalks.

Pulling up at a traffic light, the driver asked, "Ever been to Chicago before?" We admitted this was our first visit.

"Do you have family or friends living here?" We told him we had none.

"How long will you be here?" When he learned we were leaving on Monday, he guessed, "I'll bet you're going to see Don McNeil's show at the Allerton. Am I right?"

"Nope!" replied Danny.

"Too bad. They always have an outstanding show on Monday mornings."

"You're right. They *will* have an outstanding show. And we're *it.*" Danny quipped.

Grandma explained why Don McNeil had invited us to be guests on *The Breakfast Club*.

The driver, delighted to hear our story, declared, "Governor Dewey's a good man. I can't believe you know him. Chicago's pretty much a blue-collar, union town. But Dewey's got my vote. Say, my wife and daughter would sure like to meet you folks. How about after work I bring them down to the hotel? We can take a little sight-seeing tour, guided by yours truly, and then go to some place nice for supper. How about it?"

When we pulled up in front of the Allerton, the cab driver carried our luggage into the hotel. When Grandma asked him how much she owed, he responded, "This trip's on me. Yes, sir! Two heroes for grandsons. You just got to be pleased. Nope, this one's on me, all right? What if I come back around four-thirty? That'll give you time to get unpacked and wash up."

For an instant, I felt uneasy about having Danny referred to as Grandma's grandson. But I didn't have the nerve to correct the affable cab driver. We agreed to his plan, said our goodbyes, and followed the bellhop to the front desk. After Grandma checked us in and the desk clerk placed our train tickets in the hotel safe, the bellhop took us up in the elevator to our room near the top of the hotel.

When he opened our door, we gasped. Through the wide windows before us, the view was breathtaking. Tall buildings bathed in bright sunlight, a deep blue sky dotted with puffy white clouds, and the azure blue of Lake Michigan extending to the horizon.

The bellhop broke our spell by suggesting that we follow him. He led us into a large sitting room with two sofas, facing each other over a wide coffee table covered with glossy magazines. In one corner was a square table with four chairs. To accommodate room service meals, he informed us. A writing desk, a fireplace, several side chairs, oil paintings on the walls, a dozen assorted table and floor lamps, and three vases of *real* flowers completed the furnishings. A quick calculation confirmed that our sitting room had more square footage than the entire Addison house.

When the bellhop opened Grandma's bedroom door, she nearly fainted. Before us stood a white canopy bed trimmed with white lace curtains. The coverlet was a luxurious tapestry of soft greens and pinks. The carpet was a pale rose. Her bathroom was tiled in white marble. Her pristine white sink was equipped with gold fixtures. Our bedroom contained twin beds with bedspreads in dark shades of purple and maroon. After Grandma gave the bellhop his tip, a *whole* quarter, she thanked him profusely for our be-U-it-ful suite. Yes, it was mighty impressive!

Danny and I unpacked our bags, storing our clothing in one of the two chests of drawers against the wall opposite the window. We only needed one drawer apiece. We hung our jackets on the polished wooden hangers in our expansive closet. Somehow *Texaco* and *Massey-Harris* looked strangely out of place there.

Grandma entered our room. "How do you like it, boys?"

"It's swell, Grandma Compton!" Danny proclaimed. "And we even have our own bathroom!"

"Pretty nice, huh?"

"Yeah! All kinds of free soap too."

REITTER AND BADEN WERE standing in the doorways of their prison cells at Fort Leavenworth. The warning bell sounded and their cell doors slammed shut. Danny and I stood before them and watched as they sat down on their cots. They snarled at us and growled like caged animals. The warning bell rang again. When the doors opened, Reitter leaped up and dashed toward us. Then the bell rang one more time. The door slammed in his face. We laughed at him and he spat at us through the bars of his cell.

"Jase, it's the phone. Pick up the phone."

Why was Danny telling me to answer the phone? Prison inmates don't have telephones. When I opened my eyes, I had no idea where I was. Earlier, following Danny's lead, I had stretched out on my bed to rest before our sight-seeing tour. Evidently I had immediately fallen asleep. Now I was struggling to clear my head, figure out where I was, and end that infernal warning bell.

"Jase, wake up," Danny hollered.

"Hello." I heard Grandma say. "Yes. It's quite lovely, thank you. Beautiful suite. Yes. Sorry about that. We all must have been sleeping when you called. How many times did it ring? Oh, my. I'm so sorry. Yes, I believe we're all ready. Or we will be as soon as we wash the sleep out of our eyes. Where are you calling from? The lobby? Oh, I see. Okay, we'll be down in a jiffy."

When we reached the lobby, we saw the cab driver, but he was out of uniform. Instead of his leather jacket, work pants, and combination cap, he wore a sports coat and slacks. The toothpick that had been magically suspended from his lower lip was also missing. Without his cap, I could see his wavy black hair. In the brightly lighted lobby, the scar that ran from the bridge of his nose to the corner of his left eye was quite noticeable. Overall, he was a rough, but handsome, man with a very generous heart.

Standing beside him was a striking woman, deeply tanned and exotic, reminding me of the young Mexican mother at the Grafton. When she smiled, her brilliant white teeth flashed in contrast to her smooth, dark skin. The daughter was a spitting image of her mother, but softer and younger, about my age I guessed.

What a handsome family!

"Mrs. Compton. Boys. May I present my wife Maria and my daughter Angelina. This is Mrs. Compton and her grandsons, Jase and Danny. I forgot to mention my name. I am Giuseppe Biondi. But my friends call me *Guy*."

We shook hands. They were a warm, friendly family, and we all took an immediate liking to them. Angelina and I were the last to shake hands. As we were doing so, her father asked, "Mrs. Compton, is there anything special you would like to see before you leave Chicago?"

Waiting for her answer, I realized that I was still holding Angelina's hand. She didn't seem to mind. When I looked into her face, her smile melted my heart. As we walked out of the lobby hand in hand, none of the others seemed to notice.

"My cab is parked right out front. That's because I know the doorman. I pick up and drop off fares here all the time. And it's really beautiful inside, isn't it? I know this because my father was a stonecutter from a little quarry town in Northern Italy. He was brought here to help build this hotel, back in the twenties. There aren't many examples of Italian Renaissance architecture in Chicago."

He pointed to the front of the building. "Notice the setbacks, the towers, and the finish work in stone. It's a marvelous example of the style."

"Now, Guy, save that for your final exams," his wife chided with a smile. Turning to Grandma, she explained, "Since Guy got out of the Navy, he's gone back to college to finish his degree in architecture."

"Yep, I'm going to be the only one-eyed architect in the State of Illinois."

"I didn't realize you were blind."

"Yep, it happened over Rabaul. A 20 millimeter cannon round from a Jap Zero shattered the canopy of my Hellcat. Unfortunately I got separated from my buddies and was flying alone at the time. We usually paired up. It was the only way to beat those Jap Zeros. We used a tactic called the *Thach Weave.*"

THE THACH WEAVE WAS named for Lieutenant Commander John F. "Jimmy" Thach who, when commanding a squadron of navy fighter aircraft in 1941, developed a tactic for defeating the Japanese Zero. The Zero's extraordinary climb and maneuverability were a big advantage in a one-on-one encounter with any American fighter of that era.

During one intense dogfight, Thach devised his famous tactic. When a Zero pulled up behind an American fighter in his squadron, Thach radioed the *doomed* pilot to continue in a so-called scissors pattern, the first phase of which would cause the endangered aircraft to pass under Thach's aircraft. Then both Americans would circle out and return on collision courses with each other.

The unwary Zero pilot was suddenly confronted with two undesirable choices. If he continued following his prey, he would fly right into Thach's concentrated fire. If he broke off, he would subject himself to the combined fire of both Americans. There was no way out. When executed correctly, the Thach Weave was a deadly trap that neutralized the Zero's superior performance capabilities.

Years later during my own service in the Navy, I became personally acquainted with the then Admiral "Jimmy" Thach. During the summer of 1960 as a First Class Midshipman, I was selected to spend my final training cruise, prior to being commissioned, aboard the USS Valley Forge in the Mediterranean Sea. I had ranked high enough in my class to land this superb summer cruise.

The *Happy Valley*, as she was known to her crew, was a World War II Essex Class aircraft carrier. She was also the flagship of Admiral Thach who was the Commander of Task Group Alfa, one of the most effective antisubmarine warfare (ASW) hunter-killer groups afloat during the Cold War. Thus, the ship carried forty ASW aircraft, divided equally between fixed wing and helicopters, along with their pilots, support personnel, and maintenance crews.

One day after we dropped anchor in Naples Bay, I was *invited* to accompany the admiral and his family on a driving tour along the Amalfi coast. The admiral's wife thought their teenage daughter might enjoy the company of the task group's only young midshipman. During our tour, the admiral attempted to convince me to choose navy aviation as my navy career choice after I was commissioned. Truthfully I'd been considering the aviation option, but I hadn't yet made up my mind.

To influence my decision, when we arrived back at the ship, the admiral asked the ship's captain to move me in with his cadre of aviation junior officers who were quartered in what was lovingly called the J.O. Bunkroom. This large, open sleeping compartment with bunk beds was located on the far frontier of Officer's Country, way up in the ship's forecastle, right under the catapults. My fifty bunkmates were young aviators, all commissioned officers, mostly lieutenant (junior grades) and a few senior ensigns who had been commissioned after completing the Navy's Air Cadet (NavCad) program made famous by the Richard Gere movie, *An Officer and a Gentleman*. As a mere midshipman, I was by far the most junior man.

In the J.O. Bunkroom, competition between the fixed winged aviators and the *helicopter jocks,* as they were known, was fierce. Each considered the other to be inferior. They argued about it constantly. They couldn't agree on anything except that the junior man and non-aviator to boot was fare game for constant hazing. And haze they did. I really caught it from both sides. By sentencing me to the J.O. Bunkroom, the admiral all but ensured that I would choose any option other than naval aviation. Even the Marine Corps option started looking good.

In the end, I settled on being a navy line officer, serving aboard ASW destroyers which were a critical component of Task Group Alfa. During stormy weather, from the bridge of my destroyer, I often watched the spectacle of the Happy Valley, crashing into one gigantic wave after another. Each wave would lift its bow a hundred feet or more and then, in passing, thrust the bow downward again to await the next wave. Over and over for hours on end, the mammoth ship would endure this pounding. Despite the undeniable rigors of destroyer life, I always considered myself fortunate not to be among those young aviators who, for their own safety, were required to ride out the storm ignominiously strapped to a bunk in the J.O. Bunkroom.

TO DEMONSTRATE THE THACH Weave, Guy had waved his hands in the air as aviators often do. "Fortunately my buddies showed up and ran off the Jap Zero," he continued. "So I was able to make it back to my carrier and land safely. Wasn't really hurt that much, other than the damage to my left eye. But the Navy's funny. They want their fighter pilots to have two good eyes."

"Grandpa Compton's blind in one eye too," Danny informed him. "He can't get insurance so Grandma does all the driving. Right, Grandma Compton?"

"He lost it in a foundry accident about ten years ago. Says he's blind in one eye and can't see out of the other. But he still manages to shoot the feathers off pheasants better than any hunter that comes to the farm. And he reads everything he can get his hands on. So you forget that he's blind. Except when it would be handy if he could drive the car."

"Funny you should say that. Forgive me, Guy, but Angelina and I were just talking about that today. Guy does everything. Even drives a cab. So you forget he's blind."

"Don't mention *blind* in connection with this cab. Unless you want to work two jobs until I finish my degree." He laughed and then kissed his wife on the cheek. "I couldn't do this without your help, Maria." Then he turned to us saying, "Hey, jump in. Time to get this tour on the road!"

Before leaving the hotel, Guy reminded Grandma. "By the way, you never did tell me if you had anything special you wanted to see or do while you're here, Mrs. Compton."

As a matter-of-fact, Grandma did have a special request. Handing Guy a note, she cautioned, "Let's keep this a secret for adults only. Shall we?"

Adults only? Hey, what gives?

After reading the note, Guy handed it to Maria. "Got any ideas, honey?"

"What about that consignment shop on West Ontario near LaSalle? I'll bet they'd have something there."

"We better go right over before they close. Hang on to your hats, folks!"

We arrived in plenty of time. Guy double-parked his cab while Grandma and Maria went inside. Danny and I were dying of curiosity. Within fifteen minutes they emerged, smiling. Grandma was carrying a large white cardboard box.

When she reached the cab, she exclaimed, "Good luck! They had just what I wanted and the price was extremely reasonable. Thank you for indulging my whim."

The evening with the Biondi family was the highlight of the trip for me. Even more special than appearing on a national radio show that reached homes all over America. Their genuine warmth and generosity were in evidence the entire evening. And Guy Biondi was a terrific tour guide.

After all these years, it's hard to remember exactly what we saw that night because I've returned to Chicago so many times since. Like any other city, Chicago's buildings and monuments have come and gone. Many of them have even changed their names. Was it called Grant Park in 1944? What about the Wrigley Building? Or Wrigley Field? Or the Art Institute? Were they in existence then? How about the Field Museum? The Chicago Planetarium?

But there is one historic Chicago landmark that I am certain we saw that evening. I remember it clearly because on October 28, 1944, exactly one week before our arrival in Chicago, Franklin Delano Roosevelt delivered a major campaign address in which he laid out his vision for the future of America. Historians credit that address with cinching the 1944 election for FDR. It was delivered at Soldier Field, home of the Chicago Bears.

After our tour, we drove to a small family restaurant on North Rush Street. After the Biondis helped us decipher the menu, we settled down to a memorable meal. "This is where Guy asked me to marry him," Maria revealed, snuggling to her husband who feigned embarrassment. "Italian food is the key to opening any Italian man's heart."

As I stared across the table at a smiling Angelina, I considered telling Mrs. Biondi that her definition was too narrow. After all, I wasn't Italian and my heart was definitely responding to something.

"Well, I've never eaten Italian food before, but I have to say it's absolutely delicious," Grandma declared. "I wonder if Grandpa will take to calamari, especially when I tell him what it is."

"Better start him out on plain old pasta and marinara sauce. Not too much garlic. Let him work up to octopus." Guy Biondi chuckled at his own joke.

After a friendly debate, Guy finally gave in and let Grandma pay the check. I noticed that she had no difficulty computing just the right amount of tip. She asked for a receipt, as instructed by Harry Chambers' secretary. When it came, she dropped it into her purse, declaring, "Thank you, Mr. McNeil."

We all chuckled at that one as we made our way back to the taxi.

We stood in front of the Allerton for some time, not wanting to say goodbye. Guy apologized for not being able to spend more time with us before we left Chicago. But, early the next morning, the Biondis were driving to South Bend to see Guy's old classmate who was being ordained as a Jesuit priest. Best friends since they were ten years old, they'd even played on the same high school football team. It would be unthinkable for Guy not to be there to celebrate this significant milestone with his old friend.

At that, Danny elbowed me. "Wanna play some football tonight?" he whispered.

Finally we all hugged, promised to write, and said our goodbyes. The Biondis also assured us they'd tune in on Monday morning from South Bend. We watched as Guy's cab disappeared up Michigan Avenue. When we reached our room, Grandma asked Danny to hold the cardboard box as she dug the room key out of her purse. As soon as we entered the room, we realized that we were bushed. So we agreed to sleep in the next morning.

As we lay in bed, reviewing the day's events, I realized that we hadn't slept in the same place since camp. "Pete's the only Italian that I know back in Riverton. Does he remind you of Guy Biondi, Danny?"

"They both have pretty wives."

"But Pete and Mrs. Pete don't have any children."

"Too bad for you, Jase."

"How do you mean?"

"Too bad Angelina doesn't live in Riverton. Then you two could hold hands all the time."

And I thought no one noticed.

"I'VE ALWAYS WANTED TO use room service," Grandma confessed to us as we finished the last of our breakfast. "Look at all those extra little jars of jam and jelly. Make for dandy souvenirs. And isn't that red carnation perfectly lovely? Wonder where they grow them. Sun's shining brightly. It's a nice day. What shall we do? Maybe we should try to find a church service. Or maybe we should spend our time doing things we can only do in Chicago. What do you boys think?"

I reviewed the sights we had seen on Guy's tour. "Let's see. We could go to a museum. There's that one with science and industry stuff. But that doesn't sound too interesting. Then there're art museums. Or we could walk down to the pier. Then there's that Opera House. Or those theaters, the Shubert and the Goodman. Grant Park has some super fountains. And Lincoln Park. Hey! What about the zoo?"

"Yeah! Let's go to the zoo!" Danny decided for us.

Grandma stopped at the front desk for a map and a guidebook. We walked the scenic route up Michigan Avenue, past the Drake Hotel, and along the shoreline walkway. From the rolling lake, wave after wave crashed ashore generating a series of thunderous explosions and massive clouds of mist. As the mist descended around us, tiny rainbows glimmered brightly and then disappeared right before our eyes. From the misty wonderland, we admired the shimmering skyline behind us. Then we crossed the street and entered the park.

Grandma scanned her guidebook for interesting tidbits to entertain us as we walked north toward the zoo. "This used to be called *Cemetery Park.* Began as a cemetery for people who died of cholera and smallpox. Buried them in shallow graves along the lakeside here around 1850 or so. After this area became a park, the city relocated the bodies to other cemeteries. Well, I should hope so. Who'd want to go to a zoo built over caskets full of smallpox?

"Anyway let's see. Oh, when President Lincoln was assassinated, the park was renamed in his honor. Hmmm. The boundary between the park and Lake Michigan is a breakwater, to prevent flooding. See it over there? That's why there are so many little lakes and ponds here. Somebody donated some mute swans. Oh, I see. That's how the zoo got started. Lincoln Park Zoo. How about that?"

We walked through the spacious park admiring the handsome landscaping and the many statues of men we knew from our history books. Lincoln, naturally. Grant. Sheridan. La Salle. Benjamin Franklin. And even Hans Christian Andersen.

"Look at that giant greenhouse! Let's go in."

Danny wrinkled his nose at me, his silent method of registering his distain for an idea. But, nonetheless, giving way to Grandma's enthusiasm, we followed her inside. The warm, moist air hit us like a wet blanket but Grandma was in heaven. "What could those be? They sort of look like African violets. Don't you think so, boys? Can you read the name on that little stick?"

And so it went, for the next two hours or so. Mercifully, after Grandma had admired every species in the place, we departed. "I had no idea you boys were so interested in exotic plants."

"Neither did we!" Danny quipped. "Isn't it about time for lunch?"

The hot dogs were superb. The menu called them *Chicago Specials.* We each ordered two. As we ate our Specials and slurped our drinks, Grandma gave us the highlights of the zoo's history. "After the swans, came the bear pit in 1879. That didn't work so well. The bears kept getting out at night and roaming around the park. Then came the American bison. The buffalo, you know? And can you believe this? They moved eighteen sea lions, or *seals* as they're called, into the Sea Lion Pool before it was finished. All of them escaped. They wandered into a restaurant over there on Clark Street. I'll bet that was a hoot! All but one was recaptured. He was last seen diving into Lake Michigan and heading out to sea. Hee! Hee!

"Hmmm. The eagle exhibit opened in 1895. Then the Small Mammal House. Followed by the Bird House. Reptile House. Primate House. In 1931, they got a lowland gorilla named Bushman. Wonder if he's still here. During the Depression, they took in animals from circuses who couldn't afford to care for them. Hmmm.

"Last year, they bought an elephant from the Brookfield Zoo. You've heard of that, right? Only about fifteen miles west of here. The elephant wouldn't get on the truck, so they walked her here from Brookfield. Isn't that funny? This year they hired a new director from the Buffalo Zoo. Name's Marlin Perkins. Well, that's about it. Let's take a look."

What a thrill to see real, live versions of animals that we'd only seen in movies or books. Danny and I were immediately drawn to the lions and tigers. Recently we'd seen a Frank Buck movie featuring a showdown between the world's two biggest cats. The tiger won, sort of. Actually the lion bugged out before the last round.

As we stood before their cages, we were disappointed that the man-eaters preferred to nap rather than swipe their claws and growl at us as they do in the movies. And it struck us as odd that so many of the animals in the zoo seemed to be walking off cramps in their legs by pacing back and forth in their cages. What was that about? And another thing struck me. Zoos don't smell so good.

When the elephant keeper let a giant Indian elephant smooch us with her trunk, Danny wasn't sure what he thought of that. But he did observe that it tickled some. I knew exactly what I thought of it. It was wet and it was her nose. And I didn't want my shoulder looking like Sherm's jacket sleeve.

As the sun fell behind the tall buildings along Clark, we ambled back to the Allerton. "It's been quite a day, boys. Just think. Tomorrow morning you'll be on the radio. All over the country. Are you nervous?"

"I am. A little," I admitted.

"Not me," Danny asserted boldly. "I've been on the radio a *number* of times."

"What *number* of times?" I challenged.

"One!" he replied with a grin.

"IT'S A BEAUTIFUL DAY in Chicago!" Instantaneously Don McNeil's traditional opening was heard in homes nationwide over ABC's network of 350 affiliates, including WRDP in Riverton, Michigan.

The Breakfast Club was on the air!

Grandma, Danny, and I were seated at the head table with Don McNeil and *Aunt Fanny* who was a regular daily guest on the show. For twenty-five years, the role of this gossipy spinster was played by Fran Allison. (Miss Allison is perhaps best known for her later role as the only human on puppeteer Bert Tillstrom's early television show, *Kukla, Fran, and Ollie.*)

At Don's *First Call to Breakfast!* the entire studio audience rose and marched around the breakfast table, keeping time with the studio orchestra's jaunty tune. In homes across America, listeners joined in and marched around their tables as well. Every fifteen minutes during this hour-long variety show, this trademark wake-up call went out over the airwaves.

From 1933 until 1968, Don McNeil hosted *The Breakfast Club.* Millions tuned in five days a week to laugh, sing, and march with him. And to be entertained by his many guests. This Monday morning, we were his entire show.

"Ladies and gentlemen, by now most Americans have heard the amazing story of the two courageous boys from Riverton, Michigan, who single-handedly foiled a kidnapping and ransom plot perpetrated by two escaped Nazi POWs. And, in the process, saved the life of an innocent older gentleman.

"Well, I'll tell you what, folks, if you haven't heard their story, you're going to hear it today. Because sitting right here with Aunt Fanny and me are the two ten-year-old boys, Danny Tucker and Jase Addison, accompanied by Jase's grandmother, Mrs. Jane Compton. Let's give them a big hand, folks."

After the cheering and applause died down, Don looked at Grandma Compton. "Tell us what you think of these two boys, Mrs. Compton."

"Well naturally I'm very proud of them both. Their dealings with these two particular POWs go back several months. Way back to June."

Then Grandma told Don McNeil and America all about the canning-factory sauerkraut theft, our role in the capture of Reitter and Baden at Granville Park, and the resultant trial of the Libby sisters.

"All of this was very serious business. Not ordinarily the business of ten-year-old boys. But these boys are quite exceptional."

She went on to tell about the Matlock fire, Mrs. Matlock's rescue by Otto and his crew, and our successful campaign to raise funds for the homeless family. "And, thanks to the resourcefulness of Danny, the donation that pushed the campaign over its goal line came from none other than J. Edgar Hoover himself. A few days ago when Governor Thomas E. Dewey visited the Addison house, he brought personal notes for the boys from both President Roosevelt and from Director Hoover. And after these boys foiled the kidnapping plot, they each received personal telegrams from the Governor, the President, and the Director. Yes, sir, I'm very proud of them. Very proud indeed!"

The studio audience broke into applause that lasted for exactly two minutes and thirty-nine seconds. I timed it on the studio clock placed in front of us so Don could carefully keep track of his time. Don's questions for Danny and me were similar to those we'd heard from reporters at our press conferences, students at school, and neighbors at home. Those rehearsals definitely helped us answer his questions.

Then Don invited members of the studio audience to ask us questions as well. One nice, gray-haired lady asked, "Jase, what do you think of Chicago?"

"We really like it. Everybody's been very friendly — and — and nice to us."

"And what do you think of Chicago, Danny?" the lady continued.

"Friendly cab drivers. Tall buildings. Lots of cars. Beautiful Italians. Classy hotels. Quick room service. Pretty lakes. Huge hot dogs. Boring flowers. Not enough churches. Sleepy tigers. Nervous bears. Snotty elephants. Nice radio hosts. That's about it. No, wait! One more thing. Everybody here speaks with funny accents." He turned to Don and winked at him.

For once our host was speechless. Realizing that Don needed rescuing, the program director cued the orchestra that immediately broke into a rousing *God Bless America*. After that, Don McNeil announced, "Second Call to Breakfast, America!"

Grandma, Danny, and I joined the studio audience and marched around the breakfast table. When the *call* was finished, we returned to our seats. By then, Don had regained his composure. "Today we are grateful to Governor Thomas E. Dewey who helped us arrange for you to be here to share your story with America. Thank you, Governor!"

Don looked across the room at his director before turning back to us. "And, folks, we have a surprise for you. Are we ready, Joe?" The director nodded his head and Don spoke into his microphone, "Good morning, Mr. President. Can you hear me, sir?"

"Hello to you, Don. Greetings to your listeners and all those with you in Chicago. Thank you for allowing me to join you. Your young guests are a striking example of what is so amazing about America. Even our young boys can teach us all something about bravery, courage, and patriotism. Good morning, Danny and Jase. How are you?"

"Just fine, sir," we chimed.

Franklin Delano Roosevelt! I couldn't believe we were speaking with our neighborhood hero. Before remembering that all of America was listening, my immediate reaction was, *Wait until I tell Miss Sparks.*

"I heard you fellas made a radio appearance in Riverton with my opponent, Governor Dewey. Tomorrow being Election Day, I had to come on *The Breakfast Club* just to make things even. Boys, I think you know the Director of the FBI. He's here in the Oval Office with me and has something to say to you."

"Hello, boys! Congratulations and thank you for finally putting an end to Reitter and Baden. Those rascals'll never bother anybody again. Boys, Mr. McNeil will act as my surrogate there in Chicago this morning. He should be handing you each an *FBI Medal of Courage,* the highest honor that the Bureau can confer on an American citizen. I'll just read a portion of the certificate that comes with your medals."

Don held the medals high so the studio audience could see them clearly. Then he handed one of them to each of us. Danny fondled his and then looked up at me. His black eyes were as big as the Terraplane's headlights. My head was light. I realized that I hadn't breathed since FDR first spoke to us.

Was this really happening? And was Mr. Hoover really reading to us?

The Medal of Courage is awarded for conspicuous gallantry and intrepidity when facing a sworn enemy of the United States of America. Your acts of bravery have clearly distinguished you in the eyes of your countrymen. For this, your grateful Nation salutes you.

"Boys, Mr. Hoover and I salute you as well," FDR declared.

When the noise subsided, Don McNeil asked, "Do either of you boys have any more you'd like to say to the President or Mr. Hoover?"

"Just, thank you again," I squeaked.

For once, Danny was speechless.

After thanking his Washington guests once again, Don McNeil closed his program with his traditional farewell, "So long and be good to your neighbor."

12 NEW NEIGHBORS

TO KEEP OUR MEDALS OF COURAGE SAFE, WE HID them under my mattress with our other valuables. But we couldn't resist taking our certificates to school. Anxious to accompany his heroes, Sherm was waiting for us on the front walk when we emerged from my house.

"Whatcha got, guys? Let me see! Let me see!" he demanded.

Danny reminded Sherm that he didn't know how to read. But that didn't deter Sherm. So we removed the handsome, engraved certificates from their manila envelopes and allowed him to admire them.

"Ooooo! Wow! They're so — *green!* Just like money! We need to get certificates like these for FSG members. Don't we, guys? My teacher says I have artistic talons. So I can make them for us, okay?"

"Brilliant thinking, Sherm!" Danny scoffed. "With *sooooo* many FSG members, we absolutely *need* membership certificates, just to keep track of everybody. From now on, before we share an FSG secret, we'll make members show us their certificates."

Then Danny used his *talons* to give Sherm a good pinch.

"Ouch! Cut it out, Danny!"

When we reached Hamilton School, the parking area was filled with cars. "What's going on?"

The large sign next to the front door answered my question.

```
General Election
Precinct 13
```

With all the excitement, I had nearly forgotten that it was Election Day.

When we entered the classroom, our classmates surrounded us, peppering us with questions about the broadcast. "How big was the microphone? Did you actually eat breakfast during the show? Did the audience really march around the studio? Was President Roosevelt right there with you? Where are your medals? What do they look like? Are you going to frame these certificates?"

Fatigued by the interrogation, I longed for the familiar morning routine. Miss Sparks came to my rescue. "Class, please settle down. We'll start today with a reading from the book of Acts."

On our way home from school that day, I asked, "Don't you wish you were old enough to vote, Danny?"

"No! Then I'd have to choose between President Roosevelt and Governor Dewey. And I like them both." He had a point.

As it turned out, the 1944 Presidential Election wasn't much of a contest. Though aging and in deteriorating health, President Roosevelt remained extremely popular with American voters. Even with the end of the war in sight, Governor Dewey chose not to attack the foreign policy of the administration. Instead, he campaigned against the New Deal and called for less government and less regulation of the economy, especially after the war ended.

On one occasion, Dewey supporters attacked Roosevelt for incurring the cost of having a navy destroyer retrieve his dog, inadvertently left behind in the Aleutian Islands. Roosevelt turned the incident into a political coup by declaring, "These Republican leaders have not been content with attacks on me. Or my wife. Or my sons. No, not content with that, they now include my little dog Fala. Well, of course, I don't resent attacks. And my family doesn't resent attacks. But Fala does resent them."

This speech, delivered in September 1944 to the International Brotherhood of Teamsters, is credited with cinching FDR's victory over Dewey. Although he only received fifty-three percent of the popular vote, the smallest margin of victory of all his Presidential bids, Roosevelt did, however, win 432 electoral votes to Dewey's 99. Dewey even failed to carry New York and Michigan.

Four years later in the biggest surprise in the history of Presidential elections, the heavily favored Dewey would lose again to the unpopular incumbent, Harry Truman. The *Chicago Tribune's* too-early edition even carried the headline, *Dewey Defeats Truman.* After his second defeat, Dewey returned to Albany where he continued to serve as governor of New York until 1955. Then he left politics to establish his own law firm where he practiced until his death in 1971.

Regardless of his performance at the polls, because of his thoughtfulness and concern for us, Governor Dewey always stood tall in the eyes of Danny and me. "Do you think he'll come to see us, Jase?"

"Yes, he said he would. So he'll come."

Two days following the 1944 election, Governor Dewey returned home to nearby Owosso to seek solace from old friends and family. As promised, he also came to visit Danny and me. When he pulled up, we were sitting on my front porch steps, assessing our world. Neither of us recognized the car he was driving, an old Chevrolet owned by his mother. It was a far cry from the chauffeur-driven limousine that had brought him to our door just a few weeks earlier.

"Hello, boys. Nice to see you again. A lot's happened since we were last together. Kidnappings. Escapes. Radio shows. And — oh, yes — a Presidential election. Tell me all about your Chicago trip."

We shared everything about our experience, including the surprise call by President Roosevelt. At the mention of the President's name, the governor smiled slightly. "Boys, let me tell you something in confidence. I've tackled a number of tough assignments in my life, but I've never had a tougher one than running for President against Franklin Delano Roosevelt. You see, it's hard for me to say anything disparaging about the man because of all he's been through. While our politics may differ, I can't help but admire him.

"There's a reason why voters have elected him for four Presidential terms. Look at all that's happened since he first came to office in 1932. The Great Depression. Pearl Harbor. The Second World War. And him, afflicted with a disease so debilitating that he requires someone to prop him up, just to make a speech. Yet undaunted through it all, he's led our country with optimism and high spirits."

In the 1920s and 1930s, thousands of Americans, especially children, contracted polio and suffered from its crippling effects. President Roosevelt was one of polio's victims. Known as a fighter, the President founded the National Foundation for Infantile Paralysis in 1938 to search for a cure for this deadly disease.

During his radio show, Eddie Cantor urged his listeners to send any spare dimes they had to the White House to contribute to the President's fund. Over the course of this first, four-month March of Dimes campaign, the White House received over two million dimes. Combined with other fund-raising efforts including Birthday Balls held on FDR's birthday, the total collected for the fund in the first year was over two million dollars. Sixteen years later, Dr. Jonas Salk, whose research was funded by the March of Dimes, discovered a vaccine to prevent polio.

"I don't think there's a man on the face of this earth who could have possibly done a better job. Frankly I'm glad he's been there for us." Governor Dewey didn't sound like a man who had just lost the most important political race of his life. He sounded like a grateful American.

He commended us again for our courage and asked us to let him know if we ever needed anything. We shook hands and he was gone. Danny and I sat in silence. In my mind, I reviewed the extraordinary events that had brought this fine man to our porch that evening. How privileged I felt being acquainted with brave men like Governor Thomas E. Dewey and President Franklin D. Roosevelt who had willingly devoted their lives to the service of our country.

Danny sighed.

"What are you thinking?" I asked.

"I wonder if they'd like to be FSG members."

Wouldn't that be something?

AFTER GOVERNOR DEWEY'S DEPARTURE, we leaned back against the porch steps and lapsed into silence. As the moonless night slowly descended, the temperatures descended as well.

"It's getting cold. You wanna go in, Danny?" He shook his head and stared into space. "Mom should be back from Camp Riverton soon."

My mother's part-time job, teaching sewing classes to the POWs, was working out very well for all of us. With Aunt Maude lending a hand at home, Mom was able to teach several evenings each week. The familiar khaki-colored army car turned onto Forrest Street and headed toward us.

"Here she comes now."

After the car came to a stop, I was surprised when two soldiers hopped out. "Hello, Jase. Danny," said Junior Shurtleif. "This is Sergeant Nakayama. Skip, meet Jase Addison and Danny Tucker, the two boys I was telling you about."

As we shook hands, I noticed that, like Junior Shurtleif, the newcomer's chest was covered with service ribbons. I assumed that he and Junior knew each other from having served together in Europe.

"Jase, is your father home? I'd like him to meet Sergeant Nakayama."

"Yes, he's here. Please come inside. When I saw the army car, I thought you were Mom, being brought home from her class."

"We were just talking with her out at the camp. She'll be along soon."

As Sergeant Nakayama mounted our front steps, I became aware of two things. First, he had a serious limp. Second, he had the same last name as the family that owned and operated the Chop Suey Diner.

"Are you and Mr. Nakayama from the diner related?"

"Yes, he's my uncle."

"We love to eat there!" Danny piped in. "The waitresses are so friendly."

And so pretty. *Especially Nikki.*

"They're my cousins, Nikki and Mitsui. I haven't seen them since they were very young, before my uncle's family moved here from Sacramento. That's where both our families used to live."

I noticed another thing. Skip Nakayama spoke English without a trace of an accent. This was not true of his uncle's family.

"Hello, Maude. John. I'd like you to meet Skip Nakayama. Our units fought together at Monte Cassino. Although we never met in Italy, we shared stints together at Walter Reed. Skip was wounded while serving with the 442nd RCT. That's Regimental Combat Team. Thanks to some tough fighting in Italy, they earned the nickname, *The Purple Heart Battalion.*"

Between September 1943 and May 1945, the legendary 442nd RCT made up entirely of Nisei, second-generation Japanese-Americans, fought in eight major campaigns in the European Theater. During this period, the all-volunteer 442nd became the most decorated unit for its size and length of service in the history of the American military. In one case, the Nisei troops went into battle in the snow-covered Vosges Mountains to rescue 140 men from the 36th "Texas" Infantry Division. During the fighting, the Japanese-Americans suffered more than eight hundred casualties.

While serving in Europe, the Nisei were awarded 18,143 decorations, including 52 Distinguished Service Crosses. The unit also suffered an overall casualty rate of 300%. In April 1945, Lieutenant Daniel K. Inouye was one of those awarded the DSC for bravery in action near the Italian village of San Terenzo. Many years later, Senator Daniel K. Inouye would go to Washington as the first Japanese-American member of Congress. Ironically, as the Nisei fought in Europe, their family members languished in internment camps back in America.

"Pleased to meet you, Skip. I've read a lot about your outfit in the newspaper. You've compiled quite a record but you've paid a heavy price."

We all sat down in the front room. Aunt Maude offered to make coffee. The two soldiers thanked her and declined. Dad continued, "Skip, are you stationed at Camp Riverton too?"

"No, I guess you'd say I'm here on family business. In 1942, my family was taken from our home in Sacramento to the Tule Lake Relocation Center in Northern California, just south of the Oregon border. Because my two brothers and I are serving in the military, my parents are now eligible for release. That is, if my father can find employment outside the so-called *war zone*. That's basically all the western states.

"My Uncle Dai, who owns the diner here, suggested Riverton as a potential new home for them. Based on his family's experience, he says there's very little anti-Japanese prejudice in Riverton. And jobs are plentiful too. I knew Junior was from Riverton so I asked him about the town as a new home for my parents. He encouraged me to take some leave and check it out for myself."

In February 1942, just weeks after Pearl Harbor, President Roosevelt signed an order authorizing the evacuation of all Japanese-Americans from the West Coast. In a wave of anti-Japanese prejudice and hatred, 127,000 Americans of Japanese heritage, most of whom were American citizens, were rounded up and placed in one of ten internment camps in California, Idaho, Utah, Arizona, Wyoming, Colorado, and Arkansas. Many were given as few as forty-eight hours to dispose of their businesses and put their homes in the hands of rental agents. Many of those failing to do so lost these assets.

Relocation camps consisted of hastily constructed tarpaper-covered barracks without heat or plumbing. Typically, each family was assigned to an *apartment,* a single room measuring twenty by twenty-five feet. Families shared common latrines and laundry areas. Mess halls accommodating several hundred people served meager meals, constricted by a daily budget of only forty-eight cents per person. Without heated quarters, during sub-zero winter nights, internees slept in as many layers of clothing as they had brought with them and under as many blankets as they had been allotted, two per person if they were available.

Over time, the Japanese-Americans established and managed their own fire, police, and postal services. Schools, hospitals, and village governments were established as well. Ironically most internees began their day by pledging allegiance to the country that had interned them. Because internees were subject to the draft, over eight thousand men served in the armed forces, many with great distinction, including those who volunteered for service in the 442nd RCT.

"That's some coincidence, isn't it? You have family living here in Riverton. Then you meet Junior who grew up here. And now he's stationed here. What are the chances of Skip being assigned to Camp Riverton, Junior?"

"Pretty darn good! But I'm still trying to talk him into it. He really wants to get back to the 442nd RCT. I can't blame him because I felt the same way when my rehab time was up. But, if his experience is like mine, he'll learn that combat outfits frown on soldiers with wooden legs, like the two of us."

So that explains the limp.

When we heard a car pull up, Junior leaped up and hurried to the door. "Marie, please tell the driver to wait a minute. Then he turned to Skip. "When we're through here, you can go back to camp with the driver. I've got some family business of my own across the street. If it's okay, I'll catch up with you later."

"Looks like a party! Better turn off some of these lights or Mr. Shurtleif will be over here with his citation book," Mom teased, coming through the door. "Hello, everybody. Junior. Skip. Didn't I just see you out at camp?"

As Mom took off her coat, Dad asked, "What kind of work is your father looking for, Skip."

"Well, naturally my uncle offered to have my father work with him at the diner. He even wants my folks to share his house. But my father doesn't know the first thing about the restaurant business. He's a grocer. Before we were relocated to Tule Lake, he owned a small chain of stores in Sacramento. My father hopes to earn his own living and have his own home so he's not a burden to his brother."

"Where are your two brothers serving?"

"Both of them expected to be drafted so they volunteered for the 442nd. They're still fighting in Europe. That's why I'm anxious to get back."

"Your brothers were subject to the draft when they were interned in a relocation camp?" Aunt Maude asked incredulously.

"I'm afraid so. We all lived there at first. But, like my brothers, I didn't wait to be drafted. I signed up as soon as I was seventeen."

"Excuse me for asking, but how do your parents feel about you boys being in the army?"

"Well, they're both American citizens. So naturally they're very proud to have their sons serving our country."

Aunt Maude shook her head. "These are strange times."

"Please forgive me. I shouldn't keep the driver waiting. Besides I've been on a train for two days and I'm pretty bushed. I guess I'm a little out of shape. It was a pleasure to meet all of you. I'm sure we'll see each other again before I head back to Washington."

Junior walked Skip out to the car. While he was gone, we just sat there, not certain of our feelings about what we had just heard. When Junior returned, he told us more about Skip.

"Skip's quite a fellow, you know. He was awarded the Distinguished Service Cross for bravery at Monte Cassino. Carried two or three of his buddies back to safety with his leg half shot off. When he arrived at Walter Reed, he was a mess. But now look at him. All patched up and anxious to get back into it."

"I didn't want to ask him, but what happened to his father's grocery business?"

"He refused to sell it for next to nothing so it was confiscated by the War Relocation Authority and auctioned off. Same thing happened to their house. And the family doesn't expect to see any of the proceeds. It's really a shame. But, like you said, Maude, these are strange times."

Then Junior looked at Dad. "I really stayed behind to ask you a favor, John. Would you be willing to help Skip's father find a job?"

"How, Junior?"

"By saying something to Mr. Graham about Mr. Nakayama's qualifications."

"Well, yes, I could. That's an excellent idea. I'll stop by E.F.'s office on my way home from work tomorrow. Maybe I could arrange a meeting. Skip's an impressive fellow. I'll bet he could give Mr. Graham a first-rate report on his father's experience. *Skip*. I assume that's a nickname. What's his real name?"

"Shoda. Shoda Nakayama."

"Well, the more I think about it, Riverton would be a fine choice for them. Based on how people treat the Nakayamas at the diner, I'd say there's little or no prejudice against the Japanese here in Riverton."

"That's what I thought until today," Junior declared soberly. "When Skip arrived, he tried to check into the Hotel Riverton. The desk clerk snapped, 'For the likes of you, we're all full up.' Then he called Skip a *Dirty Jap* and ordered him out of the hotel."

"I can't believe it!" Mom exclaimed.

Dad shook his head. "I think I can. I've heard of similar things happening at the hotel. There's one fellow working the desk down there who's known for such slurs."

"Who's that, John?"

"A fellow who lives with his two sons over by Hamilton School. Evidently a real nasty trio named Thorndike."

Danny's eyes popped open with surprise. He looked to me for confirmation and then said, "We know a Thorndike. Quite well, as a matter-of-fact."

DAD'S INITIAL VISIT WITH E.F. Graham couldn't have gone better. Not only did E.F. assure Dad that a job was waiting for Mr. Nakayama, but depending on what he learned from Skip, he might just offer Mr. Nakayama the position of chief buyer for his whole chain of stores.

"Experience working in a grocery store earns you an average grade with me. Experience owning and operating a grocery store earns you a good grade. But experience owning and operating a *chain* of grocery stores is the major leagues. That's a grade of A plus plus! Yes, sir. I'm very interested in Mr. Nakayama and eager to talk with his son. Oh, one other thing. The work ethic I see down at the Chop Suey Diner is another reason for my enthusiasm. If it runs in the family, and I suspect it does, I will be a fortunate man indeed to have Skip's father on my payroll."

Mr. Graham's meeting with Skip was set for Friday after work. Dad agreed to be there to make the introductions. That evening we waited for Skip and Dad to return and tell us how the meeting had gone. We were on pins and needles.

"They've been down there for more than two hours. What could possibly be keeping them?" Mom wondered. "Do you suppose they went out to eat?"

At the mention of food, Danny's stomach growled.

"Well, Maude, maybe we should think about getting supper together. Whatcha think?"

Before she could answer, we heard the slamming of car doors. "Oh, good. They're back."

We all ran for the front door. When Dad and Skip entered the house, both had disappointed looks on their faces. "What happened? Tell us. What's wrong?"

Then Dad smiled and they both broke into laughter. "Boy, was that fun! We really got 'em, didn't we, Skip?"

"Oh, you! Tell us what happened. Right now!"

"Well, first of all, when E.F. Graham makes up his mind, there's no stopping him. Wouldn't you say so, Skip? And he has definitely made up his mind on a certain Mr. Takeo Nakayama who is soon to be the Graham Markets' Chief Buyer."

"Why, that's just terrific! Congratulations, Skip. I'll bet that takes a load off your mind."

"Boy, to say the least! I can hardly wait to tell my father the good news. If it hadn't been for — for all of you, it never would have happened. My folks have lived in that camp for over two years. They deserve so much more. It's time their luck changed. Thank you for putting me in touch with Mr. Graham and for everything, John."

"You're being far too modest, Skip. Your knowledge of your father's business was the clincher. You could hear old E.F.'s brain buzzing when Skip described, in great detail, the grocery chain and the control systems his father had devised to manage it. Whatever question E.F. asked, Skip had the answer. Heck, even I was impressed and I don't know a thing about the grocery business. I'll tell you something else, Skip. You don't have to worry about a job for yourself after the army. I swear E.F. would have hired you on the spot if you'd been available."

"My gosh! This all sounds so wonderful. How soon can your parents be here, Skip?"

"Well, if Mr. Graham had his way, they would have been here yesterday. He's planning to wire the offer to my father. And then wire him funds to take the next available cross-country train to Riverton. I'd say they'll be here within a week. Or ten days, tops. They won't have much to pack. When we were relocated, we could only bring what we could carry. They won't hesitate to leave Tule Lake in a hurry.

"By now, most of their friends have proved their loyalty and taken oaths of allegiance as my parents have. And most had children to help them find employment away from the West Coast. So their friends have been released and gone to jobs all over the country. With us three boys overseas, we couldn't help them. Anyway now that my father has a position, there's nothing to keep them there."

"Will you be here when they arrive?"

"No, I need to get back to Washington. I still have some more rehab. And I can do more there to pursue my goal of getting back to the 442nd and to untangle any red tape my parents might encounter. No, I'm better off in Washington. Besides my uncle's family and the Grahams are here to help them get settled."

"Will your parents live with your uncle?"

Dad and Skip smiled at each other before Skip answered that question. "You won't believe this one. They'll be living at Mr. Graham's farm. Apparently there's an unoccupied farm house on the property. Mr. Graham promises he'll have it cleaned, redecorated, and furnished before my parents arrive. And I believe him. He won't discuss rent. Says that'll just be one of the fringe benefits. That's what he called it, a fringe benefit. I'm so pleased for them."

"I didn't realize the Grahams had a farm."

"Well, they don't really. But they call it that. Their property probably consists of four or five acres. The only animals they keep are E.F.'s hunting dogs. In addition to their spacious home, there's that old farm house that belonged to the original farm that was subdivided into large lots like theirs. Once it's fixed up, it'll be a pleasant place for Skip's parents."

"There can't be any more good news, can there?"

"Well, not for the Nakayama family. But there is for two ten-year-old boys we know."

"What, Dad?"

"Mr. Graham was extremely pleased to have recovered his car, his hunting equipment, his wallet with most of his money, and his ration book. All, thanks to you boys. So he insists on giving you a reward. At first, he wanted it to be cash but I talked him out of that. Instead, next summer, Mr. Graham is sending you both back to Camp Harmony for four whole weeks!"

Danny looked at me and moaned, "Down, Shep!"

IF GRANDPA AND GRANDMA Compton had heard it once, they'd heard it from Old Nate a thousand times. Usually it occurred when Grandpa needed to discuss farm matters with him. Because Grandpa was working Nate's farm on shares, he considered Nate his partner. On those occasions, Nate felt obligated to explain, one more time, why he became a farmer in the first place.

Invariably, his explanation went something like this, "When I inherited my uncle's farm, my decision to try my hand at farming was based on family responsibility. Because I was the last living Craddock, I felt duty-bound to do so." Because he had no teeth, his words sounded more like, "Becau*thh*e I wa*thh* the la*thh*t living Craddock —."

So you can imagine Grandma's astonishment that day at the hospital when Nate surprised her with the news about the existence of his cousins, the Craddock sisters, and of their arrival two days hence.

When Nate was cleaning out his uncle's correspondence files, he learned that he was not the last living Craddock after all. This was just a few days before Reitter and Baden tied him to his kitchen chair and held him hostage in his own house. According to the correspondence, there were two distant cousins, Abigail and Lucille Craddock. After long careers as telephone operators for the Ohio Bell Telephone Company, the spinster sisters had retired and lived together in a bungalow in Dayton.

Nate thought long and hard about what to do with this shocking new information. Then he made his decision. Following the form of his uncle's will, Old Nate drafted one of his own and named the Craddock sisters as sole beneficiaries. He mailed the original, and only copy, of his will to his cousins with a carefully composed letter. From his uncle's letters, he assumed they were all about the same age. So, after introducing himself, he wrote, with the three of them *getting on up there,* he hoped the two of them could *hold on long enough* to enjoy their inheritance. After describing the farm as an agreeable sort of place, he closed by inviting them to visit anytime they wished. He mailed the letter and waited for a response.

You can also imagine the Craddock sisters' surprise when they learned of the uncle's death and the existence of a hitherto unknown Craddock cousin. And, when they read of Nate's captivity, injuries, and hospitalization on the front page of the *Dayton News,* they sprang into action. With a strong sense of family obligation, they laid down a plan to sell their house, move their possessions to the family farm, and care for their ailing cousin.

But there was one thing wrong with their plan. In their haste to settle their affairs, they had neglected to inform Nate they were coming. When they realized their error, they did what any loyal Bell employee does. They picked up the telephone, called Nate at the hospital, and informed him of their plan and their impending arrival.

Before moving in, they wanted to see the house and make any needed preparations for Nate's return from the hospital. Nate asked for Grandma's help in welcoming his newfound family to town. This was just the kind of project that Grandma relished. She could swoop in, rescue Nate, and endear herself to her new neighbors in the process. But she needed our help to make this work.

We were utterly shocked by her presence on our doorstep. First, it was an unexpected visit and second, it was very late for a farm woman to be out and about. It had been dark for hours. She arrived long after Skip had headed back to camp to share his news with Junior. And, having gone home an hour before, Danny was probably already asleep.

She got right down to business by quickly reviewing the situation and telling us what she needed. The Henrys would be at the farm first thing in the morning. Mr. Henry and Grandpa would be butchering two pigs. Among other tasks, Grandma and Mrs. Henry would be making sausage, headcheese, and preparing various cuts of pork for smoking.

The Craddock sisters were scheduled to arrive at the Chippewa Trails bus station at noon. If Aunt Maude and Mom were free, she could use their help at the farm. If Dad weren't busy, he could pick up the Craddock sisters and check them into the Hotel Riverton. Then he could bring them out to the farm where Grandma wanted to break the news about the condition of Nate's house before they saw the filthy place.

If Aunt Maude and Mom were agreeable, she would like them to join her in offering to help the Craddock sisters in the daunting task of refurbishing Nate's house. This would have to be accomplished before he came home from the hospital and before the sisters moved in on November 18th. That was just eight days away.

Whew!

"You can count on us, Ma. John, can you take us to the farm first thing in the morning? Better yet, Ma, why don't we ride out with you now? That'll save John a trip. Are you game, Maude? John, the boys and you can fend for yourselves for breakfast."

My head was spinning with all the new news that we were dealing with since Danny and I had come home from school. Within twenty minutes, Grandma and her two daughters plus Johnnie had blasted off.

The house was amazingly quiet with just the two of us there. I couldn't remember when Dad and I had slept in the house without Mom. Before going to bed, we decided to have a glass of milk and a couple of cookies. Sitting at the kitchen table, I asked, "Dad, what do you think the Craddock sisters will be like?"

"Well, if they *are* Old Nate's age, I imagine they'll be fairly fragile."

I agreed with Dad's assessment. But, little did we know, it would soon be our turn to be surprised.

DANNY ARRIVED AT OUR door wearing his World War I doughboy outfit including worn combat boots, leggings, crossed bandoleers, and his grandfather's old campaign hat. If it hadn't been for Danny's oversized ears, the enormous hat would have slipped down over his face and rested on his chin. With his ears as props, the hat floated above his head like a flying saucer from a Flash Gordon serial. In each hand, he held an American flag.

"Where'd you get the flags?"

"They're Queenie's. She bought them at Woolworths for the Armostache Day celebration today. But she won't need them now. That's why I'm wearing my uniform. I'm taking her place."

"Why isn't Queenie going?"

"She used food coloring to dye her hair red, white, and blue but it came out purple. She's *mortified,* so she's not going anywhere. I wanted to carry my shotgun like a real soldier but Dad lost the key to the gun cabinet. Don't worry. He'll find it as soon as today's over and I don't need my shotgun anymore."

Armistice Day commemorated the end of *The Great War, The War to End All Wars,* or as it's known today, *World War I.* The truce was signed in 1918 on the 11th hour of the 11th day of the 11th month. Twenty years later, Congress passed a bill declaring Armistice Day a federal holiday. Ironically war broke out the very next year. During this Second World War, 16.5 million Americans would take part and over four hundred thousand would die in service to their country. In 1954, President Dwight D. Eisenhower signed a bill proclaiming November 11th as Veterans Day, a day to honor those who served America in all wars. In 1968 at the height of the Vietnam War, a law was passed changing Veterans Day to the fourth Monday in October. But people protested, claiming that November 11th was a date of historical significance. So in 1978, Congress reversed itself and reinstated November 11th as Veterans Day.

As he entered the kitchen, Danny looked around. "Where is everybody?"

"Mom, Aunt Maude, and Johnnie are at the farm." I described Grandma's late-night visit and our plan for the day. "Wanna come?"

"Sure! What's for breakfast?"

Dad finished a couple of repair jobs before we left for town. We found a parking space across the street from the bus station. Since the Dayton bus wouldn't arrive for another half-hour, we decided to have a snack at Rick's. We found three seats at the counter. Dad ordered a frosted doughnut and coffee. Danny and I decided on chocolate doughnuts and hot chocolate.

When our order came, Danny couldn't figure out what to do with his flags. Finally he freed his hands by sticking the flag staffs into the tops of his combat boots. When we finished, we wandered into the passenger waiting room. I was eager to meet the Craddock sisters. Danny didn't bother to retrieve the flags. As he walked, the Old Glories flapped patriotically against his legs. He resembled a Riverton fire truck in the Fourth of July parade.

We didn't have long to wait. The first passengers to step off the bus were a pair of identically dressed *ladies of a certain age.* The women were tall and wiry. Their thin faces, tan from hours in the garden, showed off their white, slightly bucked teeth. Atop their neatly cropped gray hair, perched round navy-blue hats resembling large upside-down, cloth-covered pie plates. Their dresses were plain but attractive, navy-blue with narrow white piping at the sleeves and neck. Each carried a handsome gray tweed coat, folded neatly over her left arm, and a utilitarian black leather pocketbook on straps slung over her left shoulder. They were quick to smile and very approachable. We walked up and inquired if they were indeed the Craddock cousins.

"You must be Missus Compton's son-in-law. *I'm Abigail Craddock* — and I'm Lucille Craddock. *We are so pleased to meet you.* Thank you for picking us up. *Our bags are in* — the luggage compartment. *Now who are these* — fine-looking boys?"

Danny and I looked at each other. Not only did they look just alike but they sounded just alike. And they were completing each other's sentences. *How would we ever tell them apart?* After a pair of crushing handshakes, I rubbed my numb fingers and erased Dad's *Fragile-Ladies-from-Dayton* theory from my memory.

As we got in line for their bags, the sisters smiled at us and declared ensemble, "Well, we've read all — *about you brave boys.* Thank you so much for — *what you did for our cousin Nate."*

We helped Dad carry their four small, leather suitcases to the car and store them in the trunk. After we all got in, Dad drove around the block and pulled up in front of the Hotel Riverton.

"Boy, that was a — *short trip,"* the sisters remarked.

We opened the trunk and carried the bags inside. "There hasn't been a bellhop here since the Depression. The boys and I will have to do." Dad told them. "Wonder where that desk clerk's gone?"

Dad rang the bell next to a sign reading, *Ring Bell for Service.*

"Keep your shirt on out there. Can't you see we're busy?" The angry voice came from an open door marked *Hotel Manager.* "Now finish what you gotta say, Reed. Then I'll blow this joint."

"Frank, you've insulted your last hotel guest. Now be quiet and let's get this over with quickly." The door slammed shut and we heard the muffled tones of an argument.

Bam!

The door banged open. A craggy-faced man stormed past us and out the front door. The manager emerged from his office, looked out the door, and then turned his attention to us.

"Folks, please accept my sincere apologies for the unacceptable behavior of our *former* desk clerk. He used to be a good man. I probably shouldn't say it, but it's the drink." He shook his head and added, "Poor man. Got no wife now. And how's he gonna support two sons without a job? He's got such a temper that nobody in town'll hire him. I kept him on here for longer than I —. Oh, my goodness! Please forgive me. You folks don't need to hear all this. How may I help you?"

After the Craddock sisters checked in, Dad and the manager carried their luggage to the elevator and up to their room on the fourth floor. "I gave you ladies a penthouse suite at no extra charge. I hope it makes up for your terrible welcome to our hotel. Here we are."

The sisters quickly, but carefully, inspected every aspect of their room before declaring their complete satisfaction and thanking the manager profusely. They announced that they would like a few minutes to hang up some things and wash their hands. Then they would rejoin us in the lobby.

As we were leaving the room, the sisters asked, "*Do you have a hotel safe? We have something to put there.*" The manager confirmed that he did and told them he'd prepare a deposit form for them to sign. "Well, that's just dandy. *We'll be down in a jiffy.*"

As we were going down in the elevator, the manager looked closely at us. "Oh, my gosh. I was so preoccupied with my desk clerk troubles, I didn't recognize you folks. You're Mr. Addison, aren't you? You've fixed my wife's sewing machine. She thinks the world of you. And I've read all about you boys in the paper. My name's Reed. Howard Reed."

"I'm John Addison. This is my son Jase and his friend Danny." We all shook hands. "If you've read the boys' story, perhaps you'll remember that the old man who was held hostage with Danny was Nate Craddock. The ladies who just checked in are Nate's cousins."

"That's right. I thought I recognized that name. How's he doing anyway?"

"It was touch and go for a while but he's a lot better now. They say he'll be in the hospital for about another week. The Craddock sisters are moving here from Dayton to look after him." Dad paused and then added, "By the way, this isn't the first time I've heard about people being insulted or abused by Frank Thorndike."

Danny blurted out, "Yeah. What about Skip Nakayama?"

"Skip who?"

Since Danny had broached the subject, Dad described the incident involving Skip and the abusive desk clerk. Mr. Reed thanked him and asked Dad to pass along his apologies to Skip. "Tell him next time he's in town and needs a place to stay, he's welcome here. And it's on the house."

"He may take you up on that offer. His parents are in the process of moving to Riverton. His father has been offered a position with Graham Markets. Mr. Graham's fixing up the old farm house for them to live in. But, if that project gets delayed, Skip's parents might need a room."

We were standing next to the front desk when the Craddock sisters stepped from the elevator. They handed Mr. Reed a thick brown leather bag that resembled a small briefcase. The contents of the bag were safeguarded by a locked zipper. He gave them the deposit form to sign while he placed the bag in his office safe.

Rejoining us, he declared, "Safe and sound. You can pick it up any time. I'll clip a copy of this paperwork to your registration card so we won't forget it when you check out."

Danny looked up at Mr. Reed and asked, "Does Mr. Thorndike have the combination to that safe?"

"My gosh! I completely forgot! Yes, he does. And now that he's no longer employed here, his bond will lapse. I'll call the locksmith right this minute and have that combination changed. You don't have to worry, ladies. I'll stand guard until the locksmith arrives. Thank you for reminding me, young man."

As we walked out of the hotel, the Craddock sisters surveyed downtown Riverton. "Seems like a real nice town. *Lot smaller than Dayton.* We won't miss that place. *Too big.* Too congested. *Besides we grew up on a farm* — over by Owosso. *Graduated from Owosso High School.* That's a nice town too."

I THOUGHT RIVERTON WAS a wonderful place in which to grow up. During the war years, the population was pegged at ten thousand. Of course, a large proportion of Riverton's young men were away, serving their country in the armed services. And a large proportion of our young women, and older women for that matter, were working in defense plants in the area.

Factory workers could choose whether to join a carpool and commute to higher-paying jobs in Flint, Lansing, or Saginaw or to stay in Riverton for lower-paying jobs. The population was about evenly split on which choice was better. Over the course of his working life, Dad did both. Finally he decided to stay home and work full-time in his sewing-machine business.

Our town had a dozen small factories. Most of them manufactured parts and components for assembly plants located in the larger cities around us. Of course, there were also many nonmanufacturing jobs in Riverton. Businesses such as grain elevators, the stockyards, and farm implement dealers served the needs of Chippewa County farmers. The Ann Arbor and the Grand Trunk railroads were also large employers in Riverton. Many found work at switching yards, roundhouses, and repair shops or on train crews.

Riverton's population was large enough to enable its retail and service businesses to meet nearly every need of its residents. These businesses employed hundreds of Rivertonians. The downtown commercial area owed its success to Chippewa Trails whose local bus routes blanketed our city and carried both workers and shoppers to their destinations and back home again. Chippewa Trails was fond of reminding us that no home within the city limits was any farther than three blocks from one of its bus stops.

"If you can't find it in Riverton, you don't need it" was one of Mom's favorite sayings. And she wasn't alone in that sentiment. Some would say we were provincial. But I prefer to think of us as wise to stay home and avoid the smoky congestion of the larger cities.

Back then, our public school system consisted of six elementary schools, four of which had grades K through 8. And, thanks to the large fleet of school buses that covered the county, Riverton High School had an enrollment of nearly a thousand students. The school board consisted of three elected members. The superintendent's office employed two, the superintendent and his hardworking secretary. And there were two special teachers who visited each class in the system about every five weeks to share their talents in art and in music. With these limited resources and a dedicated corps of fine teachers, the relatively few students enrolled in the high school's college preparatory curriculum were welcomed by colleges all over the country, including my future alma mater, the University of Michigan.

In addition, there were two Catholic schools. One included grades K though 12. The other only went as far as the sixth grade. Teachers at these schools were nuns, more mysterious to Danny and me than anything we'd seen in the movies at the Grafton or the Chippewa.

Some would say that Riverton had its affluent and its poor sections. Riverton's founders had staked out their homesites atop the elm-covered hills north of the Chippewa River. The rest of the town, especially the south and east sides, consisted of factories, foundries, and railroad yards. Interspersed among these noisy, hot, and dirty industrial establishments were working-class neighborhoods like ours. Inexpensive homes lined dusty, unpaved streets overrun by crops of boys like Danny and me.

Each time I return to Riverton, I revisit the old neighborhood. On balance, not much has changed. The tiny houses are now starter homes for newlyweds who aspire to upgrade to better houses in better neighborhoods just as soon as their credit ratings support it. Children still use the unpaved streets as their playground.

The old neighborhood still refuses to show any sign of affluence. In that regard, not much has changed in the past sixty years. I can only hope that children growing up there today are, as we were, blessed with a full measure of character building. Freddie Holland, one of my boyhood pals from the old neighborhood recently described his perception of how it was back then. "We were poor but we didn't know it. So we just chose to be happy."

WHEN THE CRADDOCK SISTERS finished assessing Riverton, Dad asked, "Would you ladies like to go to the hospital to see Nate?"

"No, thank you. *We thought it important to meet you folks today.* Tomorrow's Sunday so — *we'll have plenty of time to visit our cousin then.*"

"That sounds logical. One more question though. I didn't ask whether you ladies had eaten lunch. If not, we can get a bite to eat before heading to the country."

"*We've only had a* — tiny sandwich on the bus — *which we brought from home.* We're starved. *Is there a quality restaurant in Riverton* — offering generous serving sizes — *and fair prices?*"

The three of us *men* looked at each other and smiled.

"You're gonna love the Chop Suey Diner!" Danny promised them.

When we entered the diner, Nikki greeted us at the door, "Wercome, radies and gentrmans. This way prease."

Without trying, we'd timed our arrival perfectly. The diner was relatively empty. Had we arrived just before or after shift breaks at the nearby Riverton factories, the place would have been packed with hungry laborers. Nikki showed us to the large circular booth in the back. This table was usually reserved for larger groups, like bowling and softball teams. But, on a slow midafternoon, our fivesome was large enough to qualify.

Filling our water glasses, Nikki described the three daily specials. As usual, they included the hot roast-beef sandwich. Steak and eggs. And, naturally, chop suey. The Craddock sisters carefully studied the extensive menu, reading aloud those selections that interested them, "Pork chop sandwiches. *Hamburger and French fries.* Chipped beef gravy over toast. *City chicken dinner.* Swiss steak with mashed potatoes — *and gravy.* Pies. *Cakes.* Egg custard. *Ice cream* — three flavors."

Confused by the great number of choices, the sisters asked, *"Please tell us.* What do you recommend?"

When Nikki returned, all of us ordered the hot roast-beef sandwich special. Of the perennial specials, this was the one we ordered most often. While we waited, Dad told the sisters about Skip Nakayama and his parents' plans for moving to Riverton. He also told them how Skip had been insulted at the Hotel Riverton. This news upset the sisters immensely. "Why are some people — *so intolerant of others?"*

As Nikki served our meals, Dad let her know we'd met Skip and how delighted we were that her aunt and uncle were moving to town. Nikki broke into a wide grin and bubbled, "Skip's my favorite cousin. When I was little, I had a big crush on him. And he's fought so bravely in the army. We're all very proud of him. Thank you so much for helping him, Mr. Addison."

Then she bowed and said, "Enjoy mears, prease."

We looked at each other and laughed. She laughed too.

Suddenly the door banged open and Frank Thorndike stumbled in. Without noticing us, he walked unsteadily to the unoccupied end of the diner. Bracing himself with both hands on the counter, he slouched down onto a stool, snatched a menu from its holder, and *burrrped.*

Shaking their heads, the sisters stated the obvious. "Looks like he's a bit — *under the weather!*"

Then Thorndike bellowed for service and Nikki hurried over to him. Glaring at her, he spat, "Don't you got no American waitresses in this greasy spoon? I don't want no yellow kewpie doll serving me. You hear?"

The Craddock sisters scowled at each other and nodded. We were stunned when they suddenly rose and walked toward Thorndike. He was hunched over the counter, examining his menu. The sisters came up behind him and stopped. Each reached out and clamped her wiry fingers down on one of Thorndike's ears. Despite his agonizing screams, using his ears, they pushed his face into the countertop. He continued to scream and struggle, but they held their grips like two giant lobsters.

"Be quiet and stop wiggling — or we'll pinch even harder. *You don't believe us, eh?* How does this feel?"

Frank made a wise decision. He suddenly gave up! His entire body relaxed and he sobbed into his menu.

Abigail Craddock looked at Dad and suggested, "John, I think you should call a police officer."

Lucille Craddock added, "We'll hold him here until the officer arrives."

Fragile indeed!

TYPICAL OF FARMERS DURING that time, the Comptons and the Henrys had formed an arrangement to put pork on the tables of both families. Grandpa, a knowledgeable pig farmer, raised the pigs. Mr. Henry, a trained butcher and meat cutter, was also skilled in the art of curing and smoking hams, sausage, and bacon. To facilitate this process, he had built a sizeable smokehouse and set aside an area in his cow barn for storing the crocks and bags of salt used in the curing process.

By the time we arrived at the farm, Grandpa and Mr. Henry had departed for the Henry's with the hams, shoulders, and flanks. In Grandma's kitchen, the four women were busily converting sundry pig parts into sausage, headcheese, and lard. They had already wrapped the more desirable cuts including roasts, loins, and chops in freezer paper and sent these along with the men for storage in the Henry's deep freeze. All the various forms of pork resulting from this day's industry would be shared equally by the Comptons and the Henrys. It was an equitable arrangement.

Dad interrupted the kitchen crew long enough to introduce the Craddock sisters who immediately volunteered their services. "Oh, don't be silly. Look at your pretty dresses, you don't want to —." Grandma didn't have a chance to finish her sentence.

The sisters removed their hats and grabbed aprons from the hook on the pantry door. "We're here. *Please put us to work.*"

"Well, all right then. We're pretty busy with this sausage. Abigail, you could check that lard kettle on the stove. And, Lucille, you could check those heads to see if the meat's ready to be picked off the bone."

Abigail marched to the stove, lifted the gigantic pot cover, and asked, "Jane, are you planning to use this lard for cooking or for soap?" Grandma told her it was for cooking. "Good. Then I'll remove the cracklings. Do you have a slotted spoon? Oh, never mind. I see one. This lard's not steaming much so it's pretty near done. Do you have some cheesecloth and a crock? I'll soon need to strain it."

Before the focus on fat and cholesterol avoidance, I enjoyed eating cracklings, the crisp particles of skin and meat that rose to the surface during the rendering of lard. While cracklings can be eaten plain, I really liked them mixed with flour and made into biscuits. The German farmers around Riverton mixed cracklings with cornmeal to make scrapple.

Lucille offered her assessment. "These heads are ready. I'll take them both off the heat and pick them over by the sink. They're fine-looking heads, so they'll make wonderful headcheese. I'll need a crock and a mold. Cheesecloth too. You'll have to tell me how you like yours seasoned."

Like many cold meats and sausages, headcheese is considered tasty to most people, providing they haven't seen it being made. In the old days, farmers took pride in utilizing every edible part of a pig. And many of the *unusual* parts became the headcheese ingredients.

Grandma's recipe used the meaty parts of the head and feet, supplemented with the tongue and heart. After cooking these parts for some time, she picked the meat from the bones. While doing this, she placed the residual liquid back on the stove to simmer until it became a concentrated, glutinous broth. Next she chopped the meat and seasoned it with bay leaf, onion, salt, and pepper. Then she strained the broth, added back the meat, and poured this mixture into a mold. After a prolonged chilling, the headcheese congealed and was ready for slicing and eating.

"Everything's pretty well under control here, boys. Why don't we run over to the Henry's and see if they need help?" Dad suggested. "Besides, with six women in this kitchen, there's no room for us."

Once outside, I realized just how hot and steamy the kitchen was. A deep breath of fresh air lessened the mild choking sensation I had experienced while breathing in some of the more unpleasant odors there. Butchering was, by far, my least preferred activity at the farm. But I knew butchering was an integral part of the way of life and livelihood for farmers in those days. So, like a loyal trooper, I pitched in when I could.

We found Grandpa and Mr. Henry in the cow barn where they were preparing for curing the various cuts of pork that were laying on a plank workbench. We exchanged greetings and Grandpa returned to his work. From a large, cream-colored crock, he dumped a sizeable amount of what looked like light-brown salt over a large ham. After thoroughly rubbing the *cure* into the ham, he made sure that it was completely coated. Then he lowered the cure-covered ham into a second crock about the size of a barrel. He explained that the larger and heavier hams went on the bottom because they would take the longest to cure. Shoulders came next and then the bacon. When the crock was full, he added a light coating of cure for good measure and covered the crock.

"After three days, we'll repack this crock to make sure each piece is in contact with the cure. Jack, we're goin' to need some more cure to finish up here."

We watched as Mr. Henry dumped salt from the large sack into the cure crock. Then he added a measure of brown sugar and a handful of pepper. "I used to weigh and measure these ingredients, but I've done it so often, I don't need to now."

We asked him how long the curing process took. "Well, it varies with the cut and with the weight of the meat. Generally it takes a couple a days per pound. Like Bill explained, you have to *overhaul* it every few days. Of course, because the curing process removes a lot of water from the meat, it lightens up on ya. We'll pour that water off.

"If we smoke it after curing, we'll brush off the cure and slip the ham, shoulder, or bacon into a *stockinette*. That's a cheesecloth bag. Then we'll hang it upside down on the 20 penny nails I drove into the joists of that smokehouse over there."

"What do you burn to smoke the meat, Mr. Henry? And how long does it take?"

"Jase, I generally use apple or hickory wood. As you know, there's plenty of that around here. But I read in the *Farm Journal* that some people use beech, sassafras, maple, or wood from any fruit or nut tree. Just don't want to use woods with resins, like pines. The trick when smoking is to have your fire burning at a distance from the smoke house and then draw the smoke in through a pipe like mine. You need ample eave vents to create that draw and keep the air moving, otherwise the meat might spoil on ya.

"How long we smoke it varies by the cut of meat and your personal taste. Hams, I leave in about five days. Bacon, three. Some people leave hams in two weeks. But that produces a flavor that's a bit too smoky for me. And the color doesn't look right either. Too dark. For me, it should come out a light-colored mahogany."

With the curing work finished, we headed back to check Grandma's progress. Mr. Henry and Grandpa followed us in the Henry car. When we entered the kitchen, the women were just cleaning up. Grandma looked up and smiled. "John! You're back just in time. I want Abigail and Lucille to see Nate's house before it gets dark. But we'll need your car to transport us over there."

All of us, except Mr. Henry and Grandpa, decided to go along. We needed two cars. The Craddock sisters rode with us. As we turned into the driveway, the sisters gasped, *"When's the last time that* — these buildings had a coat of paint?"

That was a good question. The buildings, including the house, had been unpainted and weather-beaten since I could remember. As a matter-of-fact, most everything associated with Nate was either gray or black, especially his clothing.

When the sisters walked from the back shed into Nate's kitchen, they both had the same reaction. "Oh, my Lord! *Oh, my Lord!*"

The rest of the house tour wasn't much better, although they were somewhat encouraged when they saw the stack of recently cut lumber that Nate had ordered for the construction of a new outhouse. On that positive note, we piled into our cars and went back to Grandma's house.

As we entered the house, the sisters were visibly shaken by what they'd seen at Nate's. *"We thought we'd only need a couple of days.* But that place will take us a week — *or more to get ready for* — the arrival of our furniture."

Grandma came to the rescue. "Now listen here! You're our new neighbors. So we'll all pitch in and help you get that old house in shape. We got two strong men who know how to fix things and mix paint. And four strong women who know how to scrub and paint floors and walls. We'll even put up some wallpaper if it comes to that!"

She turned to the rest of us. "Isn't that right?" We enthusiastically agreed.

"Tomorrow mornin' I'll take a load of firewood over," Grandpa promised. "I was goin' to do that before Nate returned from the hospital anyway."

When I heard Grandpa use the word *firewood,* my ears perked up. The procedure for cutting firewood always fascinated me. In the 1940s, even the oldest tractors featured belt pulleys over which wide drive belts ran portable circular saws for crosscutting tree trunks and limbs into just the right lengths for splitting into firewood. Later, of course, specialized machines were developed for splitting logs. Back then, Grandpa had no tractor, no chain saw, and no log splitter. Firewood was produced the old-fashioned way, by hand. And the entire operation took place in the woods.

Grandpa relied on Hagen Sawmill's skilled woodsmen, using two-man crosscut saws, to fell trees suitable for firewood, defined as any tree not suitable for lumber. Dead trees and scrub-wood trees were typical firewood candidates. Of course, the larger limbs trimmed from trees felled for lumber, especially the hardwoods, also made first-rate firewood.

Woodsmen cut the downed tree trunks into six- to eight-foot sections, depending on the diameter and thus the weight of the section. The section had to be light enough to be lifted by two men onto a horse-drawn sledge used to haul the section to the corner of the woods for further cutting and splitting. From the sledge, Grandpa and another man, usually a neighbor, placed the section in the *open arms* of the portable sawbuck that Grandpa had constructed from some of his lumber credit at Hagen's.

The sawbuck looked like three upright *Xs* constructed from two-by-fours, standing on a rectangular base of eight-by-eights. These components were tied together by additional two-by-fours, making the sawbuck stable, heavy, and strong enough to withstand the torque of the sawing action. Log sections placed in the sawbuck rested at the level of Grandpa's elbows, just the right height for sawing.

Unlike the one-man crosscut, the teeth of a two-man crosscut saw were designed to cut as the saw was pulled through a log. Each sawyer had to resist the temptation to *push* the saw. Pushing or *riding* the saw could bind or even bend it, making it impossible to use. When the saw was being pulled away from you, your only job was to steady the blade by keeping a light grip on the handle at your end of the saw. Depending on the type of tree and its age, even a properly sharpened saw might bind. To lessen this problem, Grandpa carried a can of kerosene to lubricate the blade. Kerosene also dissolved the pitch when sections of pine were sawed.

After the log was sawed into eighteen-inch minisections, these were then split by employing a pair of splitting wedges, a sledge hammer, and a large crowbar. An axe or hatchet could be used to make the final split into pieces of firewood, sized to accommodate the wood stoves at the house. Minisections too green for easy splitting were hauled to the house where they were seasoned for a period of time before splitting.

Needless to say, the process of producing firewood was extremely labor-intensive. So Grandpa's offer to provide Old Nate with a load of firewood was a significant gift.

Grandpa nodded at Grandma and made another promise. "After I stack the firewood in the back shed, I'll take a look around to see what paintin' we could get done in a week. Nothin' on the outside, mind you. Too cold. I'll take my tools and do any fix-up jobs that need doin' too."

"I'll come with you, Bill."

"And I'll definitely be there to help clean, Jane."

Both Henrys signed up, just like that.

"How can we — ever repay you?"

"That's easy," Danny declared. "Just be there when the next Thorndike gets out of hand."

Those of us who'd been at the diner that day reacted with raucous laughter. Within a few days, we would learn that this subject was no laughing matter.

13 TOUGH LOSSES

OVERWHELMED BY THE ENORMOUS JOB AHEAD, the Craddock sisters were eager to start cleaning Nate's house immediately. When they mentioned the possibility of beginning that very next morning, a Sunday, Grandma Compton's reaction, though respectful, was negative. So the sisters stuck to their original plan. They would use the Sabbath to rest up for the week ahead and visit their cousin Nate at the hospital. Dad offered to provide transportation.

Danny and I attended the church service/breakfast at the Mission and both services at the First Methodist Church. When Danny rose for his debut as the choir's soloist, Miss Bundy grabbed my hand and clutched it tightly until he'd sung his last note. When she finally let go, I discovered that my hand was numb, tingly, and purple, about the shade of Mrs. Mikas' plums. Miss Bundy leaped to her feet and led the standing ovation, a first for the normally reticent Methodists. In response, Danny bowed deeply from the waist. That was a first for them *too*.

When we arrived home, Dad was just pulling out of the driveway. "There you are! I'm on my way to pick up the Craddock sisters. I thought you'd be home before now."

"Danny was signing autographs for all the little girls in Sunday school." From Dad's expression, I deduced that he thought I was kidding. I didn't correct his impression. "But we want to go with you, okay?"

As we turned on to Addison Street, we saw the sisters standing in front of the hotel, visually inspecting the storefronts that lined the sidewalk. I suspected they were sizing up their new home town.

"Sorry we're so late, ladies. Danny was fulfilling some obligations at church."

Dad had believed me after all!

Since this would be their first meeting, the Craddock sisters wanted to know everything about Nate. Danny and I briefed them on every positive quality we could think of. "He's a marvelous welder. His neighbors all depend on him for that. A talented mechanic as well. And a loyal friend and neighbor of Grandma and Grandpa Compton. During his captivity, he bravely kept the kidnappers' attention on himself and away from Danny, perhaps saving Danny's life. As a young man, he wrestled a bear at the county fair. He even has a wolverine tattooed on his arm. Ordered lumber to build a new outhouse for visitors. Who else but his cousins could he have been thinking of?"

While I had run out of ideas, Danny offered one last attribute, "And he doesn't have a hint of tooth decay."

"But what does he look like? *Is he a pleasant man?*" Neither Danny nor I tackled that one.

Arriving at the hospital, Dad pulled over at the curb and shut off the engine. Then he turned around to face the Craddock sisters. "Ladies, to be honest, Nate's an old man. He's not in good health and not in good spirits. His body is bent with arthritis. He doesn't take care of his possessions, his personal hygiene, or his health. Doesn't eat well because, for one thing, he has no teeth. Refuses to wear dentures. Won't wear clean clothes, despite the tireless efforts of my wife's mother. He's stubborn and often mean. And he's been known to swear and spit some. In short, much of the time, he's a — how should I say this — a hard man to like.

"But, right now, he very much needs you to care for him. His ordeal with the kidnappers took a terrible toll. This won't be an easy task. So if this isn't something you want to take on, no one would blame you. In fact, I'd be willing to take you back to your hotel, so you could check out and be on your way back to Dayton before supper. Frankly most folks in your shoes would do exactly that."

Danny and I stared at each other. We couldn't believe our ears. *Why was Dad being so honest about Old Nate? Did he want the sisters to run away?*

Abigail and Lucille smiled and patted Dad's arm. *"Thank you, John.* Thank you. *Now we know what a loyal friend you are to Nate. And to us. We appreciate your effort to protect him from those —* who wouldn't care enough about him to provide him what he needs. *But he's our cousin, John.* Our only living relative. *We've sold our house —* and we're moving to Riverton — *just to take care of him —* like family should. *You don't have to worry.* And, with friends like you — *neither do we.* Thank you, John. *Thank you."*

Until that moment, I'd never seen my father blush. But he recovered quickly, opened the car door, and suggested, "Why don't we all go in and see how the old — *f-f-fellow* — is doing?"

As we walked to the door, Abigail took my hand. Lucille took Danny's. Then she snickered, "Tooth decay indeed." Danny gave her one of his grins.

Nate was sitting up in bed, sipping water through a straw. He was clean-shaven, neatly combed, and dressed in a light green hospital gown and a blue robe that looked brand-new. When Dad introduced the sisters, Nate absolutely glowed.

"I didn't think you'd come. I wrote to you. Well, it thheemthh like monththh ago."

The sisters smiled and came to his side. They bent over and simultaneously kissed him on both cheeks. It was Nate's turn to blush.

"Pleathhe, have a chair." The sisters took the only two chairs in the tiny single room.

"Nate, have you spoken to the doctor today?" Dad asked. "If so, what did he say about when you can go home?"

The doctor had been in earlier that day and was pleased to find that Nate's vital signs indicated that he was regaining strength. Even the soreness in Nate's ribs had practically disappeared. Barring any setbacks, Nate could go home within the week. Nate's eyes twinkled as he gave us his exciting news. The Craddock sisters responded with another pair of kisses for his cheeks.

Blush!

"Nate, I saw Junior Shurtleif this morning. He wants you to know that Reitter and Baden have been transferred from Camp Custer to Fort Leavenworth. Junior says that after reviewing the case, army lawyers are positive they'll never leave there."

"That thhoundthh wonderful. It couldn't happen to more dethherving thhcoundrelthh."

The sisters had brought Nate a stack of new magazines ranging from hunting and fishing to Hollywood gossip and everything in between. He thanked them for the magazines and for his new bathrobe which he smugly displayed by hooking his thumbs under his lapels.

"I like blue. It'thh my favorite color."

At the mention of color, the sisters launched into their redecorating plan for Nate's house that they hoped to complete during the coming week. The more Nate learned about their plan, the more he smiled. When they finished, they asked, "Do you have any objections — *with our moving forward?*"

Nate's unqualified vote of confidence in their choices was exactly what they wanted to hear.

"*Then it's all settled.* We'll start bright and early tomorrow morning. *By the time you come home* — you won't recognize the place," they promised.

"I certainly hope not!" Danny declared emphatically.

BECAUSE MOM AND AUNT Maude spent Saturday night at the farm helping Grandma complete the butchering project, Dad and I were still fending for ourselves on Sunday morning. When we left the hospital, we were famished. The only remedy for our condition, not to mention the Craddock sisters' healthy appetites and Danny's perpetual state of ravenous hunger, was the *Chop Suey Diner!*

In a rare break with custom, the diner offered a Sunday special, a full turkey dinner which we all ordered. Slabs of turkey. Mounds of moist dressing. Scoops of mashed potatoes. Buckets of brown turkey gravy. Heaps of squash. Piles of peas and carrots. Stacks of biscuits. Wedges of pumpkin pie a la mode. And mugs of coffee. All for fifty cents!

After we finished our feast, we couldn't move. We just stared at each other in a turkey-induced endorphin stupor. As an antidote, Nikki served more coffee. When we seemed to be responding, she asked us politely to wait for a moment, explaining that her parents wanted to speak with us.

The father, Dai Nakayama, was the diner's superb chef. He had the amazing ability to carry two dozen detailed orders in his head while *flawlessly* preparing a wide array of menu selections in record time. The mother, Aneko Nakayama, *flawlessly* operated the cash register, checked her daughters' arithmetic, surveyed the diner for service breakdowns, made correct change, rendered pleasant goodbyes, and bestowed mints on each departing customer.

With great ceremony, Nikki brought them to our booth and made the formal introductions. She spoke to us in perfect English and to her parents in crisp Japanese. She explained that Dad was responsible for bringing her father's brother and his wife to Riverton by finding the brother a position with Graham Markets. In response to Nikki's words, her father stood tall, reached out, and gave my father's hand a single pumping shake. Then he bowed deeply, muttered his thanks in incomprehensible Japanese, and then stood erect again. The mother *flawlessly* repeated her husband's austere ritual.

Then Nikki reminded her parents that the Craddock sisters had subdued the insulting customer, the same man who had barred Skip Nakayama from the hotel. The Craddock sisters each received pumping hand shakes and bows as well. We all bowed back several times, not knowing how many bows were appropriate.

As the senior Nakayamas returned to their posts, Nikki addressed us formally, "My parents are forever in your debt and hope someday to repay your kind acts. As an initial modest gesture of appreciation, there will be no charge for your dinners today."

Replete with warm thoughts and satiated appetites, we left the diner and headed for the farm. When we arrived, my cousins were playing catch with the bulbous football that my father had played with as a boy. He had donated it to Grandma's collection of toys, used by visiting children and stored in the gigantic wooden chest on the side porch.

I looked through the wide window from the porch into the front room. There I saw Grandpa and Uncle Raymond sitting at the dining-room table, obviously engaged in small talk. Grandpa reached into his shirt pocket and removed a small bag of pipe tobacco and a package of rolling paper. He loosened the pull string and opened the bag, removed a sheet of paper, cradled it between his thumb and index finger, and poured a thick *finger* of tobacco onto the sheet. After tightening its string with his teeth, he returned the bag to his pocket. He folded and rolled the paper around the tobacco in one quick movement and sealed it with a long lick. As a precaution against losing tobacco out the ends of his cigarette, he gave each a final twist.

Then he removed a kitchen match from a pocket on the bib of his overalls and scratched its head with his thumb. As the match burst into flames, even from the porch, I could smell the acrid, phosphoric aroma. He put the match to the tip of his cigarette and inhaled. After shaking the match out and dropping it into the ashtray on the table, he leaned back in his chair and allowed the blue smoke to escape slowly from his nostrils. I had witnessed this ritual a thousand times and each time I was no less fascinated.

After introducing the Craddock sisters to the rest of the Compton family, Grandma got right down to business. "The boys don't have school tomorrow and they want to help. With them, little Johnnie, Maude and Marie, the Craddock sisters, and your cleaning supplies, you'll need two cars to bring you out in the morning. So you'll want to take my car back in with you this evening. And, John, we'll need your car tomorrow."

Dad readily agreed to take the bus to work.

"On the way out, you'll have to stop and pick up some extra cleaning equipment and supplies. Brooms. Mops. Buckets. Scrub brushes. Scouring powder. Floor wax. What am I missing? Oh, you get the idea. The sheriff informed us that the CID has finished examining Nate's car. So it'll be back from Camp Custer tomorrow or Tuesday. Soon you'll have your own transportation, ladies," she announced, nodding at the Craddocks.

The sisters used the interruption to ask for advice. "Jane, before we forget, we need your recommendation — *on a conveniently located bank.* We have some funds we brought with us to deposit — *to start earning interest as soon as possible.* We thought we'd do it — *on our way out tomorrow."*

"The closest banks are in Granville and in New Albany. They're about the same distance from here. But the New Albany bank's on the Riverton bus route so that might be the handiest for you in case Nate's car doesn't get here." The sisters took Grandma's advice and planned to open their accounts at the New Albany National Bank the next morning.

Mom had some ideas to save time. "Maude, if you'll take my place fixing breakfast tomorrow, I'll get up early and go buy the supplies." Aunt Maude agreed. "And you ladies can take Ma's car to the hotel this evening and come over to our house after breakfast. Then we'll load the cars and head for the farm by way of the bank."

Having lived in Dayton, the sisters didn't feel comfortable with the responsibility for Grandma's car parked overnight on the streets of Riverton. "We'll just take the bus to your house. *That way Maude and you can finish what you need to do* — without having to take time to pick us up."

Mom countered, "It's not too far for us to come for you. Besides the bus routes are a little tricky, and the buses will be very crowded on Monday morning."

Before the Craddock sisters could counter Mom's counter, Danny offered a compromise. "Why don't Jase and I take the bus down and pick up the ladies at the hotel. Then Aunt Maude and Mrs. A won't have to go and the ladies will get to your house safely. Like Grandpa Compton says, we're always *up before breakfast.*"

Everyone agreed. What an ingenious idea!

We arrived at the hotel shortly after seven the next morning. Attired in gray house dresses and comfortable shoes, the Craddock sisters were signing some papers at the front desk. Abigail was holding the leather zip bag that she had just retrieved from the hotel safe.

"Thank you again for suggesting that combination change, Danny, my boy. See! The valuables are safe and sound. You better put that in your purse, Miss Craddock." Abigail took Mr. Reed's suggestion, pushing the zip bag deep down into her large, black leather purse. Mr. Reed waved and smiled at us as we left the hotel.

When we returned to our house, Dad had already left for work. And Mom wasn't back from buying the cleaning supplies. Aunt Maude, cleaning up the kitchen, explained that she still had to feed little Johnnie.

The sisters sized up the situation and announced, "With the help of the boys — *we'll just take the bus to New Albany* — to complete our banking business. *Then you can collect us from there* — on the way to the farm."

Aunt Maude could hardly say no. So off we went. We crossed New Albany Avenue and walked toward the bus stop bench that Pete had built and attached to the telephone pole in front of his store. Because we were in for a bit of a wait, I suggested the sisters have a seat on the bench while Danny and I checked out Pete's latest comic books. The sisters took our advice and plunked themselves down.

We emerged from the store just as the bus pulled up, packed with workers bound for the Burke Factory. Danny paid the four fares from the stack of nickels provided to him by the sisters. "Hey, Mr. Jenkins. Want you to meet Miss Craddock and Miss Craddock. We're taking them to the bank in New Albany. They're cousins of Mr. Old Nate Craddock. He's in the hospital. But he'll be out in a —."

"What's the hold up?" someone yelled from behind us. I immediately recognized the voice. It was Frank Thorndike.

The driver held up his hand. "Frank, you're in no condition to ride on my bus. Go home and sleep it off."

Thorndike huffed, stumbled back off the bus, and landed on the curb. Then he rendered a gesture that I won't describe. The driver closed the door and turned his attention back to Danny.

"As I was saying, Old Nate'll be out of the hospital in just a few days. And that's all, Mr. Jenkins."

The friendly driver smiled and patted Danny's arm repeatedly which had the effect of gently shoving him toward the back of the bus. Danny didn't seem to notice.

The bus was so crowded that people were standing in the aisles, steadying themselves by hanging on to the overhead straps. About halfway down the aisle, we came to a stop. "Ladies, why don't you take these seats? Hi, boys!"

Dad's gin rummy opponent, Don Paulus, was one of the two men offering seats to the Craddock sisters. As he rose, I noticed his awkward movement. Don had been severely wounded in action against the Germans in North Africa. For his courageous acts there, he had been awarded the Silver Star.

The sisters noticed his disability as well. *"Sir, why don't you keep that seat?* We'll be just fine standing." Don disregarded their suggestion and extended his hand to help them into the seat. *"Oh, all right.* Thank you —*so much.* You are true gentlemen."

When they were seated, I made the introductions.

"Some people would say moving from Dayton to a farm near Riverton is doing it backwards," Don observed.

"If you were raised on a farm near Owosso — *as we were* — it would make perfect sense."

All of us smiled at that one.

We hopped off the bus in New Albany just as the bank opened its doors. As we entered, a friendly man approached us, "Good morning, folks. I'm the bank manager. My name is Clemons. How may I help you?"

The sisters explained that they were moving from Dayton and needed to open both a checking and a savings account. They would be living with Nate Craddock, their cousin, who was a neighbor of the Comptons. And Mrs. Compton had suggested they open accounts with his bank.

"Oh, Mrs. Compton is a fine lady. And you don't have to introduce these boys. You're Danny Tucker and Jase Addison, aren't you?"

As we followed the banker to his office, he instructed his secretary to bring him the necessary forms. The Craddock sisters supplied him with all the information he requested. "How will you be making your deposit, ladies?"

"We have two certified checks — one from our bank accounts — *and the other from the sale of our home."* Abigail reached into her purse and extracted the brown leather zip bag. "The other deposit will be in the form of five bearer bonds. *They are all in this bag."*

As Abigail showed Mr. Clemons the bag, his eyes popped wide open. "Bearer bonds. Oh, my goodness! How did you happen to choose bearer bonds?"

"Our stock broker suggested them — after we cashed in our — *Bell Telephone common stock."* Abigail and Lucille looked smug. A small town banker obviously didn't have people depositing bearer bonds very often.

"Five bearer bonds! Why five?"

"If we needed funds — *we could cash one* — without disturbing the others."

Abigail reached into her change purse and extracted a small key that she used to open the tiny padlock on the tabs of the zipper. When the lock fell open, she removed it and handed the bag to the banker.

As he accepted the bag, he nodded and declared, "I'm relieved that these have arrived safely. Forgive me for saying, but I think your broker was imprudent. Bearer bonds may be cashed by anyone, without proof of ownership. If you'd lost these you'd be out of luck."

The Craddock sisters looked at each other incredulously. *"How could he have been so —* reckless? *These bonds represent a lifetime —* of investing a quarter of our salaries on a weekly basis in company stock. *The company gave us a sizeable stock-purchase discount —* and the stock's value has grown very handsomely over the years. *So those bonds represent a considerable sum of money."*

"Well, as I say, it's a lucky thing you and they made it here safely. We'll have them credited to your savings account in a few minutes. Then you'll be on your way. Let's see. What do we have here?"

The banker unzipped the leather bag and removed the two certified checks. He reached back into the bag. After moving his hand rapidly back and forth, he looked up. Panicking, he jerked the bag open and turned it upside-down over his desk blotter.

Nothing fell out.

"Ladies, I'm afraid we have a problem!"

WHEN SHERIFF CONNORS ARRIVED, the bank manager introduced him to the Craddock sisters and quickly reviewed the facts of the case as he knew them. The sheriff was all business. "Thank you for that briefing and for calling me so promptly, Mr. Clemons. I prefer to get on a criminal's trail while it's still hot." The sheriff surveyed the bank. "May I use your conference room to interview the ladies?" The banker nodded. "Ladies, please don't say anything further. I'll explain when we get to the conference room."

Mom waved at us as she entered the bank. "What's going on? Oh, hello, Sheriff. I'm double-parked outside. Please don't give me a ticket. And Maude's out there in Ma's Terraplane. What *is* going on?" The sheriff briefly described the situation. "Oh, Lord! Abigail. Lucille. This is simply awful. We'll find parking spaces and join you in a minute."

"Before you leave, Marie, I have something to say to everyone. I'll interview the Craddock ladies in private. Ask them to describe the bonds in detail including their face values. Whether the bonds have been out of their possession, when they last saw them, and so on. To protect the ladies' privacy and to prevent valuable clues from becoming known to the thief, I must be the only person, other than the ladies, to have this information. I hope you all understand."

"Sheriff, we understand completely. Please do whatever's necessary to find the thief."

After the sheriff and the Craddock sisters disappeared behind the conference room door, Danny posed a good question. "If the sheriff's interviewing the Craddock sisters privately *to prevent valuable clues from becoming known to the thief,* does that mean he thinks one of us is the thief?"

Instead of answering Danny's question, Mom shrugged her shoulders. "I better go tell Maude what's happened."

After a half-hour, the sheriff emerged and beckoned to Danny and me. We changed places with the Craddock sisters. "Boys, I understand there was a disturbance on the bus this morning. Do either of you know the man the driver asked to leave the bus?"

Danny had been so engrossed in his conversation with Mr. Jenkins that he hadn't noticed, so he simply shook his head. But I had recognized the man. "It was Mr. Thorndike. Frank Thorndike."

"Tell me what you know about Mr. Thorndike, Jase?" I described his abuse of Skip Nakayama at the hotel, his rancorous dismissal by Mr. Reed, his humiliation at the hands of the Craddock sisters at the diner, and his forced removal from the bus.

"Wow, he sounds like a real bad actor!"

"His son's not much better," Danny added. He described his run-in with David Thorndike and his rescue by Butch Matlock.

The sheriff asked us to describe in detail how we'd spent our time with the Craddock sisters that morning. When we finished, he seemed satisfied. The three of us left the conference room to join the others.

The sheriff used Mr. Clemons' phone to call his office. "The driver's name is Jenkins. I'll need to inspect that bus and talk to the driver as soon as possible. Call me on my radio when you've made the arrangements."

The sheriff turned to Mom. "Marie, I understand you folks were planning to start cleaning Nate Craddock's place this morning. I'm going to need more of the Craddock sisters' time. We can do this one of two ways. Either you can follow me until we finish and take them to the farm from there. Or you can go on ahead and I'll bring them out later. Oh, one other thing, Danny and Jase were with the ladies this morning so they'll need to come with me as well."

Mom and Aunt Maude decided to leave without us, explaining that Grandma and Mrs. Henry would be wondering what happened to us if they lingered any longer.

As we turned to leave, Mr. Clemons had a recommendation. "Ladies, this may be the furthest thing from your minds. But, so you don't have to return right away, you can just sign these signature cards. We'll open your accounts and deposit the two certified checks for you now."

After the Craddock sisters signed the cards and endorsed the checks, we were on our way. Our first objective was the bus stop in front of Pete's. When we pulled up, the sheriff shared his plan. "I think it would be better if the ladies and I inspect the bus stop first. Why don't you boys wait in the car? Then I'll come back for you."

The sisters and the sheriff walked to the bus stop. The sheriff pointed at the bench and the ladies sat down, just as they had earlier that morning. They chatted for a minute more and then returned to the car.

"Boys, please come with me." The sheriff asked us to tell him everything that had happened at the bus stop. It didn't take long. We'd walked from the house and arrived several minutes before the bus was due. The sisters sat down and waited while we went into Pete's to look at comics. When the bus pulled up, we came out and all of us got on the bus.

"Jase, was Frank Thorndike here when you came out of the store?"

"No, I don't think so. He must have walked up while Danny was talking to the driver. I first noticed him when he yelled out."

The sheriff nodded his head. Then he stooped down and looked under the bench.

Was he expecting to find the bonds under there?

Our next stop was the hotel. The sheriff asked the four of us to wait in the lounge while he talked with Mr. Reed at the front desk. We could see them through the wall of windows that separated the lounge from the lobby. After chatting for a few minutes, the sheriff pointed to the manager's office and they disappeared inside. Then the sheriff and Mr. Reed returned to the lounge. The sheriff first asked the sisters, then Danny and me, to step out to the lobby and give our accounts of what we had seen and done that morning. Again there wasn't much to tell.

After the sheriff and the Craddock sisters inspected their room, we returned to the car. The sheriff called his dispatcher and was informed that the bus and driver were waiting at the Chippewa Trails bus garage.

Again we waited in the car while the sheriff talked to Mr. Jenkins. When they boarded the bus, Mr. Jenkins pointed to where the sisters had been seated. Once again, the sheriff stooped down as if expecting to find the bonds beneath the seat. Seemingly satisfied that he had learned all he could, the sheriff returned to the car. As he opened the door, he stopped to advise Mr. Jenkins, "If Thorndike ever does that again, just stop the bus and call us."

On our way to the farm, Danny asked, "Sheriff, you said talking to us separately was *to prevent valuable clues from becoming known to the thief.* Does that mean we're all *suspects?*"

The sheriff didn't respond right away. Then he observed, "Let's put it this way, Danny. When it comes to money, all kinds of people do all kinds of strange things."

"That's good then!"

"Why's that, Danny?"

"Jase and I don't have any money."

With a friend like Danny, who needs money?

WHEN WE ARRIVED AT the farm, Danny observed, "Where are the cars? They must have gone to Old Nate's already." Nevertheless, the sheriff honked his horn. Since no one came to the door, the sheriff put his car in gear and was about to head out the driveway when Danny saw it. "Wait! There's a note on the door."

Danny popped out of the car and ran up the steps. "It's for the C sisters!" he exclaimed as he popped back into the car. "Here!"

The Craddock sisters read it aloud, *"Dear Abigail and Lucille,* I am so sorry to hear of your loss. *At the moment, you must feel just terrible.* But the Lord has a way of looking out for good people like you. *So I'm confident that your loss will be restored in no time.* Regardless of what happens, *you can depend on my support and friendship.* Your neighbor, Jane Compton."

Danny confessed, "I like the way you say everything together. Have you always done that?"

"Yes, Danny, we have. Because we're identical twins, we think just alike. *We can't remember ever —* doing it differently."

So now we knew.

As soon as we walked through Nate's kitchen door, Grandma threw her arms around the sisters. "What a day you've had. I'm so sorry."

"Thank you for your beautiful note, Jane. *It means so much to us."*

Turning to the sheriff, Grandma inquired hopefully, "Any news, Sheriff?"

"No, Mrs. Compton. Afraid not. But it's still early and we do have a suspect."

"Don't worry, Grandma Compton. Jase and I aren't suspects. Too poor!" Danny assured her. Those of us just arriving in the sheriff's car chuckled.

"Sorry I kept your *hired hands* with me so long, Mrs. Compton. Now you can put 'em right to work, especially these boys. If it's all right, Mr. Henry, I'll telephone your house if we come up with anything."

Mr. Henry readily agreed.

After the sheriff left, Grandma noted, "Isn't it strange? Here we are, standing in Nate's house just days after the kidnapping, discussing yet another crime affecting the Craddock family? You poor dears."

"Oh, that's where you are wrong, Jane. *We have our savings, proceeds from our house sale, and our pensions.* We have our health and our optimistic dispositions. *And, for the first time in many years, we have family.* But most important — *we have splendid new friends* — all of you. *We are far from poor, dear Jane.* Far from poor."

The first order of business was to remove the trash from Nate's house. *Trash* was loosely defined as anything not bolted down. Furniture. Clothing. Stale food. Magazines and newspapers. Broken kitchen utensils. All of this had to go.

The women rounded it up and we men carried it outside and dumped it into Nate's wagon that was parked just outside the back shed. Next we swept the floors clean and dusted the window sills and woodwork. By the time we finished culling and cleaning, the sun was setting in the west. We called it a day.

"I'll bring a team over tomorrow and haul this load to the woods," Grandpa promised.

"I'll lend a hand, Bill," Mr. Henry promised as well.

Because Mom and Aunt Maude decided to stay at the farm again, Abigail drove us home in Dad's car. Mom had convinced the Craddock sisters that it was perfectly safe to park our car on the street near the hotel, but they wanted to be sure that Dad agreed.

When we got out of the car, Dad opened the front door. "You're back! How'd it go?"

Suddenly I realized that Dad didn't know about the missing bearer bonds. "To be honest, we've suffered — *a bit of a loss,*" the sisters admitted. "But the sheriff — *is hot on the trail of the thief.*"

"Thief?"

We all pitched in to give Dad the complete story. "My gosh! I'm sorry about what happened. You ladies have had some introduction to Riverton. Kidnappers, nasty desk clerks, and now thieves."

We stood in our front room shaking our heads. Then suddenly Dad had a brilliant idea. "I think I know how to cheer you up. Are you as hungry as I am?"

"The Chop Suey Diner!" we all chimed. So off we went.

At dinner, Dad confirmed that the sisters should plan to use his car every day until Nate's was returned by the CID. Dad confessed he didn't mind taking the bus at all. This gave him an opportunity to converse with the bus-riding Burke workers about sports and other manly subjects. So, after dinner the sisters dropped us off, before running Danny home. At first, Danny thought he might come inside with Dad and me. When Dad reminded him that this was a school night, Danny didn't complain. Besides we were all exhausted after our long day of hard work and emotional distress.

Later, Dad and I sat in the front room in our pajamas. "Dad, how much money do you think those bearer bonds are worth?"

Dad was adept at making complex calculations in his head. Rolling his eyes back, he booted up his *cranial computer.* "Let's assume they worked for about forty years and contributed a quarter of their salaries for that period. I would guess their average salary was. Hmmm. Plus the appreciation of the stock during that period was about. Hmmm. Well, let me see. That's approximately. Oh, my gosh. I can't quite believe the number that I just calculated in my head. Just a minute, Jase. I'll double check it."

Dad went into the bedroom and reappeared with paper and pencil. "Okay. Now let's start over. That's — yep. Times — yep. And the result is —. My gosh! I was right. Please don't mention this to anyone, Jase. But my figures indicate that those bearer bonds are worth ten thousand dollars apiece for a total of fifty thousand dollars!"

"Fifty thous —." I couldn't believe my ears.

Frequently, I had heard Riverton men state that they were lucky to be making fifty cents an hour. I quickly made a calculation in my head. Working 2500 hours a year at fifty cents an hour, these men only earned $1,250 a year. They would have to save every penny of their wages for forty years to accumulate fifty thousand dollars.

"Dad, do we know anybody who has fifty thousand dollars?"

"Not anymore, we don't, Jase. Not anymore."

THE SHERIFF HAD ADMONISHED us all to keep the theft under our hats. In these cases, he explained, it was better to keep the story out of the newspapers and to squelch any rumors concerning the theft. This strategy was designed to give the thief a false sense of security. Confident that he'd gotten away with his crime, the thief might be inclined to take more risks, brag about the caper to his buddies, or even attempt to contact the Craddock sisters.

To increase his chances of nabbing the villain, the sheriff had sworn us to secrecy. When school reconvened on Tuesday morning, it was all Danny and I could do to keep our lips zipped.

Wouldn't Miss Sparks and our classmates flip if they learned the two of us were working on yet another case with Sheriff Connors?

"Good morning, class. I hope you enjoyed your long weekend. Yesterday, we had our last Red Cross workshop. Now all Hamilton School teachers are certified to teach first aid. We'll be integrating these techniques into your health classes as the year progresses. I know some of you must have had interesting weekend experiences that you would like to share with us. Anyone? Just raise your hand. Yes, Danny. What would you like to share?"

I couldn't believe it. After the promise we made, my pal was going to spill the beans. What would the sheriff say? What if the thief got wind of the sheriff's stealthy method of tracking him down?

"Yes, Miss Sparks. I do have something to share. This past weekend Jase and I did absolutely nothing! That's right, Miss Sparks. We have nothing to report. Nothing. I mean *nothing*. Do you understand, everybody? Nothing. Nothing. Noth —."

"Well, thank you, Danny. That was most enlightening. Anybody else?"

At recess, we were inundated with questions about what we *really* did over the weekend. Danny's response was to lock his lips and throw away the imaginary key, a gesture fully understood by every red-blooded sixth grader in the land. He was American and Americans don't blabber.

I was relieved to have the school day come to an end. Butch joined us for our walk home. That day, we decided to take the dump route. Just as we turned onto Trumble Street, we noticed them following us.

"Who's that guy with David Thorndike, Butch?"

"That's his older brother Bobby. He was in high school with my cousin but got kicked out for fighting and stealing, I think."

"David knows better than to mess with us. Isn't that right, Butch?" He shrugged his shoulders and kept walking. The Thorndikes picked up the pace and were gaining on us.

"Hey, *pukes*. Wait up! We got something to say to you." It was the snarling voice of Bobby Thorndike. "I said, wait up!"

While we decided to ignore him for as long as possible, we neglected to take Bobby's speed into account. He silently ran up behind us and, before we knew it, he had grabbed the back of Danny's and my jacket collars.

"Stop! I ain't gonna hurt you."

Butch reared back and prepared to charge. "Back off, muscles! All I want to do is talk, okay?"

He released our collars. So we let him have his say. "I know you two *town heroes* may not give a hoot about this, but our dad spent last night in the county jail. And I have a sneaking suspicion that you had something to do with it."

My reaction to Bobby's news was twofold. First, I was pleased that Frank Thorndike had spent the night in jail and would have been more than happy to have had something to do with it. Second, besides telling the sheriff about Frank Thorndike's nasty disposition and rude behavior, information that the sheriff could have gleaned from any number of Riverton sources, we had nothing to do with his jail time. Figuring that Bobby would prefer my second reaction to my first, I insisted, "We had nothing to do with it!"

"Whether you did or not, I'm warning you. Our dad may not be as goody-goody as your old man but he's our dad. Got it? And we don't want no sniveling *pukes* like you getting him in trouble with the sheriff. Got it? This is your last warning."

Then Bobby turned to Butch. "As for you, muscles, you ain't gonna be able to baby-sit these *pukes* constantly. There'll come a day when you aren't around and —."

Bobby had crossed the line. And waggling his finger in Butch's face was a tactical blunder. Instead of being intimidated by the finger, Butch saw it as a tempting morsel. So he chomped down on it. At the same time, he placed his hands squarely on Bobby's chest and began to pull back on the finger. I developed the strange expectation that Bobby's finger would soon start to stretch, and, when Butch released his bite, it would snap back into place like a rubber band.

And, oddly enough, instead of crying out, Bobby didn't utter a sound. His face just got redder and redder, the longer Butch held on. And, for whatever reason, David seemed glued to the ground. He made no effort to rescue his poor older brother. Instead, like Danny and me, he stood immobile, absolutely astounded by Bobby's predicament.

Rrrrrrr!

Suddenly the short burst of a police siren broke the silence. We turned to see Sheriff Connors' patrol car rolling toward us. I figured that Butch would let go, but he simply hung on until the sheriff tumbled out of his car.

"Okay, boys. That'll be enough. Let him go, son." Butch dropped his hands and opened his mouth. At that instant, Bobby let out a deafening ***yeeeoooooow*** that probably rattled the windows of houses a mile away.

"You Thorndike boys. You need to come with me. I want to release your father this afternoon, but I'm not letting him go until you're there to take custody. He's still not in very good shape. Go over there and sit in the car. I'll be right with you."

When the Thorndike boys were out of earshot, the sheriff looked at Butch, then at us. "You boys remember our conversation about secrecy, right?"

"We didn't say a thing, Sheriff. Honest."

"Okay. I just wish for once I could have a case that didn't involve the two of you."

He gave us a mean stare. Then he broke into a wide grin and patted each of us on the shoulder.

"Go on home and stay out of trouble. And that goes for you too, Master Matlock."

Before we knew it the sheriff had disappeared with the Thorndike brothers, and we were alone. Butch looked a little shaken. "Are you okay, Butch?"

"I guess so but Bobby's right. I can't always be there to protect you. I'm scared for you guys. They're not a pair to mess with."

We walked in silence past the dump, over the railroad tracks, and onto Milford Street. We stopped in front of the Matlock house, thanked Butch one more time, and said goodbye. Then we headed for my house.

"Danny, what are we going to do about the Thorndikes?"

He didn't answer right away. But, when he did, his answer amazed me. "They're just scared. Afraid something will happen to their father. So, maybe, we should make friends with them."

Was that possible?

THE REST OF THE week rolled along smoothly. Our class mastered the technique of tying a tourniquet around someone's arm or leg. But Miss Sparks was a little disturbed when Danny attempted to tie his around Millie Zack's neck. Of course, Millie was delighted to be the focus of Danny's attention, even if it meant having to endure some strangulation.

Still there was no break in the bearer bonds' case. In fact, aside from the incident with the Thorndikes, we hadn't seen the sheriff all week. We honored our vow of silence and were hopeful that something would break soon. By all reports, Grandma's cleaning, fix-it, and painting crew had made excellent progress.

With Mom and Aunt Maude still at the farm, Dad and I continued our bachelor life all that week, including our regular supper date with the Craddock sisters at the Chop Suey Diner. Since Nate's car had arrived from Camp Custer, the sisters now had their own transportation, and Grandma had exclusive use of her Terraplane again.

Nikki introduced us to Skip's parents who had finally arrived from the West Coast and were just as polite as their diner relatives. Because their new Riverton home at the Graham farm wasn't quite ready, they were using the Grahams' guestroom. Of course, Mr. Reed was disappointed that they hadn't accepted his offer of free accommodations at the Hotel Riverton.

All week, the *Riverton Daily Press* ran front-page articles about the possibility of an undefeated season for Coach Comstock's football team. Their last game was against Saginaw Arthur Hill and would be played at Waters Field on that very evening. While we all wanted to attend, we weren't sure we could because this was the Craddocks' moving day!

Danny and I were standing on our front porch when Sherm spotted us. He ran toward us shouting, "We gotta have an FSG meeting! We gotta meet. It's real important."

Danny responded with his usual, calm understanding, "We're not having a meeting today, Vermin. Get used to the idea. We got other more important business to take care of. Don't you know this is the Craddock sisters' moving day? You dope!"

"But we gotta! It's something reeeally important for *all* members. Pul-leeeze!" Sherm's plea fell on deaf ears. An exasperated Danny went inside to see his mother who had offered to help with the move. "Geez, Jase! We just gotta have a meeting. Honest!"

"Tell you what, Sherm. How would you like to go to the farm with us and help with the move?" I thought this might placate the poor fellow and turn off his unending *need-a-meeting* tape. With Mrs. Tucker driving the station wagon, there would be plenty of room.

Sherm went bananas. "Yes! Yes! Yes! Yessssssss!"

"Okay, Sherm. Sherm, okay! Go home and ask your mother. Then get back here right away, okay?"

Sherm shot across our front lawn, past the cottonwood tree, and across Forrest Street. He was home in no time flat and he returned in a flash. "I got permishshum! Permishshum!"

"Okay, Sherm. What's in the gym bag?"

"My lammy. The puppet Mr. Zeyer gave me. And some other important stuff."

"When do you have to be home, Sherm?"

"I got permishshum to stay out real late."

"Well, then it's lucky you brought your gym bag. You'll have your lammy in case you fall asleep." Sherm replied by tugging on his pants bottom and wiping his nose on his jacket sleeve.

Danny poked his head out the front door. "Jase, you want to ride with us?"

"Sure. Sherm's coming. He can ride with us too."

"What! How did *that* happen?" I confessed that I had invited him.

"Oh, all right. On one condition though, worm. No more talk about an FSG meeting! We've got to work. You got that?" Wisely, Sherm nodded his head without saying a word.

When our two-car caravan arrived at Nate's, cars belonging to Grandma, the Henrys, and the Craddock sisters were parked in a row perpendicular to the driveway. Mrs. Tucker and Dad pulled off the driveway and took up position in the orderly row.

As we entered Nate's house, I was awestruck. The change was unbelievable. Where once there had been nothing but gray-black grime, there were polished floors, brightly papered walls, gleaming woodwork, new curtains, and the delicious aroma of cookies baking in the oven of the sparkling kitchen stove. Grandpa and Mr. Henry were tapping the last carpet tacks in the new runner that led up the stairs to the second floor.

"It's beautiful! Absolutely beautiful," declared Mrs. Tucker. "Well done, folks! Miss Craddock, do we have any idea when the movers might be here?"

"I called just before we left the hotel this morning. According to the dispatcher, they should be here any minute. We gave them detailed directions so they shouldn't have any trouble finding us."

Sure enough, within minutes we heard the *chugging* of the moving van pulling into the drive. With hissing brakes, the truck came to a stop next to the front porch. Two husky movers stepped down from the van. "Morning, ma'am. Nice to see you again. I assume we're at the right place. I'd like to come in and look around before we start unloading, if that's all right."

The driver mounted the front steps and entered the house. "Wow! The insides look a whole lot nicer than the outsides of this place. I was worried there for a minute. Yes, siree. Nice looking insides, ma'am."

Well, that was all Grandma and her crew needed to hear. Compliments from the moving-van driver somehow officially approved all that they had done to ready the house for his arrival. Grandma repaid him by offering a cup of coffee before he got started and inviting him to join us for the massive picnic dinner that she and Mrs. Henry had prepared for later.

The driver took it all in stride. "No thanks on the coffee, ma'am. But that dinner offer sure sounds great. Thank you!" The Craddock sisters' furniture was not what I expected. For some reason, I had imagined lacey, spindly, and puffy. But I should have known better. They were far too sensible for that. Their furniture was sturdy, plain, and practical. Woods and leather. A cross between Stickley and Shaker, if I were to characterize the style. I was relieved. Old Nate just didn't strike me as the doily type.

The movers were very efficient. The furniture came off the truck more quickly than I thought possible. The expansive front porch became the staging area, enabling the sisters to review and select the next piece for placement inside the house. As the movers carried each piece inside, the sisters would name the destination. "Front bedroom. Kitchen. Dining room. Front room."

Systematically, the movers transported each piece and *plunked* it down, right where the sisters indicated. The thermometer read in the low forties. But, from the perspiration on the foreheads of the movers, you would have thought it was the middle of August. With about half the load in the house, the driver called for a break. He and his assistant agreed to a cup of Grandma's coffee and sat on the front porch surrounded by our curious crowd.

"You know what, folks, this is the farthest north that either me or Ed, here, has ever been."

Everyone reacted in one way or another to his news. Frankly I never considered Riverton as being that far north, south, east, or west. I always thought we were right in the middle.

The movers tackled the more difficult tasks first. So the second floor furniture and boxes were in place well before those destined for the first floor. This enabled Lucille Craddock and Grandma's crew to begin unpacking boxes of linens, pictures, and other items needed to complete the second-floor bedrooms. The system worked very efficiently.

By two in the afternoon, the truck was empty, and the driver and Ed were ready to stand down. Mrs. Henry and Grandma took that as their cue to set up the picnic dinner. True to form, it was too much, too good, and too bad for anyone who missed it.

There weren't enough places at the large oak dining-room table so Danny and I opted to eat our dinner sitting on the steps in the back shed behind the kitchen. Sherm, our shadow, joined us there. After we'd finished second helpings and thirds, we stared blankly out the back shed door at Nate's welding garage. We were indeed mellow.

Sherm seized this opportunity. "Guys, can we have our meeting now?"

Danny looked at Sherm, then at me, and then back at Sherm again. "I give up. Okay, Sherm. Let's get it over with."

Sherm leaped up, ran into the kitchen to retrieve his gym bag, and immediately rejoined us in the back shed. He closed the kitchen door because, as he explained, this meeting was to be *Top Secrete*.

Danny frowned and called the meeting to order. "This FSG meeting is called to order. Only three members are present. Jase Addison, Danny Tucker, and Sherman Vermin. Any old business? Seeing none. Any new business? Seeing none. This meeting is —."

"Wait! Wait! Look at these!" Sherm reached into his gym bag and pulled out some papers.

"Sherm, what are these?"

"FSG membership certificates! I kept tellin' you guys we needed them. Sooooo, here they are." He handed them to me. At the top of each of the five documents, Sherm had used an orange crayon to inscribe the name of an FSG member.

"Sherm, I want you to show these to the Craddock sisters."

"What's wrong? Don't you like them?"

"Sherm, they're absolutely beautiful. And the Craddock sisters will think so too."

"Okay, Jase. Be right back."

As Sherm disappeared into the house, Danny and I looked at each other and shook our heads.

"So Sherm stole the bearer bonds!"

Danny chortled, "We better tell the sheriff it worked."

"What worked?"

"Keeping the case a secret. Sherm never suspected a thing!"

AFTER THE SHERIFF ARRIVED, we assembled in the front room. By then, the Craddock sisters had kissed Sherm so many times that his face was permanently crimson. He must have been mystified as to why the membership certificates, created from those papers he had found, merited such adulation. But he didn't say a word.

"Well, ladies. Jase and Danny. I officially declare this case closed. You are released from your vows of silence. I'm sure everyone wonders how this happened. Miss Abigail, let's start with you. Please tell the folks what you told me in the conference room at the bank this past Monday."

"Certainly. If you recall, we retrieved the locked leather bag containing the bearer bonds and certified checks from the hotel safe that morning. We were preoccupied with the cleanup day here at our house. Danny and Jase had met us at the hotel and brought us by bus to Jase's house. Because Maude was still busy with the baby, we decided to take the bus to New Albany and open accounts at the bank there. Jase and Danny agreed to come with us so we wouldn't get lost in the Riverton bus system.

"The bus wasn't due right away so Lucille and I sat down on the bus-stop bench in front of Pete's store. While we waited, the boys went inside to look at comic books. As we sat there, I realized that I hadn't checked the contents of the bag since retrieving it from the safe. So I removed the key from my change purse, opened the bag, and removed the contents. Everything was there. Two certified checks and five bearer bonds. These bonds," she declared, holding Sherm's membership certificates high so everyone could see them.

"But, when I unlocked the bag at the bank, the bearer bonds were missing."

"Thank you, Miss Abigail. Sherman, can you tell us where you found the membership certificates?"

"Uh, huh. They were stuck between the telephone pole and the side of the bench at the bus stop in front of Pete's."

"When did you find them, Sherman?"

"Pretty early on the Monday morning when we didn't have school. I saw them there when I came out of the store. Mom sent me to buy milk."

"Oh, my. I must have dropped them by mistake," Abigail lamented. "I was sure I put everything back in the zipper bag just the way it was. But I had a lot on my mind and the bus was just coming to a stop. Oh, me. I have caused everyone, including Lucille, a lot of concern. I'm so very sorry."

"Sheriff, am I going to get in trouble?"

"No, Sherman. You're not. We're all relieved that it was you and not some dishonest person who found them. Thank you, Sherman." Sherman blushed some more.

"Sheriff, I kinda thought Mr. Thorndike took them. He was there at the bus stop when the bonds were there, wedged between the bench and the pole. And he had the combination to the hotel safe, before Mr. Reed had it changed."

"I was thinking exactly the same thing, Jase. That's why I brought him in for questioning. But, to be honest with you, on Monday morning, I don't think Frank Thorndike could have focused his eyes enough to spot those bonds, if you catch my drift.

"After he spent a couple of nights with us, I questioned him again, and he didn't strike me as someone who had recently stolen a large sum of money. And, to put it bluntly, I don't think he would have known what to do with those bonds if he had found them. He's not exactly a financial whiz, you know?"

"Any other questions?"

"I have a question, Sheriff."

"What is it Sherman?"

"You're not going to take away our FSG membership certificates, are you?"

14 JUST REWARDS

DANNY AND I HAD JUST ARRIVED HOME FROM
school. We sat in the front room as Aunt Maude excitedly shared
the contents of her letter from Uncle Van. His team of
communication technicians had been billeted temporarily in a
town not far from the front. Later, I would learn that this town was
Liege, Belgium, just a few miles from where the Allies broke
through the Siegfried Line to enter Germany for the first time.

Because inclement weather had temporarily postponed the
Allies' eastward advance, their stay in the town was extended.
Having time to kill was a new experience for Uncle Van and his
men. For the sake of good order and discipline, he decided that
occupational therapy was just the ticket. On the day they'd arrived,
he noticed that their new *hometown* had no operable phone
system. That afternoon, he sought out local telephone company
officials and offered the expertise of his team to help restore the
town's phone service.

Utilizing their extensive telephone experience, coupled with a
bit of U.S. Army hardware and cable, the team made the necessary
repairs and restored service to a significant portion of the town's
population. And, over the course of the next few days, local
telephone workers under his team's supervision completed the job.

The mayor and citizens were extremely pleased and expressed their appreciation in a most delicious way. Each evening, when Uncle Van and his team arrived back at their quarters, they were treated to giant baskets, overflowing with freshly baked bread and rolls, a wide assortment of cheeses, smoked ham, goose-liver paté, and a selection of the region's finest wines.

The mayor apologized profusely for his inability to include local beers as a part of the town's gift. During the years of Nazi occupation, thousands of Belgian brewers had been forced to shut down after the Germans confiscated their gigantic brass brewing vats and turned them into shell casings for the German army. Nonetheless, Uncle Van and his team were touched by the generous gesture of the Belgians who could ill-afford these gifts, after having suffered years of deprivation and mistreatment at the hands of the brutal Nazis.

Aunt Maude folded the letter and smiled at us. Because the letter had taken some time to reach Riverton, we were unaware that the Allies, including the French, had already broached the German line at Beffort Gap to reach the Rhine. The Russians were making similar advances on the German eastern front.

When that news finally reached us, optimism surged and wild speculation about the European war's early conclusion dominated conversations throughout Riverton. But we were also unaware of the impact of the worsening weather and of the resolve and resourcefulness of a cornered German army.

Just after Dad returned home from work, we heard a knock at the door. When I opened it, there stood E.F. Graham, Skip Nakayama, and Skip's parents.

"Anybody home?" asked Mr. Graham. "Sorry to drop in unexpected, but we were looking at some warehouse space not far from here so we stopped by to say hello."

"Delighted you did, E.F. Come in, please." Dad held the door wide open. "Welcome, everybody. Skip! Nice to see you again. Does your presence here mean what I think it does?"

Skip smiled sheepishly and admitted, "I'm afraid Junior was right. Returning to the 442nd RCT isn't possible. So I've settled for a posh assignment at Camp Riverton. Officially, I report for duty in a couple of days. However, I saw Junior, and he's been kind enough not to say, 'I told you so.' "

"That's excellent news. Welcome to Riverton! With your parents here, this is an ideal place for you."

Dad shook hands with Mr. and Mrs. Nakayama who smiled and bowed slightly. "I'll bet you folks are glad to see your son."

"Yes, Mr. Addison, we're very happy and so appreciative of the role you played in arranging with Mr. Graham to make all of this happen."

SKIP'S FATHER, TAKEO NAKAYAMA, was an Issei, a first generation Japanese-American. Born and educated in Japan, he had immigrated to America as a young man. As the owner and operator of a chain of grocery stores providing services to Sacramento's English-speaking community, he spoke near-perfect English without an accent. His wife Yumiko had also been born in Japan but was educated in America. A graduate of the University of California, she had taught high school physics in the Sacramento public school system.

They were forced to abandon her job, his business, and their home to join thousands of others of Japanese ancestry in hastily constructed government relocation centers across the west. More than two-thirds of the 127,000 Japanese-Americans interned at the time were American citizens. Being forcibly uprooted would have been traumatic enough, but Japanese families from the Sacramento area were sent to Tule Lake Relocation Center, the most turbulent and conflict-ridden of the ten War Relocation Authority camps. At this camp, many prisoners demanded restoration of their constitutional rights by demonstrating and striking.

Camp internees could affirm their loyalty to America by answering the two questions on loyalty questionnaires:

Question #1:

Are you willing to serve in the Armed Forces on combat duty wherever ordered?

Question #2:

Will you swear unqualified allegiance to the United States of America and faithfully defend it from any or all attack from foreign or domestic forces and foreswear any allegiance to the Japanese Emperor or to any other power, foreign government, or organization?

As a result of the pervasive hostility and defiant resistance there, over forty percent of Tule Lake internees answered *No* to both questions as compared to ten percent at the other nine camps. Those who answered *No* to only one of the questions were deemed to be *Disloyal* and ordered to be held in a newly designated *Segregation Center* which, because of its large proportion of disloyal internees, was established at Tule Lake. Over 18,000 internees were jammed into this camp which had been designed to accommodate no more than a fraction of that number.

In November 1943, an uprising against WRA officials at Tule Lake caused the camp to be placed under the army's direct control. In the Segregation Center, Japanese schools were formed to teach children about Japanese culture. Anti-American sentiment ran strong among Tule Lake internees. Pro-Japan organizations at the camp convinced many Nisei to renounce their American citizenship. Over five thousand did so. And over seven thousand Tule Lake internees applied for repatriation to Japan. Order was restored only after two thousand dissident leaders and Issei were relocated to Department of Justice prison camps. Clearly the situation at Tule Lake Relocation Center was not one to inspire optimism among the pro-American families like the Nakayamas.

In December 1944, the U.S. Supreme Court declared the detention of loyal citizens unconstitutional. In January, internees were released and given $25 and a train ticket back to their former homes. Shortly thereafter, nine of the relocation centers were closed. But, because of its special nature, Tule Lake remained open until March 1946.

WHILE WE MEN SAT in the front room, Aunt Maude and Mom took Mrs. Nakayama to our bedroom to see Johnnie. I could hear him cooing in response to all the motherly attention he was receiving.

Mr. Graham looked at Dad and smiled. "John, Mr. Nakayama is the best thing that's ever happened to Graham Markets. Initially I had thought of his role as just a buyer for our chain. But he's convinced me to broaden my thinking. If we can buy for our chain, why not buy for others in the Riverton area? Independent grocers. Restaurants. Hospitals. Schools. Produce, meat, and grocery distributors that serve Chippewa County truck all the way over from Flint, Saginaw, or Lansing. We can provide quicker, better service by being headquartered right here in Riverton.

"Yep! It's a dandy idea. And in less than ten days, my new *Vice-President for Distribution* is going to launch this new business. We're planning to hire sales representatives, truck drivers, and warehouse workers. If you know someone looking for a good steady job, one that will extend beyond the end of the war, just let us know."

We all looked at Skip who squirmed and smiled nervously.

"E.F., naturally I'm delighted it's worked out so well for all concerned." Then Dad turned and said, "Congratulations on your new position, Mr. Nakayama. Having Skip here with you and your wife is such good news. And from what we're seeing in the papers today about developments in Europe, God willing, you'll be seeing your other two sons before long."

"You're very kind to say that. This has certainly been one of the better turns in our lives. Thank you again for your part, sir."

As the women reentered the front room, Dad asked, "What's the status of the Nakayama house, E.F.?"

"That's the best news, John. The folks will be moving in tomorrow. The last bit of furniture arrives in the morning. If I don't say so myself, it's turned out beautifully. Hasn't it, Mrs. Nakayama?"

"You're so right, Mr. Graham. Soon, Mrs. Graham and you will have your privacy again and we will have a lovely new house. Thank you so much."

After we said our goodbyes, Mom expressed what we were all thinking. "Can you believe it? The Craddock sisters got their bearer bonds back. Old Nate's due home from the hospital tomorrow. Uncle Van is doing wonderfully in Europe. The war's going well there.

"Skip's back in town, probably for good. His parents are here with their relatives. Skip's father has a fine position with Mr. Graham. Mrs. Nakayama has a new house. Mr. Graham is happier than we've ever seen him. Jim Comstock's Riverton team beat Saginaw Arthur Hill so they're undefeated. And Grandpa and Grandma Compton have new neighbors. Boy! None of us has a thing to worry about anymore!"

We would soon learn just how mistaken Mom had been.

EARLY THE NEXT MORNING, Danny arrived at our kitchen door just in time for breakfast. There was nothing unusual about that. But he was accompanied by a most unlikely companion. Queenie! Since it was quite chilly, I immediately invited them into the kitchen where they joined us for breakfast. At first, I thought maybe I'd forgotten something. Had we all planned to walk to school together? I was hesitant to ask why both of them were there. And Danny didn't help. He acted as if this were a normal occurrence. After breakfast, we adjourned to our front room to wait until it was time to leave for school. I still wasn't sure what was happening.

As I was about to ask, I heard a faint knock at the front door. When I opened it, there stood Sherm with a sheepish grin on his face. "Are Danny and Queenie here yet?" As he entered, he blurted out, "I came just like you guys told me. What did Jase say, you guys? Did I get here on time? Huh, you guys?"

Thump! Thump! Thump!

I was startled by an exceptionally heavy knock at the door. Rising to open it, I quipped, "I'll bet this is Butch Matlock. That would mean that the Forrest Street Guards are all present and accounted for." I opened the door and there he stood. "Come on in, Butch. We've been expecting you."

Butch took a seat. "Sorry I'm late, Danny."

"Okay, everybody. I give up! What's going on?"

"We have some bad news."

"Bad news about what, Queenie?"

"About Mr. Thorndike. He's really angry with you and your father. He's threatening to hurt both of you."

"Why would he want to hurt my father? And me?"

"What's this?" Dad entered the front room with Mom and Aunt Maude right behind him. "You better start at the beginning, Queenie. First of all where did you hear this?"

"From David Thorndike. He came to warn me."

"David Thorndike?" I couldn't believe my ears. "When? What did he say?"

"Late last night, because I couldn't sleep, I got up and went down to the front room. I was sitting on the davenport reading a magazine when I heard a noise outside. I went to the window and looked out. David was standing on the bottom step of our front porch. He looked confused. At first, I thought maybe he'd been drinking, like his father does. Anyway I went to the door and opened it. Just a crack."

"Weren't you frightened?" Aunt Maude asked.

"No, for some reason I wasn't. Maybe it's because I've known David for as long as I can remember. He's tough and has a bad reputation. And I was real angry when he started the fight with Danny, but basically he's a nice boy. Anyway when I opened the door, it must have startled him because he leaped off the porch and ran down our driveway. I called his name and he stopped. When he saw it was me, he looked relieved. He said he needed to talk to me but was worried that my folks would come to the door and be mad because it was so late."

"What time was this, Queenie?"

"After midnight. Everyone at our house was asleep."

"What's a boy David's age doing out so late on a school night?"

"Well, that's just it. After his family was evicted for not paying their rent, his father made him drop out of school. He's in my class, but he hasn't been in school since last week. He got a job, setting pins with his brother down at Grafton Bowling. They've been sleeping there at night, back behind the pins. Says the manager feels sorry for them."

"Where's Frank Thorndike hanging out nowadays?"

"David wasn't sure but he thinks he's staying with an *old drinking buddy*. That's what David called him. Over on the west side of town, somewhere out by the Chippewa Sugar Beet factory."

"So why's he so angry with Jase and me, Queenie?"

"David told me that his father believes the Addisons are to blame for all his problems. David repeated his father's exact words so I would know how angry he is. His father claims that you and your *dirty Jap soldier boy* got him fired from the Hotel Riverton. Because he had no money to pay rent, he was evicted. Then your *old lady friends* embarrassed him in front of the *yellow Jap rats* that run the Chop Suey Diner.

"And Jase got him *tossed off the bus* for no reason. And you *sicced the sheriff* on him for stealing something he hadn't stolen. And Jase *got his boys in hot water* with the sheriff down by the dump. Finally you got that *old Jap POW* a job with Grahams. They got a *pretty new house* to live in for free while he and his boys are *living on the street.*"

"So Jase and I did all that, did we?"

"Yes — I mean — that's how Mr. Thorndike sees it. And David is very concerned that his father might do something crazy. He's been drinking for days, David says. That's why he came by to warn us."

"Any idea what Bobby thinks about this?"

"Apparently Bobby's very concerned that his father might do something he'll regret. He doesn't want his father to get in trouble, but he doesn't want anybody, like your father and you, hurt either."

"Sherm, is your father home?"

"Yes, he is, Mr. Addison. He goes to work about the same time we leave for school. Sometimes he gives me a ride in his patrol car."

"Wait here, kids. I'll go down and ask Sergeant Tolna for advice on how to handle this."

In a few minutes, Sergeant Tolna pulled up in front of our house. He and Dad got out of the car and came inside. Dad asked Queenie to repeat her story. When she finished, Sergeant Tolna went outside to call his chief on the car radio. After talking for a few minutes, he returned.

"Queenie, you did a real fine job reporting all that David revealed to you. We've issued a countywide bulletin to pick up Frank Thorndike. One of our officers or the sheriff's men should spot him shortly. Meantime, we'll take some precautions. John, why don't you and I cart these kids to school? Then I'll post a squad car there to keep an eye on things.

"If we haven't picked him up by the time school is out, we'll send another car to pick you up and bring you back home this evening. Don't leave before the car arrives, okay? Then we'll be back here in the morning, if necessary. Any questions?"

"Why are Danny and I always involved with the police or the sheriff, Sergeant Tolna?"

"Boy, Jase, you got me!"

"I know why," Danny declared. "Just good luck, that's why!"

Good luck, so far, that is!

DESPITE THE CONCERTED EFFORTS of the Riverton Police Department and the Chippewa County Sheriff's office, at the end of the school week Frank Thorndike was still at large. Riding back and forth to school in a police car was becoming old hat. Even the students at Hamilton School had stopped staring when we pulled up each morning. On Friday afternoon, our chauffeur was Sergeant Tolna himself. After dropping off Butch and Queenie, he took Danny and me to my house to wait for Dad's return from work. Mom made a pot of coffee and treated us to large slices of the snow-apple pie that she had just baked.

"Hello, Jeff," Dad said as he came through the door. "Any news about Thorndike?"

"First of all, we still don't know where he is. We tracked down his so-called drinking buddy, Charlie Maxwell. You remember him. He was in school when we were. Lived over off West Main Street. He's been in and out of trouble with us for years. Always seems to be out of work. Lives in his parents' old place. They passed away a few years back. As you know, he was their only child. The way Charlie turned out, it may have been a blessing. Charlie worked as a handyman at the Hotel Riverton for a couple of years before being fired for drinking on the job last year. Apparently he and Frank started carousing when they worked together at the hotel."

"Have you talked to him?"

"We identified him as Frank's pal within an hour of my leaving here on Tuesday morning. Took a couple of cars around to see if we could surprise the two of them at Charlie's place. But no one was there. His folk's old Plymouth was gone too. Looks like they left town. We've been keeping an eye on Charlie's place, but no luck so far."

"In a way, it's comforting to know they aren't here in Riverton. Maybe tempers will cool and this will blow over."

"John, I'd like to hope so, but my experience says that irresponsible bullies, like Frank, are fueled by resentment. Resentment of authority of those who have more than they do and of people who are different. Like the Japanese. They always blame others for their own failures. Never take personal responsibility for anything that happens to them. And they like bullying weaker people.

"In Frank's case, his sons have always been his punching bags, especially since his wife died. Now he appears to be focusing his resentment and anger on Jase and you. No, I wouldn't count on this blowing over."

"Have you talked to the Thorndike boys?"

"A couple of times. The first time was about their father. I got all I could from them one morning down at the bowling alley. Later I returned to talk to them about their situation. I wanted to know why they weren't in school. It won't surprise you to know that Frank bullied them into dropping out. Made them feel guilty about not contributing any money to the family after he lost his job. He kept after them until they dropped out of school just so he'd stop badgering them.

"Technically neither one is old enough to drop out. Sometimes when school officials deal with tough cases like these two, they overlook the age rules and simply let 'em quit. It's too bad because the two of them are pretty bright. Not your typical delinquents."

"Is it true that they're living in the back of the bowling alley?"

"Afraid so, Marie."

"Well, that's not right. Something has to be done."

"Exactly. While it may not be the most desirable place in town for two teenage boys, what would you say to the Good Mission Church as a temporary solution? At least they'd have a clean bed and three hot meals a day. And they'd stay out of trouble there."

"That's a fine idea, if they've got room. During the cold months, their number of residents grows as hobos and the like want to sleep indoors. When we finish, we can walk down and talk to Reverend Squires."

"By the way, you two boys will be interested in this. When I asked Bobby and David if they had any friends they could stay with, the only names they came up with were yours. Does that surprise you?"

I was astounded by the news. "Yes, Sergeant Tolna, it really does."

Clearly, Danny wasn't. "That's why David came to warn Jase and Mr. Addison. I told you they could be our friends, Jase."

He was right again.

We entered the Mission through the back door. Buddy Roe Bibs was setting tables in the auditorium/dining hall. Keith Squires was in the kitchen starting to put supper together.

When Bibs looked up and saw Sergeant Tolna, he announced in a loud voice, "Cheese it! The cops!"

Of course, Bibs was joking, but several of the residents, lounging around waiting for supper, took him very seriously. Their natural aversion to police kicked in, causing them to scurry from the room and out the front door. Bibs seemed surprised by the melee he had created and yelled after them, "Can't ya take a joke? It's just our neighbor, Sergeant Tolna!" Then he turned to us, predicting, "They'll be back. We've got chili tonight. And that's one of their favorites. Besides it's cold out there. It has to be in the teens."

"Good evening, men. What can I do for you?" Reverend Squires approached with a smile on his face. "Jeff, hope you're not here on official business."

"Semi-official, Reverend."

Dad and Sergeant Tolna summarized the situation and asked Reverend Squires what he thought about having two younger guests. He rubbed his chin and thought for a long while before speaking. "I can't think of any reason why not. They're a bit different than the others here. But I think that might be good for all concerned. The boys could see where a life of sin can lead. And the sinners could see what they were like before their sinning careers began. Yep, it just might be good for both sides."

"Have you got openings so I can bring them over tonight, Reverend?"

"Sure have. Several of our veterans got it in their heads to take off for warmer climates this afternoon. Their freight train ought to be passing into Ohio about now. But they'll be back next spring. Too many mosquitoes for summer camping down in Florida."

"Fantastic! The boys work until eleven o'clock on Fridays. I'll bring them over then, if it's not too late."

"That'd be fine."

Sergeant Tolna headed back downtown to deliver the news to the Thorndike boys and to check one last time on the whereabouts of their father. We walked back to our house. When we arrived, Mom and Aunt Maude were setting out supper. "We're having chicken and dumplings tonight. One of your favorites, Danny. Want to stay?"

Talk about a rhetorical question! Of course, he wanted to stay. Danny always made the cook feel appreciated. It was more than just the sheer amount of food he consumed. It was his sound effects. His *oohs* and *ahs* and *hmms* and *yummies* really got to Mom. You had to admire his technique. After the last of the dumplings had disappeared with the final *hmm,* Mom suggested a game of gin rummy. Dad begged off, saying he needed to check the progress of the war in the afternoon paper. Just as we settled into our game, there was a hurried knock at the door. Before Dad could open it, the knock came again. It was Mr. Shurtleif.

"John, there's been a terrible fire. Junior just called me from the hospital. Apparently earlier this evening, Frank Thorndike and another man set fire to the Nakayama's new house. A number of folks were burned very badly. I don't know the details. Junior says that Jeff Tolna is there with Thorndike's sons. They're very upset about their father. He's in pretty bad shape. Jeff thought you and the boys might like to come down. Skip and the Grahams are there too. That's all I know."

We thanked Mr. Shurtleif, threw on our coats, and rushed to the car. Aunt Maude, who stayed home with Johnnie, waved goodbye as we raced up Forrest Street.

Within minutes, we were walking into the hospital waiting room. People stood in small groups, talking softly to each other. We were comforted to see that Mrs. Nakayama was unharmed. She was talking with Sergeant Jeff and another police officer I didn't recognize. Bobby and David were being consoled by Mrs. Graham and Skip Nakayama by Mr. Graham and Junior Shurtleif. I was surprised to see the Craddock sisters standing alone on the far side of the room. Seeing us, they looked relieved and headed our way.

"I guess you know there's been a terrible fire. Mr. Nakayama was burned, has a cut on the head, and is suffering from smoke inhalation. *He's in serious condition but is expected to recover fully.* Another gentleman — *a Charlie Maxwell* — died earlier — *of extensive burns.* And the boys' father — *Mr. Thorndike* — was burned extensively as well. *We don't think he has* — much of a chance — *from what the doctor said."*

"We're a bit surprised to see you here. How'd you hear about the fire?"

"We went to the early show at the Grafton — and then stopped to drop off some clothing for Nate — *who comes home tomorrow.* We saw Mrs. Nakayama and the Grahams — *and innocently asked what had brought them here tonight.* When they told us — *we thought we might be of some assistance* — so we decided to stay. *Now that you're here* — maybe we'll excuse ourselves and head on home. *We have a long, dark drive ahead of us.* And we have to be back here — *first thing in the morning."*

Dad thanked the Craddock sisters for their concern and for filling us in. He assured them that, under the circumstances, they should feel free to leave because there were enough people present to stand vigil. Having said their goodbyes, they departed. Mom joined the group consoling Bobby and David. We waved at the two boys who seemed pleased to see us and, with Dad, joined the Sergeant Tolna group.

"John. Boys. Glad to see you here. I believe you know Mrs. Nakayama. She smiled at us and bowed slightly. This is Officer Reynard." We shook hands and gave him our names.

Then Jeff briefed us on what had happened. "Our worst fears were realized tonight, John. Evidently Frank and Charlie got back to town earlier this evening. Charlie was driving his folks' car when they stopped at the gas station, out West Main Street near the city limits, where he usually does business. The attendant asked Charlie where he'd been lately. He said they'd been working for a building contractor in Flint for the past week and were home for the weekend.

"The attendant concluded that they'd been drinking heavily. After Charlie topped off his tank, he asked to borrow a gasoline can and a siphoning hose. The attendant didn't think anything of it until later."

Sergeant Tolna turned to Mrs. Nakayama and asked, "Will my telling these folks about what happened at your house be too upsetting for you, ma'am?"

"No, not at all. They're friends who were threatened by the same man who did this to us. They deserve to know what happened."

"Thank you, ma'am." He continued his report. "We think they drove directly to the Graham farm from the gas station. Must have turned out their headlights because no one saw them turn into the driveway. As you may know, it's a long driveway, probably couple of hundred feet, that passes the new Nakayama house on its way up to the Grahams' main house. Charlie pulled off the driveway and parked beside the new house out of sight of the front door.

"Presumably they siphoned gasoline from the tank into the can and then splashed it over the sides and porches of the house. A pile of leftover lumber next to the back porch made good kindling for the fire. Our guess is they replenished the can more than once because it looks like they left the siphoning hose in the tank."

"Were you and your husband in the house while this was going on, Mrs. Nakayama?"

"Yes, Mr. Addison, we had had a long day, so we went to bed early. I was asleep when my husband smelled the gasoline and went to investigate. When he saw what they were up to, he ran back into the bedroom, woke me, and gave me my instructions. I was to leave the house by the back door, run to the Grahams' without being seen, call the fire department, and tell Mr. Graham to come quickly and bring his gun.

"As I started up the driveway, I looked back. I saw my husband struggling with two men on the porch. Then one struck him with some tool, perhaps a tire wrench or something, and shoved him back into the house. When they tossed a burning pack of matches onto the porch, there was an immediate explosion. Fire spewed in all directions. Their clothing caught on fire. They panicked and ran toward their car. I turned around and ran back toward the house to help my husband. I saw one of the men stop near the back of the car."

Sergeant Tolna interjected, "We think that was Charlie. Stupidly, he must have stopped to retrieve the siphoning hose and replace the gas cap before driving off. Mind you now. His clothes were on fire, and he grabbed a gasoline-soaked siphoning hose. Sorry to interrupt, Mrs. Nakayama."

She nodded and continued. "That's when the car exploded. I rushed into the house and dragged my husband outside. By that time, Mr. and Mrs. Graham had seen the fire and called the fire department. My husband was unconscious but still breathing with some difficulty because of the smoke he'd inhaled. And his head was bleeding from the blow. His robe had caught fire and his arms appeared to be burned somewhat. But I rolled him over and over on the ground until it was out.

"We loaded my husband into the Grahams' car. But the other two men were lying too near the burning car for us to reach them. They didn't look like they could have survived the fire and explosion so we left them for the fire department and brought my husband here to the hospital. He regained consciousness when we arrived. The doctor saw him right away and assured us that, with a couple of days' rest, he will recover fully. But the other men, the arsonists —."

She stopped and looked at Sergeant Tolna who picked up the story. "By the time I arrived, the firemen had given up on both the house and the car. Not that the car was anything of value. But that beautiful house! What a shame!

"Those two nuts paid a heavy price for their folly. Charlie was pronounced dead on arrival, and Frank's not expected to make it through the night. Because he was standing in front of the car, away from the gas tank, he was barely able to survive the explosion. What a pair of nincompoops they were. In the first place, who'd use gasoline to start a fire? And grabbing the siphoning hose when your jacket's on fire! Some people are just plain stupid."

"We loved that house, Sergeant Tolna, and we'll miss it. Houses can be rebuilt but families can't. That's the saddest part of the story. Frank Thorndike may not have amounted to much, but in the eyes of those two boys —. Yes, that's the saddest part."

"Well, at least they've got us as friends, haven't they, Jase?"

Mrs. Nakayama smiled and patted Danny on the back.

AS WE WALKED FROM the hospital, snow began to fall. By the time we reached the car, we were covered with heavy flakes. It was refreshing to be outside in the cold, snowy night.

As we pulled up to Danny's house, Dad proposed, "The temperatures are falling. This snow's going to stick. How about going rabbit hunting in the morning?"

"That might be just the thing to get your minds off all of this," Mom observed. Danny and I readily agreed.

"Good! Why don't I go in with Danny and see if his father wants to come with us?"

In a few minutes, Dad returned to the car. "Sam thinks that'd be a fantastic idea. He's going to drive his station wagon. You ladies can have the car tomorrow. Mrs. Tucker'll come over right after we leave. Says she's got a great plan for how three rabbit-hunting widows can put this car to good use. Something about some sales she saw in the paper."

Mom laughed, "Are you sure you can afford to go rabbit hunting, John?"

Aware of the slickness of the road surface, Dad focused on his driving and carefully pulled out onto New Albany Avenue before answering Mom. "Marie, I've learned something about you Compton women. When it comes to spending, you talk a much better game than you play. For you, as well as your sister and mother, parting with a penny is a difficult chore. I don't think I have anything to worry about. Thank goodness!"

"Jase, doesn't that sound like a challenge to you? For some reason, I feel like proving your father wrong. I think I'll tell Aunt Maude what he said. Then the three of us will go out and do some real *buck burning* tomorrow. That'll teach him to be so overconfident. Can't be too predictable, you know?"

As we walked through the snow from the driveway to the front door, Dad gave me a piece of advice. "Jase, whatever you do, don't get married. Your wife will drive you to distraction. I suggest you and Danny run off and join the French Foreign Legion. Or go to Tibet and become Buddist monks. Otherwise your life will be miserable. Just like mine."

At that, he threw his arms around Mom and gave her a big kiss. They both giggled.

The next morning, Danny and his father pulled up in front of our house well before dawn. Because of the frigid temperatures, they didn't come in, choosing instead to wait for us in the warmth of their car. Dad opened the door and waved to them through the storm door. Then he held up a single index finger, letting them know that we would be there in one minute.

After saying goodbye to Aunt Maude, Johnnie, and Mom, we slipped on our hunting gear, picked up our shotguns, and headed for the car. The snow, about two inches deep, sparkled under the bright street light in front of the Shurtleif house. The sky was clear and blue-black. All the houses in the neighborhood were dark. This was Saturday, a sleep-in morning for many.

It was still dark when we pulled into the circular driveway at the farm. From the light in the cow barn, I knew Grandpa was well into his morning chores.

"I'll help Grandpa, Dad. Then maybe he can come hunting with us."

"Dandy idea, Jase. You know just the way Grandpa likes his chores done. The rest of us will go inside and have a cup of Grandma's coffee." Then he suggested, "It'll be hot in the kitchen. We better leave our coats on the side porch."

Chores in winter took far less time than in summer. For one thing, there were fewer animals and chickens to feed. After fall butchering, a good proportion of the summer population now existed in the form of jars of bully beef, stockinettes of hanging ham and bacon, or packages of frozen chicken, beef, or pork resting in the Henry's deep freeze. And those animals held over for next summer were all housed indoors, making it easier to feed them.

Also the Plymouth Rock laying hens and the Holstein milk cows gave miserly amounts of eggs and milk during winter. It was not unusual to extract ten gallons of wholesome milk from an adult Holstein in July, but in November you were lucky to collect a single gallon. So the reduced daily production was quickly gathered and processed. Grandpa and I finished in no time.

Dad had just begun to describe the tragic events of the evening before when Grandpa and I entered the kitchen. "You're just in time, Paw. John was just about to tell Mr. Tucker and me about a terrible fire on the edge of town last night."

It didn't appear that Danny shared things like this with his father. I wondered why. But the thought slipped from my mind just as soon as Dad started his story.

When he finished, Grandma asked, "What's going to become of those Thorndike boys? No parents. No school. No home. Living in the Mission with a bunch of —. It's just not right."

"You're right, of course. But we had to find them some place to stay. They couldn't continue sleeping at the bowling alley. The Mission will do until we make permanent arrangements for them. First thing Monday morning, Jeff's going to speak with the principals at Riverton High and at Hamilton School. We're confident that they can be reenrolled without too much trouble. According to Queenie, David's a darn fine student despite his troubles. And Jim mentioned last week that Bobby had the same reputation among his teachers. Looks like the boys were going to succeed in spite of their father."

As an afterthought, Dad added, "Oh, I almost forgot. We saw the Craddock sisters at the hospital last night. They told us Nate's coming home today."

"Yes, they stopped by here on their way into town yesterday. Said they wanted to come by and see us today after they get Nate all settled. I invited them all for dinner. Why don't you stay too?"

"Thanks, but Sam and I have to get back before all our money's spent. Your two daughters and Christine Tucker have threatened to go *buck burning* at some sales in town. You don't suppose they were serious, do you?"

"Wouldn't surprise me one bit!" Grandma replied with a guffaw.

As we were preparing to leave, I noticed that Mick was pretending to be asleep in his bed next to the kitchen stove. He knew he wouldn't be invited to hunt that day. When hunting rabbits after a newly fallen snow, you didn't really need a dog, especially a runner like Mick.

Rabbits were located by tracking. Old rabbit tracks would be covered with newly fallen snow. As long as you knew the difference between rabbit and the nearly identical squirrel tracks, you were in great shape.

Early in the morning, the curious rabbit would venture out of the fencerow, stand of brush, or pile of weeds where he'd bedded down the night before. On cold mornings, the rabbit's desire for warmth exceeded his curiosity. He would quickly duck back into his bedroom, leaving a short loop of telltale tracks pointing to his location. One kick was usually enough to dislodge the napping bunny. Once your shooting eye adjusted to this fast-moving target, bagging rabbits was fairly easy. And, if you happened to miss your shot, rabbits never ran far. So you could track your prey to his next hiding place and deliver a second kick.

Even though rabbit season opened in mid-October, we waited until after a hard frost and a long cold spell before hunting them. Rabbits were often infected with tularemia, a bacterial disease contracted from ticks and fleas. This disease was also transmittable to man. A rabbit infected with the disease would not survive a cold spell. Just the same, we always let the rabbit run to prove his state of health before wasting a shot on him. As a further precaution, we field dressed each rabbit we shot and discarded the carcass if we discovered any white or yellow spots on the animal's liver. Finally rabbit meat was always thoroughly cooked.

I have always believed that the unpleasant task of field dressing rabbits was the first step in the development of my aversion to hunting animals. But I confess to still enjoying the taste of well-prepared pheasant and rabbit.

We had extremely good luck that day. Our team of five hunters bagged seven rabbits in just under three hours. And all passed the health check. Danny was the only hunter whose eye was off the mark. He claimed it was a faulty batch of 4-10 shotgun shells. As usual, Dad took first place with three to his credit.

We finished skinning and cleaning the rabbits and laid them out on newspaper in the back shed, ready for Grandma to cut into pieces just the right size for fricasseeing. By midmorning, the temperature had risen into the thirties so we stored our hunting coats and guns in Mr. Tucker's station wagon. After cleaning our boots well, we entered the kitchen.

Beep! Beep!

From the driveway, came the sound of a familiar car horn. I looked out the window and was amazed to see Dad's car.

"It's Mom!" I yelled.

"Now what do you suppose they're doing out here?" Dad asked. "And who's that with them? Oh, it's Queenie and Chub! Your whole family's here, Sam."

The new arrivals filed into the kitchen and announced they'd brought a special treat for dinner! Opening the box, they displayed four freshly baked apple pies. "That pie I baked yesterday tasted so good, I thought I'd do it again," Mom explained.

"You baked pies, Mom? I thought you were going shopping."

"We did go shopping. We bought flour and these apples. We already had the lard." I knew the apples had come from Grandpa's supply in the cow barn where everyone in the family *bought* their apples each year.

"Wonderful! The Craddocks are coming too. I wondered what I would have for dessert. Thank you, girls. Now you can help prepare the rabbits your men bagged today. There are seven of them out there in the back shed."

The heat from the cooking activities in the kitchen expanded into the front room where we hunters had taken refuge. One by one, we fell asleep. After what seemed like an entire night of slumber, I awoke to the sound of familiar voices.

"Well, look who's here! So nice to see you up and about, Nate! Welcome! Welcome!"

Shaking the sleep from my head, I rose from my chair and entered the kitchen. The Craddock sisters were standing on either side of a nicely dressed gentleman whom I barely recognized. His handsome black double-breasted suit was set off by a freshly starched white shirt and bright red tie. The flawlessly polished toes of his black shoes told me that they were new. His hair was neatly trimmed and his clean-shaven face radiated a rosy, healthy glow.

Smiling, he turned to me and spoke, "Afternoon, Jase."

Old Nate didn't look *old* anymore. Even his bent body seemed to be straighter and taller. Aside from his new wardrobe, there was something else different about him, but I couldn't put my finger on it.

"Hello, Mr. Craddock."

When he smiled a second time, I realized what it was. He hadn't called me *Jathhe*. Thanks to a brand-new set of false teeth, he had spoken without *hissing!* By convincing Nate to wear dentures, the Craddock sisters had succeeded where Grandma had failed. But, as the Craddock sisters were quick to point out, Grandma had played a significant role in creating Nate's new look.

"Jane, thank you for Nate's new suit. *Doesn't it look marvelous on him?* It's a perfect fit. *How did you know what size to buy —* when you were in Chicago?" Evidently the Craddock sisters were unaware of Grandma's role as Nate's dresser.

"I'll bet that suit was in that adults-only, secret cardboard box. Right, Grandma Compton?" Danny was now standing beside me admiring the new Nate. "You look pretty sharp, Mr. Craddock." Nate was taken aback by Danny's flattery.

"Well, there's the groom! Who's the bride?" Nate turned as Grandpa entered the kitchen. "Good to see you out of the hospital, Nate. I guess you heard that your two POW buddies are sitting in prison cells out in Fort Leavenworth, didn't you? Boy, I wish they could see you now. Nice having you home, neighbor." Grandpa shook his hand.

"And what a home I returned to. I can't thank everybody enough for all you did to make the house into a place where Abigail and Lucille would feel at home. I guess I'd kind of let things go a bit over there in recent years. But from now on, things'll be different."

Nate thanked Danny and me again for rescuing him from Reitter and Baden. Then we men, once again, adjourned to the front room. While the ladies put the dinner together, we described the day's hunt to Nate who wanted to know exactly where we had found each rabbit. Then he recounted his own luck at that particular spot or one nearby. He seemed determined to let us know of his rabbit-hunting prowess, even though he hadn't been with us that day. We promised to include him on our next outing.

The crowd was so large that the dining-room table was reserved for adults. Queenie, Chub, Danny, and I enjoyed the delicious meal at the kitchen table. When it came time for dessert, we were invited into the front room. Each serving of apple pie was supplemented with a large slice of sharp cheddar cheese, another one of the lady shoppers' purchases. This pleasant addition provided my father with yet another opportunity to remind us, "Apple pie without the cheese is like a kiss without the squeeze."

No matter how many times he said it, Grandma responded in the same way, "Oh, John, for crying all night. Where do you hear such things?"

Dad once confided to me that he had first heard the *old saw* from Grandma herself. But that was something I never mentioned. Sharing a secret with Dad made me feel like an adult.

The Craddock sisters took it upon themselves to replenish everyone's coffee. When they returned from the kitchen, Abigail was carrying a large manila folder that I surmised must have been retrieved from her mammoth leather purse. The image of bearer bonds popped into my head. When Lucille sat down, Abigail remained standing.

"Ladies and gentlemen, we three Craddocks have something important to tell you. We've made a number of decisions that affect everyone here today. Normally it would not be proper to discuss such matters outside our family but, as you will see, there's an important reason for us to do so on this occasion.

"Before getting into that, we want to express our profound gratitude for the generous way you have welcomed us into your community. And for years of caring for and protecting your neighbor and our beloved cousin Nate.

"We were overwhelmed. By the way you took charge of the project to convert Nate's house into a beautiful home for the three of us. Your visits to the hospital. For working Nate's farm all these years. And for immediately making us feel welcome in your home, just as if we were a part of your family."

Grandma shook her head and waved a hand as if to say, *Aw shucks, it was nothing.*

"Being welcomed into a family like yours is something very special to us because we have no family other than the three of us. No one to carry on our family name." She paused to catch her breath. "No one with whom to share our family estate. And, let's face it, we're getting on in years. So we've decided to share it with you. We asked Harry Chambers to draw up two documents that the three of us signed this morning at his office."

Abigail turned to face Grandma and Grandpa. "If Jane and Bill agree to the terms, which we think they will, they'll have to go to Mr. Chambers' office and sign the first document. I won't go into all the legal intricacies but here's the gist of it. Nate has decided to change his will and leave his entire estate, consisting mostly of the family farm, to Bill and Jane Compton."

Grandma gasped, "No, that's not right."

"Let me go on, Jane. I think you will agree that it's quite right. Now, in return, Bill must agree to continue working the farm for Nate on shares, just as he has for the past few years. And you must agree to allow whoever among the three of us is left to continue to occupy the house until we pass. Then the farm is yours, free and clear."

Grandpa looked at Grandma who nodded. Then they both looked at Nate. "Are you sure that's the way you want things, Nate?" Nate nodded and smiled. "Then we are most grateful. You can count on us to take care of the farm and of the three of you just like you were family. Because that's how we think of you. Both of us sincerely thank you."

Abigail smiled and continued, "The second document establishes a trust that will be funded initially with two of the five bearer bonds that Sherman was kind enough to return to us last week. When Lucille and I pass, the remainder of our estate will be placed in the trust. The purpose of the trust is to provide full university scholarships for the children of five very-deserving families. The Addisons, Tuckers, Tolnas, Matlocks. And we think you will like this last-minute addition, the Thorndikes. Appropriately, the trust is called the *FSG Scholarship Fund*. And I'm sure you'll approve of the person that we named as trustee. Can you guess who he is?"

We were all stunned by Abigail's news. Full scholarships for the children of some of Riverton's poorest families! It was unbelievable.

Abigail looked around the room. "Anyone have a guess?"

We all shrugged our shoulders.

"I understand he was once known as *Gentleman Jim.*"

15 GIVING THANKS

WHEN WE RETURNED FROM THE FARM ON SATURDAY evening, we read in the *Riverton Daily Press* that Frank Thorndike had died from burns suffered in the Nakayama fire. According to the article, his two sons were his only survivors. Because he was indigent, he would be given a pauper's burial by Chippewa County. With my parents' blessing, Danny and I pulled on our coats and headed for the Mission to see Bobby and David.

When we arrived, Reverend Squires was holding a special vesper service in the Mission auditorium. Before long, it became clear that the reason for the service was to acknowledge the boys' loss and to provide emotional and spiritual support for them in their grief. Reverend Squires was at his best, extending comfort and encouragement to the boys while Edith played her piano softly. I was pleased we'd come. From our seats in the back, we could see both Bobby and David clearly. They seemed in shock.

Reverend Squires reminded us of the staggering losses that the two brothers had suffered during the past year. He counseled that no one could undergo such traumatic change without being profoundly affected. Finishing his service on an optimistic note, he promised that he and Mrs. Squires along with the brothers' personal friends (Danny and me), members of the community, and fellow Mission residents were there for the boys to lean on.

After the service, as if to reinforce the Reverend's point, all of the Mission residents filed by the boys, extending their condolences and reminding them to keep their chins up. When we presented ourselves, the brothers seemed pleasantly surprised. Evidently they hadn't seen us come in. They stood up, smiled, and their dispositions changed for the better.

When the auditorium emptied as the residents returned to the dormitory to prepare for bed, Danny and I sat down to chat with the Thorndikes. In keeping with the positive nature of our visit, I related all the good news I could think of.

"Did you hear about Sergeant Tolna's plans for Monday?" Yes, he had informed them today at the hospital. They were eager to return to school.

"Have you heard about the Craddocks' scholarship fund?" Yes, they were excited. Earlier that day, Jim Comstock had dropped by the Mission to tell them. They planned to buckle down in school so they could pass whatever college entrance tests were required. They'd even brainstormed various careers they might pursue after earning their college degrees. Bobby was considering being a lawyer while David wanted to be a veterinarian. Danny and I hadn't planned that far ahead yet.

"Do you know anything about Mr. Nakayama's condition?" Yes, in the past twenty-four hours or so, he had improved greatly. He's sitting up in bed and bugging the nurses about getting out of the hospital. That was good news!

After the Thorndike boys successfully answered all my questions, Danny thought he'd give it a try. "Do you know how many rabbits we shot today?" They were stumped. So Danny described our day of hunting in excruciating detail. He insisted that the day had been absolutely idyllic with one huge exception. Those darned faulty 4-10 shotgun shells.

Mercifully he neglected to describe the obligatory field dressing. His omission made sense because, during this procedure, Danny had turned his back, jammed fingers in both his ears, and whistled very loudly. His aspirations to be a Big Game Hunter were in serious jeopardy. Today he'd washed out of *Big Game School* at the bunny level.

When the clock on the front hall table chimed ten, all four of us yawned. We laughed at the coincidence and decided to call it a night. After agreeing to meet the next morning at the Mission for breakfast and church service, Danny explained that this was our normal Sunday morning routine. They suggested we go to the hospital after church to check on Mr. Nakayama. We agreed.

Danny and I parted company at Mrs. Mikas' alley. As I walked toward my house, I reviewed all the amazing events that had occurred just since we left school on Friday afternoon. I was relieved that the police wouldn't need to take us to school on Monday. When I remembered the reason, I felt a twinge of guilt. A lot had happened, all right. Still there were many unanswered questions. Where will the Thorndike boys end up? They can't stay at the Mission forever. They have to find a permanent home with someone.

And what will the Nakayamas do for a house? They probably aren't anxious to move back in with the Grahams. They could stay at the Hotel Riverton, at least for a while. Perhaps they could stay with Mrs. Libby like the Matlocks did when their house burned down. But that would be a long stay because, with winter on its way, it would be months before they could break ground for a new house. Besides, this being wartime, securing building materials and skilled construction labor remained a serious problem.

I must have been punchy because a strange thought entered my mind. Frank Thorndike had called the Nakayamas *POWs*. So wouldn't it be logical to have Otto's crew rebuild the house for their fellow POWs? *What was I thinking?* Exhausted, I entered the house and fell into bed. By the time my eyes closed, I was fast asleep.

After services at the Mission, Danny and I convinced Bobby and David to join us at the First Methodist Church. When I mentioned that Danny was the choir soloist, they thought I was pulling their legs. But Danny's delivery of a few short bursts of *Ave Maria* brought them around. Arriving well before the first service began, we entered the front door and took the stairs to the basement where Danny hoped to see the choir director. Since he'd missed all the choir practices that week, he wanted to find out if he was in hot water.

On entering the basement, we were amazed to see the Craddock sisters standing outside the kitchen door talking to Reverend Noble, Miss Bundy, and the Carmodys. After greeting us, they expressed their sorrow about Mr. Thorndike's death and inquired about the welfare of the boys. Everyone seemed pleased that the brothers were with Danny and me.

"We didn't expect to see you ladies here," I told the Craddocks. "Are you planning to join this church?"

"Oh, no, we're planning to — attend the Barrington Church of Christ — *with your Grandmother.* She's told us all about your friend RJ — *Reverend Johnson.* We're here this morning — *just to see the facilities* — one last time before our — *Thanksgiving Gala."*

We must have looked mystified because the Craddock sisters immediately apologized. "Oh, please forgive us. *You don't know* — anything about our idea, do you? *It was so last minute* — we decided that Thanksgiving Day was an ideal time — *to thank the community* — formally, you know — *for all the blessings* — that have come our way — *from so many of our new friends and neighbors.* That involves a lot of people.

"So we decided to rent a church hall. One with ample tables and chairs. *A stage.* A well-equipped kitchen with the capacity to produce — *a full, traditional Thanksgiving dinner for dozens if not hundreds of well-wishers.* Only one church in town could meet those criteria — *the First Methodist Church.*

"The celebration starts promptly at two o'clock so tell your families. *Jim Comstock will be our Master of Ceremonies.* And these four fine volunteers from the First Methodist Church — *will take charge of the kitchen and dining-hall operation.* And I suppose you can guess which big-hearted grocer in town — *is furnishing all the turkeys and trimmings.* And your friend Pete practically had to arm wrestle Mr. Graham — *for the right to furnish soft drinks and ice cream.*

"We ladies will bake the pumpkin pies and rolls. *Make the stuffing.* Special dishes and so on. *We won't bore you with details.* Just be assured that we have them all worked out. *Don't forget, two o'clock on Thanksgiving Day.* Remember, tell your families."

To make it back to Barrington in time for church, the sisters said goodbye and flew up the stairs and out of the church. Reverend Noble spoke for everybody. "Their energy level almost makes me tired."

"Reminds me of Miss Bundy!" Danny quipped. Miss Bundy blinked in surprise, then smiled approvingly.

Mel Carmody remarked about the Craddocks' generosity. "The scholarship fund is truly unique. You boys and the other recipients are indeed fortunate to have the Craddocks as your benefactors."

Bobby Thorndike offered an important thought. "All this talk about Thanksgiving dinner makes me hungry. Does anybody else have that reaction?"

"I do and I've got just the remedy." Anne Carmody turned around and opened the gigantic box of cupcakes on the table behind her. "We ordered far too many for the number in Sunday school today. Please, help yourself."

"You're a lifesaver, Mrs. C!"

Danny always knew just the right thing to say.

E.F. GRAHAM AND MRS. Graham greeted us as we entered the hospital. Having just finished a long visit with Mr. Nakayama, they planned to have lunch in the hospital cafeteria and invited us to join them. We sat at a large table overlooking the hospital grounds.

Two young girls and a teenage boy were feeding mallard ducks from the nearby river. Because the girls looked too young to visit a patient in the hospital, we surmised that the boy was caring for them while their parents visited a friend or relative. All three were dressed nicely so we also assumed that they had attended church earlier that morning. Since none of us recognized the three duck-feeders, we agreed that they were from out of town.

Our story, created to explain their presence, satisfied us all. Speculating about who people were and why they behaved as they did was a popular pastime among Rivertonians.

It wasn't until after we finished lunch that E.F. Graham revealed his reason for inviting us. "I'm glad to have this opportunity to talk to you Thorndike boys before you go upstairs. I need to ask you a very important question. I hope you'll give me an honest answer."

Bobby looked startled by the question but quickly responded, "Why, sure, Mr. Graham. Why shouldn't we?" David nodded his agreement.

"There's a lot at stake here. That's why I asked. I'm certain you know your father held certain opinions about the Japanese and he didn't hesitate to express them. I need to know what you boys thought of his opinions."

Although Bobby and David could be tough and nasty, I'd never heard them direct their anger at any particular group of people, like the Japanese. But I wasn't sure how the brothers would answer this question.

Bobby spoke first. "Mr. Graham, our father was not a perfect man. First of all, he was raised on a small farm near Springfield, Missouri. He used to tell us they were dirt poor. When Grandpa Thorndike landed a job with the railroad, the family ended up in Riverton. They moved here when my father was about my age.

"Anyway not long after they arrived, our grandfather was killed while working down in the railroad yards. Our grandmother kinda went crazy. She left my father here with a family friend and headed back to Missouri. Dad never saw her again. He dropped out of school and worked odd jobs around town as you probably know." Bobby hesitated and then apologized, "I realize I'm taking a long time to answer your question, Mr. Graham."

"Don't worry about that. Take as much time as you like. Besides it helps me to know about your father. Helps me understand him. That's why you're telling me, isn't it, son?"

"Yes, sir. It is. My father once told me when he was growing up he didn't know any adults who weren't members of the Ku Klux Klan. Apparently that's just the way things were down there at that time. Well, naturally, it rubbed off on him too. But our mother wouldn't let him use racial slurs and the like. And growing up, we didn't hear that stuff.

"But, after Mom died, he began drinking and started saying those kinds of things. His anger seemed to build up and it came out in very bad ways, especially when he was drinking. If my mother were still alive —."

Bobby was so choked up that David took over. "Bobby's trying to say that we don't feel that way about the Japanese or any other people. We know there are German and Japanese soldiers killing Americans right now. But we go to school with a lot of kids with German names and Mom used to take us to the Chop Suey Diner. We liked going there mainly because of the Nakayamas. Mom admired how hard they worked and how polite they were to everybody. We like them too.

"No, sir. We don't feel the way our father did. Or acted like he did anyway. It used to embarrass us a lot. To be honest, we were ashamed of his drinking, his anger, and his name-calling. It would have hurt Mom a lot if she were still alive."

"You feel that way, Bobby?" Bobby nodded his head vigorously, still unable to speak.

"I admire your courage for telling me the way you have. It's hard to speak poorly about your father, especially just after his death. But I'm relieved to know the truth about how you boys feel. I have some decisions to make regarding the estates of Charlie Maxwell and your father. And your attitudes make my job much easier."

"Estates?" Danny was just as mystified as I was.

"Yes, this morning at church, Judge Morrison, the Chippewa County Probate Judge, asked me to act as executor of the two estates. He made a preliminary determination that neither of the two men had a will and neither had heirs, except you boys in the case of your father. Was he right about your father not having a will?"

"Mom was always after him to go to a lawyer, but he claimed it was too much money. No, he never had a will."

"Then the judge was right on that score." Mr. Graham paused and turned to his wife before continuing. "The judge asked me my opinion about who should be appointed as legal guardian for you two boys. He thought I would make an ideal candidate. I mentioned this to Mr. Nakayama and his wife. But they've asked me to tell the judge that they would like to be appointed as your guardians. As you could guess, it was important for me to have this talk with you before I called Judge Morrison."

Bobby spoke for all of us. "After what our father did to them, the Nakayamas want to be our guardians?" He was incredulous.

"You heard me right. They are very forgiving people. They believe it's time to put this anger and bitterness behind us and move ahead. So, boys, do I make that call?"

Bobby and David smiled at each other and then turned to us for our opinion. We nodded our heads enthusiastically. "Please call the judge, Mr. Graham. We'd like that very much."

Mr. Graham left the cafeteria to make the call. When he returned, he announced, "The judge was pleased to appoint the Nakayamas as your guardians and to accept some other suggestions of mine as executor. For one, I think there will be enough money in Charlie's estate to cover the costs of his and your father's funerals. They won't be fancy, but they'll be a cut above the pauper's burial provided by the county."

Bobby and David looked a bit stunned, almost as if they had forgotten about the need for a funeral for their father. After they thanked him again, Mr. Graham continued. "Don't worry about this, boys. I'll see to the arrangements tomorrow. Now, as to my other piece of news. I think we should go upstairs so the Nakayamas can hear it at the same time."

As we took the elevator to the third floor, Danny looked at me and shrugged. We were dying of curiosity. When we entered the room, we were greeted by friendly smiles from the Nakayamas. E.F. broke the news. "The judge liked your idea, folks. Meet your new charges, Robert and David Thorndike." Mrs. Nakayama walked over to the brothers, extended her hand, and then, thinking better of it, gave each of them a big hug. Tears welled up in every eye in the room.

"Well, that's not all the news from Judge Morrison." We all turned to Mr. Graham. "You have a new home. I mean an *interim* home until your house at the farm is rebuilt next spring. The judge has ordered that you may occupy the Maxwell house. He stated it was only right. Charlie helped burn your house down so you should live in his house until yours is finished. How's that sound to you?"

The Nakayamas smiled broadly. Then Mrs. Nakayama asked, "How big is that house? How many bedrooms?"

"There are two on the second floor and a large master bedroom on the first floor. Why do you ask?"

"Then Bobby and David can live with us."

"Well, in that case, we'll have to rebuild your house at the farm with three bedrooms as well. What do you think of that idea, boys?"

Naturally Bobby and David were overwhelmed. "When can we move into the Maxwell house?"

"As soon as we complete some minor cleaning, fixing, and painting. It's in pretty decent shape actually. So I'd say in a week or so. In the interim, we'll get a couple of rooms at the Hotel Riverton for the four of you. These boys'll need to rest up. Unless I miss my guess, they'll be back in school by Tuesday. And there'll be school work to catch up on."

Bobby and David were excited about the positive turn their lives had taken. Even though they were eager to move into the hotel, they asked if they could spend one last night at the Good Mission Church. They wanted to tell Reverend and Mrs. Squires all about their good fortune and to thank them properly. And they wanted to say goodbye to all the Mission residents who had befriended them during their brief stay there.

MR. AND MRS. GRAHAM dropped the brothers at the Mission before proceeding to our house. As we pulled up, Danny asked, "Mr. Graham, why do you think the Nakayamas are doing this for Bobby and David?"

He answered with a question of his own. "Why did you want to be friends with them after they tried to hurt you, Danny?"

Danny answered without thinking, "Because they're really nice boys and what their father did doesn't change that."

"You've answered your own question, Danny."

I asked the Grahams to come inside and tell Dad, Mom, and Aunt Maude the news.

"Wow, things really moved fast, thanks to you, E.F. I imagine the boys are overjoyed. How'd you talk the judge into it?"

"John, if anything, I've always found Judge Morrison pragmatic, as well as creative in finding ways to do the right thing for all concerned. Plain fact is he's an upright man with a big heart. He always looks out for the underprivileged and the underdog. I've always admired that about him so I was pretty sure he'd go for my idea.

"If this were a huge estate with heirs fighting for every penny, he'd probably have gone by the book. But, in this case, he chose justice over an arbitrary timetable for getting the estate settled. If it takes a few more months, who's hurt? More importantly, who's helped by doing it the way he chose?

"In the end, it wouldn't surprise me to see the proceeds from the Maxwell estate, mainly the sale of the house, set aside for the benefit of the Thorndike boys or, if not that, donated to a deserving charity. You can trust Judge Morrison to do what's right."

"Mr. Graham, I'm not sure you've heard about the scholarship fund established by the Craddock sisters. The beneficiaries include the Thorndike brothers."

"No, I haven't. Tell us about it, Marie." Mom gave the Grahams the details of the Craddock scholarship fund including Jim Comstock being appointed trustee. "Well, I'll be. Jim has certainly come up in the world since the Libby sisters' trial. Hasn't he? Reinstated as high school teacher. Coached his football team to their first undefeated season ever. And now being given the fiduciary responsibility for the college educations for how many? Fifteen or twenty boys and girls?

"I know you folks think a lot of him. This is another example of how everything works out for the good of all concerned. Who says there's no such thing as Divine Providence in this world? Good for the Craddocks, good for Jim, and good for all those future college graduates!"

Since the temperature was falling rapidly and the winds had picked up, the Grahams offered to drop Danny off at his house on their way home. He was grateful. He too was eager to get home and share all the news with his family. We waved goodbye and sat down again in our front room. Owing to the whirlwind of recent events, I wasn't sure that I had mentioned the Craddock sisters' plan for Thanksgiving at the First Methodist Church. "Do you know about the Thanksgiving Gala?"

Aunt Maude stopped rocking Johnnie. "They stopped by this morning and announced their plans. With so few days until Thanksgiving, we were amazed that they decided to undertake this. They suggested that we put together a list of people to be invited. Where'd we put that list, Marie?"

Mom looked around the room. "It's there on the end table. Why don't you make sure we have everyone you think should be included, Jase? Aunt Maude and I really couldn't think of anyone else."

I sat down on the davenport, picked up the list, and quickly reviewed the alphabetical list of families:

Thanksgiving Invitations

1. Addison
2. Chambers (Harry and Family)
3. Compton
4. Comstock (Jim)
5. Connors (Sheriff)
6. Craddock (Nate & Sisters)
7. Giamo (Pete's Store)
8. Graham
9. Harrison
10. Henry (Farm)
11. Johnson (Church of C.)
12. Klump (Otto & Crew)
13. Kolarik (School Bus Driver)
14. Libby (Neighbor)
15. Matlock (Neighbor)
16. Mikas (Neighbor)
17. Morrison (Judge)
18. Nakayama (Diner)
19. Nakayama (Grocer)
20. Nakayama (Skip)
21. Nichols (WRDP)
22. Petrov (Garden)
23. Prella (POW Guard)
24. Reilly (Neighbor)
25. Shurtleif (Neighbor)
26. Sparks (6th Grade Teacher)
27. Squires (Mission)
28. Thorndike (Brothers)
29. Tolna (Neighbor)
30. Tucker
31. Zeyer (Neighbor)

After thoroughly reviewing the list, I said, "Aunt Maude, the Craddock sisters told me that Reverend Noble, Miss Bundy, and Mr. and Mrs. Carmody will be helping at the church that day. And I think we should invite Bohunk Joe and Buddy Roe Bib Overalls too."

"Excellent additions, Jase. Anybody else?"

"Just one more. For Danny's sake, let's add Millie Zack's family. Wow! Thirty-seven names. If each family represents just three people, there will be over a hundred attendees."

"Well, Jase, the sisters are planning for two hundred."

For some reason, my mind began to calculate the number of turkeys, pumpkin pies, and quarts of gravy required to feed two hundred hungry, but thankful, people. Just as I was coming close to nailing my answer, I threw away my numbers and restated my premise.

Make that one hundred ninety-nine hungry, but thankful, people plus Danny.

Laughing aloud, I concluded given that premise, the numbers would be too large to calculate in my head. So I shut down *my* cranial computer.

THE NEXT MORNING DANNY and I were sitting in the front room watching the kitchen clock. We didn't want to leave too early because overnight temperatures had plunged to two below zero, a near-record low for November 27th. If we left now, we'd arrive at school before the doors were opened for the students to enter. Neither of us felt inclined to stand around the school yard in the gusty wind that whined outside.

Thanksgiving had come late that year, falling on the last day of November. It felt more like Christmas than Thanksgiving. With this turn of weather, fall was definitely behind us and winter was here to stay, for a number of months at least.

We heard the *beep* of a car horn out front. Without thinking we put on our coats, hollered goodbye, and ventured out into the cold. We struggled into the back seat of Sergeant Tolna's patrol car where Sherm was all bundled up in his new snowsuit. He waggled his mitten-covered fingers at us without saying a word through the scarf, wrapped tightly around the lower half of his face.

It wasn't until our driver spoke that I realized our mistake. "With the danger of Frank Thorndike a thing of the past, you boys don't really need a police escort this morning. But it's pretty bitter out so I thought I'd offer anyway. Besides I'm taking the Thorndike brothers to arrange to have them reinstated in school."

Danny looked at me rather sheepishly.

"We knew that, Sergeant Tolna. We really prefer to walk but we'll keep you company."

"Harrrumpf!" was the sergeant's response.

When Sergeant Tolna left the car to get the Thorndike brothers, Danny turned to his favorite target and asked, "Sherm, did you hear about the Craddocks' college trust fund for kids in our families? Where are you going to college?"

"I'm not going to college," mumbled Sherm through his scarf.

"Oh, whattaya going to do then?"

"I'm going to be a doctor."

"Okay, numbskull, where do you think doctors learn how to be doctors?"

"At the hospital." Before Danny could retort, Sergeant Tolna returned with the Thorndikes.

When we pulled into the school parking lot, as usual, no one paid any attention to us. "Wait here, Bobby, I shouldn't be long. If I get tied up, I'll come back and get you. Don't want to burn any more gas than necessary. Danny and Jase, why don't you fellows come with David and me? You can get a head start on your school day."

The school door was still locked, so Sergeant Tolna tapped on the glass until he got the attention of a teacher whose classroom was near the entrance. She opened the door and led Sergeant Tolna to the principal's office. We followed them until we came to our classroom. Through the glass door, we saw Miss Sparks writing our spelling words on the board.

When we opened the door, her immediate reaction was, "Oh, my. Good morning, boys. Did the bell ring? I must have missed it. Come in and sit down. I'll just finish this list and be right with you."

She quickly finished, glanced at the clock above the blackboard, and then looked at us quizzically. "How did you boys get in so early? Oh, forget that! I read about the terrible fire in the paper this weekend. How are you boys faring with all this? And what about the Thorndike boys?"

We filled her in on all that had happened since school ended on Friday afternoon. By the time we finished, the bell had sounded and our classmates were filing into the room, removing their boots, and hanging their wraps in the coat closet.

When the second bell sounded, announcing the start of class, she looked at us and vowed, "As usual, you boys have more details than the *Riverton Daily Press*. From now on, I'm not wasting time reading the paper. I'll just wait till I see you the next morning. Good morning, class. Everybody ready to get down to business?"

As Miss Sparks fetched her Bible, Danny whispered, "We have to let her know about the Thanksgiving Gala."

"Let's tell her at recess." When I suggested that, I didn't realize recess would be four weeks and ten days away. At least, that's how long it seemed. After the morning ritual, Miss Sparks announced a special treat. Butch Matlock was going to present a particularly informative report, for extra credit we learned later, on the history of Thanksgiving.

By the sixth grade, even the slowest student among us could give a full report on the history of Thanksgiving with one arm tied behind his back, for goodness sake. Every fall since entering school, we'd concentrated on this subject for what seemed like weeks. We knew the story backward and forward.

Butch was aware of our shared level of knowledge of his subject, so, to make his report truly unique, he added content not normally included in the standard rendition. Specifically, he chose to add the first and last name and the *relationship* of every pilgrim who was on the Mayflower passenger list.

It might not have been so tedious, if he hadn't considered it necessary to list all these names on the blackboard. You see Butch was an extremely slow chalk-writer back in those days.

- John Alden
- Isaac Allerton
- *Mary* Allerton (wife)
- Bartholomew Allerton (son)
- *Mary* Allerton (daughter)

Danny groaned, apparently at the mention of a mother and daughter bearing the same Christian name.

- *Remember* Allerton (daughter)
- Don Allerton *(no relation to other Allertons)*

"Hold it right there, Butch," Danny demanded. "My information says that *Don Allerton* was a son as well. Mother *Mary* just forgot about him for a while. She had a bad memory. That's why she named her second daughter *Remember*. She didn't want to forget her."

Butch was undaunted. Without correcting his list as Danny suggested, he forged ahead.

- Don Billington
- Eleanor Billington (wife)
- Frances Billington (relation unknown)

We all waited for Danny's objection but for some reason, he allowed Butch to proceed unscathed.

- William Brewster
- Mary Brewster (wife)
- Love Brewster (son)
- Wrestling Brewster (son)

"Now wait a minute, Butch. Isn't *Love* kind of a sissy name for a boy? Were they trying to make up for that by naming the next son for a *sport?* By the way, was that *Arm Wrestling* or the regular kind?"

Butch didn't have an answer for Danny. "Then how do we know it was *Wrestling?* Maybe it was *Football Brewster.* Or how about *Basketball Brewster?* Or maybe *Bowling Brewster?* How about *Bullfighting Brewster?* Or *Boxing Brewster?* Those last two are pretty macho."

"Danny! Please don't interrupt Butch's presentation. I'm sure there'll be time for questions when he finishes." Butch shook his head violently. Miss Sparks smiled encouragingly and urged, "Please continue, Butch."

- James Chilton
- Susanna Chilton (wife)
- Mary Chilton (unknown relation)

Danny couldn't resist one last jab. "Wait a second, Butch. How could a relation be *Unknown?* Let's say your *Aunt Susanna and Uncle James* come to your house. They have this new kid with them. Name's *Mary,* right? So you ask them, 'Hey, who's the new kid?' And they say, 'Oh, she's just *Unknown.'* Does that make sense? If she's a *relation,* she's got to be *known* by somebody. What kind of a family is this *Chilton* family anyway?"

"Danny!" Miss Sparks was about to lose patience. "Now, who's giving this presentation, you or Butch?"

Danny's gave her a broad grin.

"Well, who is it?"

"It's *unknown,* Miss Sparks. *Unknown!*"

That brought down the house. When the laughter subsided, Butch pressed on.

Despite having taken four weeks and ten hours to get there, this recess was more interesting than most. When we reached the schoolyard, we saw David Thorndike punching arms with the rest of his gym-class buddies. Obviously he'd been readmitted to school. When he saw us, he smiled and waved. That was good news.

During the weeks leading up to that morning's deep freeze, the Hamilton broad jump (now called *long jump)* pit had filled with about a foot of rainwater. Overnight, a thick layer of ice had formed. Danny and I took it upon ourselves to break this layer into as many ice cubes as we possibly could, before the bell sounded ending recess.

Our stomping and splashing caught the attention of the herd of Hamilton underclassmen led by Sherm and Chub. One by one they joined us in the pit. It got so crowded that Danny and I decided to take a break and simply watch. From the sidelines, the stompers resembled a crazed crew of stunted Sicilian winemakers at grape-harvest time.

Before long, there wasn't a piece of ice worth stomping, so Danny and I organized a small test of courage for our under-classmen associates. We positioned the two dozen snowsuited neophytes about twenty feet away from the broad-jump launch point, a rectangular rubber pad nailed into the ground at the edge of the pit. When the recess bell sounded, we yelled, "Follow us!" We dashed madly toward the launch pad. When we hit it, we leaped as high and as far as we could. After landing in the center of the pit, we kept on running, through the ice water and up onto the steps of the school.

Before going inside, we looked back just in time to witness the pile up. Instead of maintaining an interval between jumpers, Sherm, Chub, and company had run furiously, en mass toward the small launch pad. The first two jumpers' legs somehow became tangled. Each did a magnificent belly flop right in the middle of the frothy pool of ice cubes and frigid water. Like lemmings, the rest of the snowsuited jumpers leaped into the air and came down right on top of Sherm and Chub, creating an enormous pile of arm-flapping, splashing miniature Eskimos.

By the time the trail of soaking wet snowsuits reached the steps where we stood, each Eskimo was bawling. Frost had formed a white powder, coating their faces and clothing. Abandoning our roles as Riverton's two courageous heroes, Danny and I panicked and absented ourselves from this potential scandal and rushed back to class.

Very innocently, we hung our wraps and took our seats. Just then, the principal's special bell sounded, calling all teachers to her office. By the time the sodden-suited underclassmen made it back to their classrooms, their suits were so frozen their zippers wouldn't open. So a command decision was made to send the shivering, ice-coated boys home in the company of responsible upperclassmen. Each kid was asked to name a trusted guide to accompany him home. Danny and I assembled in the hallway near the front door with the other trustees.

We were given careful instructions on our duties. We should slowly escort our wards to their homes, taking care to ensure that our sniffling ice-balls didn't tumble over and spend the rest of the winter as permanent fixtures embedded somewhere in Riverton's snow-covered landscape. Upon arrival at their houses, we should take them inside and stand them next to the stove. If their mothers were home, our obligation ended.

If no mother was present, we should wait until their snowsuits thawed. Then we should remove their suits and immerse our wards in a hot bath, if we could arrange it. If not, we should cover them with blankets, seat them in front of the stove, and stay with them until their mothers returned.

As we left school, through the window of our classroom, we saw Butch, chalk in hand, plodding ahead with *The History of Thanksgiving, Part II.* Looking down on frosty Chub and icy Sherm, we decided that we had the better of two undesirable choices for how to spend a frigid Monday afternoon in Riverton.

THE CRADDOCK SISTERS AND their small army of helpers had less than a week to transform the concept of a Thanksgiving Gala into reality. The selection of the First Methodist Church was a brilliant stroke of genius. The facility itself was ideal for the occasion. A spacious modern kitchen. Sturdy new tables and chairs. Knowledgeable Methodists who volunteered to help. And finally, a factor no one valued until the last day or so before the event, its close proximity to the Forrest Street neighborhood. The majority of help and support came from women who lived only a short walk from the church.

No one could beat the Craddock sisters when it came to thorough planning and intelligent execution. And when teamed with Grandma Compton and her daughters there was practically nothing beyond their capabilities.

As it turned out, the sisters were also masters at identifying key contributors to an affair like this. And they wisely ensured that those vital contributions, whether from wallets, talents, or time and energy, were formally acknowledged. The sisters, who formed a *steering committee* of key workers, were evidently very experienced at organizing volunteers and contributors for events like this one.

Of course, the key to success of this Thanksgiving Gala was the appropriateness of the celebration. Thanksgiving of 1944 was perhaps the first time since before the Great Depression that Americans had considerable reason to celebrate. In Europe, across a broad front, the Allies had pushed the Germans back behind the Siegfried Line. In the Pacific, recapture of strategically located bases like Guam, Tinian, and Saipan enabled American B-29s, using Norden bombsights from Riverton's Burke Factory, to destroy war materiel factories in and around Tokyo.

Indeed, recent news from the war was definitely encouraging. Moreover, many in the room that Thanksgiving Day had much for which to be personally thankful. Our masterful Master of Ceremonies, Jim Comstock, decided to utilize this opportunity for people to share their heartfelt feelings of gratitude and thanksgiving with each other.

By half past two, every one of the nearly two hundred thankful diners had been served. Early reviews of the dinner were outstanding. Every hostess dreams of a Thanksgiving like this one, where everything comes out perfectly. By three o'clock, people were turning down offers of seconds and thirds and groaning about their tight belts.

That was Jim's cue. He stepped to the podium and spoke into the microphone. "Happy Thanksgiving, everyone! How was your dinner?" The response was wild applause and cheering. "That reaction ought to make our steering committee very happy. I think it would be fitting to acknowledge those folks right here and now. Please stand when I call your name. First, let's have a big round of applause for the two ladies who originated the idea of this First Annual Thanksgiving Gala today, Miss Abigail Craddock and Miss Lucille Craddock.

"And Mr. E.F. Graham for providing the turkeys and the trimmings for our dinner. And Mr. Pete Giamo for the soft drinks and desserts. Mrs. Jane Compton and her daughters, Marie Addison and Maude Harrison, who worked hard to bring about this event. And the able support from the First Methodist Church. Reverend Noble, Miss Elizabeth Bundy, and of course Anne and Mel Carmody." When each name was mentioned the crowd responded with a generous round of applause.

Jim allowed the audience to settle down a bit before continuing. "I don't have to tell any of you the meaning of Thanksgiving. It's been a national tradition since the pilgrims first set foot on American soil more than three hundred years ago. We celebrate Thanksgiving with families, friends, and neighbors each year. It's a time for spiritual reflection. A time to count our blessings and to be thankful for the love and support of those around us. In time of war, we're thankful for those loved ones in the armed services who've been fortunate enough not to have sustained physical harm. And we are truly grateful to those who've sacrificed life and limb for the rest of us.

"Here in Riverton, we've experienced the war differently from other American communities. Camp Riverton has made our town unusual in that regard. The Forrest Street neighborhood is different as well. We have not been spared the suffering of war. A number of our friends here today have lost sons, brothers, or fathers in the war. They have suffered wounds of the heart. Others here today have returned from the war with wounds of the body.

"Based on my conversations with some of you, I thought it would be fitting for each of us to spend a few minutes silently contemplating the reasons we are thankful today. And then I would like to ask you, if you desire, to share your feelings of gratitude with us, your neighbors and friends."

The room was absolutely silent for nearly five minutes. Gently, Jim brought us back from our contemplation by asking softly, "Who would like to share?"

"I think I would, Jim." Harry Chambers rose to his feet. "Naturally I'm thankful for my health and that of my family. But I am also blessed with some of the best friends a man could have. I'm especially proud of two of them. Both were my classmates and fraternity brothers at the University of Michigan.

"Who other than Tom Dewey would have taken time from a tight Presidential race, on more than one occasion, to see that two Riverton boys, Danny and Jase, received the thanks they deserved for their acts of courage and bravery. Even though he didn't win the election, Tom won the respect of his opponent and of the country for returning class and dignity to Presidential politics. Yes, I'm thankful to call Tom Dewey my friend.

"My second friend suffered the terrible loss of his wife and his daughters in a tragic accident a few years back. Nonetheless, Jim Comstock emerged from his depression and testified on behalf of the Libby sisters, perhaps helping to lessen their prison sentences by years. And, after his reinstatement as teacher and coach, it only took Jim one season to transform Riverton High's football team into a state champion, by way of the team's first undefeated season ever.

"Congratulations, Jim! I'm proud and thankful to be your friend."

Dressed in his new black suit, white shirt, and classy red bow tie, Nate Craddock spoke next. "Five years ago, frankly, I didn't give a hoot about living. I had chosen the life of a farmer and failed miserably. I became a bitter and angry man. Most of my neighbors laughed at me. Then I met my new neighbors, Bill and Jane Compton, who treated me as a friend.

"Bill worked long hours to turn my land into the finest farm it could possibly be. And Jane, bless her heart, tried and tried to turn me into the finest man I could possibly be. Bill encouraged me to start my welding again. And, in that way, I regained the respect of my neighbors. And my own self respect. I was thankful to have the Comptons as neighbors. But I still didn't fully appreciate life, not the way I do today.

"That came to me after a run-in with a pair of rotten Nazis who beat the tar out of me. If it hadn't been for Danny Tucker and Jase Addison, I'd be dead. I guess it took coming close to death for me to realize what life really could be. In a funny way, I'm thankful for those Nazis. If it hadn't been for them, my cousins Abigail and Lucille might not have come into my life. And the Compton cleanup crew would never have refurbished my old house so my cousins could live there with me.

"Yep, I have a lot to be thankful for. I'm thankful to have my health back. My cousins in my life. Good neighbors and good friends. Yes, life's real good now."

Bobby Thorndike raised his hand. Jim nodded. "Go ahead, Bobby."

Mr. Nakayama patted Bobby on the back as he rose to speak. "I wasn't going to say anything, not that David and I aren't really thankful today. Gosh! Who wouldn't be? But when Mr. Craddock said that he was thankful that the Nazis had beaten the tar out of him that's when I decided to say something." He glanced at David before proceeding.

"Last night, my brother David and I were talking about the exact same thing. If our father, bless his soul, hadn't burned down the Nakayamas' house, David and I wouldn't be here today telling you that we're the two luckiest boys in town. Just a few days ago, we didn't have a mother. Whisky had taken our father. We'd dropped out of school. And, because we had no home, we were sleeping in the back of the bowling alley.

"But today that's all changed. From the ashes of that house came some real blessings for David and me. Most important, Judge Morrison has made the Nakayamas our guardians. They told the judge they wanted to do this for us. And they want us to live with them in the new house that's being built for them by Mr. Graham. This week Sergeant Tolna talked to our principals so we're back in school.

"And we have two new best friends, Danny and Jase. Oh, please forgive me, I nearly forgot. The marvelous Craddock sisters have set up a trust fund so David and I, as well as a number of other kids in this neighborhood, can look forward to going to college. All this is a miracle to us. We are so thankful that so much good has come our way in such a short period of time. We just hope that we don't wake up one morning at the bowling alley and find out that all of this was just a dream."

"Maude, please go ahead."

Aunt Maude stood holding Johnnie for all to see. "Isn't he just beautiful?"

The crowd responded with a unanimous *awwww!*

"Thank you. As you can imagine, I'm very thankful for this healthy baby boy, John Jason Harrison. Little Johnnie! And I'm thankful that I continue to receive letters from his father who's fighting on the front lines in Europe. Everyday, I pray for Van's safe return. I know others of you pray too. So far our prayers have been answered.

"I'm also thankful to be living with my sister Marie and her family, John and Jase. As you all know, our nextdoor neighbor, Mrs. Mikas, who's sitting here at our table, has two gold stars hanging in her window. I'm very thankful, and I know everyone shares this sentiment, for the sacrifice that Ivan and Theo Mikas made for the rest of us. And I'm thankful for the way Mrs. Mikas has shown us how to deal with such loss by the courageous way she faces each day.

"Finally I'm thankful to live in our neighborhood and in Riverton. I'm thankful that Johnnie was born in America, not in some other place in the world where he would be in constant danger. We have a wonderful country. And I'm proud and thankful to be an American citizen today."

Mr. Graham rose to his feet. "I'm thankful for the people in our community, like those who have spoken here today. Isn't it marvelous to hear such good things about the people you know and respect? That's what community is all about.

"I'd like to mention some others for whom I'm thankful. The first is John Addison for suggesting that I bring Mr. Nakayama into the Graham Markets organization. Without John taking that first step, Mrs. Graham and I would not have been blessed with the friendship and fine example of two exemplary Americans, Takeo and Yumiko Nakayama. The Nakayamas were deprived of their livelihoods, stripped of their assets, and forced to accept the humiliating life as relocation camp internees. Yet they turned their cheeks and took the Thorndike boys into their family. Yes, I'm thankful to be able to witness, firsthand, the character and integrity of the Nakayamas. I feel privileged to be their friend.

"I'm also thankful for my friendship with Bill Compton who invited me and my business associates to hunt at his farm. And for Jane Compton who offered her generous hospitality to me and my friends. And when the two escaped POWs tried to ruin the experience by making off with my car and our equipment, I'm thankful for Sheriff Connors who, with the help of Danny and Jase, put an end to the criminal careers of those Nazis. As you may have seen in the paper yesterday, those two rascals were sentenced to a life of hard labor which they will serve at Fort Leavenworth. So, naturally I am thankful for our system of justice. Finally I would like to thank the wonderful Craddock sisters for their idea to bring us all together, here on this Thanksgiving Day."

Jim took that as his cue to ask the Craddock sisters to say a few words. As usual, Abigail took the lead. "Thank you, Jim and Mr. Graham. Oh, my! Where do I begin? I guess my sister and I feel a little like Bobby Thorndike. Only a few short weeks ago, we were living a quiet retired life in Dayton, Ohio. Then we received a letter from Nate Craddock, a cousin whom we had no idea existed. Before we could absorb this reality, we read in the paper about his being held captive and the injuries he received at the hands of the bad POWs. It was then that we decided to move to Riverton. And since that decision, life has hardly been *quiet.*

"Our life is filled with new neighbors and friends, challenging adventures, a new home, and most of all, our own flesh and blood, Cousin Nate. So many people have made this possible. But I have to start with Jane and Bill Compton and their daughters, Marie and Maude. And our neighbors, the Henrys. Of course, we'll always be eternally thankful for Nate's resourceful rescuers, Danny and Jase.

"It's hardly a quiet life, but *talk about fun!* We couldn't be more blessed than we are. Nor more thankful. Thank you all for welcoming us to your community."

Before the day was over, nearly forty people stood, expressing their gratitude for the many generous acts of family members, neighbors, and friends. RJ thanked Danny and me for making his camp experience *so interesting.* Miss Sparks thanked us, too, for making her classroom *so interesting.* Mrs. Libby thanked us again for helping to capture the POWs before her daughters got into deeper trouble. For the thousandth time, Mrs. Matlock thanked us for saving her life and organizing the fund-raiser to rebuild their house.

Bibs thanked us for not telling Mrs. Squires about certain transgressions relating to a bottle that he kept under the Mission back porch. Of course, Mrs. Squires was sitting right behind him at the time, so he was in trouble *again.* Bohunk Joe thanked the neighborhood for allowing him to recycle their trash and for the knife sharpening business they sent his way. He also thanked Jim Comstock for the delightful years that the two of them had spent together as our neighborhood bums.

Chuck Nichols thanked Danny and me for having brought him *so many interesting* stories over the past six months. Sergeant Tolna thanked us for the way we included Sherm into our FSG ranks. Danny smiled and took full credit. *What a guy!* Mom and Mrs. Tucker rose together to tell Danny and me how thankful they were to have sons like us, during which Chub wrinkled his nose and Queenie carefully examined her nails.

When everyone had spoken, Jim reassumed his position at the podium. "I can't think of a single person who wasn't appreciated and thanked here today. Don't know about the rest of you, but this is the best Thanksgiving I've ever experienced. How could next year's Thanksgiving Gala possibly top today's?"

Jim looked around the room. "Have we said it all? If so, I'll ask Reverend Noble to deliver the benediction."

"But we haven't said it all, Mr. Jim."

"Danny, what haven't we said?"

"Aren't you thankful for something you haven't told us about? And don't you think this would be a good time to tell everybody about it?"

Jim's face turned red. Suddenly he left the podium and returned to his table. He took Louise Libby's hand and she rose to his side. She whispered in his ear. He nodded and turned toward the audience.

"Danny's right. There *is* something more to be said."

People looked at each other quizzically and shrugged their shoulders.

"Louise Libby and I are pleased to announce our engagement. We plan to be married in the spring."

A hush fell over the room. Then, suddenly, an explosion of cheers and applause filled the air. As the celebration subsided, Danny stood and walked toward the podium. When he reached the microphone, he raised his hands for silence.

Then Danny delivered a benediction of his own.

"All's swell, that ends swell!"

I couldn't have said it better myself.

ACKNOWLEDGEMENTS

We have been blessed with an overwhelmingly positive response from literary critics and readers of *Cottonwood Summer*. Particularly meaningful for me was the reception we received from the people of my hometown, Owosso, Michigan. I would especially like to acknowledge and thank the following people and organizations:

Pat Vaughn, my seventh grade English teacher, who challenged me to abandon my collision course with academic disaster and dared me to excel. My classmate and good friend, Brenda Jordan, who with Pat organized the Owosso launch of *Cottonwood Summer* in May 2004.

The local newspapers that generously shared the story of *Cottonwood Summer* with their readers. Dick Campbell at *The Argus-Press* and Bill Constine at *The Independent*.

The community organizations and their leaders who invited me to speak to their groups: Beta Sigma Phi, Brenda Jordan and Janet Walker; Corunna Rotary Club, Linda Sovis; Current Topics Club, Pat Shaw and Piper Brewer; Owosso Kiwanis, Dave Shepard; Owosso Rotary Club, Joane Ford and Carol Vaughn; Shiawassee-Owosso Kiwanis, Jon Greenway and Mary Nuechterlein; and St. John's United Church of Christ, Rev. John Downing and Judy Elliott.

The enthusiastic students and teachers from the elementary schools where I spoke at assemblies and those who made the arrangements: Larry Audet, Superintendent of Schools; Lorraine Ross, Communications Specialist; Principals at Bentley Elementary, Janet Drews; Bryant Elementary, Steve Brooks; Central Elementary, Lori Bailey; Emerson Elementary, Mark Erikson; and Washington Elementary, Chris Perry.

The libraries that sponsored my "Behind the Book" talk. Ken Uptigrove at the Owosso District Library. Sue Huff at the Corunna Public Library. Mary Alice Campbell, Anna Annese, and Judy Batteen with Friends of the Corunna Public Library.

The Book Mark and its manager, Janet Bates, who promoted and hosted a successful book signing for *Cottonwood Summer* and who continue to provide the Cottonwood series to Shiawassee County readers.

The Owosso High School Class of '57 women whose annual luncheon was the first event in our successful launch in Owosso. My many school friends who have shared their memories of our times at Washington, Roosevelt, Central, and Owosso High School.

The members of the Curtis, Farley, Hildebrant, Mrva, Nichols, Shrenka, Smock, Steiner, Williams, Wing, and Worthington families who continue to share their memories of our old neighborhood during the 1940s.

My relatives who encouraged me to capture the times that meant so much to all of us: Uncle Jim (James H. Waters) and Aunt Tiny (Kathleen Waters Kurz) who both were able to read the manuscript before they passed away just months before *Cottonwood Summer* was published, and my cousins: Ivan Conger, Mick (Leonard) Mitchell, and Jim Waters whose passion for those early times motivated me to create the Cottonwood series.

If I have failed to acknowledge any Owosso friends, I trust they will be as enthusiastic in their forgiveness as they are in their support.

Thank you again, Owosso!

Gary Slaughter
Nashville
October 2005